Books by Catherine Curzon and Willow Winsham

Single Titles

The Star of Versailles

The Star of Versailles

ISBN # 978-1-78686-116-0

©Copyright Catherine Curzon, Willow Winsham 2017

Cover Art by Posh Gosh ©Copyright 2017

Interior text design by Claire Siemaszkiewicz

Pride Publishing

Published in 2017 by Pride Publishing, Newland House, The Point, Weaver Road, Lincoln, LN6 3QN, United Kingdom.

Pride Publishing is a subsidiary of Totally Entwined Group Limited.

THE STAR OF VERSAILLES

CATHERINE CURZON
and
WILLOW WINSHAM

Dedication

CC— For Rick, the most rakish of all Colonial gents!
WW—For Debbie, there right from the start!

.

Chapter One

There was more than mud on the streets of Paris today, something other than earth drawing and sucking at the feet of the thousands who trod here, heads bowed and shoulders hunched against the summer rain. From the Place de la Révolution a roar erupted, louder than thunder and more violent than lightning, the sun disappearing behind a jet-black cloud in deference to the violence below.

Held fast in the grip of the Terror, the city trembled, and everyone, from the highest to the lowest, had their secrets. For some, like the residents of a fine house on the Rue Saint-Honoré, secrets had seen a father chained in the Conciergerie, awaiting his date with the National Razor, whilst for others they were currency, life itself.

Every morning William Knowles woke in his unassuming room and donned the identity of Yves Morel as other men might step into a favorite pair of comfortable shoes. For two months, he had existed under the name of a man feared from the south of the country to the north and that, he knew, meant that his time could only be running out.

Here in Paris, Morel was known as a figure of unflinching cruelty, those who could put a face to the name all safely occupied with the business of government hundreds of miles away. Yet one day, and he knew it must be soon, one of them would return to Paris. Before that happened he would be gone, vanished once more into a world of shadows and secrets.

Tomorrow, perhaps the day after that, the last surviving conspirator of the Rue Saint-Honoré would climb the steps to the scaffold and take with him the only hope William had of a successful completion to this most lucrative of missions. Valuable days had been lost on the journey to Paris in response to reports of Philippe Plamondon's arrest, William expecting to find the man dead by the time of his arrival. Instead, he found him deep within the Conciergerie enjoying the special attentions of Vincent Tessier, the Butcher of Orléans who could, so rumor had it, convince a man to confess to any number of crimes, both real and imagined.

One chance, William told himself as he opened the window in an effort to dissipate the stifling heat.

One chance, then the last link to the Star of Versailles was gone forever.

A cheer rent the air and he shuddered. There came a second then a third explosion of approval from the distant crowd, each one louder than the last. As the day grew darker, he bowed his head and pictured the blade being hauled back to the skies, the shuffling feet on their way to the scaffold, the moment of silence before the razor edge fell and ten thousand spectators released their breath at once.

Then came the next soul, the clattering thunder of the guillotine and on and on it went until the blade grew dull and the crowd grew hungry for something more tangible than blood.

Another shudder ran through William and he drew the window down with a note of finality before picking up his coat as he crossed the bare boards to the door.

Sometimes, William reflected as he stepped out onto the landing, deep undercover work was boring, pointless hours spent reading dispatches and copying out messages. On other occasions, it was dangerous, dodging bullets and torture, and once in a while, deep undercover work, even as a revolutionary firebrand, meant traveling for a week to spend one hour with a man beyond rescue.

If he knew anything at all.

For all the excitement among the Academy's members over recent developments, there was really nothing here but more rumor, nothing tangible whatsoever besides the usual anti-Revolution pamphleting and some ill-advised rabble-rousing.

Now and again, Professor Dee would send a dispatch to his agent and William would follow it to the letter, stealing from his bed to creep through the house as everyone slept and copy this paper or that missive. During these excursions, he had learned from experience that Tessier, his genial host, was given to sleeplessness. After midnight, he roamed the rooms, pacing the stairs up and down or sitting in his study staring at the darkness beyond the window, still as marble and just as cold.

Two evenings earlier Tessier had sat there as William, snooping just for the sake of snooping, pressed back into the wall and barely breathed. For long minutes, they'd shared the same space, William clutching the documents he had been reading by moonlight when the door handle had turned, his knuckles bleached white.

That had been the last time he'd searched the study after dark. Now he confined his efforts to the gray hours before dawn when the house had yet to wake. Where once these walls had echoed with the whispers of those who carried messages through Paris for Philippe Plamondon and his counter-revolutionaries and watched fleeing prisoners escape to a new life, now it was silent, Tessier's thin voice the only sound that occasionally ended the quiet.

Not so long ago, the house had rung with a child's laughter, with the gentle lullaby of Claudine Plamondon and the cheery greeting of her husband, but now those memories were as gossamer as a dream. The homely building was a shadow of its former self, picked apart by its new tenant, so consumed was he by his search for the illustrious treasure. Carpets and rugs were torn up until the floorboards themselves were pried apart, paper stripped from the walls and furniture dismantled to no avail. After two months in residence, Vincent Tessier was no closer to the prize, the jewel that half of Europe searched for proving utterly elusive.

At the top of the stairs William paused as something, he hardly knew what, stilled his tread.

Footsteps.

Somebody in Tessier's study?

Finally convinced that there was, indeed, someone else in the house, William made his way along the landing with all the care he could muster in his heavy boots, taking each step with utmost delicacy.

For a moment, he peered at the bare floorboards where Philippe had been caught as he'd fled and where, local gossips had told him in the alehouses, 'his spilled blood had stained the most beautiful rug you ever did see'.

'It stank like a butcher's slab. They had no choice but to burn it. You can still see the stain on the boards. That dark patch, that's where they caught up with Monsieur Plamondon. That bonny wife and little François, well, they'll catch up with them too one day and it'll be all the worse when they do.'

'Such a lovely family...'

And with each telling the tale grew more grotesque, the violence more bloody and the stain deeper and darker than before.

'That house has seen its share of sadness – we used to have such lovely times with Madame Plamondon and the little one, and what do we have now?'

'Men talking politics from dawn until dusk, paddling mud and blood and Lord knows what across the rugs and up the stairs.'

'Mark me, there's more than one stain in this house.'

Once word had gotten around as to who they were addressing the gossips fell silent and William stopped frequenting the alehouses, marked out as the man in Robespierre's pocket. It was a compliment of sorts, he supposed, that he could be so convincing as a monster to whom betrayal and punishment were second nature.

Though Vincent Tessier makes Yves Morel seem like an amateur.

As he trod lightly, William realized that the gossips were

right. The house was pockmarked with the scars of battle and the dark stain of Philippe's blood on the board was the most tangible of them all. William stilled before the door and breathed in the atmosphere of damp that lingered about the place when the rain fell. It felt heavy, twisting his stomach for no more than a second.

As the door swung open beneath his hand William stepped over the threshold, his eyes fixed on the man who stood with his back to him. The intruder was beside Tessier's desk, head bowed low. William found his attention drawn by the stranger's vibrant blue outfit, more suited to the opera than a filthy day in Paris. As William watched, the man spun to face the door, one hand held up in surrender.

"Alexandre Gaudet?" William asked, momentarily wrong-footed by the unexpected appearance of the toast of London theater here in this fetid city. It made sense, of course, yet he would never have expected a dandified playwright, more used to perfume and silk than muck and politics, to make such a dangerous trip. With that thought in his head William lowered his voice and asked, "You're looking for your sister?"

"Claudine," Gaudet confirmed, searching William's face with green eyes. His voice was almost convincing but there was just a trace of a wobble, a small break that betrayed his fears. "This was her home—"

A veil of realization descended over his face then his gaze dropped to William's hands in a search for the leather gloves, Vincent Tessier's trademark.

"You're Morel," Gaudet breathed after a moment, taking an involuntary step backward. "Please—"

A hundred possibilities presented themselves then, chief among them being the fact that this man, this pampered society darling, was the last free link to the Star of Versailles. If indeed it had left Paris with Claudine Plamondon when her husband had been dragged to the Conciergerie, then might Alexandre Gaudet be able to find her? Wouldn't a brother know the mind of his sister, the places she might hide herself?

"Trust me—" William began, the words silenced by the sound of a slamming door and voices from below. There came the heavy thud of damp boots crossing the stripped, bare floorboards of the entrance hall and William whispered, "Say nothing."

He knew that the words were wasted as the feet continued on and up the staircase. Praying that they would pass by, William weighed up his choices, not sure what he could do to help this possibly God-sent new arrival without giving away his own subterfuge.

Gaudet made a run for the door. The force with which he hit William sent him careening into the dresser. The intruder wrenched the door open, seeking escape and, instead, came face to face with Vincent Tessier. Behind him, three men were clustered and, anticipating nothing more thrilling than an afternoon of politics and debate, they were quick to respond to this unexpected excitement.

As William recovered his footing, Gaudet was dragged from the room and William followed, too late to witness anything but a commotion of feet on the stairs. He knew that the intruder's efforts to escape would be hopeless— Tessier would not allow Alexandre Gaudet to leave the house a free man.

That's if he even leaves it alive.

William descended the stairs quickly, reaching the hallway in time to see Gaudet being hauled toward the door. His arms were pulled back at a painful angle and a thick loop of rope encircled his wrists, tight enough to draw a thin streak of crimson that just made its way down the pale skin of his hand.

Tessier looked to William with malice glittering in his eyes and told him brightly, "I owe you a debt for this, Morel—a valuable head."

In the seconds before he was pushed into the street and taken away, Alexandre Gaudet glanced over his shoulder at William. For a moment, their eyes met and he recognized in Gaudet's gaze the flare of hatred that the name of Yves Morel always provoked.

William decided that he would not remain in this skin for long, bowing his head and turning back to the stairs.

Soon it will be time to travel on.

Chapter Two

"Hand," Sylvie Dupire commanded, folding her arms across her chest and waiting for the child to comply. "Bastien, hand."

He shook his head, clenching his fist even more tightly for a moment before she said, "Now, Master Dupire."

Another moment passed before Bastien puffed up his cheeks and let the air escape in a long sigh of annoyance, each finger of the fist slowly uncurling itself. As a couple of dull coins were revealed, Sylvie held out her own hand until he dropped his bounty onto her palm.

"Who did you steal this from?"

"I didn't steal it." He shrugged. "I found it."

"Found it how?" Sylvie offered her son the opportunity to tell something that at least resembled the truth. "By dipping into the pockets of passers-by?"

Bastien furrowed his smooth brow at the accusation of theft before he let out another sigh of disappointment and shook his head slowly, switching expertly from chastised son to wounded innocent.

"My hand may have slipped on occasion."

"Bastien!" Sylvie threw her hands up, voice clipped when she said, "You're going to end up getting us all in big trouble, young man."

"A few coins…"

"A few coins." Sylvie leaned forward then and jabbed a finger at him, Bastien fighting his desire to take a step back. "'A few coins' has put boys on the scaffold!"

"So I'm not getting it back, then?" Bastien asked, the unspoken disdain turning to annoyance when she returned to the ragged clothes she had been examining without replying. "But I've been all over the city for that!"

"Consider it your board."

"What bloody son pays his ma to live in a filthy hole like this?"

"Deliver milk, you keep the money," she explained calmly, tucking the coins into her apron. "Dip into pockets and pay board. Your choice, Bastien."

Bastien stared at her for as long as he could before the need to blink overcame the need to at least attempt to make his mother feel guilty. Only then did he climb onto the table to sit beside the pile of rags, picking up a frock coat and examining the tattered finery absent-mindedly.

Here and there were still traces of the rich deep green it had been, a tantalizing suggestion of gleaming gold on the mud-soaked frogging, the woolen frock having once warmed and cocooned someone on the cold Parisian evenings. Now it was rags, the back stained black and stiffened with blood. Used to the routine, Bastien pulled at the tarnished brass buttons that still remained and added them to the growing pile on the table.

"What you reckon?" He held out one of the frock's dirty sleeves and Sylvie closed her hand around it, her eyes narrowing as she rubbed the fabric between her fingertips as though it was the finest silk.

She paused to chew her bottom lip, frowning before she lifted the other sleeve and examined it closely. Finally, an almost conspiratorial smile spread across her face and she asked, "Do you think anyone told this poor bugger where he was headed? From the state of this, he'd dressed for a summer ball, not the scaffold!"

"If they did it to me, I'd take my britches off," Bastien announced with a nod of satisfaction, raising his head to peer down his nose as he adopted more aristocratic tones. "You can chop off my head, my good man, but here's my arse to kiss while you're doing it."

"Watch that mouth." His mother laughed, picking up

a shawl that was more holes than fabric. "I'm not having people say I brought you up to swear."

"That Sylvie Dupire," he replied, still in his theatrically plummy tones, "has brought her son up to say 'arse' — what a bloody scandal."

Sylvie shot him a warning glance, pointing in his direction momentarily, and he went back to the task in hand, tearing the sleeves from the frock and throwing them to the pile of so-called 'good' rags. He dismembered the garment expertly and dropped the panels onto the various piles, ready for his mother to take with her when she went out selling, building her meagre empire.

Here on the Rue du Faubourg-Saint-Antoine, safe in the house and heart of Thierry Charron, Sylvie and Bastien no longer slept in the gutter. As Charron spent his days in the cabinet workshop downstairs, she made the apartments comfortable, kept her lover and her son well cared for and finally gave up sleeping with one eye open and a knife in her hand.

'*Always have a way out,*' she'd told Bastien more than once. '*Put a bit of money away and don't be beholden to nobody, they're all bastards in the end.*'

That's fair enough, Bastien thought, *but you just took mine off me, so how can I tuck it away?*

They worked in silence for a while, sifting and sorting through the rags until he slid down from his perch on the table and went to the window, looking out into the glaring sun.

"You off?" Sylvie asked, not glancing up. "If you're going to pinch, make it worthwhile."

Bastien gave a sullen nod then, with a quick peck at Sylvie's cheek, darted from the kitchen and onto the landing. He took the stairs two at a time, pausing to shout a passing farewell to Charron, who called, "Keep away from the square, your mother doesn't like it!"

The boy pulled open the door and ran into the street, swept up in the tide of people. Even if the rain had finally stopped after what seemed like endless days and nights of deluge, the ground was still a bog, sucking and dark. Where others did their best to edge around the quagmires as though they were bottomless pits, Bastien darted through gaps in the thickening crowd without any care for the mud that splattered his feet and legs.

By the time he reached the Rue Saint-Honoré, the jeering spectators were virtually at a standstill, their catcalls and whistles echoing through the street and drowning out the rumble of wheels and the sound of hooves. As the tumbrel rolled into view, he peered at the two men aboard, one carelessly holding the reins whilst the other was stooped, an old man who seemed ready for his grave. A stern-faced priest followed as he had a hundred times before.

"Who is it?" Bastien looked up at the old woman beside him, her hand raised to jab furiously at the sky. "Oi!"

"Plamondon." At the word, his eyes widened in surprise. Philippe Plamondon was a man in his thirties, tall and confident who shared Charron's air of unshakeable solidity. Could the Conciergerie really have transformed him into a man more than twice his years, small and frail on his way to the scaffold?

Seized by the need to see if this really was Plamondon, Bastien crouched as he ran along the line of dark-uniformed soldiers who separated the crowd from the street. Within seconds, he had drawn level with the tumbrel and recognized the man who had kept so many late-night appointments in the cellar of Charron's workshop. They thought Bastien ignorant of their politics, of course, believed that he had slept whilst they had plotted, but though he might not have known what they had been saying, he knew what they were about.

News of Plamondon's arrest had shaken Charron and Sylvie to the core. If their fear went unspoken, their eyes told him all, the starts and jumps every time there was a knock at the door or a sound in the street. Vincent Tessier had taken Plamondon and now they expected him to come for them, to round up those who had joined the meetings in the cellars and carry them all off to face the blade.

Yet nobody came.

Eventually, his mother seemed less tired and Charron spent more time working rather than haunting the windows, back to his cabinets and hearth. Soon enough, life returned to normal, even if the meetings in the cellar seemed to occur with less frequency.

Plamondon's arrest was big news on the streets, of course, because his wife and son had been nowhere to be seen by the time Tessier's men had come knocking.

And now Vincent Tessier lives in your house.

As they passed the building, Plamondon lifted his head to look at the place that had been his home, and in eyes that had once been full of life, there was nothing but despair. Bastien followed his gaze and caught sight of Yves Morel in a lower window, his face a shadow on the glass. He had seen Morel about the streets since his arrival from the south and was always struck by the man's strong features, more adventurer than bureaucratic torturer. He was a commanding figure, tall and broad in a way that the men of the Convention never seemed to be, lacking their fastidious neatness or the studied chaos of Danton. He was a solitary one, too, even setting himself apart when he was in the company of others.

As Morel turned away from the glass, Bastien dashed along the grim procession to where Vincent Tessier rode at the head of the column on a sleek black horse, no emotion showing on his face. Behind him came another man who Bastien didn't recognize, stumbling along uncertainly with his wrists fastened behind his back and a soldier flanking him on either side.

Whoever this was, his fine clothes suggested that he hadn't been a prisoner for long, though his left eye was swollen shut, ashen skin blooming black and purple. If Philippe Plamondon seemed broken then this stranger was lost, good eye darting back and forth as he took in the baying figures that hemmed them in on either side. In his eleven years, Bastien Dupire had seen everyone from beggars to monarchs make this trip to the Place de la Révolution and none of them had appeared as bewildered as this well-dressed stranger.

Beats thinking about what's up ahead, I suppose, Bastien decided as he walked alongside the procession. *Not a bad turnout for the merchant Plamondon.*

Still, nothing surprised him as much as Vincent Tessier.

The so-called Butcher of Orléans enjoyed a reputation so fierce, so horrifying that Bastien had expected much more. He had imagined a bear of a man, a figure whose physical appearance would match the stories of titanic cruelty that had arrived in Paris long before he had. Yet where there should have been the devil there was just, as Charron observed, a bloodless provincial clerk.

But make no mistake, there's blood on that man's hands. It doesn't matter what he dresses like.

For now, Tessier seemed to be exactly what he was, the man in charge. His eyes were fixed on the road ahead and he was a pale shadow all in black, the bright silver buttons on his coat catching the afternoon sunlight to spark like flint on tinder. One gloved hand held the reins and the other rested on the pommel of the sabre he wore, while his face was a white mask, thin lips set in a dead straight line. There was a sharpness to his features, a suggestion of cruelty in the hard lines of his face that made Bastien instinctively dislike him.

At the sound of a bang, Bastien jumped back into the present and looked over at the tumbrel to see that the driver was huddled low, one hand holding his hat on his head as rocks rained down on the prisoner, the priest spattered by mud and worse. Even now, Plamondon was unmoving, and Bastien wondered whether he even knew where he was, what was happening.

It's better that way.

At the Place de la Révolution the crowds pressed in even

more tightly and Bastien dropped almost to his knees. There, low to the ground, he moved through the sea of skirts and breeches. The smell was acrid and a couple of times he found himself coming up for air, stomach lurching at the metallic tang that stung his nostrils and burned the back of his throat as he neared the heavy wooden scaffold. On days with smaller crowds, he would climb as high as he dared on Liberté, but today the spectators were too tight to move back so instead he pressed forward, closer and closer to the platform.

Tessier dismounted his horse and climbed the steps, gesturing for the manacled man to follow. The prisoner stumbled after him and, as he stood before the guillotine, Bastien almost saw him snap into the present, his wits returning in the shadow of the National Razor.

The man with the black eye turned in a full circle and took in the scene, stepping back to get a glimpse of the instrument of punishment before him. His mouth fell open, slack and terrified. He spoke then, and though his words were lost in the racket, Bastien saw very clearly what he had said.

'*My God.*'

If one of the soldiers hadn't made a grab for the prisoner's arm, Bastien was sure he would have fallen, but instead he was wrenched upright and a rope was lashed through the chain of the manacles and knotted tightly to the rail on the side of the scaffold. Only then did Philippe Plamondon make his way up the steps, eyes downcast yet he walked to the bascule without any sign of struggle or emotion. A buzz of expectation passed through the spectators as the straps were fastened. Bastien leaned closer, swallowing hard.

"You're Charron's messenger?"

"Bloody hell!" Bastien started, twisting to look up at the new arrival. He found his efforts frustrated by the press of the crowd, the man's heavy-collared coat and large hat incongruous in the summer heat.

"Give this to your master." He passed a sealed letter to

Bastien, a hand on the boy's shoulder keeping him staring straight ahead. "Tell him it is from the ninth Scholar."

Bastien kept his eyes on the scaffold. He pushed the letter into his sleeve with a nod, the mention of the Scholar leaving him in no doubt that this was a man to be obeyed. Bastien swallowed hard and shuffled to keep his footing, the crowd pushing forward just slightly to watch the bascule being moved into place, securing Plamondon beneath the blade.

"People of Paris, let this be a lesson to all of you," Tessier announced, clasping his hands behind his back as he trod the scaffold. "Enemies of the Republic will never be tolerated, no matter how much wealth and influence they believe themselves to wield."

"They call me the Butcher of Orléans, and make no mistake, I will become the Butcher of Paris if the Republic demands it of me. Today we witness the execution of Philippe Plamondon, a man who is an enemy to us all — a man who has brought into our country a spy in the pay of the British crown."

"My brother-in-law has had no trial." The man who had seemed so lost protested uselessly, blinking as if waking from a nightmare. "Have we no rights?"

"You gave up your rights, sir, when you entered France as a spy." Tessier gestured to the well-dressed prisoner. "See how the celebrated *Gaudet* returns to Paris! I deduce no reason for a playwright to come to this city, sir, but I see *every* reason for a spy to do so."

Gaudet stared at Tessier, his mouth opening slightly as though he meant to speak, then he looked wildly about himself, tugging once more at the rope that bound him. Whatever he said was lost to the wind and Bastien edged forward. Now he was so close to the scaffold that he was virtually among the furies, the man's hand on his shoulder carrying him along, too.

Many years ago, his mother had taken him to watch a carnival and he thought of it now, remembering the way the audience had whooped and cheered, and the atmosphere of a party about the gathering. He had only felt that in one other place and it was here in the Place de la Révolution when the condemned stood before the great guillotine and the thousands who gathered here became one great colossus, a surging, amorphous beast that bayed for blood from the pit of its stomach.

And here I am at the head of it.

I am its eyes today.

"So welcome home to Paris, Monsieur!" Tessier went on, warming to his performance. "Your public is glad to have you back!"

"You cannot do this," Gaudet reasoned, as though that could do any good when faced with the righteous fury of Vincent Tessier. "Think of his wife and child!"

Tessier shook off the pleas with a toss of his head. The words were evidently nothing but the buzzing of an irritating fly. Then he crossed the scaffold to the guillotine and stooped to peer at Plamondon. For a moment, the prosecutor regarded his prisoner with all the fascination of a man watching a new species of exotic insect, a second before he stamped on it with his boot. "Have you anything to say, Monsieur Plamondon?"

The crowd took in a breath as one, listening intently as the man on the bascule licked his cracked lips and turned his eyes to the figure who stood beside him.

"The Star of Versailles will never be yours."

Tessier leaned forward to listen to Plamandon's words.

"You have already lost, Monsieur Tessier."

"A pity," Tessier replied, "that you will not live to see my victory."

There was no executioner, Bastien realized, even as Tessier reached up a gloved hand and seized the *déclic*. When the blade thundered down, Gaudet started forward and let out a cry of protest, his words lost on the riotous exuberance from the mob that seemed to go on forever. Bastien couldn't turn away from the sight of the body that stiffened and grew still, the spray of crimson blood that painted the wood a darker shade, as fascinating now as the circus had been in his infancy. Even the pain he'd felt when the Scholar had squeezed his shoulder did nothing to tear his attention from the sight.

"People of Paris, take this as your warning! Enemies of the Republic are not welcome in our city," Tessier bellowed in triumph.

As the crowd cheered, he stooped to retrieve Philippe Plamondon's head from the basket where it had come to rest, blood still pumping from beneath the fallen blade. He twined his fingers in hair that was matted with filth and held the head up as a macabre trophy, keeping it at arm's length to avoid the blood that dripped from the raw neck.

"*Vive la République!*"

With that proclamation, Tessier swung his arm and hurled the decapitated head into the mob. Bastien flinched away from the scrum that erupted a couple of hundred feet away. When he turned to ask the Scholar for a few coins for the delivery, he was not surprised to find that the man was gone.

Chapter Three

William sat before his bedroom window and stared out into the darkness, replaying the moment when the blade had fallen again and again, even when his eyes remained open. He remembered the final spark of defiance that had lit up Philippe Plamondon's face, heard the tone of triumph in Tessier's words and the thud of the head as it had hit the basket, but beyond any of that, he couldn't escape the look of terror in Alexandre Gaudet's eyes.

Gaudet hadn't been watching him, of course, his was just one face amid thousands. Yet in all his adventures, all the horrors he had witnessed, he had never seen anyone look so afraid, so hopeless. How could so many be in rapture when one was so petrified?

Because there is no humanity in the mob.

And we can all lose ourselves as a part of something bigger.

Behind the closed doors of his home, Tessier was a quiet man, considered and studious, yet up on the scaffold before the ravening faces he was a ringmaster, assured and flamboyant.

A monster.

What does Alexandre Gaudet know? he wondered, gazing at the moonlight beyond the glass. With the arrest of Plamondon, the last hope of recovering the Star had seemed lost, yet was it renewed in the shape of the playwright from Rouen, newly arrived in Paris from his London liaisons?

No man would travel into the heart of the Terror to save his sister, surely, but a diamond more valuable than a king's ransom? Well, that was something *worth* putting oneself in danger for.

Sisters can take care of themselves.

Since that evening, Tessier's chambers had been secured day and night. From behind the locked door came the familiar sound of floorboards being lifted, wallpaper being torn away in the ceaseless search for *something*, the same *something* that Gaudet must have been searching for, too.

Tomorrow things would be clearer, William decided — he would make contact with Thierry Charron and what was left of Plamondon's network. If the fates smiled, he might finally hear from Professor Dee and perhaps even receive some measure of guidance in this most directionless mission.

With that thought in his mind William rose to his feet, letting out a sigh as he stretched his aching arms and pressed his hands into the small of his back for a second. He walked across the bare boards and slipped beneath the blankets, hoping that sleep wouldn't continue to evade him tonight.

* * * *

When William opened his eyes again, the gray light of dawn was creeping across the room, the street outside seemingly already bustling. With the sun came a new sense of optimism and he sprang from the bed. He dressed quickly with the intention of heading straight for the cabinetmaker's workshop where Thierry Charron plied his seemingly innocent trade.

A knock sounded at the door just before he reached it and one of the maids who toiled to keep the house running called, "Monsieur Tessier begs an audience in his study, sir."

Damn the man and his timing. He kept the less than gracious thought to himself though, opening the door to tell the girl, "I will be with him directly."

It was no more than a minute before William rapped at the door of Tessier's study, the inhabitant already speaking as he entered.

"The city is restless."

As William stepped into the room, Tessier rose from behind the enormous desk, one of the few ornamental pieces he had kept when he'd taken over the home of the Plamondon family. He was more bureaucrat than butcher now, hands clasped behind his back and his plain gray coat a world away from the jet-black frock he had worn for the execution. Gone was the glint of furious excitement that had sparked in his eyes, and instead, he was almost placid, his voice measured and quiet.

"Monsieur Morel." He gestured for William to sit, waiting until he obeyed. "I am sorry you could not join us on the scaffold yesterday—you apprehended Gaudet, after all."

William bowed his head in acknowledgement, telling Tessier, "One cannot put personal pleasure before the greater good, Monsieur."

"I had hoped that the sight of his brother-in-law on the scaffold might focus Gaudet's mind somewhat." Tessier resumed his seat. "But it did not. Today I intend to move onto more rigorous methods of persuasion—might you be free to accompany me to the Conciergerie?"

William felt his heart quicken at the invitation, the thought of setting foot inside the prison one he had not dared to anticipate. Accompanying Tessier in the interrogation of Alexandre Gaudet was something he'd neither expected nor relished, and he realized now what that meant, how far he might have to take his role today.

"It would be an honor," he told Tessier carefully.

"You are aware of the Star of Versailles?" Tessier did not wait for a response before he went on. "I believe it was taken by Madame Plamondon when she fled Paris. Her brother, I am sure, holds the key to her whereabouts."

"A woman." He sniffed, even as he watched the other man. "You think she would be capable of such a thing?"

"Oh, Monsieur Morel, I am surprised at such…*small-mindedness*." Tessier held William's gaze. "The Star represents largesse, the obscenity of monarchy…all that we have toiled so hard to overcome. The widow Capet taunted me with it until the very morning of her death and I will not see it pass to another over-privileged, ermine-clad poodle."

"So, we must track the woman down"—William returned the look unflinchingly—"and Gaudet must be made to speak."

At that, Tessier drew in a breath. "I intend to ensure it is kept in Paris for the people."

William smiled, nodding even as his mind drifted back to the guaranteed buyer waiting in England, though the Prince of Wales's own depleted coffers might make the transaction interesting.

Dee's problem, not mine.

"Then we shall make a visit to Alexandre Gaudet," Tessier decided, "and see if we cannot convince him that he would be happier if he unburdened himself."

* * * *

Within the hour, the two men were in Tessier's carriage en route for the fortress on the Seine. It did not escape William's attention that his companion had changed into a black suit once more, the scars hidden beneath supple leather gloves. As they traveled in silence he studied Tessier, as he had so many times, taking in the narrow face and thin lips, the pale skin that seemed as though it had never seen the rays of the sun. He was tall and almost painfully thin, yet when he headed the procession to the guillotine or strode the platform in the midst of his Revolutionary fervor, Tessier seemed an enormous figure. After all, a reputation like his was not won on words alone.

Nor were scars like those that wrecked his flesh.

The noise and bustle of Paris did not diminish on their approach to the glowering building, but the place seemed infected by despair, a malaise that hung heavy in the air itself. Those who shuffled here kept their heads down, the children scurrying around the carriage and the stench stronger than ever.

There was no question of detaining this most important of visitors and, without any preamble, Tessier and William were admitted to the prison. Despite all that he had seen, the adventures he had known, William was unprepared for the scene that greeted him. The fortress buzzed with life, prisoners and guards sharing the same space in air so fetid it turned his stomach.

It was utterly repulsive, everything he hated most about mankind crammed into this heaving, stinking space, but he kept his expression clear of it all, face remaining closed, impassive. The smell was breathtaking, a stink that burned the back of the throat, and William found himself momentarily stilled by it. Tessier pressed on, the guards clearing a space for him as he went, William following in his wake. It occurred to him that a man with the wealth of Gaudet must have been able to, at least, buy himself some moderate comfort away from the rabble. Yet, as they descended deeper into the fortress and the air grew heavier, all sunlight fading into a dirty haze, William wondered if their next stop would be Hell itself.

Tessier hardly stopped speaking for the duration of their walk, warning that Gaudet was a man of extraordinary intelligence and fortitude, that William would do well to watch for him. This was in marked contrast to his knowledge of the man who was the toast of London light theater. Gaudet's plays were not exactly noted for their challenging intellectual content.

In fact, as William well knew, the man Tessier sought was not Dee at all, because that estimable character was safely concealed in a farmhouse some miles from the prison. Whatever Alexandre Gaudet may or may not know, he was simply a man in the wrong place at the worst possible time. No matter what William might wish, what heroics others might believe he should perform, there was nothing to be done to save Gaudet now.

"What," he asked Tessier, "are your intentions?"

"That the spymaster will give up his secrets." After rounding a final corner they stopped before a heavy door. "And here we are."

The guard who had led the way through the prison produced a heavy bunch of keys and selected one, knocking at the door in a mockery of manners before he called, "Visitors to the salon, Monsieur Gaudet!"

"Dignity," Tessier said with a sharpness in his tone that surprised William. "We are not here to torment, Jacquet."

"Monsieur," he said, bobbing his head in a gesture of apology.

"Morel," Tessier introduced William to the guard, who regarded him with a nod, "is here to speak to our playwright."

"He's having a look at life from the other side — those who had nothing have made good, those who had it all are in the sewer," Jacquet explained with a sly smile. "A few years ago, my son scraped for a coin, but when the widow left the Conciergerie on her way to meet her maker, he was the person watching the gate. The last few years have brought opportunities for some that they wouldn't have known otherwise."

"And he behaves meek as a mouse." Tessier smiled indulgently. "Our spymaster."

"Don't you worry about that," Jacquet assured him. "He knows better than to upset Jacquet, unless he likes the taste of his own teeth."

With that he turned the key in the lock and the door opened on the private cell in which Alexandre Gaudet now rested, a world away from the fine salons of London that had been his home since his departure from France half a decade earlier.

William had expected that Gaudet's wealth might have bought him some comfort, yet in this dim cell, with its small barred window set high into the wall, he saw no such thing. As if on cue, a rat scampered over his boot and through the door, leaving the confined, festering room as soon as the opportunity arose. There was no shred of gentility in the place where William now found himself, just a thin covering of straw on a floor that swam with the filth of innumerable previous occupants. Manacles hung on the damp wall and, despite the heat, he shivered, forcing himself not to jump when the door slammed shut behind them.

Alexandre Gaudet sat on a chair toward the back of the room, hidden in shadow. From the angle of the playwright's shoulders William could see that his wrists were bound. His head hung forward until his chin almost touched his chest, the only movement the steady rise and fall of his breathing.

"Monsieur Gaudet." Tessier's voice was as bright as though he were visiting an old friend. "I have brought another *illustrious* visitor. Yesterday Robespierre, today Citizen Yves Morel, visiting from the south."

When Gaudet gave no signal that he had heard, Tessier went on, "You would do well to consider him a man deserving of your full attention—not a village is left standing after he passes through it, nor a man left breathing that ever crossed him."

"Perhaps," Tessier said when Gaudet still did not speak, careful to keep any hint of emotion from his voice, "Monsieur Gaudet is not receiving visitors today?"

When William could no longer avoid it, he let his eyes settle on the prisoner, hardly recognizing him as the richly dressed character he had encountered just days earlier. The flamboyant coat and waistcoat were long gone, a once crisp white shirt filthy and torn, stained with blood here and there. His feet were bare, bright blue breeches muddied with dirt, and dark bruises bloomed wherever his skin was exposed

"He won't eat," Jacquet informed them. "Won't do anything."

"Why will you not eat?" Tessier leaned close to Gaudet, who raised his head, peering at them through the blackened eye. After a moment, he let his eyes slide across to William, holding his gaze until Tessier told him, "Then you can starve, sir, it is of no concern to me."

"And neither should it be." William found that he had to glance away for just a moment, Gaudet's gaze too haunting. "He will talk, either way."

Tessier reached into his waistcoat for a key and slid it into the lock that held the manacles. As soon as they fell to the ground Jacquet dragged Gaudet from the chair and flung him onto the floor. Clearly already used to this, the playwright curled into a ball. Tessier advanced on him, landing a kick to his spine as he said, "Tell me where I might find your sister, Gaudet."

The playwright said nothing, body curling tighter in response, and Tessier said, "This, Gaudet, is nothing but the beginning."

Chapter Four

There was a time not so long ago when Paris had meant something to Alexandre Gaudet. For a young man with money and celebrity it was a playground of hedonistic delights, of days lost to drink and nights abandoned to beauty, sights that he would never forget and scenes that he wished he could remember, and all of it, seemingly, lost to another lifetime.

Where he had once known pleasure he now saw nothing but terror, swift and deadly as Robespierre had promised, and uncompromising as time itself.

How had he ended up here, where the sunlight couldn't shine and the air itself felt damp, where a cloying darkness gnawed at him through his every waking moment, where men told him he was a spy?

A spy?

The very thought of it would be laughable if the consequences weren't so serious. After all, Alexandre Gaudet's private life was anything but—he had reveled in scandal, had enjoyed the favors of the finest gentlemen London could offer. Had dressed in the most flamboyant fabrics and had been found at a different dance every evening and a different salon every day, had been able to light up even the dullest party with his presence and always had a story to tell that was guaranteed to entertain and, even better, to shock.

And yet they think it possible that I, a man who can't keep even his own secrets, could trade those of the very nation where he was born?

Not in this lifetime.

He would say all of this if he could form the words, if he weren't so preoccupied with the pain in his shoulders and the weals on his wrists, or if his throat weren't lined with sand and broken glass.

He didn't know what time it was, or even how long Tessier had been standing before him, silent and still in the hours since the man he called Morel had left them. The few strands of light that pierced the bars had all but disappeared and a flickering candle threw dancing shadows onto the wall. Each passing hour was lost to him and a deep shudder ran through his body as he heard Tessier shift from one foot to the other, leather boots creaking.

Just speak, he wanted to scream but he couldn't muster the energy — *say something, please.*

Don't just stand there watching me as though I'm some sort of animal.

"You came into my home," Tessier said eventually, his voice as quiet and steady as ever. "And you will not eat — is this what passes for gentlemanly behavior in England?"

"Is this really your idea of hospitality?" Gaudet asked, eyes still closed.

"I have treated you very well, sir," Tessier told him quietly. "Believe me."

"You have blackened my eye —"

"You broke into my house and resisted arrest."

"And kept me without sleep for three days," Gaudet reminded him. "The best you can offer me now is food not fit for a dog and 'hospitality' in the form of imprisonment."

"Life in France has grown harder since you left for England — your kind don't belong here," Tessier explained as though the reasoning should've been be obvious. "This isn't your country anymore."

"You are killing our land," Gaudet murmured, lifting his head to watch Tessier, who responded with a bloodless smile that didn't extend to his eyes. "You and your kind."

"We are cleansing it."

This time it was Gaudet's turn to smile and he wetted his

lips, feeling the dry skin rough on the edge of his tongue.

"Even *you* cannot believe that, Monsieur Tessier."

Tessier's hand darted forward like a snake striking at its prey, the gloved fist hitting Gaudet's jaw with more force than he would have expected from such a slight figure. He jerked his head away uselessly as a second punch landed, the salty taste of blood filling his mouth almost immediately. Then Tessier turned away and began to pace the room, kneading his still-clenched fist into his open palm.

"Tell me about the Star, Gaudet," he demanded with an urgency that hadn't been there previously. "Where is it hidden? Where is your sister?"

Gaudet shook his head, unsure of how he could say anything other than the truth that Tessier had already rejected as the weakest of lies. He swallowed the blood in his mouth and squeezed his eyes together, a roaring in his head threatening to drown out the whole world.

"Where"—Tessier wrapped his fingers in Gaudet's hair as he had the dismembered head of Philippe Plamondon— "is the Star of Versailles?"

He jerked Gaudet's head up sharply, fixing him with those unblinking eyes, a blue so pale as to be virtually colorless.

"I don't know where your diamond is." Gaudet gave a gasp of pain, his stomach knotting at the darkness that seemed to cloud Tessier's face. "I came here for my family—"

"Where is the Star?" Tessier asked the question for what seemed like the millionth time. "Tell me and the pain can end."

Gaudet's hair was pulled so tight that he felt as though it might rip out from the roots, yet still he could only whisper, "I write plays. I am no spy."

Tessier began to pace again, the shadow from his slender figure enormous and black as night in the single candle flame. Gaudet could understand now why this man commanded such fear, why people spoke of him in whispers.

The Butcher of Orléans.

"Have you seen it, Monsieur Gaudet?" Tessier's pacing ceased and he linked his fingers behind his back, breath audibly faster and a trace of admiration in his voice. "I think you know where it can be found. I have never known a man with such fortitude."

"If I had your Star, believe me, I would give it to you."

I know where Philippe is, of course, I can't forget that. It haunts me even now.

Whatever else happens, that will always be with me, the look of a man barely thirty-five years old ashen and stooped, silent and broken.

That will be with me to the grave.

"My hospitality only extends so far, Monsieur Gaudet— you have just exhausted it."

With those words, Tessier left the room. As the key turned once more Gaudet let out a long-held breath, screwing his eyes shut when he leaned over and spat out a mouthful of blood. His mind was jumbled and he couldn't form anything resembling a coherent thought, brain racing as he tried to find one thing to hang on to, some kind of a rock in the current.

And it can't be the sight of Philippe on the guillotine, the faces of the mob contorted like medieval devils – nor can it be Claudine and her child lost in France waiting for help that is never going to come.

I will die here.

The thought lodged in his head, and when two of Tessier's soldiers returned to the cell Gaudet felt as though he was barely there, looking down on his own body as he was dragged toward the back of the room. After three days without food or sleep his struggles were always going to be futile, but Gaudet gave them as much of a fight as he was able until the younger of the two slammed the stock of his pistol down into the back of his head then, when Gaudet was suitably subdued, they slammed their prisoner into the wall.

Gaudet felt his senses return as the manacles were removed from his wrists, but any relief was short-lived when a length of rope replaced them, pulling his arms roughly upward and fastening them to an iron ring. After so long without movement, the violence of the action tore through the stiffness in his shoulders and Gaudet winced in agony, flexing his fingers in the air. With some effort, he managed to twist enough to watch the door, where the soldiers had turned their backs on him, lost in a muttered conversation as though they were waiting for a tavern to open rather than readying a man for torture.

The sight of Tessier's shadow looming on the wall of the corridor filled Gaudet with new terror. He pulled at the rope as the jailer dismissed his warders then, once again, closed the door. Gaudet turned his face to the wall and waited, hearing the *swoosh* in the air before the riding crop hit his back. He couldn't hold back his cry of pain, body arching away instinctively with every muscle tensed in agony.

"Where is the Star of Versailles?" Tessier asked with an insane calm, the whip connecting a second time.

Gaudet couldn't have answered had he wanted to, teeth clenched when the leather crop slashed his skin again and again. A cool breeze chilled his spine where his shirt hung in tatters and warm rivulets of blood drew webs where the whip found them. Gaudet was conscious of nothing but pain, of the sense that his whole body was being hung on hooks, burned above hot coals.

"Before I kill you, you *will* tell me," Tessier promised as minutes and hours stumbled together. "And before I put you to the blade, you will watch your sister and her son die."

Gaudet said nothing, his breath coming in harsh bursts and his head hanging below the level of his shoulders, every nerve ending exposed and raw. Heartbeat crashing, he was aware of the sickly stench of claret when Tessier's face filled the space where the meagre light had been.

"You will tell me everything, Gaudet," Tessier told him in

a tone as cold as night. "And when Morel has finished with you, you will *beg* for my *kindness*."

I know nothing, Gaudet screamed inside, hot tears stinging and blinding him behind his clenched eyelids as one set of feet receded and two more returned.

"Poor bastard," he heard one of the soldiers say, then the rope was unfastened and the manacles closed over his wrists once more, every movement hot needles in the fresh wounds. This time there was no struggle and they dragged their rag doll prisoner across the cell, dropping him down onto the straw. Then there was a calloused hand supporting the back of his head and a tankard at his lips for a few moments as the guard shared the few remaining sips of beer with him. Gaudet gulped the bitter alcohol down, but it swam in his body. If it hadn't been for the man who held his head up, he knew he would have choked.

"Tell them what you know, son," an older voice told him. Gaudet's head fell to the straw as though made of lead. He barely registered the guard's next words. "Morel won't muck about like Tessier does."

There were too many footsteps to count then, comings and goings until the door closed. Somewhere in the fog of pain Gaudet sensed the presence of another. In so far as he could think of *anything*, he knew that there would be more suffering. There seemed little else in his life anymore. Behind the bars, he had no sense of night and day, just cruelty and the pain it left behind, the angry words and agonizing touch of Tessier.

Now Gaudet lay in the darkness and listened to his ragged breathing, tasting a foul mixture of beer and blood in his throat. He hardly dared move for the agony in his upper body. It felt as though every muscle was smoldering, his skin a mass of tiny flames that burned still. The world around was all darkness, the pain that consumed him without end. He heard a groan that couldn't have been his welling in his throat, low and barely human

"Alexandre Gaudet," a man said and he flinched,

unconsciously, anticipating more punishment. "They have summoned me to torture your secrets from you—have you any to tell?"

At the sound of the voice, Gaudet drew his tongue over his lips and realized that they had split, a tang of blood still lingering there. The unseen man's boots trod across the floor and Gaudet opened his eyes. He watched the shadows on the wall grow and change as the new arrival lifted the candle and walked toward the straw. Laid on his side, Gaudet was surprised to hear the man give a gasp of something that he supposed must be horror at his wounds, setting the candle on the floor and placing something heavier beside it.

"Where is your sister?" The words were low, even, the sound of a cloth being wrung out following a moment later.

"My sister," he heard a voice that didn't sound like his own rasp. "Please—"

"If you want to see her again"—the unexpectedly gentle press of a wet cloth to his tormented skin almost made him cry out—"you must tell me everything you know."

The straw shifted when Morel sat beside him, one hand still on the cloth and the other coming to rest on his upper arm. A few moments passed, then he wrung the cloth and applied it again, touch assured and firm, but there was gentleness there, too. He worked at the slashes in silence, dabbing the solution across the whip-straight slices that crisscrossed Gaudet's spine in a map of suffering. The only sound came from the water that wrung into the bowl and the grating breaths that escaped his bloody lips.

"Why?" There was the hint of frustration in the words. "Why will you not speak?"

"Why," Gaudet turned his head, the world swimming in and out of darkness, "will I not give up my sister to the Butcher of Orléans and his torturer from the south?"

Unsteady though his vision might be, Gaudet thought for a moment he caught a flicker of disquiet in the gaze of the man who watched him, the gentle ministrations pausing as

Morel weighed up his response.

"Things are not always what they seem."

"Do I strike you as a spymaster?" Gaudet raised a tired eyebrow as he posed the question.

The man considered this for a long moment, holding his gaze when he countered, "Do I strike you as a man who would torture hundreds?"

"Tessier looks like a thin-lipped bureaucrat." Gaudet sighed deeply, thinking of the little girl he had left lodged in Paris. "And you are Morel."

The careful touch resumed and Morel again stroked the cloth over Gaudet's stinging back, his voice quiet when he murmured, "You must eat."

"If I do not eat, I will die all the sooner."

"If you do not eat," he was informed, "you will not be the only one to die."

"When I am gone, you will *never* catch Claudine." A tear threaded from his eye at the thought of it, of his sister and her child lost forever in France.

"Tessier wants the Star." As Morel spoke, Gaudet found himself being turned slightly, the cloth soft against his brow. "He will not stop until he has it in his possession."

Gaudet shivered at the thought of those hands, the scarred flesh stretched over gnarled bones, yet he said nothing, not willing to give in to kindness where torture had failed.

"Tell me." There was a pleading note now. Whatever had been added to the water eased the smarting bruises on his face. "Tell me where she is."

"If I knew," he reasoned, "I would be with her, not searching for clues in her house."

"Are you *always* this bloody stubborn?"

"You are Robespierre's man." Gaudet shifted to assuage the pain in his back. "And one day *you* will face the guillotine."

"I am nobody's man." There was an edge to the words, yet the touch remained gentle as Morel brushed the cloth lightly over his bruised eye. Gaudet let it soothe him despite himself, glad for this momentary break in the torture, for the kindness that he *knew* was feigned, was intended only to break him further.

"Let me help you."

"Never."

"Never is a long time." The words were deadpan.

There came a knock at the door of the cell then, Gaudet tensing when Tessier ventured politely, "Morel, might I enter?"

"One moment," Morel called back, and when he spoke again, his voice was low and urgent. "I am on your side."

He turned his gaze back to Morel, reaching for his hand and for a long moment they stayed there, Morel's expression, for one brief flicker, one of fear. With a brief nod, however, the impression was broken and Morel got carefully to his feet, bucket emptied into the corner and the cloth vanishing a moment later.

Tessier strode into the cell, his fingers knitted together before him. He took in the scene with a cold smile and said, "Gaudet, you are to return to the Rue Saint-Honoré. I believe you and I will soon reach an understanding there."

"It seems our playwright is not one to speak freely," Morel told Tessier coldly. "Even the candle flame could not induce him to talk."

"You will see" — Tessier crouched before Gaudet, dragging his head up by the hair — "how well I treat my houseguests, *sir*. Jacquet, the manacles!"

Morel stood aside as the guard entered with the requested chains, the memory of them making Gaudet's entire body cry out in protest after the all-too-short reprieve.

"And you and I" — Tessier clapped his leather-gloved hand to Morel's shoulder — "shall enjoy an excellent claret while we wait."

With that, he led Morel from the prison cell as Gaudet collapsed back onto the straw, submitting to the chains once more.

Chapter Five

Fouquier-Tinville set down his coffee cup and steepled his fingers before his face, dark eyes fixed on Tessier's pale gaze.

"Saint-Just and I took a trip to the Conciergerie today, Tessier," he said in a measured voice.

Tessier nodded, trying and failing to read the apparently benign expression on the lawyer's face, the silence growing more uneasy with every passing second.

"We thought we might look in on our Monsieur Gaudet," he went on finally, still not blinking. "And yet the strangest thing, we could not find him *anywhere*."

"Indeed."

"We wondered if perhaps he had escaped or perhaps, *somehow*, we had missed his trial, and yet it appears not," Fouquier-Tinville commented, his voice steely. "Where is our spy, Tessier?"

How dare you. Tessier curled his fingers around the arm of his chair, holding himself in place before his temper erupted. *Who do you think you are to challenge me?*

"With the greatest of respect, as you are left to practice law, leave me to interrogate my prisoners." Tessier smiled coldly. "He is in a safe place under the watchful eye of Yves Morel."

"If Morel is in Paris then we expect to see him before the Convention—he has been silent in all but the briefest correspondence."

"I shall speak—"

"And now there is an empty cell at the Conciergerie," the other man said, standing and executing a stiff bow of thanks. "Return Alexandre Gaudet to it within twenty-four hours or the Convention may decide it suits *you* better than the Rue Saint-Honoré."

"I highly doubt that." Tessier smiled, utterly confident in the support of Robespierre. "I think your influence will be wasted if that is your intention."

"My intention is simply to ensure that the country benefits from *all* our actions," Fouquier-Tinville informed him. "Rather than suffering through our own desires for revenge. Good day, Tessier."

"Good day," Tessier replied, standing to return the bow and staring after the figure of the lawyer as he walked down the steps of the coffee house and disappeared from view.

Could he break Alexandre Gaudet in twenty-four hours?

I need him in the house, right there in the place where every floorboard, every window pane is a reminder of his sister and the child, for it is that memory that will split his resolve in two. He might grit his teeth and bear a whipping, hold his breath so he doesn't scream when I apply a candle flame to his skin, but he won't be able to withstand the thought of his sister out there somewhere, lost and alone.

He must give her up, for her own good.

Tessier drank what was left of the bitter coffee and bowed his thanks to the young woman who had served him. Despite the season, he pulled the leather gloves over his scarred skin and stepped out into the sunlight, nodding to signal for his carriage. Waiting for his transport to arrive, he surveyed the packed street and those who made every effort not to catch his eye even as he saw them glance his way anxiously or even point him out to their companions, throwing a glimpse in his direction with feigned disinterest.

And they should look — let them know me and let them fear me, every one of them.

Let them know what happened in Orléans, whisper about it and use my name to scare their misbehaving babes.

Vincent Tessier, the Butcher of Orléans.

They will write that on my tombstone.

He stepped back to avoid the filth thrown up as the ebony carriage rolled to a halt, then he climbed into the cool interior, pulling the door closed behind him. There was a pause as the usual two soldiers clambered into position on the back of the vehicle and they set off again, clattering over the surface of the streets in the direction of home.

The day had been an unusually hot one and the stench hung in the air across the city, filthy and cloying. He would lay down his life for this country, and though Paris was the jewel in the crown of his homeland, its stink was less majestic.

And the noise, that thunderous, rumbling racket that never seemed to fall silent. When he stood on the scaffold it was like oxygen, pushing him forward and filling him with extravagant pride, but in everyday life it was an unwelcome and deafening din.

And there is nothing that shuts it out other than the blade and the whip, the welcome moment when a man is lost in his work.

The carriage slowed to a halt when it passed the crowds in the Place de la Révolution. Tessier leaned forward to see Sanson on the scaffold, continuing a proud father's legacy. He knitted his fingers beneath his chin and watched three people go beneath the blade, his heartbeat quickening as the crowd roared its approval. Tessier's lips parted in anticipation as the fourth and final soul went to the bascule, the sun glinting on her white-blonde hair. She fought like a tiger with her escorts, even as the straps were tightened around her thin frame, mouth contorted with raging oaths. The twisting and wriggling went on until the very moment that the *mouton* drove the blood-blackened blade down onto that swan neck. Tessier tightened his fist and let out a wordless exhalation of triumph, his breath coming faster now.

Finally, the carriage rolled on and he caught the occasional snatch of a shouted complaint, an obscenity hurled in the direction of the postilion after yet another pedestrian jumped out of the carriage's unswerving path.

Once again, Tessier remembered Fouquier-Tinville's barely concealed threat and felt a surge of annoyance that he and the upstart Saint-Just presumed to interfere in interrogations, matters that were not their concern.

Let Fouquier-Tinville look down his nose and Saint-Just threaten me with a cell. They will celebrate me as a true hero of this Republic, the man who stole the queen's last, bitter victory from beneath her pretty nose.

And they will have their playwright back in prison tomorrow, because by morning, I will have wrung the truth from his contorted, screaming body.

He will tell me his secrets. By the time we part company, he will be begging me to listen to his every sin, however slight.

I will be his final confessor.

Then he too will meet Sanson in the Square.

Tessier clenched his gloved fists and stared through the dirty window, lost for a moment in a memory of a very different time in Paris, when a younger man had burned for revolution, when ideals had been all he'd possessed.

That man had never expected to be here, had never even held a gun, let alone found the beauty in a dying man's last confession, the perfect, unguarded moment when there was only truth.

Had I really been such an innocent once?

Perhaps.

Tessier shook his head to banish all thoughts of the past and flexed his fingers again, feeling a stiffness in the joints. No warmth came from the pale summer sunlight and he shielded his eyes and squinted past his reflection at the same route that had carried the widow to her death.

The thought of the Star of Versailles brought back a stark and clear memory of the woman who had once been queen, diminished and frail yet still she held his gaze, challenged him at every turn. How Tessier longed for his time alone with the Widow Capet, dreamed of tearing the missal from her slender fingers and showing her a little of the cruelty the world thrust upon those who did not have the fortune to be born an archduchess.

He could not escape the feeling that she had beaten him, that through their long hours of conversation and verbal sparring, she had never been anything other than a monarch, her civility condescending and her patience an offensive mask. Her eyes had flickered just once, gaze shifting when he'd tested what he was sure could be no more than a rumor and mentioned the Star of Versailles. The words had frozen her usually demure countenance for no more than a moment before she'd pursed her lips and gone back to her treasured book without a second glance.

Then, after so much silence and with hours before she felt the blade, the widow had sent for Vincent Tessier. He'd found her kneeling in prayer, head bowed and hands clasped so tightly that her knuckles had been as white as her hair had become. Tessier had waited for her to talk to her imagined God, standing at the door until she'd crossed herself and risen to her feet, turning to fix him with that glittering gaze.

"You have asked me about the Star of Versailles, Monsieur," Marie had stated simply, her voice clear and calm. "And I have remained silent but I can do so no more."

He had held his breath, waiting for her to unburden herself.

"It is the most precious thing in the world to me," she'd explained, tears that never fell shining in her eyes. "And the Lord will see that you never hold it in your filthy hands — you may send me to my death, sir, but believe me when I tell you that as long as the Star remains safe, you have lost."

He heard her words as though she stood beside him and flinched away from the steel in her tone even now, even as he knew she was no more than an echo in history.

'You have lost.'

And it was at that moment that he'd known he must possess it, no matter what the cost — he would not be beaten by a spoiled whore.

Again, Tessier clenched his fists and the tight flesh

stretched beneath his gloves, the leather grown supple from wear until it was a second skin that hid the evidence of his infamy. He felt no shame in the scars, but the weather could be cruel so he preferred concealment nowadays. Though there was a certain undeniable *frisson* about the first touch of flesh when the gloves came off. Only now did Tessier realize that the carriage had halted before the house. He threw open the door and emerged, disappearing into the building.

Without pause he made for the staircase. As he climbed, he stripped off the gloves, the two men who guarded the door leaping to their feet, straight-backed and silent.

Tessier acknowledged them with a nod and took the key from his waistcoat, about to slide it into the lock when Jacquet told him, "Citizen Morel is already inside, sir."

Still silent, Tessier pushed the door open and stepped into the room, where he saw Morel before the boarded window, hands knitted behind his back and his eyes fixed on the new arrival. His face wore an expression of annoyance at the interruption and he asked, "Monsieur Tessier?"

"I have come to see our Monsieur Gaudet," Tessier replied with a lightness that belied the slam of the door. "Paris is quite dazzling today—it seems as though a beautiful evening is in store."

He tilted his head to one side and regarded the man who was, once again, in the chair, arms behind his back. Tessier fully expected that his words would find no reaction. He was right, there wasn't even a twitch. Gaudet was bent forward at the waist as far as his painful position would allow and his head hung as though his neck was snapped in two. The shirt that had once been carefully tailored for this so-called *gentleman* was now torn and stained more crimson than white. Deep black bruises bloomed where his skin was visible, welts and weals showing up a furious red.

Tessier smiled thinly and told his prisoner, "I bring good news, sir."

He crossed the room and took Gaudet's hair in his fist,

pulling his head up to stare into the blackened eyes, hardly recognizing the face that had once been considered so handsome.

I always hated your sort.

Gaudet opened his eyes. He peered at Tessier with no trace of emotion, his gaze moving back and forth as though trying to focus as Tessier said, "It seems your fame is not limited to the theater." Tessier darted his eyebrows up and added, "Robespierre has taken a personal interest in you."

"Robespierre," Gaudet muttered through what was left of his voice and the prosecutor recognized a flash of fear in his eyes. "I don't—"

"Tomorrow you return to the Conciergerie," Tessier confirmed. "And from there, it is a short journey to the scaffold." He released Gaudet's hair and addressed Morel. "He has told you nothing?"

"Nothing," came the confirmation. "I have seen nothing like it in all my years."

There was a creeping sense of admiration that *anyone* could resist both Morel and himself, that a supposedly dandified playwright could show such fortitude.

"Very well, very well," Tessier said, dismissing Morel with a curt bow as he turned back to his prisoner and said, "Our time is limited, Monsieur Gaudet, and we have so much left to discuss."

Chapter Six

The night drew on, bringing rest in some degree to all who slumbered in the house, from the prisoner on his sorry mattress to Tessier, who slept soundly in the once marital bed. Yet the man they called Yves Morel was wakeful, making his way through the building as silent as a shadow, escape the only thing on his mind

He was not Yves Morel, of course — the commander who had terrorized the south of the land now lay rotting in a pit with a hundred of those he had sent to their death. That politician, brutal and uncompromising, had run into an equally dedicated figure in the shape of Viscount William Knowles and it was the peer who had put him in his grave, his identity an easy and convenient one to assume.

There were always hazards with taking the name of another, he knew, but when it put a man one step closer to the Star of Versailles, the risks were worth the reward.

And with a diamond like that, a man can be done with adventuring, with danger and having nowhere, no one *to call his own.*

With a diamond like that, a man can start again.

Retrieving Alexandre Gaudet from the Rue Saint-Honoré was never going to be an easy task, he had known that from the start, though it was a world away from the Conciergerie. Here he had two guards and a madman to deal with and yet, until word reached him from Dee, he dared do nothing to act.

As the hallway clock struck two, William made his way to the dark kitchen, where Bastien waited behind the kitchen door. He greeted the child with a coin, thinking how unnoticeable Dee's people had become, how deep in the fabric of Paris they were woven.

"You found your buried treasure yet?" the little boy asked with a cheeky smile. "I know you've got a playwright in your nursery with no skin on his back, but what about this diamond?"

William stood quietly for a few seconds and absorbed all that, brushing an unseen speck of something from his sleeve. He turned the words over in his head, eventually telling Bastien, "Supposedly it's as big as your fist. If Madame Plamondon is carrying *that* in her petticoats, she'd better keep an eye on her skirts."

"What happened to Morel?" Bastien enquired casually as they strolled away from the house. "And how it is nobody so much as questions you?"

"He had the misfortune to come home to meet me." William shrugged. "And he came off worse. I took his correspondence and sowed the seeds as I traveled north — he is known to Robespierre and Saint-Just alone. As long as I avoid the two of them for the next few days nobody need be any the wiser."

They walked on in silence to the cabinetmaker's shop, then, with a glance back at the street, William slipped inside. Here, he was greeted by Charron and Sylvie as though he were an old friend, their hospitality warm and welcome after the frozen horror of Tessier's house. Over a welcome ale, he told them of the playwright, of the torture and the sure knowledge that Gaudet *must* know something, that nobody would be stupid enough to come into the heart of the Terror without possessing the knowledge of how to escape again.

As he outlined his plans to help Gaudet escape, Charron studied William more closely than he had ever been studied before. He saw a slight twitch in Charron's hand, his fingers tightening around Sylvie's. The cabinetmaker chewed at his lip and turned to consider the woman who sat beside him, his eyes searching her face for something.

"Sylvie," Charron said finally. "What would you have me do?"

"I would have you take me to Vienna." She smiled, her face lighting up with mirth. "And dress me in silk and diamonds, *but* if we can't do that, I would have you do whatever you believe is right."

"I can't endanger Sylvie and Bastien," Charron concluded, returning his eyes to William. "I *am* sorry."

Sylvie pulled her hand free and reached out for William, catching his arm as he went to stand. "If this man dies, what is lost?"

"He is searching for his sister and her child," he explained with a shrug, well aware that might not be enough to sway Charron. "But it seems he holds the key to the whereabouts of the Star of Versailles."

Sylvie's eyes widened and she asked urgently, "So it's true — it's here in Paris?"

"So it would seem," William answered. "Dee believes it is held by Madame Plamondon."

And if he believes it, then it is true.

"I won't put you and Bastien in danger for a bloody trinket," the cabinetmaker told them, leaving no room for argument. "But I would do it for Madame Plamondon and her son if you would give me your blessing, Sylvie. Philippe was one of the finest men in France."

Say yes, William silently prayed, so much depending on the woman before him. Candlelight danced in her eyes and something sparkled in the gloss of her black hair as she looked from William to Charron and back again.

"Bring your Monsieur Gaudet here," Sylvie told him finally, squeezing his arm in a gesture of support. "What do you need?'

"I'll fetch a sleeping draft from Madame Masson," Bastien exclaimed. "You can walk him straight out of there and bring him and his diamond to us!"

"It is miraculous, as though God himself created it," Tessier had told him that morning. "Every angle exact and it shines so brightly that there might be a flame within its very heart."

And yet the Prince of Wales would scream and rave about it being the rightful property of the British crown, yet destined for France.

"Bring him," Charron agreed as Bastien turned to William with a grin of triumph. "And do it tonight, if you can."

There was nothing William wanted less than to re-enter the stinking cell, the memory of his last visit there all too fresh in his mind. He closed his eyes briefly, opening them again at the sudden and vivid reminder of Gaudet's face. The expression in the broken man's eyes when the playwright had clung to him had been like a drowning man, the barest flicker of hope he had seen more painful than the grip on his hand.

"Get home," Bastien said excitedly, the little boy alive to the possibilities of the drama. "And I'll be there in an hour with your draft!"

Returning to the house, he wondered what it would have been like when the elusive Madame Plamondon had lived there, a flicker of irritation again that her brother had not seen fit to be slightly more useful during their brief encounter. He would not be sorry to leave that shell of a household behind and it should not, he was sure, be too hard to extract the Frenchman, if only his luck would hold.

After pouring a glass of brandy, William settled in the now threadbare drawing room to await the boy's arrival. Once again, he thought of that damned jewel, of the prince who would spend its wealth on women and the gaming table, then he thought of his own existence, of risking life and limb for rich men who had nothing better to do with their money.

Just before nine, he left his seat and went to stand out in the empty alleyway behind the kitchen, ready for the delivery. After a few moments, he saw Bastien clamber over a wall thirty feet from where he stood and drop nimbly to the ground.

"As requested." Bastien smiled, handing over a small bottle of clear liquid, and William passed him his usual coins. "Half of this and they'll be out after five minutes — you will be careful, won't you?"

"When" — he gave a small, rare smile — "am I not?"

Bastien acknowledged him with a nod and darted off along the alleyway, disappearing into the shadows as William returned to the kitchen. At the sound of the heavy door knocker falling against the front door he froze, his breath catching in his throat for a moment. Quickly he dropped the bottle into his pocket and paused at the top of the kitchen steps as one of the maids hurried to answer the door.

Robespierre.

William stepped back into the shadows, the lawyer's attention thankfully taken by the sight of Tessier descending the staircase. William saw then that the riding crop was tucked beneath his arm, a splash of blood staining the pale flesh of his cheek and coloring his white linen cuffs. When he saw the visitor, Tessier visibly straightened before nodding a welcome, curt and brisk.

Pausing at the mirror, he wiped the blood away with a handkerchief and said, "Citizen, I — "

"The playwright," Robespierre told him, already climbing the staircase. "Now."

"Take this," Tessier hissed as he tossed the whip toward the maid.

She caught it with a grimace, her palms sticking on the bloodied leather. Barely daring to breathe, William melted back into the shadows, listening intently for any noise from above. Finally, after what felt like an excruciatingly long time, footsteps sounded once more, the two men descending and heading out into the night.

Another pair of feet pounded on the stairs then as one of the guards thundered down, calling, "I'll see what food there is to go with the beer and all!"

Seeing his chance, William stepped from the shadows,

seemingly in all innocence, saying conversationally, "I am due to *visit* Gaudet shortly. I shall bring your beer up with my own."

"Citizen," the guard exclaimed with a panicky bow, "my pa said as he'd met you at the prison, it's an honor, sir!"

This is Jacquet's son? This boy, the offspring of that villain? He hasn't inherited his father's manner.

"Go back to your duties," he told the young man, wondering at what the world had come to. "I shall be up directly."

"We was saying to each other," the young man remarked with a smile, his father suddenly writ on his face, "he's a funny one, never makes a sound, just takes the beating. I tell you this, I reckon *I* could get it out of him. Give me that sister of his to go at, he'd soon talk then!"

William felt a flash of loathing when he repeated, "Return to your duties, citizen."

With a bow, the boy retreated, taking the stairs two at a time whilst William made his way to the kitchen. It took no time at all to fix the drink, thanks to the bottle from Bastien. His thoughts were firmly on the task ahead when he returned upstairs and announced, "It must be thirsty work watching a traitor. Drink, with my blessing."

"Much obliged, sir!" The older guard laughed, taking one of the mugs of beer as the younger Jacquet snatched his own with a greedy thanks. He guzzled at the ale, pausing to turn the key and admit William to the room that had once been the nursery of the Plamondon child, now pungent with the smell of blood and sweat, a pitch-black torture chamber illuminated by a single candle.

"Am I to be executed?" From where he was strung up by his wrists, Gaudet tried to lift his head, yet failed, in even that simple gesture. His split lips parted for a second before any more sounds came out. "Robespierre says I die at dawn."

"Well, now," Jacquet growled. He threw open the door and commented, "That was quite a draft you gave us,

Morel."

"What is the meaning of this?" William had a split second to decide to brazen it out. "Tessier will hear of this intrusion."

"He'll hear about you drugging folk, coming in here to cozy up to this molly," the young man agreed. "I saw Morel speak in Bordeaux and I say you're *not* Morel."

"And I say that you are mistaken, Citizen."

"They'll pin a fucking medal on me," was the guard's response as he drunkenly lifted his gun, hand trembling.

In reply, William took two steps forward and a smack from his elbow sent the weapon flying.

"Call—" the guard began, though if any of the meagre domestic staff had heard, no one seemed to be rushing to answer or assist. The call for help was cut off a moment later when William's own pistol fired once and struck true, the man crumpling to the floor.

"Sir?" the voice of Madam Bonnay, Tessier's cook, floated upstairs, alive with the chance of gossip. "Is all well up there?"

"Everything is as it should be," William called back, already working to release Gaudet.

The rope burned his fingertips but eventually the ends of the knot were free and he tugged it away from the wall, Gaudet's body falling against him for a moment when his bonds were finally removed. Only William's arms around his waist stopped them both from hitting the floor and he steadied them awkwardly, limbs that must have been in agony wrapped loosely around his body.

"I'll get you to safety," he told the injured man, "but you have to work with me."

It was at a painfully slow pace that they made their way toward the door, William taking most of Gaudet's weight as he managed, with some effort, to get the door open. He listened to the house below, praying that their luck would hold when they stepped around the drugged guard.

"I can't…"

"You can't what?" William stared at the playwright with something akin to amazement. "Would you rather wait here to die?"

"The nursery—" Gaudet winced, stooping at the obvious flare of pain. Suddenly he straightened, pulling against William. "I have to get the locket, Claudine is alone and nobody is there and—" His voice rose in pitch and volume before he cut the words off, shaking his head.

"Locket?" William was utterly lost by this new twist.

"We had a hiding place in the nursery, I didn't think." With that, Gaudet turned back to the cell and dragged William with him. In the darkened shell of the once cozy nursery he paused, fevered eyes roaming before the cold fingers William held slipped free of his grasp.

Gaudet dropped to his knees as though in prayer, patting his hands on the floorboards as William told him, "They've had the boards up, there's no way—"

"It's not under the boards," Gaudet hissed and there was such urgency, such conviction in his voice that William dropped to his knees beside him in time to hear him say, "I need a knife, something sharp."

William reached into his coat, wordlessly handing over the blade, even as he questioned the sanity of tarrying.

"The child…" Gaudet gasped. "He cannot be left."

"You are not making any sense," William heard himself mutter in exasperation, as though *anything* here made sense.

Gaudet used the blade to lever up one of the boards, setting it on the ground, doubling over with a gasp of pain as his body caught up to the adrenaline-fueled exertions. "I won't get another chance."

After a moment, Gaudet pressed the tip of the blade to a point in the grain and began picking at it with fingers that were already bruised black, what was left of the ragged nails catching on the rough wood. He lifted the board to reveal a small cavity, and before William had a chance to intervene, Gaudet slipped his hand into the gap.

With utmost care, he withdrew his fingers and there was

the tinkle of a delicate jewelry chain, a tiny locket safe in his palm. The treasure was no bigger than a fingernail. Gaudet put it to his lips, murmuring as he clutched it in a surprisingly strong fist.

"Now we go," William told him, sure they had already tarried long enough.

Gaudet's reply was to rise shakily to his feet and hold out his slender hand, graceful fingers curling around William's own. Their progress out of the room was hampered by Gaudet's obvious suffering, and William halted them at the top of the stairs, attention fixed intently on the gloom below.

Then he heard it, the tread of footsteps climbing the staircase, accompanied by Madame Bonnay's voice trilling a soft song on her way to bed. A dim candle flame illuminated the darkness in which they stood, both rooted to the spot with nowhere to go and every moment bringing discovery closer. Though he knew it was a futile effort, William pulled at Tessier's locked door as the broad figure of Madame Bonnay emerged from the shadows.

"What's this? What on earth—?" Madame Bonnay asked, tone steady and disapproving.

"It's me." Gaudet lifted his head and the woman gasped in shock. "André?"

"Shame on you." She drew her head back and spat on Gaudet. "Be on your way, traitor."

If that was as good as they were going to get, William was happy to grab it with both hands, calling his thanks to the woman as he pulled the spittle-flecked Gaudet along with him. They were halfway down the stairs when he heard her voice again.

"Marie!" Madame Bonnay called, her voice raised in alarm. "Run and get the master from his club!"

"Damn it, man, move!" By sheer determination, he got them to the bottom of the stairs, William praying the door was unlocked.

"Through the kitchen," Gaudet told him weakly, "The

lanes are a warren…"

Reassured that he was not rescuing a man completely deficient in sense, William changed course, the journey through the kitchen taken as quickly as he could pull Gaudet along. There was the sound of footsteps from the stairs but he didn't even glance back, letting out an exclamation of relief when the cool air of the night hit them at last.

When the thunder of wheels sounded at the end of the long, narrow lane from which there seemed no easy escape, William froze, Gaudet a dead weight in his arms. He stepped back into the shadows as a simple carriage clattered to a halt and the door was flung open.

From within the familiar, brusque tones of the spymaster Tessier sought in vain called out, "Get in, quickly!"

William didn't need telling twice. He dragged Gaudet toward the carriage, piling him through the door before climbing in after.

"Tomorrow," Dee said firmly, his mouth a tight line, blue eyes flashing with annoyance as he addressed William, "you and I will discuss this."

With that he turned his attention to the playwright, shaking his head.

'Discuss.' William was, he knew without a doubt, in a certain degree of bother—just what amount that was he would have to wait to find out. It was, however, a better position to be in than the one of a few moments previous, and William allowed himself the briefest of moments to gather himself, turning his gaze to the window.

He watched a group of men hurrying toward the house, pistols drawn, no doubt roused by Marie's cries for help. Gaudet, meanwhile, huddled in a tight ball in the corner of the squabs, shaking his head furiously at Dee's assurances of his safety.

"You're safe," William found himself telling the broken man suddenly, Gaudet's terror grating on his already jarred nerves. "Don't you understand that?"

"Safe?" He spat the word as though it were poison and

Dee, frowning, retrieved a folded page from his own coat and held it before Gaudet's eyes.

"From your sister," Dee said as though addressing a child. "You are with friends and on your way to shelter."

Then, William decided with no small amount of relief, *I can wash my hands of you.*

"Morel," Dee said as the coach drew to a halt. "This is your safe-house tonight, Gaudet and I will go on. Await my contact."

"I am, as always, at your service," William couldn't help the dry edge to his tone. With a final glance at Gaudet, he gladly exited the carriage, looking from left to right before making his way to the door, the Frenchman's face in his mind as he did so.

Chapter Seven

The rain, which had been nothing but a light mist when Bastien had arrived to collect William just after dawn, had grown heavier during the last hour as they walked mile after mile along a narrow, muddy track toward Butte aux Cailles. With the weather worsening so too did the conversation dwindle and now they traveled in silence, Bastien almost prancing through the mud in bare feet, shoes thrust into his tattered pockets.

In the last seventy-two hours, William had been transformed from a well-dressed hero of the Revolution into something slightly less grand. Yet even concealed beneath the clothes of an innocent citizen, he could not escape the fear that every sound in the night was Vincent Tessier, seeking out the traitors in his midst.

Dee's appearance in the city left William with no doubt that things had progressed, that his rogue decision to free Gaudet had led to trouble. He had been on a mission to watch and gather information, to learn more about the unknown traitor who had informed on Philippe's people, allowing the counter-revolutionaries to be systematically smashed by Tessier. Instead he had surrendered his cover, saved a man who might know nothing at all and caused the spymaster himself to appear in the heart of the action, an unthinkable development. Dee was a name on dispatches, a polite meeting in the club of a European capital. He was sober and polite and, to any passing gossip, nothing but an upper-class gent touring Europe. Now he was in Paris and William was on his way for an audience.

"Gaudet's better than he was already, thanks to Ma,"

Bastien told him. "Asked after you this morning… Says he's going to put you in a play."

"If he tries that," William said, "I'll send him to the block myself!"

"He don't make no sense most of the time," Bastien admitted. "But he'll get there."

It swiftly became apparent that their destination was a large stone farmhouse on the horizon. William gathered himself for the calling to account, let alone the inevitable trip back to England. Where he would go then he didn't know, the world being a lonely place for someone with no friends to call their own.

"Here you are, then," Bastien told him when they reached the courtyard where chickens watched from their coops, safe from the battering rain. "Good luck!"

He was going to need it, of that William was certain. Bidding the boy farewell, he strode purposefully across the yard to the farmhouse and the rotting wooden door. He raised his hand once, let it fall, and lifted it again before finally knocking, counting the seconds and listening for sounds inside.

As he readied his hand to knock again, the door opened just an inch and a tiny, frail old woman appeared in the gloom beyond. She blinked at the visitor through a single milky eye and rasped, "Yes?"

"Good morning," he bowed low. "Have you any melons today?"

"Finest in the north," she confirmed. She stepped back and opened the door wide, ushering him into the house.

William had to twist sideways to fit between his hostess and the wooden crates piled at either side of the hallway, yet it was the smell that took his breath away, something between a pig sty and a stable. As he took a moment to acclimatize, the woman walked slowly away, gesturing her guest to follow with a crook of her weathered fingertips.

"Melons…" The woman's sniff of a voice seemed even older and more decrepit than its owner.

William slicked the rain from his hair as they moved through the house. Closed doors flanked them on either side and the only light was that which escaped down the narrow staircase they passed yet still he followed the shuffling, stooped woman. Her clothes were stained with dirt and soil that might have been as old as she was and as they walked she muttered to herself at a furious pace. Here and there she paused to correct the position of the myriad dust-shrouded trinkets and baubles that decorated every surface.

When they came to a halt at a latched door, William noticed that the woman's finger was gray and hardened with age, the skin calloused like that of a farmer might be. She eased her fingertips beneath the latch and lifted it, nodding William through. He was surprised to find himself at the foot of a narrow staircase that seemed to have no natural position within the house. The old woman retreated and let the latch fell before she called, "He's upstairs, in a devil of a mood..."

William drew in a deep breath of the suddenly fresh and cool air—the gloom of the house was replaced by natural light. Any respite was short-lived, though, a shadow falling over him as a silhouette appeared at the head of the stairs.

William recognized Dee's Dublin burr telling him, "I have come by some marvelous tea. Come and try it."

"Is that before or after you tell me off?" William regarded the man calmly, lifting one hand to shield his eyes.

"I never tell *anyone* off," he replied as William reached the landing, Dee's somber face brightening with the barest hint of welcome. "Just ask my daughter."

Two minutes later, the men were sitting in armchairs that had seen better days, a plate of bread and cheese and the much-vaunted tea on the table beside them. Dee's latest surroundings were a far cry from his usual meeting places, clubs and offices where he seemed to be permanently behind one oak desk or another. There the walls were decorated by oil paintings depicting bewigged kings and peers, yet here in this rambling, decaying farmhouse, he had lost none of his gravity. Dee picked up a sheaf of papers from the small pocked table and leafed through them, humming as he did so.

"Your role, your *express* purpose," he said finally, steepling his fingers beneath his chin, "was to gather information on the comings and goings of Tessier's household. What on earth possessed you to give up your cover and perform a *prison break*?"

"Tessier was going to have Gaudet killed," William told Dee smoothly. "His sister has the Star and he is the best chance of finding his sister. There was no time to send word or ask for instructions."

"I set you to infiltrate Tessier's household for three reasons." Dee leaned forward, holding up three fingers. "First, your French is as fluent as a native. Second, you actually managed to kill Morel, a man many have targeted, and third…" He paused, folding down two fingers and obviously trying to find the right words to go on. When he did, William could tell he wasn't quite satisfied. "Third, I thought you had a cool head."

"I respectfully disagree." William bowed his head, the playwright's pleading face in his mind again. "I did what was necessary."

"Gaudet will mend, given time." Dee took a sip from his teacup. "Since you have already formed something of a relationship with him, I would like *you* to guide him to the coast, so that we might return him to England. Along the way, I expect you shall be able to tease his sister's whereabouts from him…"

"Me?" William couldn't help the disbelief in his tone, unable to keep the shock from his voice or face. "I have no more of a relationship with the man than you do!"

"I have a few tasks for you to complete at the border — deliveries, paper drops and the like." Dee picked up the papers again as though William hadn't spoken. "Three weeks today, I expect to see you at Charron's cabinet shop ready to accompany our playwright to his ship."

"Do I have *any* say in this?" He felt Gaudet's fingers clasped around his again, the inconsequential weight of the playwright leaning on his shoulder.

"No." Dee furrowed his brow. "Young Bastien tells me that the locket Gaudet retrieved from the house contains a cryptic message, but I have a sense that our playwright will not share it. Build your relationship, become friends. Monsieur Gaudet and his sister will be reunited and can go wherever the fancy takes them and we…"

Dee paused to take a sip from his cup, shrugging carelessly when he finished the thought. "Well, we will relieve her of the responsibility of the Prince of Wales' diamond and be on our way, richer, happier and with a perfectly delighted house of Hanover at our beck and call."

It sounded, William reflected, almost too good to be true. Then there was the part where he would have to actually spend time with Gaudet. He opened his mouth to protest, closed it again, and settled instead for a quick pace around the room, finally telling Dee, "If that is what you think is for the best."

"He seems a quiet fellow *at the moment*," Dee stated. "Of course, he may suddenly spark into life, he *does* have a reputation…"

"Apparently," William recalled Bastien's words, "he wants to put me in a play."

"Well, everyone loves a hero," Dee replied dryly, his bright blue eyes sparkling with mirth. "Even the French."

William peered at Dee, strongly suspecting that the other man might be having a joke at his expense. "Then he can put one of *those* in his play instead."

"He is given to fancies, flamboyance. *Don't* indulge him. You must pass unnoticed."

"As always" — William gave a dry smile of his own — "you make it sound so easy."

"It is a simple escort, what could possibly go wrong?" Dee added, his smile sanguine. "Though make up will stand out in the villages—discourage the rouge."

"Where is he going to get rouge *from*?" William shrugged. "That will be the least of our worries."

"And no heroics?"

"I will do my utmost"—he turned to regard Dee over his shoulder—"to refrain."

"Then I will see you at some point between here and the coast." Dee smiled, rising to his feet. "It will be, I am sure, a pleasure."

Chapter Eight

Although the world had hardly expanded since Gaudet had left the Rue Saint-Honoré, there was no denying that his surroundings had improved. He had little recollection of the carriage journey through Paris, nor did he know where his new residence was, but it was enough to know that the beds were soft and the food plentiful, no more locked doors and scraps of moldy bread. Better still was the dirty window that offered views over the rooftops of Paris where the sun and moon shone in their turn, even the rain a welcome sight when it beat on the pane.

Apart from a vague impression of the window and the sense that he had been well cared for by someone, Gaudet's recent past was blighted by shadows. If the feeling of the whip lashing his flesh was as fresh in his mind though so, too, was the gratitude he still felt for the unknown man who had saved his life. There were moments he could recall, the feeling of assured fingers washing and binding his wounds, the taste of excellent claret and the welcome warmth of a fire on his freezing skin. It was something of a blur until now, focusing on the dying sunlight that cast a pall of shadows across the room.

Gaudet shifted beneath the covers and let out a small gasp of pain as the wounds on his back twinged, but the sensation was nothing like he remembered, those tiny blazes all but extinguished now.

And somehow, I'm still alive.

Another movement shifted the blanket. He reached up and drew it down to his waist. His gaze raked across his naked body, taking in the deep black bruises that seemed to cover almost every inch of skin. Dark red scabs had formed over the wounds where Tessier had cast down the crop or whipped Gaudet with the iron manacles. He closed his eyes at the memory of it, a deep shiver running though his bones as he pulled the blanket up once more.

Gaudet studied his arms, where the rope burns were beginning to fade and even the patches where Tessier had held the candle flame to him were paler than they had been. The agony had passed, but there was a dull, thudding ache throughout his body and he stretched gingerly, feeling as though he had been trampled by a whole herd of horses.

After a few minutes, Gaudet turned his head to look out into the bedroom, focusing on the pale walls and a low ceiling held in place by stout, dark beams. A fire burned brightly in the grate before which was set a low chair, and through the dim light he saw a woman sitting there, her face turned away to the needlework she held in her lap.

"Claudine?"

She started at the sound of his voice, dropping the thread she held and rising to her feet. He felt a sharp stab of disappointment at the realization that this wasn't his lost sister but a stranger, her hand clasped to her heart in a gesture of shock.

"Monsieur, you startled me!" A smile spread across the woman's face and he was struck by her unexpected beauty, a welcome sight after the nightmares of the past who knew how many days. "I'm not your Claudine, I'm afraid — I'm Sylvie Dupire."

"Sylvie," Gaudet repeated in a whisper. "Hello."

"Brandy." Sylvie said the word as a fact, not a question.

He closed his eyes again, opening them when she returned to the bed and handed him a glass. With some difficulty, he managed to raise himself to his elbow and took a sip, savoring the taste as it warmed him.

"I've looked after you this past week," she told him, refilling the glass he held and offering another bright smile. "And you've slept or babbled through just about all of it."

"This is still Paris?"

"The Rue du Faubourg-Saint-Antoine," Sylvie confirmed. "Thierry says you're to stay here as long as you need."

"And Morel?" His voice was more urgent than he had expected, heart beating faster as he fixed her with his gaze. "Mademoiselle Dupire, is Morel here, too?"

"It's Sylvie." She shook her head and took back the glass to sip from it herself. "He took himself off that same night — disappeared like a proper spy."

Gaudet nodded but barely heard her words and instead returned his head to the pillow, glad of the sensation of comfort after what felt like so long in pain.

"Give us another tot of that," Sylvie said pointlessly after she'd taken another drink. "You hungry, Monsieur Gaudet?"

"Perhaps a little," he admitted and Sylvie rewarded him with a beaming smile that lit her entire face.

She brushed her glossy black hair back behind her ears and held his hand in her own for a moment, the gesture immediately reassuring. "Call me Gaudet, please."

"Not Alexandre?"

"Gaudet," he corrected with a smile. "To my friends."

"Gaudet it is." Sylvie squeezed his hand. "You look as though you've been to Hell and back."

Something like that.

He said nothing in response but shifted slightly, oddly embarrassed to be here in bed, a beautiful woman kneeling at his side with a glass of brandy in her pale hand.

I wish I had something witty I could give you, some charming little nothing.

I wish I could be me.

"I'm sorry," was all he could manage. "I'm just…"

"It's to be expected," she said, kindly sparing him the search for the words he couldn't find. "I'll get you something to eat if you like."

"No," Gaudet replied finally in response to her offer and her hand left his as she stood. "I don't want to be any trouble—just having me here must put your household in danger."

"If I didn't want any trouble, I wouldn't be living with Thierry Charron." Sylvie shrugged, and he thought again how she was almost too perfect to be in this small, provincial room. With her glittering gaze, the perfect symmetry of her features and the arch of her eyebrow, she seemed to have been sculptured from marble by a master craftsman.

Even her voice was angelic, a perfectly tuned melody escaping her pursed lips as she walked across the room. At the door, she turned to ask brightly, "Shutters open or closed?"

"Open," he said a little too quickly, remembering the darkness of his cell. "Thank you."

"Don't you go anywhere, Gaudet." She executed a perfect curtsey. "Your wish is my command."

Left alone once more, Gaudet focused on the fireplace, the minutes ticking past as he waited for the return of his gentle hostess. In fact, when the door opened again it didn't usher in Sylvie but a small boy, his pale skin streaked with dirt and his clothes obviously having seen far better days. He crept into the room and, seeing that Gaudet was already awake, abandoned any pretense at silence and darted toward the bed as though he was being pursued.

"Alexandre Gaudet?" The boy's skinny hand shot out and Gaudet took it in a daze. "Bastien Dupire, assistant to your rescuer."

"Morel?" Gaudet pushed himself up against the pillows to address the child. "You know him? Is he safe?"

"He's long gone," Bastien assured him and, though he smiled, there was a shadow on him, too, a slight downturn of the mouth that broke up the brightness in his face. "And he weren't really Morel—that murdering bastard's dead and buried."

"I don't—" Gaudet began, unsure of what he wanted to say. "Morel saved my life, what do you mean?"

Bastien shook his head and rolled his eyes as though

Gaudet was stupid not to understand.

"Well, put it this way," he said. "In Paris, he was Morel, but he ain't in Paris no more. He's a spy —"

"A spy?" The realization left Gaudet's lips as a whisper. He stared at Bastien Dupire, hearing the crackle of the fire and feeling, once again, the gentle hands bathing his wounds when all hope had seemed lost.

"Anyway, you're not to worry," Bastien said finally. "He didn't have to get you, you know, he could've left you to it if he'd fancied."

"I know." Gaudet nodded. "I know."

"You missing anything?" The question was innocent enough, the child's voice a sing-song timbre and Gaudet bolted upright as he remembered the cool solidity of the locket in his hand on that last night, the way he had wrapped the chain around his fingers and clung on to it like a rock in the middle of a storm-swept river.

"Where is it?" Gaudet barked with more urgency than he had intended.

Bastien's smile faded as, like a Mesmerist, he drew something from the pocket of his jacket. For a moment, the tiny silver pendant hung in space, suspended from a chain narrow as a spider's web, then the boy cupped it in his hand and offered it to the playwright.

"Ma took a liking to it," he explained, his eyes flashing a challenge. "But I've been looking after it for you, reckoned she'd be wearing it otherwise."

"Sylvie is your mother?" He held out his palm and saw, too late, the wounds his own fingernails had dug into the flesh, recalling in that instant the sound of the whip slicing through air on its merciless path toward his spine.

If the boy saw his hesitation then, he gave no indication and, instead, took a step forward until he could drop the locket into Gaudet's outstretched hand, the chain a delicate shower falling into his clenching fist.

"Thank you," Gaudet whispered and the child nodded, watchful and silent as Bastien opened his hand and looked down at this most precious of treasures.

"You're lucky I'm honest. That must be worth a bit."

Gaudet had forgotten the child was still with him and he raised his gaze, seeing Sylvie in her son's face, but, if she was beautiful, he was alive with barely concealed mischief, a small smile playing at the corners of his mouth though the joke went unspoken.

"I've seen you before," Bastien admitted eventually. "Up on the scaffold with Philippe—you were bloody *petrified*."

Gaudet's shrug appeared more casual than he felt and he replied, "I was."

"You'd better be all right, Monsieur Playwright," Bastien said, his words more grave than Gaudet would have believed possible. "My mother's all I've got and if Tessier follows you here, I'll give you up in an instant—he's not getting his hands on her."

What happened to childhood?

Is this what France has come to?

"I wouldn't expect any less."

"So long as we understand each other." Bastien nodded, his business concluded. "And don't forget who it was took care of that necklace for you when *I* need a favor in return."

The darkness in the boy's face lifted as he dipped to pick up the glass of brandy and emptied it in one swig. He lifted his other hand to refill the glass before he gave his mother's wink and said, "She's got the good stuff out for you."

With a peal of laughter, he dashed back across the room, almost through the door when Gaudet called after him, "Bastien, wait a moment."

"Sir?" The word was polite enough but the tone was annoyed, this child obviously having far more important things to do.

"Can you get a message to Morel?"

"If I can, and I'm not saying I can, mind." He lowered his voice and glanced over his shoulder. "What would you want it to say?"

What would be appropriate?

Are there even words strong enough?

"Just thank you," Gaudet decided, wishing there was something more. "And tell him that, if he is ever in London, I would very much like to take him to supper."

"Sir," Bastien replied in an exaggerated upper-class accent, swinging his arm round before him as he bowed and trotted from the room. "How *could* he refuse?"

The room fell silent. Gaudet slid down on the mattress, trying to find a position that was comfortable for the injuries that mapped his back. The locket grew warm in his hand and, if its presence was unexpectedly comforting, so too did it jar, pricking and nudging at him to be up and out of bed, starting out into Paris in search of Claudine.

Despite all it must have witnessed, the locket was undamaged when he examined it, its painted face decorated with a vivid red poppy that sprang from the white surface, even beneath the layer of grime. Gaudet rubbed the pad of his thumb over the painting until it was clean once more. He remembered the day that Claudine had been given the locket, her tenth birthday celebrated as though it was a coronation. He, like all good big brothers, had recognized immediately how much this trinket had meant to her and had resolved to hide it and give her a fright. The sound of her hysterical reaction upon waking to find it gone rang in his ears afresh, more than a decade after the thrashing he had received.

Since then, Gaudet didn't know if he had ever seen Claudine without the locket clasped around her slender neck, the necklace becoming a part of her. Now, clutching it in his hand, he spoke a silent promise to it, to *her*, that she and her son would soon be safe. He stroked his thumb across the surface once more before he slipped it over the gold edging and clicked the clasp, the locket springing open at his touch. What Gaudet had hoped to find, he didn't know, yet he felt a stab of disappointment at the contents, the hopes that rested on this discovery teetering at the edge of devastation.

His eyes found nothing within, other than the long-since familiar portrait of their mother in her youth, as striking and pampered as she had made her son. Yet when Claudine had written to her brother in London she had promised that, should anything happen, he would find the clue in this locket. Instead, he found *nothing*.

But Claudine would not have made such a mistake.

Unless Tessier found it first, he realized, and it was like a knife to the heart.

And yet something about it seemed out of kilter. After all, Tessier wanted nothing more than his precious Star of Versailles, the flogging and burning a means to an end. His torture was meant to achieve something beyond pain, and if he already had what he sought, Gaudet had no doubt that he would have followed Philippe into a mass grave, another victim of the guillotine.

"What have you left for me?" Gaudet asked the empty air, tipping the locket face down into his palm. The small portrait of his mother didn't move at first and he shook the pendant until it gave way and dropped weightlessly into his hand, followed by a tiny square of folded paper.

Gaudet's usually graceful fingers felt clumsy and ungoverned after so long without movement. He fumbled his efforts to unfold the delicate paper, cursing himself as he slipped his thumbnail beneath the corner, finally revealing its secrets.

And it was good to see that Claudine hadn't lost her sense of the absurd.

François wants to see where Uncle André tried to drown Mama. Come and find us.

Beneath the words, she had drawn a tiny, five-pointed star and he stared at it until tears welled in his eyes. A dash of his hand cleared them away, Gaudet furious with his sister for playing games at a time like this.

The words, those tiny, perfect letters, meant nothing to

Gaudet and he cursed himself for not caring, for forgetting all that she had wanted him to remember.

I was never one for family and sentiment.

And now I can't remember.

He thought again about Claudine's dripping wet hair, matted to her face and slick with sand and how his father had shouted, called from a meeting to deal with his errant, apparently murderous son.

And my God, what a thrashing I received...

There was an older man who tried to intervene in the punishment, he recalled, *but he had only heightened father's fury.*

Then it began to unravel like wool on a loom and he could see the ships his father had been appraising, could hear the calls of sailors and smell the salt in the air as he had run up and down the gangplanks and made futile attempts to scale the rigging.

The older man had been the captain of one of these vessels, one of the many his father was sure had been embezzling the cargo before the late Monsieur Gaudet could turn raw product into money. His son had run away after the beating and had had a fancy he would stow away on one of those ships, but he'd been caught and returned for another whipping, of course. His father eventually deciding that there were too many temptations in this particular port, too many opportunities to escape his parental guiding hand.

I do not miss him, Gaudet thought bitterly, catching the sentiment too late to banish it. Yet as it occurred he knew with a sudden and shocking clarity exactly where he had been when he'd pushed Claudine into the English Channel.

"Le Havre."

As the words left his lips, Gaudet squeezed the locket in his fist and a wave of emotions rippled through his heart. He knew then that his time as a guest in the home of Sylvie Dupire must soon reach its end, that his sister awaited by the sea.

Soon he would leave for Le Havre and there he would, somehow, find Claudine and François, with a triumphant return to England surely on the near horizon. How he would trace his sister and nephew could wait until later, because, for now, there were plans to be made and farewells to be given to the charming Sylvie, though he would miss the restorative powers of her beauty, if not her consommé.

The small square of paper disappeared into Gaudet's clenched fist and he rested it against his chest, letting his head fall back onto the pillow as the fire spat and crackled across the room. Bathed in the sunset, he lay unmoving, breathing in a cool breeze that carried the scent of roasting meat from somewhere nearby. He toyed with the locket, opening and closing it rhythmically, the chain rattling against the bed now and again as it moved.

"I will come to you," he promised, wishing that Claudine could hear, had left him something more solid than this. "And find you."

With some effort, Gaudet turned onto his side and focused on the fire, his vision filling with the dancing flames in the grate until the tears had dried and there was nothing left but a bubbling mixture of anger and despair that was like a lump in his chest. When he had been in that filthy cell with Vincent Tessier there had been no meaning in anything, no sun or moon, no comfort or respite, yet he had survived somehow, holding on to the thought that nobody else could, *would*, help Claudine. Now he was free, yet no less a prisoner, helpless and alone, even with the clue she had left him.

Without giving it a second glance, Gaudet folded the note and returned it to the locket. The catch clicked into place once more and he held on to it like a talisman as he finally let his eyelids fall, every movement exhausting.

Somewhere in his dreams, he was dimly aware of the door opening and a soft tread upon the boards, the clatter of the manacles jolting him awake with a gasp of remembered pain. Within a moment, the unyielding wall at his back had become the soft mattress, the torturer transformed into Sylvie Dupire and Gaudet realized, with embarrassment, that the sounds that had seemed so terrifying were no more than a spoon rattling in a bowl of steaming soup. His hand instinctively opened with the violence of his start and he heard the locket fall, striking the rug beside the bed with a dull thump.

"Not feeling so good?" Sylvie perched on the edge of the bed and frowned her sympathy, her head cocked to one side to peer down at the fallen locket. "What's this?"

"It's nothing," he lied as she stooped, her slender fingers closing around the pendant. It was like watching the world being snatched away, his voice betraying something like panic. "Madame Dupire, I—"

Sylvie turned her sparkling eyes to him, the fingers that held the locket uncurling, and he watched her gaze flit down appraisingly for no more than a second.

"Is it 'Madame' now?" Her words might have held a challenge but her expression was mischievous and he felt his anxiety dampening when she raised one of those arched eyebrows teasingly. "It's always 'Madame' after they meet my Bastien. I'm not married, Gaudet, I'm—"

She paused for melodrama and looked over each shoulder before leaning in to him and whispering, "*A fallen woman.*"

"Then we shall get along splendidly," Gaudet replied, his eyes meeting hers. Sylvie put her hand to his, closing his fingers around the locket. "*Mademoiselle.*"

"I've told you," her voice low, smile brighter now. "It's *Sylvie.*"

Chapter Nine

Gaudet watched Charron silently, the burly man working with utmost care as he applied another layer of polish to the small jewelry box he was making, every spare moment spent on the gift for Sylvie. He had a remarkably delicate touch for one so bullish and if he seemed ill at ease in conversation, in the workshop he was a master.

The physical injuries that Tessier had inflicted were healing well and, weeks since his escape, Gaudet was growing restless in his convalescence. In England, he was used to tailored clothes and evenings at the theater, late nights at Ranelagh or Vauxhall, dancing through the lamps with someone or other on his arm and through all of it, he'd never given this a second thought. As he'd squired actresses and debs, mollies and sailors, even the occasional duke or two, it had never crossed his mind that this could have been happening in the country of his birth, that the land he loved was cracking open at the roots.

When news had begun to cross the Channel of the problems in France, Claudine had still been at Versailles as lady in waiting to the queen. Of course, there had never been any real doubt that she would come to England. Why would she not?

Then came the first letter.

My loyalty is to my lady and where she goes, I will follow.

So many letters had followed that, each more horrifying than the last, yet still Claudine had told him not to find her, that Philippe had work in Paris and she was traveling with the royal family, that they would find safety in Austria, that there was still hope.

I cannot risk a sea voyage, but when the little one is born, we shall come to join you in England.

Then there had come the dreadful news across the water, stories of arrest and trial and finally, execution.

My lady is dead, all hope is lost. We have business in Paris. Pray for us, pray for François and with God's grace, we will be with you before the first snow falls.

That was when the silence had fallen and he'd pranced merrily into Paris to retrieve his lost sister, little wondering what fate awaited him.

The night before Gaudet had left England had been riotous and, as he sipped a glass of brandy, he allowed himself a slight smile, remembering the tenor who had perched on his lap at the Theatre Royal and tilted a glass of claret to his lips, his free arm snaked around Gaudet's neck as the chap had put his mouth to his ear and robbed him of any interest in the drama. As midnight rang out he'd danced in Cavendish Square until the Duke of Devonshire had raised merry hell and there had been a moonlit swim in the Serpentine with someone who may or may not have been engaged to a minor European prince.

As though he could read Gaudet's mind, Charron straightened up and looked at him, annoyance clearly fighting a losing battle with loathing before he returned to his work.

"Is it Sylvie's birthday?" Gaudet asked lightly, craning to examine the small trinket box that Charron was fashioning from walnut. It was an undoubted work of art and one that Charron seemed as devoted to as he was to the woman and child who shared his home. "Or gift for the sake of a gift?"

"The latter," Charron said, not glancing at him again.

Gaudet winced at the craftsman's exaggerated sigh, half-expecting Charron to be angry. Instead, he seemed resigned to being disrupted and folded his arms, leaning back against the work table.

"Sylvie's worked and struggled all her life," he explained and Gaudet recognized the unspoken sentiment of *not that you would understand.* "And she's never lost her spirit, never done anything but the best for Bastien. Now she sorts through rags and lives with a man who harbors fugitives for a few measly livres — she deserves something special, something that hasn't belonged to someone else."

"It's a nice piece," Gaudet replied, setting down his glass and clasping his hands together. "At my house in London, I have a lacquered Chinese —"

"Excuse me," Charron cut him off and Gaudet frowned, annoyed at his interruption. "This needs concentration."

A long sigh escaped Gaudet's lips and he stood to pace across the workshop to the window, where he rubbed his hand through the grime and peered out into the street at the world passing by.

"Get away from there!"

At Charron's snapped warning, he stepped back, then went forward again to pick up the meagre bits of rouge and powder Sylvie had supplied him with.

"I am away," he told Charron haughtily, "to put on my face!"

At that moment, there came a knock at the door, the sound repeated a moment later, in what seemed to Gaudet a precise pattern of knocks, and had the grumbling Charron moving quickly to answer. Shrinking into the shadows of the staircase, he watched as the man he had known as Morel stepped into the house and the men exchanged low murmurs. Ears straining, Gaudet chanced to descend a couple of steps, yet still he was unable to pick up anything of the conversation until Morel shook his head and gave an exclamation.

"Well!" Morel declared as Charron departed back to his work. "*Well!*"

"Sir," Gaudet said cheerily, setting the makeup on the stairs before he descended. "I trust I look a little brighter to you today."

"You will need to be." Morel regarded him with narrowed eyes. "For you and I are to take a trip together."

"To a tailor, I hope." Gaudet gestured to the plain breeches and shirt he wore. "And I will go *nowhere* without my girl."

"There is no time for talk of clothes, sir." There was a pause, a shadow of consternation flickering across Morel's face. "And nor for whatever lady friend you have cause to think of either."

"She is but two years old." Gaudet's lower lip quivered at the thought of the beloved little girl. "I cannot leave her here alone."

"You—" His companion was clearly having difficulty, closing his eyes briefly as he pinched his nose. "I was not told of this."

"I will not go without Papillon," Gaudet said, folding his arms petulantly. "I would rather die."

"That can be arranged…"

"Charron." Gaudet bristled. "Summon the tall fellow with the blue eyes. I will not travel without Papillon and my life has been threatened."

"Your life is threatened every moment you remain in this city," Morel pointed out with a long-suffering sigh. "Where is this 'Papillon' to be found?"

"She is with Monsieur Abel on the rue de la Harpe," Gaudet told him. Seeing a chance for an extra something, he added, "Along with four suits Abel was making alterations to, perhaps you might collect those, too?"

"Suits?" The eyebrows raised even farther. "You left her with a *suit* maker?"

"No." Gaudet sighed, thinking this gentleman might not be as worthy of a lead role as he had hoped. "I left her with a gentleman who happens to be able to do marvelous things with fabric. He has girls of his own. They are practically cousins."

"Then would she not be better off remaining with them? Our journey is likely to be fraught with danger, Monsieur…"

The thought of it sent a jolt through Gaudet, eyes growing wide as he imagined life without Papillon, never knowing what became of her, let alone how a girl who was virtually a princess would manage in a Parisian backstreet.

"A girl" — Gaudet blinked away tears at the very thought of it — "should be with her father."

"Then what do you propose?" Morel threw up his hands in an almost comical fashion.

"We shall go tonight after dark and collect my girl."

"Just the girl," came the wary response. "No suits. Nothing else."

"If we are there, anyway..." Gaudet sucked in his cheeks, pursing his lips for a moment. "It would be absurd to abandon my suits."

"We are going to be fugitives," his increasingly irritated companion declared. "One suit and your girl."

"There are four suits, sir, and I will take them all," Gaudet decided haughtily. "What name am I to call you by?"

"Have you never heard of the concept of *compromise*?" The man he had known as Morel peered at him as if trying to make some sense of the situation. "Of course you haven't, you're French."

"Are you not French?" Gaudet frowned, peering closer. "Something is afoot here."

"I said nothing of the sort," the man peered back. "No wonder the country is in the state it is."

"I am not sure I trust you." He pouted. "I wish to travel with the one with the blue eyes, I believe he is trustworthy — you are somewhat roguish."

Morel's rolled his hazel eyes, a murmur that might have been a petition to the heavens following a moment later. "The 'one with the blue eyes' has charged *me* with the godforsaken task of getting your *derriere* and the rest of you safely out of Paris — I like it no more than you, sir, but we shall have to make the best of it."

"Then *what* do I call you?" Gaudet set his hands on his hips. "You are far less amenable when one is not being tortured, sir. If you do not give me a name, I shall call you... *chérie*."

"Bobbins," came the unimpressed response. "You can call

me Bobbins."

"You are *English*!" Gaudet's eyes widened and he shook his head. "I am not going *anywhere* with an Englishman with an English name. We will be dead within the week."

"Then make it sound French," the man retorted. "I am your only chance of getting out of here alive, sir, and you'd do well to remember that."

"I have many followers in England. It is hardly surprising someone has charged you with rescuing me," Gaudet said confidently, flattered that one of his many patrons had done so. "Tonight, we collect the suits and my girl, tomorrow we leave to collect my sister..."

"You have had news of her whereabouts?" The man who was now Bobbins grew serious. "Where is she hiding?"

"I should have to see the one with the eyes before I could tell you that."

At that, Charron turned from his work and said grumpily, "This man is your savior, Gaudet. Your late brother-in-law and sister were as family to me and you may trust Bobbins, or whatever you are calling him, with your life."

"There." Bobbins' expression was one of relief. "Anything you know, anything at all, you must tell me."

"Le Havre," Gaudet said finally, sure that Charron would not lie. "Where, I do not know, but in Le Havre."

"Then we are heading for Le Havre," Bobbins said firmly, "as soon as our *errand* here is completed."

"I shall go and assemble my things," Gaudet told this odd Bobbins character, who he remembered being far more chivalrous when he'd been in Tessier's custody. "And put on a little powder."

Chapter Ten

For three days and nights following the escape of Alexandre Gaudet and the man who called himself Morel, Paris burned. Violence rent the streets and tore through the slums as Vincent Tessier's men ripped apart the city in their search for something that might lead them to their quarry, but if they found anything, it was misery that already ran deeper than the Seine. Blood coursed from the scaffold in a spreading stain and the blade grew blunt as, again and again, it slammed home, sending Tessier's message to the people who cared to listen.

Take this as your warning.

We have all grown complacent.

Yet still he found nothing, even as he smashed his way through the denials and tears of those whose names had been mentioned to him for one reason or another, ripped useless confessions from the lips of sobbing women and broken men and found dead ends and empty words. The peddlers of herbal potions and powders were detained and questioned, their filthy hovels put to the flame, and still there was not as much as a whisper in the wind about Gaudet and the spy, the viper in his home.

But they must be somewhere and somebody knows something.

Somebody supplied the opiate, the escape means…

Somebody gave them shelter.

Somebody else was involved.

With Plamondon's death, he had done nothing more than cut the head off the snake. Its body remained wound around the city, muscles constricting and squeezing all that was right out of the world. Another serpent had already risen to take its place and this one had found its way into his very home, had struck him with its venom and retreated to its nest. Yet they had reckoned without Vincent Tessier. Those who opposed him might be reduced in number and means without their wealthy patron, but he had no doubt that they would grow strong again and every day they enjoyed this victory, their strength increased.

And mine is diminished.

He could barely stand to be in the house any longer, still haunted by the memory of that missing floorboard…the knowledge that *something* had been hidden there all along.

Right there under his nose

Or under his feet.

The moment of clarity came, as they so often did for him, as he made a seemingly inconsequential trip to speak with Robespierre, to try to shore up his suddenly weak position. There, he sat in a covered carriage outside the Pavillon de l'Égalité, summer rain beating a tattoo on the roof and the chatter of voices passing back and forth. On the dog-eared paper in his gloved fingers was written the names of those who had been sold out under interrogation, dozens of them. Some of them had even been willingly, even eagerly, handed over without coercion and all of them were as unremarkable as the next.

Those are always the innocent ones, of course – a name given freely is the name of an enemy, a vendetta for the settling.

Those are the chaff, burrs on the wind – these are the names of the innocent.

The names on the second list, however… Well, those are a different matter.

When a name is bled out of you, it isn't the name of a rival or the man who took your wife, it is the truth.

I know the truth when it lies bleeding before me.

Tessier had studied the names until he knew them by heart, yet still he returned to the list, reading every word with a frown in the hope that something might, somehow, spring to life before him and declare its guilt. Somewhere among the Marcs, the Pierres, the Bastiens and the Maries, he knew there was the person who would unlock the mystery, no way that one man had planned and executed the rescue of Alexandre Gaudet.

Or Professor Dee, as his associates refer to him.

And you will all die for what you have done, every last one of you. Neither this country nor Vincent Tessier will forgive and forget this treachery.

The scaffold will run with your blood before autumn comes.

He still sought Morel everywhere — each figure on a street corner was scrutinized and studied, from the beggars with their filthy bundles to the drunkards who blighted the thoroughfares. Yet in his heart Tessier knew that he was hunting a ghost, a memory.

In so many ways, it is like he never existed at all and like all phantoms, he is vanished with the dawn.

Yet somebody always knows something.

Always.

They had pulled in all the known opiate peddlers and, as one of them breathed her last, she had told them everything, sobbed out a story about a little boy who had come to her for something that could put a burly man to sleep and keep him there for a night.

'*Little Bastien,*' she told him through bloodied sobs, '*his mother keeps house for the cabinetmaker, Charron. He's a good boy at heart, he wouldn't mean anything by it.*'

'*He has his schemes. He's never done no harm to no one.*'

Now Tessier stood in the gloomy workshop of that same cabinetmaker's rooms as his men went to work inside, securing the occupants. The night outside had been the coolest of the summer, but at the top of the stairs the air seemed stale and he smelled the aroma of over-boiled vegetables and the stench of dirty rags that had filled his own childhood room.

That was a long time ago.

Tessier unballed his fists, the creak of the gloves lulling him into the familiar role of the Butcher of Orléans. He nodded to the guard at the top of the stairs to step aside, closing his hand around the doorknob and taking a final moment to control himself.

Let them all fear me.

The kitchen was illuminated by a fire that spluttered weakly in the grate. Before the open window was the pot that must contain the food he could smell outside, a faint steam rising from it into the night. A large man stood beside the window, his wrists bound, and he started forward when Tessier entered and asked the new arrival, "What's happening? We've done nothing!"

Tessier looked down his nose, seeing nothing he hadn't seen a thousand times before. He might command respect in his tavern or with his woman, but with his limbs secured, there was nothing to fear from him.

With their hands bound they are helpless as babes.

"Where is the boy?" Tessier ignored the man and spoke instead to the guard who stood beside a closed door, two deep scratches still wetting his cheek with fresh blood.

"Locked in there with his mother," came the reply and the guard glanced at Charron before adding, "She's a bloody harpy, that one — did this with her nails, watch yourself."

Tessier raised his eyebrows in mock indignation then rapped at the door and called out, "Open the door, woman!"

"You'll have to bloody break it down!" Her response was shrill, but where there should be fear there was fury, the futile gesture of a mother protecting her young.

"Madame," Tessier said, his own voice soft and steady, as though he were addressing a lunatic. "I wish to talk to your son — you have nothing to fear by sending him out."

"Piss off," she hissed.

Tessier's face slackened at the obscenity, his heart slamming in his ribcage. A glance at Thierry Charron swelled his annoyance as the bound man matched his gaze with a sullen stare of his own, bitter amusement growing in his expression.

"Open. The. Door."

"Piss. Off," she replied.

He could hear the humor in her voice, feel it like a slap to the face.

"Break it down," Tessier instructed the guard, stepping aside to allow him access. "Now."

At first, the door held beneath the repeated efforts of the guard to charge it. Tessier grew more agitated with every failed attempt, his temper growing thinner and thinner. The woman within matched each thud and splinter of the wood with catcalls and laughter for what seemed like hours then, miraculously, she called, "He's going to break his bloody arm. I'll unlock it, but you're not taking my Bastien away."

"I shall be the judge of that," Tessier replied as the key turned in the lock and the door began to open slowly, a candle flickering within. He moved quickly then and slammed his hand into the wooden panel, forcing the door open. That elicited a cry of annoyance from the woman as her child hid behind her skirts, clutching at her white nightgown with his thin fingers.

"Madame," he said as he stalked into the dimly lit room, "you have led me quite a dance tonight."

"And not just tonight," Sylvie Dupire said with a small smile as she emerged from the shadows, her hands resting on her hips and her next words a whisper. "Isn't that right, Monsieur *Vincent* Tessier?"

Chapter Eleven

"Look at me," Sylvie said through a smile as she turned and surveyed the bare room where she stood, her hand resting on the damp stone wall as though she might be able to soak up some past memory from it. "Living like a queen at last."

The irony of the statement wasn't lost on Tessier. He smiled at the cold humor of it, his eyes never leaving the woman before him, an angel in her white nightgown, a red shawl thrown over her shoulders. He had seen the Widow Capet within these walls a hundred times but she had never transfixed him as this creature did now, never brought such an air of perfect calm to the rooms that had been her cell.

"Where's the young one?" her voice was soft. "The little king."

"We are free from the tyranny of kings," Tessier reminded her. "The child is in his rooms at the Temple."

"From the Tuileries to the Temple." Sylvie shook her head with a rueful smile. "And I thought *I'd* fallen on hard times."

"I found her here on that final morning." He gestured at the floor where Madame Capet's cushion had been. In his mind's eye, he watched her run the rosaries through her fingers, lips moving in silent invocation. "She would pray for hours at the end, they always do."

Sylvie nodded once and walked toward him, drawing her shawl around her body before she asked, "Did she kneel to pray?"

"Always." Tessier nodded, surprised when Sylvie fell to her knees where Marie Antoinette herself had kneeled, her

85

hands clasped before her breast.

"Like this?" Her eyes blinked in the gentle glow of the flame when she turned her head to glance up at him, the tip of her tongue darting out to wet her lips. "Was she very pretty?"

"She was not."

Sylvie nodded, her green eyes sparkling in the flickering candlelight that danced on the stone walls of the former queen's final, miserable, deserved lodgings. Even without the clamor of children that filled their rooms at the Temple, this room still rang with that quiet, sing-song voice reading aloud from the damned missal as though her very soul depended on it. Now, though, it was more silent than he had ever known, the only sound his own breathing.

"You thought me very pretty once, Monsieur." Sylvie smiled in place of prayer. "Do you still?"

"Your son—"

"Granted, I'm not as young as I was, but am I still your pretty girl?" She turned her head again, her clasped hands unmoving. "You're still my boy, you know."

"Please, Mademoiselle Dupire..."

Tessier's words petered out and Sylvie turned on her knees and put her arms around his waist, pressing her face against his thigh. He dimly thought he should push her away, but instead, he linked his hands behind his back at the stark realization that she might see the scars and, somewhere in the distance, his own breath caught.

"My boy," she murmured. "My good, good boy."

"Mademoiselle Dupire," he whispered, hating the way his voice almost shook as her hands brushed back and forth over his buttocks, bringing back too many memories with every caress. "Please don't."

"I watched you," Sylvie said softly, her words almost lost in the darkness. "Just look at you—standing in the Conciergerie with the queen on her knees."

I wanted you more than you ever knew, he wanted to say, longed to surrender to her as he had on so many evenings in another lifetime. *You were always the other side of me.*

"Tell me about your son—who did he supply with the tincture of opiate?"

"Have you missed me?" Sylvie's mouth pressed to his breeches, and a decade or more fell away when he hardened at her touch. "You did, didn't you?"

"Who did he supply?" Despite himself, he put his palms gently to her cold cheeks, easing her away.

She slid her gaze across to the scars for no more than a moment, then took his right hand and brought it to her lips, kissing the skin where it stretched and glistened. Softly, tenderly, Sylvie slipped his index finger into her mouth and encircled it with her tongue.

His heart pounding, Tessier went to lift her from her knees, but instead she drew him down until he was on the ground beside her, the rough earth floor digging into his flesh. He felt nothing but her mouth over his, lips parting and his body growing warmer despite the cold air.

"I missed my boy, too," Sylvie cooed into the kiss, her hands moving deftly to his shoulders. "I would hear about what you'd been up to and I was so proud."

"I looked for you," he muttered, lowering his head until he could rest it against the swell of her bosom. "Why didn't you come to me?"

"How could I?" Sylvie wrapped one arm around him and pressed him close to her breast, the nipple hardening beneath the thin fabric. Despite the darkness and the linen that separated their bodies he could almost see the milk-white skin, feel the softness of her against him. "A boy has to make his own way in the world, doesn't he? Look at what you've become."

She reached round to work at the fastening of Tessier's breeches and she slipped her hand inside to take hold of him, a touch he had never expected to feel again. Her grip tightened until a gasp of pain escaped his gritted teeth. He kissed the nightgown beneath his lips hungrily, pulling her to him. As she murmured and encouraged, Sylvie worked her hand faster and faster, squeezing her fingers until every touch was exquisite agony. At the suggestion of her fingernails, he finally let out a cry and felt the release that he hadn't experienced in so long. She kept working until there was nothing left within him, that he had given all he could. The world swam before his eyes and a deep sigh escaped his chest. He breathed her in with the next breath, lost in the woman who cradled him.

"You're a good boy," she whispered into his hair, drawing her hand out of his breeches. "Am I to follow her to the guillotine now then? Will you put your girl to the razor?"

"If I must," he muttered, fumbling at the lacing with stiff fingers as he tried to regain some sort of control. Yet the slender arm around his shoulders kept him from lifting his head from her breast, holding him to her. "No exceptions, Sylvie."

She said nothing but took his hand in her own and placed it on her breast, massaging her body through the linen until her other hand left his shoulder. Then he could move again, bringing his lips to kiss the point in her throat where her pulse beat.

"No exceptions, Vincent," she told him, a statement more than a question. "But you'll always remember me here in her cell at the Conciergerie, more a queen than she ever was?"

"You are more than a queen to me," he replied, tracing the line of her throat with kisses.

The laugh that escaped Sylvie's lips was low and the disbelief he detected in it sent a pang of sadness through his body. In reply he pulled her closer to him as though that alone might convince her of the sentiment.

"I bow before you now as I always have," Tessier whispered as she put her hand in his hair and dragged his head roughly upward, until their eyes were level.

"We'll see, Monsieur Tessier," she replied, putting her parted lips to his again. "We'll see."

Chapter Twelve

With night having fallen over the city, William found himself peering up at the house at where he was to perform another, unexpected, rescue. The news of Gaudet's child had filled him with both surprise and irritation, the additional burden and distraction not one he had bargained for. Not only that, but the celebrated playwright smelled like a deb's posy, the journey through Paris delayed by Gaudet's insistence on reminiscing at every street they passed, seemingly having forgotten his very life was on the line.

"Are you certain," William whispered, "that this is the house?"

"This is Abel's home." Gaudet nodded toward the small, narrow building where a dim light burned in one window. "And my girl will know we are close by."

"We knock, we get her and we go." He glanced around, cautious to the extreme, every second one that could bring discovery. "Understood?"

"Thank you, *chérie*." Gaudet clapped excitedly and rapped at the narrow door. From within came a cacophony of yaps and barks, the sound of scratching, as though a dozen dogs were clamoring at the panels and, somewhere beneath it, a wavering old male voice cooed, "Quiet now, angels…back to your beds."

William waited with as much patience as he could muster and, as soon as the door opened, announced, "We're here for the girl."

The tiny old man within gave a cry of delight and declared, "I believe the little one already knows." At that came the unmistakable sound of paws racing down the distant wooden stairs. A tiny white poodle flew along the hallway and leaped into Gaudet's arms, lapping at his face as he cooed happily, Monsieur Abel beaming with obvious adoration.

"The girl," William pressed, certain they had no time to spend coddling animals. "Where is she, Monsieur?"

"Papillon, say hello to Bobbins." Gaudet held out the poodle, its glittering dark eyes regarding William shrewdly. "Papa has missed you so, princess."

"I don't understand." William realized, even as the words left his mouth, that this was an almost permanent state of affairs where Gaudet was concerned. "This is a dog."

"And your suits are ready and packed." Abel pottered back into the house. "I had thought you were arrested. I did not tell the mademoiselle, I had not wanted to worry the poor child."

"It's a bloody dog!" William felt as if he were fast losing hold of reality.

"Let Papa collect his suits, Angel," Gaudet cooed, cradling the poodle beneath his arm. "Then we are off to find Auntie Claudine and little François…have you had a splendid time?"

"Is anyone listening to me at all?" William tried, pinching his nose.

"Are you to carry the suits?" Abel asked, leading them along a darkened hallway. "You will need a carriage."

"We don't have a carriage—"

"Then you will need strong arms." He threw open the door to a workroom in which were piled what seemed like dozens of bright, folded fabrics, far from the four suits Gaudet had mentioned. William took it all in in astonishment, not quite believing this was happening when Abel said, "Here are the suits, all ready for you."

"We cannot take them," William declared flatly. "You can take what you can wear, Gaudet, and that is it."

"You said, I think, I might take ten?" Gaudet asked innocently, the pout already returning to what was, supposedly, one of the most enchanting faces in London. If it *was*, its attraction passed William by as he stared at the playwright, once again wondering what madhouse he had landed in.

"Take what you can carry," William turned for the door. "I want no part in it."

"I cannot carry suits *and* my girl!" Gaudet gave a theatrical sigh. "You must carry Papillon, she would not like the mud in the streets, I know."

"She does not," Abel agreed warmly, "and she will only sleep on the green silk I brought up from Calais...we have gone through an ocean of it."

A moment later, William found himself with his arms full of poodle, the dog regarding him with an expression he did not find entirely comfortable. "Right. We go now."

"I must select the suits I adore above all others," Gaudet decided. "Monsieur Abel, the remainder will be a gift to you." Abel agreed readily and there then passed what seemed like *hours* as Gaudet deliberated over this shade of green, that hue of blue, sorting through acres of silk and lace, brocade and threads and all the time the poodle stared at William, eyes bright.

"Your dog," he told Gaudet, "is staring at me."

"Do I want the blue of a summer sky or the blue of the tall chap's eyes?"

"Does it matter?" William shook his head. "Blue is blue. Can we *go*?"

"Blue is blue?" Gaudet repeated, he and Abel laughing uproariously and, at the sound of it, William froze, widening his eyes.

Gaudet's laugh was unlike anything he had ever heard, piercing through him in a way that had him fighting the urge to drop the confounded dog and clap his hands over his ears.

"Will you *please*," he managed through gritted teeth, "choose a *damned* suit?"

The laughter ceased suddenly, William surprised to find

that the panes of glass in the window had not actually been shattered by it, and Gaudet said, "Two more minutes, *chérie*…"

"Two minutes…" He gave a sigh, thinking longingly of a particularly fine brandy that he had not tasted in far too long. "Two minutes."

What must have been close to an hour passed and finally Gaudet stood, his arms laden with an enormous amount of clothing.

"No."

"I do not *do* no."

"I do not," William felt his last remaining thread of patience snap, "give a *fig* for what you do or do not do, sir. I have been charged with your safety and you cannot carry that pile of *gaudiness* all the way to our destination." Shifting the poodle into one arm, he approached the playwright, pulling out a suit at random. "This one. Take this one. Leave the rest. I will hear no more on the subject."

"Oh." Gaudet's face dropped and he looked to Abel and said, "Her late majesty's favorite, God rest her." Both men exchanged a suitably forlorn frown and Gaudet sighed, handing it to Abel. "I shall also take the shirt from Bordeaux, you know the one…have you a portmanteau?"

"Of course." The old man nodded. "And if there is any way to send the rest of the items to you in London, I shall find it."

William felt a flicker of something he recognized a moment later as guilt, before crossly pushing it aside. "Your safety," he pointed out in an attempt to ameliorate his perceived unfeelingness, "is more important than clothes, Monsieur."

"She adored the blue," Gaudet said wistfully as Abel set the clothing into a portmanteau. "You have chosen well, *cherie*."

"Well." He cleared his throat, certain no good could come of quibbling the name at this point. "Shall we go?"

"Monsieur Abel, you are a saint." Gaudet kissed the old man's cheek. "Thank you, sir."

"Go safely," the elderly man replied. "And I shall send the suits on."

Still clutching the poodle, William made for the door, listening carefully for any sound out of the ordinary before opening it. Finally, he gestured for Gaudet to follow, slipping out into the night with the playwright trotting alongside, swinging the portmanteau.

As they went, William was acutely aware that the poodle was still staring at him, a fact he did his best to ignore when he muttered to Gaudet, "A dog… I thought we were rescuing a child."

Gaudet answered with a *hmph*, clearly too pleased with his bounty to argue. On they went through the darkened streets. The dog's gaze remained locked on William. They were almost at the door of Charron's workshop when William saw a vision that he knew too well, his stomach jolting at the sight of two armed soldiers standing beside a jet-black carriage. He had ridden in that vehicle many times since his arrival in Paris, *always* with Vincent Tessier.

"Get back," he whispered to Gaudet, grabbing the Frenchman's arm and bustling him into the nearest alleyway.

The whinnying of one of the two horses at the head of the carriage split the silence. Then there was a click as the polished ebony door of the carriage opened. A single foot emerged first, the delicate filigree shoe buckle catching the moonlight before Tessier unfolded his tall, thin frame from within, every inch the figure of menace so feared in these streets. As though someone had called his name, he paused and looked around, face pallid and drawn beneath the moonlight. He wore the outfit of the execution day, a shadow in the funereal black frock coat with its silver buttons, scarred hands that had beaten and burned not covered by those well-worn leather gloves.

William held his breath, faintly aware that his fingers were digging into Gaudet's arm.

"Those scars…" Gaudet murmured. "Gloves for a

beating—he took them off for the lash…"

And those burns—long since healed but the gnarled skin left ravaged—stretched glistening and taut across prominent bones like a stripped-back anatomical drawing. William hated having to shake those hands, to see them knitted on the desk, handling food, holding the bloodied crop when Robespierre had made his unexpected visit.

"Shut up," William snapped. "Do you want to get us killed?"

Tessier turned in a full circle to survey the street, tilting his head up to peer at the windows where an unseen audience would, no doubt, be watching. After a moment, he turned his head from side to side slightly then, almost deliberately, took the black leather gloves from his coat and pulled them on. He peered toward the shadows where the pair were concealed. A moment passed before he pushed his gaunt face forward just a little and those blazing, almost colorless eyes narrowed. The expression he wore grew hawk-like and he squinted into the gloom, flexing his fingers as he tried to focus.

"Home," Tessier instructed the coachman suddenly. "I believe it is too late for politics."

William did not let out his breath until Tessier was in the coach. There was another pause before the horses were coaxed into life, the carriage moving off at a steady pace a moment later.

"I write plays," Gaudet said, his hand closing over William's for a second, as though it were a confession, his shoulders sagging. "That's all I really do. I write plays and I enjoy life. I'm not made for this kind of thing."

You are not the only one, William responded silently, instead murmuring a moment later, "I have promised to see you safely home." He found himself holding the playwright's gaze then as he added, "I am a man of my word."

Gaudet inclined his head and admitted, "I believe that is true."

"But you must tell me one thing," William added, the two

of them very close now in the darkness.

"Go on," Gaudet urged.

"Why is that confounded animal still staring at me?"

"She is quite enchanted," Gaudet deadpanned with a wry smile, "by your exquisite beauty."

William could only stare at Gaudet for a long moment at that, wondering again how his life had become *this*. "We need to get inside," he concluded. "Come on."

It was with a sigh of relief that William stepped into the workshop and, once Gaudet was safely beside him, closed the door. One look at Charron told him that something was wrong, the cabinetmaker sitting before the window, the walnut jewelry box gleaming in one hand and a polishing cloth in the other. Without acknowledging their presence, he worked the cloth over the already perfect surface slowly, back and forth as though setting a rhythm.

"What is it?" William asked after observing for a long moment. "What has happened?"

"Tessier took them away," Charron whispered, his hand stilling. "They put me in a cell for a couple of hours and then they brought me back here… I don't know what happened to Bastien or Sylvie…"

William closed his eyes briefly, his orders from Dee clear in his mind. "I have to get Gaudet out of Paris," he murmured finally.

"The herbalist, Madame Masson, gave Bastien's name under interrogation… She made the sleeping draft," Charron explained. "There are spies everywhere — once Tessier started asking around, plenty of people would have been happy to point the finger…"

"I cannot help them." William hated himself at that moment. "I am sorry."

"I know," Charron assured him, staring out into the street. "I could do nothing for Plamondon, you can do nothing for Sylvie and Bastien…you must go tonight."

"We must," William agreed, meeting Gaudet's gaze. "Be ready to leave shortly, Monsieur."

"I wish you both well," Charron said simply. "If I can get them out, if we can follow. Where are you heading for?"

"Le Havre," William informed the shattered man. "We are headed for Le Havre."

"Go safe," Charron told them, his head whipping round at a heavy knock on the front door as a second knock sounded from the back.

"Open the door," came a shout, that familiar jet black carriage drawing to a halt outside the window. "Open the door, Charron."

"Go," he barked. "Now."

Gaudet and William virtually threw themselves over Bastien's straw bed and up the staircase into the living quarters as downstairs there was a flurry of noise. First came the heavy bolt, then two or three pairs of boots on the floor before that careful, quiet voice floated on the night air.

"Monsieur Charron," Vincent Tessier said. "Where are they? Sanson cannot be left idle at the guillotine."

"The window," William told Gaudet. "We have to jump. Go first, I'll throw the dog to you."

"Someone else could take her place in the Conciergerie, on the scaffold, even," Tessier mused quietly. "Somebody who knows something, who might tell what he knows."

Gaudet shook his head and pulled William across into the room where he had spent his recovery. He opened the linen press, dragging out Sylvie's collection of rags and piling them on the floor. William grimaced in distaste as moths fluttered up from the fabric, fascination growing when Gaudet reached into the cupboard and, with a click, the back panel swung open.

As boots reached the staircase, Gaudet nodded toward the barely visible passageway that had been revealed, gesturing for William to join him. With no choice, he did as he was bade, what light there was extinguished when Gaudet replaced the false panel and plunged them into darkness.

Somewhere in the world beyond he could hear the

heavy footsteps and muffled voices of the guards. Gaudet gripped his wrist, the gesture oddly reassuring even as he encouraged them onward. William reached out blindly, a sense of panic building in his gut when his hands found what seemed to be rough fabric, then a wooden surface that felt less permanent than the darkness, a sensation of movement beneath his palm.

As the cupboard door swung open they were both propelled into a small room, falling onto the bare wooden boards. Gaudet's breath escaped from his lips as though he had been punched in the stomach. Pap in turn let out a small woof of triumph, peering around the unexpectedly flamboyant bedroom.

It was like falling into another world, William decided and he looked about, half expecting to hear Tessier's voice at any moment, to feel a hand on his shoulder. "Where the hell are we?"

Gaudet smiled then, mischief twinkling in his green eyes for a moment before he confided, "Sylvie told me this is a brothel, Monsieur. It was in their interests to leave the secret door in place, too. Sometimes prostitutes have to beat a hasty retreat…"

His life was, William thought, turning into something similar to one of Gaudet's famed plays about which he had heard so much. "A brothel."

"A molly brothel," Gaudet confirmed as, from the bed, a rather pretty young man sat up and peered at them through bleary eyes. Quickly the playwright leaped to his feet and bowed deeply, saying, "Good evening, sir!"

"We aren't staying." William got to his feet with as much haste as he could manage. "Just passing through!"

"We have come from Monsieur Charron's workshop," Gaudet replied courteously, offering a nod of acknowledgement. "Via the linen cupboard."

"I confess I have little to do with linens." The young man's eyes widened theatrically and he extended his arm with a flourish to indicate they were welcome to pass, his gaze sweeping over Gaudet. "Though I wish that I'd had a root through that cupboard if *you* were hiding in there."

"Perhaps another time." Gaudet bowed. "Thank you for being so understanding and so *bloody* gorgeous!"

"Pleasure," the young man beamed. Then his gaze shifted to William and he sniffed. "Nice poodle."

"It isn't mine," William was quick to point out. "I'm just holding it for him."

"Is *he* yours?"

William glanced from the man to Gaudet and back again, managing a somewhat baffled, "For the foreseeable future, yes."

"*Adieu*, pretty lady." Gaudet dropped into a courtly bow, eyes widening as they alighted on a coat of rich red. "How much for that *gorgeous* garment? I must have it—*look* at these rags, if you could but see my usual—"

"Oh, take it," the clearly enchanted young man told him. "Red isn't my color, anyway."

"An *angel*!" Gaudet picked up the coat and, with another bow, hurried from the room.

Utterly bemused, William followed. "We must get out of here."

"Tessier is in the house next door," an older man was shouting from the landing below, a flurry of movement all around the house. Clinging to the poodle, William followed Gaudet through the building, vaguely processing the nature of the establishment as they went.

"We've come from next door," Gaudet told the older man. "Which way is freedom?"

"Take those stairs"—he gestured—"and out the back door. If you are fleeing Tessier, good luck."

William didn't need telling twice and, with Gaudet following, hurried toward freedom and the night visible beyond the open doorway. With relief, he gulped in the cool air for a moment before catching Gaudet's arm, sure that to stay still now meant certain capture.

"Sylvie and her boy—" Gaudet blinked. "We—"

"We cannot." William's tone was harder than he'd intended and his grip tightened on Gaudet's arm, pulling him on into the city.

"Give me my girl." Gaudet reached for the dog, who strained toward him. "They helped me—gave me their home..."

"And what fine repayment it would be for you to end up dead?" William kept hold of the poodle, certain it was the only way to guarantee some control over Gaudet as he dragged him along. The city seemed too quiet, every footstep echoing to give them away, every beggar a watchful threat of betrayal. They could not, he realized, leave Paris that night—they needed somewhere to stay, to lie low until the morning.

"Give me Papillon," Gaudet snapped. "Please!"

"Not"—William kept walking—"until we reach safety."

"If we leave them, what will happen?" Gaudet's voice betrayed panic and uncertainty. "The child...he is just a boy."

"I will send word to someone who may be able to help," William promised, cursing the playwright afresh for putting him in this position. "That is the best I can do."

They pressed into the night, out of the fetid city and toward the open fields and, William hoped, somewhere they might hide for the night. A barn, a farmhouse, anything to put distance between them and Tessier's search. He was silent as they went along, anger and frustration burning alongside a growing despair.

They would have to sleep in the woods, he knew. I was not safe enough to chance the roadside. Yet the thought of a night cold and hungry and listening to the playwright list his, no doubt, many complaints only added to his ill temper. Finally, lights were visible in the distance and William told Gaudet, "Look, there."

"Another hovel." Gaudet scowled, slipping his arms into the red brocade coat. "Do I *look* like a man who sleeps in rural taverns, Bobbins?" Despite Gaudet's obvious temper the coat seemed to mend his manners somewhat and he twirled in the moonlight, the elaborate garment swirling around him with undeniable panache. "This is more like it... I am saving the suit for a special occasion but this, this is my sort of style."

"Would you prefer a hovel?" William asked with a scowl of his own. "Or sleeping in a ditch?"

"This coat is exquisite." Gaudet ran his hand over the red fabric, a delicate silver pattern catching the moonlight. "Perhaps a little less vibrant than I am used—" He froze suddenly, an expression of horror falling over his face.

"What?" William reached for the pistol he kept concealed.

"I forgot my rouge and powder!"

William found he could only stare, managing after a long moment, "Would you have us go back?"

"I am not an imbecile, Bobbins." Gaudet set his chin defiantly, sucking in his cheeks. "Let us potter on."

The lights belonged to a coaching inn that stood almost directly on the road and William frowned at the sight of it, gloomy in the darkness. A crowd milled around the exterior, drinks in their hands, yet they showed no interest in these new arrivals, this not being a place where questions were asked. As the men approached, the door opened and a customer was ejected by his unseen host, letting off a barrage of abuse from where he landed in the mud. From both the assembled drinkers outside and those within there came the sound of raucous laughter and voices raised in mirth. The promise of life spurred William toward it, perhaps too enthusiastic for some company.

"Here," he told Gaudet. "We will stay here tonight."

"Will we share?" The playwright clapped one hand to his mouth. "Will I be safe alone? I am a wanted chap."

William pondered that for a moment before conceding. "It might be safer."

"And Pap must have supper."

"They'll have scraps, no doubt..."

"*Scraps?*"

William rolled his eyes and pushed open the door to reveal an interior as busy as the yard outside and he paused, scanning the patrons. If the troublesome playwright was as chaotic as he appeared, then that meant he would have to be watchful for both of them. There was no doubt in his mind that Tessier would still be searching for his escaped spy. Still, it amused him that anybody could mistake this hapless, vain creature for Dee, as watchful and strategic in his decisions as Gaudet was flighty and foppish.

A few murmured words, coins were passed across, and a room was secured, not to mention a hearty meal for two, along with enough to fill the belly of the pampered pet that Gaudet carried beneath his arm.

In the minutes that had passed since they'd entered the inn, Gaudet had apparently already managed to ingratiate himself with a rather shapely woman who had abandoned her duties behind the bar to address him. She listened to the story he was spinning, with her head cocked to one side, wide eyes fixed on the handsome figure before her as though he were a prophet. The barmaid chewed at her rouged lower lip and lifted one hand to play absent-mindedly with the few strands of hair that fell from her bun to brush her cheek, everything about her positively screaming sympathy. She reached out to touch Gaudet's arm and leaned forward on the counter to confide something, coincidentally displaying an extra inch or so of her pale bosom as she did so.

"We will need an early night," William informed the playwright. "We must be away at dawn."

"My husband calls," Gaudet pouted, eliciting a laugh from the girl. "*Adieu*, beautiful lady."

"Do you think," William whispered, leading him away, "that you could refrain from drawing *quite* so much attention to us?"

"I have not been outside in a month," Gaudet snapped. "I am simply enjoying a few moments before the next trouble."

"There will be no more 'trouble,'" William shook his

head. "We will make our way calmly to Le Havre, collect your sister, and get everyone safely to England."

"And will we walk all the way…?" Gaudet took a seat. "My nerves will not stand it. Might we pick up a carriage tomorrow?"

William sighed, sitting with a long, deep breath, not willing to admit that he had no idea how they would reach the coast. In Paris, things had been possible, plans could be made and the very geography of the capital had lent things a certain sort of sense, even though it was a maelstrom. There was protection in numbers there, safety in the fabric of the city from the catacombs of the Ossuary far beneath his feet to the buildings that rose overhead, pressing into the narrow streets from either side. If the spies of Paris could watch from windows or doorways, then here there was too much space for safety, an apparently unending expanse of land in which two people traveling to Le Havre would be either utterly anonymous or dreadfully, fatally exposed.

And with Alexandre Gaudet in his crimson coat, laughing with that shriek and carrying a white poodle, we cannot not hope to be invisible.

"Do you ride?" William asked Gaudet, hoping that the answer would be yes. "Horses will carry us to the coast, if so."

"At Versailles, I was feted for my equestrian skills. I do not *ride*, I *excel*." Gaudet preened at his hair for a moment. "And you shall see only my fine derrière, disappearing into the distance."

"That is a delight," he told Gaudet with a sniff, "that I shall manage to live without."

"I will have you know that the fineness of my bottom has been discussed in parliament."

"Well," William stated, "they do tend to struggle to find matters of interest."

The food arrived then, two bowls of rather worrying stew and a plate of meat scraps for the poodle. Both canine and master frowned at the offerings before Gaudet told William,

"This will not do, not at all."

"You are at liberty to eat it or go hungry," William told him curtly.

"You wish us to starve?" Gaudet's mouth fell open and he exchanged a look with the poodle, both turning their noses up as one.

"There's hell on that road tonight," an elderly man said as he hobbled to the table beside their own, his inconsequential weight leaning on a knotty stick of wood. William saw that his left leg had been amputated at the knee, a pale stump just visible beneath the frayed hem of his breeches. "They're burning Gustave's farmhouse — it's up like a tinderbox."

"They'd burn the land out from beneath our feet if they could," the landlord agreed to a chorus of approval, heads nodding all over the inn. "And the Committee who fan the flames."

"I'm not a man who loved his king and queen," the old man went on, sucking at the stem of a long pipe, "but it seems to me that we're as hungry under this lot as we were with the last. Pray for rain tonight, for Gustave's sake."

"It doesn't do to pray these days," the landlord warned with a smile. "Somebody might tell our Supreme Being."

"Let them tell him." He shrugged, a plume of gray smoke rising from his pipe into the night. "From what I hear, he's buggered anyway."

As William was distracted by the exchange, Gaudet snatched up Papillon and left his seat to return to the counter, where the barmaid once again welcomed him with a beaming smile. She had applied fresh carmine to her full lips and listened to his story with rapt attention, eyes wide with awe. Within less than a minute a second dish of food was produced for the poodle, this one hot enough to steam and giving off a rich aroma of beef gravy. Papillon devoured it greedily as her master watched in obvious adoration, stroking the dog's head.

With a sound of annoyance, William turned away, the playwright's utter lack of comprehension as to the seriousness of their situation starkly clear to him then. He forced down the food before him, appetite gone as he considered the days ahead, the weeks that would follow after his mission was completed, the danger of having time to think about his life and what it had become. Shaking his head, William pushed back his bowl, drained his glass and stood. *He* would heed the hour even if Gaudet would not and bed was the answer, he was sure.

"I must go," Gaudet told the barmaid who emerged from behind the bar, summoning both men to follow along a corridor and up a steep, narrow staircase to the first floor.

The landing opened out and a hallway disappeared into the gloom, but it seemed that their destination was a little closer. Humming a gentle melody, she turned the key of the door nearest the staircase and pushed it open to reveal a room that seemed far too snug for two.

"It's all we've got left," she said by way of an apology, before the men had even seen the space where they were to spend the evening. "The cattle market brings in a lot of custom."

"I'm sure we'll manage," Gaudet replied, sharing a ghost of a smile with the barmaid. She bobbed in what seemed like an abandoned curtsey and handed the candle to him, hurrying downstairs before they had a chance to complain.

With Gaudet on the landing, William surveyed the room, though that seemed like a very grand description for what was essentially a slightly larger than usual cupboard. It held one bed and a chest of drawers on which was a bowl and water jug, a threadbare armchair pushed up beneath the small window. By the light of the tallow candle, he could see that the dark green bedcovers had obviously seen far better days and were more darn than fabric, whilst the smell of previous residents still lingered on the air. The expression of disgust on Gaudet's face amused William just a little and he wrinkled his mouth into a scowl then grimaced, shaking his head at these insalubrious surroundings.

"I cannot sleep here, Bobbins."

"Then stay awake, it makes no difference to me."

"Then I will," Gaudet stated, opening one of the shutters to peer out into the darkness, the dog cuddled close to his chest.

William sighed, sitting on the edge of the bed to remove his boots. There were several responses he could think of but he kept them to himself, realizing suddenly just how weary he was, adrenaline lessening now they were in relative safety.

Gaudet set down the poodle, who climbed up onto the bed and curled into a tight ball despite her master's complaints. Leaving her to settle, he stripped off the red coat and poured water into the bowl from the jug that sat atop the dresser, sighing very deeply. For a second, he seemed about to remove his shirt but instead sat in the threadbare chair, lowering his head for a long moment.

"Sleep," William told the dejected man. "Everything will look better in the morning."

"I will let you have the bed." Gaudet smiled faintly. "I sleep badly."

"Do I have your word that you will not do anything stupid?" William peered at Gaudet. "You must not leave this room."

"Do you think I would put my sister and her child in danger?" William saw the playwright positively bristle at the thought of it, his voice rising in pitch and volume. "I have been brought to the brink of death already, sir, do you believe I did so lightly?"

"I do not believe," he decided after a moment, "that you knew *what* you were getting into."

"I thought she would be in Paris," was Gaudet's quiet admission. "That I would bring her to London…"

"I am sorry," William found the words slipping out unbidden. "The world has become a cruel place."

"Go to sleep," Gaudet said gently. "Pap will keep watch."

"It is big enough for two," William spoke without thinking. "You will need to be well rested for the days ahead."

"I do not sleep any longer," Gaudet told him with a forced lightness, "until I have absolutely no choice."

"Why?"

"Did you not see me lashed to the wall, my back raw from the whip?" Gaudet asked furiously, virtually leaping from the chair. "Beaten to within an inch of my life, burned, slashed, starved and you ask why I do not *sleep*?"

William remembered the scene too well, the haunted shadow in Gaudet's eyes having disturbed his own sleep during these last few weeks since parting. "I am not quite the unfeeling monster you suspect, Monsieur."

"I worry…" The fight seemed to go out of Gaudet and he sank onto the bed. "If I cannot get to them, you must find them, sir. They have nobody — see them safely to England?"

"I will see you all there." He put his hand on Gaudet's shoulder. "I have been given a task, Monsieur, and I have not failed yet."

"My back is still troubling me." It clearly took a lot for the playwright to broach the subject. "I wonder, might you help me bathe it? Mademoiselle Dupire had helped but she is… Well, God help her."

William wanted to refuse, to plead exhaustion, crawl under the frayed blankets and block out the world. Instead he nodded, reaching into his pocket for the small bottle that contained the liquid that had soothed Gaudet's wounds that night in the prison. "Of course."

"I would not ask, you understand, but I think the day's exertions have rather told…"

"I will do it" — he got to his feet, adding a couple of drops to the water — "if you will try to sleep."

"I will try," Gaudet agreed, taking a deep breath before he pulled his shirt over his head.

The marks left by the whip hadn't fully healed, yet the angry crimson wounds were now dulled, as were the black bruises that time had rendered disappearing gray shadows. He dipped his head as William wet the cloth and sat on the bed again. Gently, he pressed it to Gaudet's body, trying his best not to think, preferring instead to concentrate on cleaning the marred skin.

There was the slightest sound of discomfort before Gaudet bit his lip, breath coming quicker. William winced in turn and muttered an apology, doing his best not to aggravate Gaudet's back further as he breathed in the delicate fragrance of the water that filled the air.

"I would not have guessed that you were an Englishman," Gaudet said eventually, his tone too cheery to be anything but manufactured. "If you ever wish to turn your hand to the stage, come and find me."

"I would not be suited to it," he told Gaudet firmly. "Besides, my hands are busy with other things."

"Tell me about her," was the cheeky reply, "and cheer me a little."

"There is nothing to tell." William was powerless to stop the coldness in his tone. "My work keeps me busy enough."

"As you say."

"I do." He fought the absurd need to explain, to make Gaudet understand, pausing as he struggled with conflicting emotions that he did not have time for.

"Thank you for all you have done," Gaudet told him. "Now let us try to sleep?"

"That is the most sense you have spoken since I have known you," William decided with relief, lowering the cloth. "Sleep."

Chapter Thirteen

Sylvie moved her hand over her face, feeling the tender skin and increased heat where Tessier's fists had landed that morning. Her lip was split in at least two places, she knew, and her left eye had swollen badly enough to suggest that it might be black, the vision reduced to just a fraction of what it ought to be. For the so-called Butcher of Orléans, he had proved reticent when it came to her punishment, and she had found herself encouraging him along, telling him to use his fist rather than his palm, to put his force into every swing.

The rope with which he bound her was as loose as her shawl and she urged it tighter so that her flesh burned and prickled with blood, letting him throw her to the floor until her white nightgown was filthy and torn, hair disheveled and full of dust.

"Now I look like a real prisoner," had been her answer when he'd begged for her forgiveness on his knees, his face resting on her stomach. "You've done a good job."

Abandoned on a pile of straw that stabbed at her skin, Sylvie felt like a real prisoner, too, the bare hopelessness of the royal suite a virtual palace compared to where he had placed her in preparation for Charron's arrival. Bastien had been brought to his mother after her beating and he lay curled in her arms, his head resting in her lap and his body moving with the steady rise and fall of sleep. Even now he refused to cry, but she saw the despair in his eyes, the pain that filled them when he saw the injuries that blighted her beauty.

"I never saw them guillotine a kid before," Bastien had

confided before he'd finally given in to exhaustion, "so I suppose I'll be special in a way."

"And just like I said, I'm going to show them my arse before they do."

She stroked her bruised hand softly over his dirty hair and studied his peaceful face, recognizing herself in his childish features and more than that, in his strength. To put a scrap of food in his skinny belly she had been through things she would never share with anyone, from a simple dip in a crowd to going down on her knees for a so-called gentleman behind the Délassements-Comiques. Even here in this hell of a prison, he clung to her like a babe, all that bravado forgotten in the moment he'd seen her bruises.

"You're not going to have nothing to worry about," Sylvie whispered. "You've got your ma looking out for you."

If I have to give Vincent Tessier the occasional treat then so be it, it won't be the first and it won't be the worst.

"Better than the guillotine," she concluded aloud, her head snapping up. The door opened and a guard shoved Charron into the tiny cell, the sound of the manacles he wore waking Bastien from his sleep.

"Thierry!" Bastien pushed himself upright and shuffled closer to Sylvie. The door slammed again, the heavy lock sliding into place a moment later. "See what they did to Ma!"

"Sylvie," Charron said earnestly, putting his manacled hands on her shoulders and studying her face.

"It's not as bad as it seems." Sylvie made an air of putting on a brave face.

Thierry shook his head, Bastien pulling at his sleeve for attention as he asked with a child's optimism, "They'll bring help then, won't they?"

"Nobody's coming for the likes of me," Charron whispered. "But I got you two a deal."

"What have you done?" Sylvie searched the face of the man who had put a roof over their heads, saved them from more than he would ever know. "Who'd come for us in here?"

"I fed Tessier a line and he went for it, told him that Gaudet was headed for Spain and had taken off that first night."

You really believe that Vincent Tessier might believe your fairytales. She almost smiled — it would be funny if it weren't so tragic.

"But that's not true," she leaned closer, dropping her voice. "Is he safe?"

"He's bound for the coast," Charron told her, a shadow clouding his face when he added, "I told Tessier I smuggled them out, so…"

So I will be next to meet the executioner.

"No," Bastien cried, his head whipping from his mother to the man who had been a father to him. "That's not fair! No!"

The boy wriggled his small frame beneath the manacles to force an embrace from Charron, who squeezed his eyelids together and told the child, "You've got to take care of your mother now, all right? Don't give her a hard time."

"I'll kill Tessier," Bastien promised, fury and sadness in every word. "I swear I will."

"And what good would you be to Sylvie then?" Charron shook his head as Bastien edged out from beneath the chains that bound his wrists and fixed him with his gaze. "Sylvie needs you — that's the most important job in the world."

Sylvie cocked her head to one side and watched their exchange, recognizing now in these final moments that this man was the father her son deserved, that in less vicious times the family they had become might have been enough to carry them through.

A shame you're not the one with the diamond or we could have been so very happy.

I might even have loved you one day, given time.

She straightened when Charron addressed her directly, blinking back into the dank cell and the damp, filthy air that was almost a presence in itself.

"Gaudet's sister's in Le Havre," he told her and she knew that this was the truth, no line to string Tessier along. "Roucelle's Dee's man in that part of the world."

"Le Havre." She turned the words over in her mouth, feeling the sting of triumph. "He's headed for Le Havre."

"I want you to try and catch up to Gaudet. I can tell you the safe houses I have given him but that's all I can do." Charron closed his eyes again and she listened as he went through the locations where they might find help, revealing the secrets of his escape network, the concealed places in the house she had shared where this information could be found. Through all of it, Sylvie kissed her lover and murmured soft reassurances, tried to tell him that execution wasn't necessarily guaranteed, that they could still walk free through the streets of the city again.

"I made you a gift, a little box for your buttons," he whispered, kissing her chastely. "I wanted to give it to you, but…"

She felt another twinge of pity at his simplicity, to be talking of boxes and buttons when much greater riches were at stake. "Don't worry over that now. We'll find Gaudet, you've got my word on that."

"Where is it?" Bastien asked urgently. "That box?"

"The workshop hearth…" Charron fell silent as the door swung open and the guard entered, his demeanor as casual as a man strolling by the river.

"Come on, son," the guard told Bastien, taking him under the arms. "Let's be having you."

"Put me down!"

"You're lucky today," he informed the child. "Not every lady who's slept in this here cell got to go home with her lad."

Though the boy fought and swore the guard carried him effortlessly out, slamming the door and locking it behind him. With freedom suddenly impossibly near, Sylvie could hardly keep her eyes off the cell door, straining her ears for the sound of the key jangling, the heavy lock sliding back.

Now she had what she needed she longed to be away from here, this place that had become a charnel house.

"I'm sorry," she told Charron with something close to honesty, "that it had to end this way."

The door swung open again and this time the visitor was more than a mere guard, Tessier a slender shadow in black. He executed a curt bow and tucked the horsewhip he carried beneath his arm, a thin smile on his bloodless lips.

"Have you said your goodbyes?" As he spoke, Tessier took Sylvie by the elbow and hauled her to her bare feet. Her stomach felt as though she had swallowed poison and she turned her eyes to the floor. She was sure that Charron would read in them what she had done, the bargain she had made with herself. "Not many have walked free from this cell, Mademoiselle, don't dawdle."

Such a good man.

"Before you go," Charron called after them, his voice strong for the benefit of the interloper, "tell me you love me one last time — let me die with that in my ears?"

It would be a kind lie, the right thing to do, the *only* thing to do if she were any sort of a decent person. Sylvie thought again of who she was, of what had brought her here, and what she intended to do, and the words stuck in her throat, bitter and unspeakable. At the door she turned, heart hardening as she knew it would have to if they had a chance of surviving.

"I can't say it, Thierry," she told the too-trusting man who had given them so much. "Because I never did."

Chapter Fourteen

For the first time in weeks and no doubt as a result of his utter exhaustion, Gaudet slept through the night, wakened by Papillon's decision to carry out her morning promenade up and down the bed. After treading heavily on her master, she snuggled down between Gaudet and William happily, sinking back into a deep sleep.

"It's over there," the still sleeping Englishman muttered, one arm lifting slightly. "There!"

"Shh," Gaudet hushed, happy to return to sleep, his eyes not even opening. Instead he snuggled closer and draped his arm around the waist of what he *believed* was a rather pretty Parisian molly. There was silence then, punctuated by the occasional sigh as William dreamed in the warm and comfortable bed, Gaudet's face resting against his hair.

"I could put you in a play," Gaudet whispered, trailing his hand lazily over his companion's chest. "You have such presence."

It was the sort of statement that should, he was certain, be met with a positive response—excitement, perhaps, and gratitude at the very least. The irate exclamation of shock was decidedly out of place and he cracked open an eye to find himself face to face with the man he now knew as Bobbins.

For a long moment, Gaudet gazed at his companion, then, with a shrug, closed his eyes and snuggled closer again, thinking Bobbins was really quite acceptable company at the moment. The man beside him was still and silent, and he almost drifted off again before he heard the words, "I am *not* being in a play. Never, sir!"

At that, Gaudet lifted his head and asked, "Why are you holding my hand?"

"I am not—"

"Yes"—he held up their linked hands—"you are."

"You, sir," came the eventual reply when the fact couldn't be denied, "are holding *my* hand. I would like it back immediately."

Gaudet straightened his fingers, proving beyond a doubt that he wasn't the one doing the holding, then laughed. "Sir, you like Frenchmen?"

"Not at this particular time," was the dry response, Bobbins pulling his hand away a second later.

"I dreamed you were a gorgeous bedfellow"—Gaudet sighed, careful *not* to mention the gender of the bedfellow in question—"with whom I had passed a night of debauchery."

"You must be horribly disappointed." Bobbins attempted to sit up.

Pap leaped onto Bobbins' chest, tongue lapping at his face as Gaudet laughed, clapping. "She is kissing you hello!"

"I don't want her to kiss me at all," the Englishman exclaimed, batting with his hands. "Get her off."

"She likes English boys."

"Well, *I* do not like French poodles."

Gaudet's face dropped into a pout and he wondered how *anyone* could not like French poodles, especially one so angelic as the little girl who had followed him through hell and high water. "*Well*."

"Not like that," Bobbins quickly clarified, Gaudet's hopes rising again. "I mean I don't like them like *that*. It's a *poodle*."

"Who likes poodles like *that*? That would be a very strange way for a chap to like a poodle." Gaudet clamped his hands over the dog's ears. "Pap is too young for such talk. She has no interest in carnality. She is very spiritual."

"Well!" Bobbins seemed even more perturbed, though quite why, Gaudet couldn't fathom. "Now we've established *that*, do you think I might get up?"

"You already are." Gaudet laughed, casting an arch glance at his companion's breeches.

There was nothing to see at all, of course, but he enjoyed the devilment of it nevertheless. The utterly scandalous claim was more than worth it, Bobbins pushing both man and poodle aside as he sat up, fixing Gaudet with what he could only describe as a *look*. Gaudet cared little and instead lay back in the bed, hands pillowed beneath his head as he watched Bobbins make for the long-cold water and splash some over his face. He appeared tense, and if the sleep had done his companion good it did not show.

"Would my lovely coat cheer you?"

"I do not want to wear your coat." Bobbins was clearly finding the idea difficult to process, and Gaudet wondered again at what an odd fellow he was.

"I *adore* fashion." Gaudet sat up against the thin pillow, dreaming of the room full of clothes in London, the gleaming jewels, polished shoes and acres of silks and lace. "Antonia—Her Majesty to you—and I used to pass *hours* in the pursuit of it. She always said I was the finest hairdresser at court, far better than those supposed *professionals*."

"Congratulations." Bobbins dried his face, peering over the towel at Gaudet. "You dress hair?"

"Now and then." Gaudet sighed, shaking his head. "They cut off her hair, you know...and her poor children... This country is going to Hell."

"Which is why we're getting out of it." Bobbins seemed animated at last. "Get up. Get dressed. We must be on our way."

"We had such times... The last time I saw her, we gave a little soiree for the children, had a little ball for them..."

"We need to go," Bobbins cut into the reminiscence.

He was right, of course. Gaudet knew that, even as he gathered up Papillon and slipped from between the sheets. Le Havre seemed a million miles, a hundred years away and he thought again of the sister and her infant child, of Vincent Tessier and those rooms in London where everything was just, *just*. Under Bobbins' impatient stare Gaudet tidied himself as best he could, the new coat bringing some comfort as he slipped it on, adjusting it with a sigh of satisfaction.

"I am *very* famous, you know," Gaudet explained, smoothing down the fabric. "I do not usually dress like a gutter peasant, as you will see when we dine in London."

"Dine in London?"

Gaudet wondered for a brief moment if the man might be just a trifle idiotic, the look of surprise on his face at the simple statement giving him cause for concern.

"You and I, when we are safely home, I will take you to dinner at my club by way of thanks for all you have done."

"There is really no need," Bobbins protested.

"Nevertheless, it will be done." He clapped. "I am *sure* Queen Charlotte would *love* to meet you for supper. I know the princesses would *adore* you. I am always popping along to see them."

"Princesses and poodles…"

"And perfume, too."

Bobbins seemed pained at that, muttering, "Oh, for a drink…"

"It is some way to the coast," Gaudet commented with a frown, brightening when he realized, "but I shall cheer you all the way with tales of theater. Have you seen my plays? You must have, I imagine?"

"I have not," Bobbins admitted. "I rarely visit London."

"I *love* London, and Brighton, of course, but London… London is the center of the universe." He laughed, thinking wistfully of the place. "Well, outside of France, of course."

"I much prefer the country," Bobbins told him.

The thought was utterly inconceivable to Gaudet. The countryside was so quiet, so still—there was no hope of being recognized in the cornfields, after all.

"You are a strange fellow, Bobbins." Gaudet nodded curtly at the polite rejection, thinking it quite the gentleman's loss. "As strange as your name."

Bobbins' response was to head for the door and, with a sigh, Gaudet followed, dreaming of the gaming room on the Strand, his home on Berkeley Square and the soft, marvelously ornate bed where he longed to rest his head once more.

"Horses," Bobbins was muttering as they took the stairs. "We need horses."

"Pap will travel safe in my coat." Gaudet swung the portmanteau as he walked, the poodle trotting alongside, her tail swishing happily. She too would benefit from a return home, he knew, back to her own wardrobe and jewels. Bobbins appeared to have no reply to his comment and, instead, approached the bar, leaving Gaudet to tell Pap the plans. "You will travel with Papa, you are too small to reach the stirrups, flower."

After some negotiation and a decidedly unhappy Englishman parting with a few coins, the deal was apparently struck, Bobbins gesturing for Gaudet to follow him out into the yard. As he strolled after his guide Gaudet allowed himself a wink in the barmaid's direction, finding himself greeted with a most coquettish wave in reply.

Really, he thought with a smile, *perhaps I am just born this way!*

"You won't be smiling after a few hours in the saddle," Bobbins was almost too quick to warn him as they emerged into daylight. "And for heaven's sake, make sure you don't drop the dog."

"I will wager it isn't a fine steed you have secured for me..."

His suspicions proved correct as a stable hand appeared at that moment, leading two mounts that had most certainly seen better days. Of course, Gaudet was hardly to be outdone and spent some time circling the animals, studying them with a practiced eye before he decided, "Pap and I will take the chestnut, sir — we will let you have the gray."

"Why?" Bobbins peered at the horse suspiciously.

"Because," was the arch reply as he watched Bobbins closely, "it will have a longer gait and since *I* am an excellent horseman, you will need all the help you can get. Now let us away and you can tell me all about the one with the eyes…"

With a long-suffering sigh, Bobbins pulled himself into the saddle, muttering something to himself that Gaudet couldn't quite catch. Instead, he fastened the portmanteau containing his precious suit to the saddle, tucked Papillon into the front of his coat and nimbly mounted the portly horse, straightening in the saddle as though it were a prize Lipizzaner. For a few moments, he fussed with his clothes, smoothing down the lines, then decided, "I believe I am ready."

"Then let us be off," Bobbins declared. "And may nothing untoward await."

Chapter Fifteen

The sun had begun to sink what felt like a hundred miles ago and the saddles grew less comfortable with each passing hour. Gaudet's occasional chatter had given way to complaint until even he had fallen silent, the dog sleeping happily cuddled to her master. Now, they were in the first safe house that William knew they could trust, concealed in a hayloft, much to Gaudet's chagrin.

He knew Gaudet by reputation, of course. Everybody in London knew Gaudet by reputation. Occasional scandals kept him from rehearsals, ticket sales were never better than when the diarists had his name on their lips, and he reveled in it, a stranger to neither the gossip pages nor the finer things in city life, though William wished he would stop *talking* about them.

"Are you not tired?" William asked hopefully when an infrequent lull in Gaudet's monologue presented itself.

"Should I be?" Gaudet blinked and continued on his tale of a saucy encounter between a bishop and two leading ladies, accompanied by much uproarious laughter and those excitable, childish claps. On and on he went, fueled by the brandy their host had provided, settled on his impromptu bed of straw. William found himself drifting, watching the Frenchman as his tale went on, wondering as he did so if the man was ever going to shut up.

"How long shall we stay here?" Gaudet waved a piece of straw away from his nose, hopping to another subject like a particularly dapper frog in a lily pond. "It smells like horses."

"Tonight." William forced himself to focus on what the

man was saying, with effort. "We cannot afford to tarry."

"I must tell you of the time His Majesty and I—" Gaudet frowned, looking at him. "Are you listening?"

"Listening?"

"Are. You. Listening?" Gaudet peered very close then and enunciated as though William were stupid. "What did I just say to you? What story did I just tell of Mrs. Siddons, Lord Chatham and I?"

"There was drinking involved," William hazarded a guess. "And dancing."

"You were not listening," Gaudet concluded. "Have you no rip-roaring tales of your own to share?"

"But when it comes to interesting tales, I cannot beat you."

"Why do you dislike me so?" Gaudet's tone was light, but his gaze, William noted, flitted away. "I am sorry that you do."

"I do not dislike you."

Gaudet's answer was a silent shrug before he nestled down into the straw and blankets, turning his back to William. There was the sound of a delicate chain being drawn from his pocket then the click of a locket opening, the Frenchman utterly silent.

"I am just not one for actresses and peers."

"I believe I should do well enough traveling alone," Gaudet said without turning. "Rather than *endure* me, you are free to go. After all, you are not here for the good of your health…"

"It is not in your hands," William told him, the thought of Dee's fury if he abandoned Gaudet hardly filling him with confidence. "I am getting you to the coast, come Hell or high water."

"Why on earth would you?" Gaudet rolled over to gaze at William. "I have offered no money, nothing in return…"

Why indeed? How to explain that he felt he owed it to Gaudet, that he should have somehow been able to prevent the torment sooner? Not to mention the fact that the missions given to him by Dee were the only thing to bring any semblance of meaning to his days, that he had nothing, was nothing, without these carefully scripted tasks.

"I gave my word," he offered as hopelessly inadequate explanation, wishing that he had a drink.

"If I stop talking, I will start remembering." Gaudet's voice had lost its lightness. "Let us talk about something that will interest you."

"I am not very interesting, Monsieur," he told his companion. "You have a knack for conversation and small talk that I find I quite envy."

"I have never done well with silence."

"Do you read?"

"I do."

"Well." William seized on that. "What do you like?"

"You tell me what *you* like first," Gaudet urged, smiling as Papillon hopped into William's lap. "Mistress Pap enjoys all the classics, of course, and the scandal sheets, too."

"History," William admitted. "It is comforting to know that everything has been entirely messed up many times before."

"But the lessons are never learned, and innocent lives are the price that is paid."

"If we are going to start talking like that," he decided, "we need a drink."

"You were very annoyed at my chatting to that charming bosomy barmaid." Gaudet sat up and reached for the carefully discarded crimson coat. As he went on, he slipped his hand into the pocket and retrieved a silvery flask, adding devilishly, "But it paid off."

"What is it?" William was surprised before realizing he probably shouldn't be. "And how did you manage that?"

"Brandy in this one" — a second bottle appeared — "and claret in the other. It took a smile, a wink and a flutter of my exquisite eyelashes."

"Impressive," William had to concede, something making him add, "but I cannot deprive you of your bounty."

"Then we shall save it for another day," Gaudet said,

replacing the flasks.

"I don't dislike you." William yawned, feeling suddenly helpless. "I am just used to being alone."

"Whereas I cannot bear it—a fine pair we are!" Gaudet shook his head and decided, "Let us try to get along…"

William looked at Gaudet, the apparent sincerity in the playwright's face finding him nodding in agreement. "It might be an improvement over bickering."

"We will still bicker," Gaudet assured him with a cheeky wink. "And it will keep my mind alert."

"And no doubt your tongue," William heard himself add.

"My tongue is never short of a task…" Gaudet arched one immaculate eyebrow. "Taken alongside my bottom and myriad *other* delightful qualities, you are quite the chap to be envied."

"You think there are others who would want to be in my position?"

"I *know* there are many who would—really, I am usually pursued by everyone from duchesses to actors and everything in between. How I have remained a virgin is a mystery," Gaudet told him piously.

William wondered briefly how the conversation had taken this particular turn, more certain than ever that anything was possible when the Frenchman opened his mouth. "I would not want to venture an explanation for that."

"Of course, when I bared my arse to a passing scandal rag publisher in the Strand, I was beset by marriage proposals. It is quite exhausting being me. You should feel privileged." Gaudet gave a long-suffering sigh and shook his head. "We should travel by night, I cannot risk my skin. It has taken *forever* to attain this natural paleness. I will not be burnished."

"We must travel when it is *safe* and expedient to do so," was William's well-drilled response. "Day and night."

"When we are back in England, I will take you out on the town to say thank you." Gaudet's smile faded just a little before he recovered it, though his green eyes grew darker.

"And I will *never, ever* try to be the hero of the hour again."

"There are no such things as heroes," William told him quietly, his own memories too close for comfort. "You are either lucky, or you are not."

"I had not seen the guillotine before that day," Gaudet admitted, all levity gone. "I shall not soon forget it. Did you see what that *animal* did to Philippe? There is no dignity afforded, even in death…"

"Turn your mind from it," William advised. "Otherwise it will drive you quite mad."

"When they come to England, they must know no more sadness, no more loss…"

"That is impossible," was William's rueful reply. "But I believe you will make sure they have less than most people."

"And you…you are…what? Are you a secret agent of some sort? Are you Dee?"

"Dee?" The very thought that he might be that controlled, organized spymaster filled William with amusement. "Goodness no, I am not."

"I had my doubts about you from the start." Gaudet yawned. "For a torturer, you did precious little actual torturing. The tall chap has the gravity of a spymaster whereas you do *not* have that look."

"Indeed. And what *do* I look like, then?"

"A man who is no stranger to confusion."

William considered that for a long moment, deciding not to ask if that was a compliment as he examined the sleeve of his coat. "Hm."

"You should 'hm' at such a drab garment—my wardrobe on Berkeley Square fills an entire room, a second houses my shoes, jewels and make up. One should *shimmer!*"

"I have no time nor need for any of that." William shook his head, no words to explain what his own *shimmering* life had once been, much less what had brought him here. "Not anymore."

"Why would one choose *not* to shimmer and sparkle?"

Gaudet enquired, clearly perplexed.

"Do you ever —?" He cut himself off. "We should sleep."

"Do I ever?"

Want to give up? Feel as though everything is utterly worthless? Wish you could undo the last five years and have a chance to put things right?

Gaudet was watching him expectantly and William settled for, "Wonder what the *point* is."

"The point" — Gaudet was suddenly on his feet and William thought for one awful moment that he might burst into song — "is to *sparkle*. We have but one life, it is for living!"

"I have the impression that you will live enough for both of us." Feeling suddenly bone weary, William unfastened his coat, slipping out of it with a tired sigh.

"What is your name?" Before William had a chance to reply, Gaudet spoke again, telling him, "Your real name — just the first one if you wish?"

He deliberated on that, turning what should be a simple request over in his mind. Dee would tell him to use a false name, he knew, even as he admitted, "My name is William."

"A nice name — it suits you."

He had nothing to say in response, closing his eyes briefly as he fought the ridiculous urge to take it back, to reclaim the name that was used by so few now.

"Guillaume." The French version of his name rolled off the playwright's tongue with almost indecent decadence and he found, absurdly, his cheeks coloring.

"Indeed."

"Guillaume Bobbins." Gaudet dropped into an extravagant courtly bow. "Good evening."

"You look as if you are about to ask me to dance." William had to smile when the playwright offered his hand for a second, as though they might be about to take a turn on the floor. "It has been a long time since I danced."

Gaudet sighed and turned away, murmuring, "Or smiled. Or laughed." With that, he settled on his own meagre bed of straw, twisting and turning as he clearly tried to find some respite from the still-healing wounds on his back. Finally, though, he drew the poodle to rest beside him and said, "Goodnight, Guillaume and Papillon."

"Goodnight," William murmured in return, though he suspected he would not sleep, despite his weariness. Instead he lay peering into the darkness until he drifted off, Gaudet's pronunciation of his name following him into dreams.

Chapter Sixteen

Tessier swilled the coffee that remained in his cup and looked through the murky glass to the clouds that swirled above, black as night in the middle of the day. They seemed to press down on Paris, threatening to engulf the filth and the chaos, to choke those who traveled its thoroughfares and lived wretched lives within its walls. He had seen the city from both sides in his thirty-four years on Earth, had been turned away from church by a ruddy-cheeked, gout-hobbled priest who feared that the little boy's bare feet might offend the ladies who came to open their purses and confess their decadency. There had been precious little gold in his life, the color of the altar cloth more dazzling than any he had seen and, refused entry to this most holy, most palatial of places, the boy who had grown to be Tessier had spent his days at the door, hands clasped in prayer whilst his eyes had seen nothing but excess.

He had been both repelled and fascinated by the gaudy, painted creatures who'd fluttered past him as though he were another rat in the gutter to be ignored. They'd thrown the occasional coin to appease their good Catholic consciences even as they'd pressed fresh, white handkerchiefs to powdered noses and turned away from the half-starved wretch who'd bowed his head in deference. He could still recall the sound of their rustling silk gowns as they'd passed, the hoof-like clatter of brocaded shoes on the nave and the empty, simpering platitudes of the priest and his hangers-on.

So pious as they'd swept past him, so brazen as they'd left…

There was nothing sacred about the gods they worshipped.

The women had been intoxicating in their exoticism. He would watch his mother with her blackened teeth and sagging skin and try to imagine her as one of the ladies who frequented the church. In his mind's eye, he took her patched, tatty clothes and redrew them as gowns of silk and lace, painted her sallow cheeks with powder and rouge and covered her lank hair with a tall wig, ringlets framing a face that he could not imagine had ever been anything other than tired.

Then the woman was no longer his mother and he'd found her so much easier to loathe, to blame.

What kind of woman births a bastard in this unforgiving world?

Sometimes, Tessier would catch a glimpse of one of those sorry figures who sold themselves in the street or fell senseless with drink into the mud and see not the face of a stranger. Instead he saw the mother he had abandoned when he had been just seven years old, the woman with no time for the son who had become a burden. She hadn't even bothered to draw the curtain around her bed on that last night, no sense of shame as she'd fumbled and rutted with another man whose name she would never know. In that freezing room that had been their tiny world, he'd turned his face to the wall and thought of the perfumed ladies in their silk, the god who granted only the prayers that came plated with gold.

Better an orphan.

So, he'd left her sleeping as the church bells had struck midnight and set out alone, a child without parents on the streets of Paris.

And it was the making of me.

In the mind of the boy, the church door had been as impregnable as the Bastille, open yet barred to him, and though he'd passed it many times as he had grown from an innocent child to a young man whose belly was filled with the fire of revolution, he never again uttered a prayer. On the day he'd turned his back on the God he had once believed in as fervently as he now believed in the Republic, he'd rejected the miraculous. It was simply luck, good, bad or otherwise that had brought him to the Champs-Élysées on the August afternoon that would change his life.

The dappled gray horse had been fractious all the way down the road and the slight woman who'd ridden it struggled and shifted in the saddle, panic twisting her face as she'd careened through the other riders and pedestrians, who had scattered in her wake. There had been nothing heroic behind his instinctive reaction to reach up and seize the dropped reins, no intent to save anyone beyond himself as the beast bore down on him, eyes rolling and nostrils flaring wide. With his hands as they had become, he would have no hope of taking control of the animal, but there had been no scars to tighten and stiffen in those days and though the horse had bucked and snorted, the crisis appeared to have been averted by nothing but the quick thinking of the lowly milk seller's apprentice.

And life had changed in that moment, everything turned on its head by the sobbing woman who'd slid from the saddle. Never once did she reject the filthy child before her or stare through him as though he was litter at her feet, but instead she'd looked him in the eye and taken his hand, gasping her sympathy when they had seen that the reins had flayed the skin from his palms.

Josette and Hugues Tessier had taken the boy from the milk seller and his brutal thrashings and apprenticed him to their own groom. The work had been hard and the hours long but the groom had been kind and the horses fine and he'd settled into this life as he had no other, his mother's face invading his conscience less and less as the days had passed.

In fact, the boy who was known simply as *Vincent* had made more of an impression on the childless Josette Tessier than anyone had guessed and she had become ever more attentive to her savior. By the time he had grown to be ten years old, the Tessiers had given him their name and he'd left the stables for a life of education. This boy who'd had so little was now learning not only the fundamentals of education but also what it meant to be human, to really *think*.

For Hugues there had been no simple decisions, no required learning and no prescribed rules, there had simply been the desire to install in the boy a sense of what was right and what was, fundamentally, wrong.

'No man should bow before another, Vincent. That is the first thing you should learn.'

'And we are all humans, no matter what our station.'

These people had made him the man he had become, nothing left of the boy who'd kneeled before the church and stared at those exotic, immoral women and their braying, politicking men. Within the walls of the Lycée Louis-le-Grand, Tessier had found himself with friends, something entirely novel for a child who had always been solitary.

Those friends have served me well, he thought with a smile, *and France, too.*

Hugues had been the first to die, falling from a horse ten years earlier, and in 1790 a disorder of the lungs had taken Josette as Tessier had held her hand, bitter tears coursing down his face and a hundred useless words of adoration pouring from his lips. He had never felt more alone, a lost child once more, just as he had been in that Parisian hovel.

She was all a woman should be – no rouge and powder, no paint and horsehair beneath which to shelter.

She was all that was good and beautiful in a world without color.

Those enormous church doors had been diminished when Tessier had returned as the silver-buckled rulers of Paris stumbled before the onslaught of revolution. He had flung them wide open, incense mingling with a less holy smoke as they put that den of immorality to the flames. The whole place had been stained with decadence and idolatry, too tainted in his memory to serve as a Temple of Reason. Instead he had folded his arms and closed his eyes as the building had burned before him, a warm orange glow dancing behind his closed lids. The priest who had flung that ragged child from the church into the gutter had long since gone, but another had stepped into his worthless shoes, and even as the defenders of reason filled his church he had fallen to his knees before the altar and prayed, fancying himself another Beckett.

And who am I to disappoint?

For all his holiness, the priest's blood was as red as every other man from king to pauper – we are all alike under the skin. I have seen enough men bleed to be sure of that.

And yet, I can still be beguiled in that search for something innocent, that is where true holiness lies. It is as fleeting and false as the gospels that had no room for the likes of me.

We are all ruined.

Tessier bowed his head until his forehead rested against the cool glass of the window, his own reflection returning his stare, dark and unwavering. For a few moments he watched himself in the glass, traced the narrow skull and dark hollows of his face where finely rendered cheekbones left him gaunt even as they had made his mother beautiful in his childish fantasies. He sucked his lips in and moistened them, watching as his face barely moved and he saw more clearly than ever the now familiar mask of the Butcher of Orléans, a figure of fright to keep children from disobeying the commands of their parents.

The stories they must tell about me…

I am the devil himself nowadays.

And yet, I think, not always.

Tessier allowed himself the briefest suggestion of joy at the memory of Sylvie's face when the locked door to the bedroom had finally opened and she had stood before the man who hadn't seen her in over a decade, one hand on her hip and a coquette's smile on her face. He had long since considered her lost to him, gone off to Lyon with her strapping bootmaker as she found her charms no match for those of politics and debate. Without her, he had been adrift, mourning Sylvie as one would the dead, his life seemingly shattered by her departure. And now here she was in Paris, ten years older but more beautiful than ever, as perfect as one who had been preserved on canvas.

His memory strayed to the sensation of her fingertips on him, the softness of her voice as she had whispered and encouraged and he closed his eyes again and breathed in the scent of her nightgown, felt the rise and fall of her breasts beneath thin fabric. In the Conciergerie, he had kneeled beside her chair as she had recovered from her time in the cell, and the need to touch her, to hear her words of praise again, was almost overwhelming. To have Sylvie so near and yet so disinterested in his presence was an exquisite agony. He'd clasped his hands behind his back and bowed his head, raising his eyes to her as though awaiting a benediction when she had run her fingers through his hair for a brief, wonderful moment.

Tessier stepped back from the study window at the sound of heavy footsteps on the stairs and turned from his unwelcome reflection, snapping into a more comfortable role as there came a knock at the door.

"All the men are here," Jacquet said, hardly entering the room as Tessier pulled on his gloves and prepared to leave. "They're in the kitchen."

When Tessier entered the kitchen, the six men were already standing straight and silent, waiting for this general to address his troops. He paced the line back and forth a couple of times before he told them, "Gentlemen, we are fighting a war."

Their eyes stayed on him, every man waiting for his next words as he knew they would, each of these guards hand-picked for their loyalty, their ferocity.

Their dedication to our cause.

"Our country is assailed by parasites—creatures bred on our own soil seek to destroy us, to unsettle the nation we have built through blood and toil."

"We all know of the Academy and its cowardly

operatives," he went on, warming to the theme. "They come from their nests to poison the citizens of France, to attack and destroy the very fabric of our Republic. The vermin are hidden within our own walls."

"Those responsible for the enslavement and starvation of the *sans-culottes*, who have assisted the enemies of the Republic, who have *murdered our own sons*." Jacquet closed his eyes for a moment, nodding in emphatic agreement, and Tessier paused before him as he concluded, "All will be found, apprehended and shown the true meaning of justice."

"Today we leave Paris and we will not return without the man they call Professor Dee and all of the rats who swarm around him."

Because, Monsieur Gaudet, you have written your last farce.

Chapter Seventeen

"I wonder if the cabinetmaker was saved," Gaudet mused after two more days on the road, two more nights hiding in stables and outhouses. "I hope so."

With that, he kicked his horse into a trot, not wanting to see the frown of doubt that he knew would be on his companion's face. The cool wind that buffeted him as they rode was refreshing in the heat and Gaudet closed his eyes for a few moments, listening to the refrain of drumming hoof beats. Tessier would be scouring the land for them and Gaudet could do nothing more than hope that this seemingly aimless cross-country route would confuse them, because if it didn't, they might well have run out of schemes to outfox their pursuers.

"Perhaps one day you might find out." The response from William as Gaudet spurred his own horse on was surprisingly positive for once.

"I cannot help but think of that poor, poor child…"

"It is a sorry business." William's horse began to pull ahead. "Think of something else, Gaudet, do not dwell."

"That Dee character was rather a fine figure of a man." Gaudet caught up with William. "Wouldn't you say, *Guillaume*?"

"I hardly judge men on their figures."

"It keeps my mind from darker thoughts," Gaudet confessed quietly, the fineness of men's figures being one of his main interests. "What has happened to my country? In the south, the land is scorched, in the north, drowning in blood…"

"Perhaps the world is ending," William suggested. "It

would be about time…"

"No, it cannot be, because I am still a virgin and that would not be fair at all!" As the mischievous words left his lips, Gaudet flashed past William on his chestnut mount, Papillon offering a cheeky bark of triumph. There was the sound of laughter before William gathered speed behind him, the two horses chasing each other along the road.

"What a lovely view you must have," Gaudet called, offering a wiggle of his bottom. "The finest in France!"

"You make a bold claim there."

"I have the finest face in the land, so my bottom must likewise be unsurpassed."

There was no response from his companion as they raced down the road, one pulling ahead for a moment, only to fall behind again at the next.

"Actually, ahead you go," Gaudet tried a different tactic, "so that I might see *your* arse and appraise it."

"I will be too far ahead for you to see my bottom or anything else."

"Not the size of it. I would see it from Rome!"

"Damn you Frenchman." William gave chase again. "I will win this race."

"I am not racing," Gaudet said, all innocence as he settled into a gentle trot. "I am enjoying the scenery, thinking about my beautiful coat…"

"You cannot give up *now*."

"I cannot hear, drop back and say again?"

With a growl of frustration William did so, repeating, "You cannot give up now, sir."

"Give up?" Gaudet frowned, urging his horse into a gallop with a cry of, "It is *you* who has fallen behind. Like all Englishmen I've known, I've outridden you."

"I am not *all* Englishmen, Monsieur." William pushed his horse even further, breathing hard with exertion. The animal thundered on until, quite suddenly, it decided that snacking was far preferable to racing and veered off the road toward a patch of apparently irresistible grass.

Unprepared, William barked an oath before he tumbled unceremoniously into a ditch and the horse carried on a short way without him, finally coming to a lazy halt.

"Guillaume, *chérie!*" Gaudet could barely manage to call for laughing as he reined his own horse in and pottered over to the mud-soaked Englishman. He peered over the edge of the ditch and said sweetly, "I believe your enormous bottom proved too much for this delicate French horse. You are *very* muddy now."

"Of course I'm bloody muddy. I'm in a bloody ditch!"

"Why are you in a ditch? I thought we were going to Le Havre."

The next few moments were lost in ranting that was, to Gaudet's ears, rather incoherent. "I need to get up."

"That should be easy, just think of my *stunning* bottom."

William's expression at that was priceless, the spluttering continuing for a good few moments.

Finally, Gaudet slipped from his horse and, settling Pap and his red coat on the saddle, held out a hand as he warned, "Don't you *dare* get mud on me, Guillaume."

He realized his mistake as soon as William seized his hand, but by then it was too late, he was already toppling into the ditch. For a moment, Gaudet was silent, then he let out a shriek of dismay, hands flailing in a wild fury as he shouted, "Look at my clothes. What have you done? I am *filthy*...my hair!"

As Gaudet watched in shocked disbelief, William actually laughed, a sound that grew in volume until he was positively shaking with humor, overwhelmed by it.

"Do not *laugh*," Gaudet shrieked, though in truth, it was infectious. "Stop it."

"You — *We* —" William guffawed. "Look at us!"

"I am filthy." Gaudet looked down at his muddy hands before, with some difficulty, he clambered out of the ditch. Safe on the grass once more, he stripped off the muddy shirt, pausing to tell Pap, "See what Uncle Guillaume has done to Papa!"

"Don't listen to him. I did nothing." William was still laughing as he hauled himself out of the ditch. "That bloody horse."

"Mud will do one's skin no harm—indeed, I do like the occasional mud mask at home." Gaudet tried and failed to convince himself, hardly able to imagine how dreadful he might look. "Find me some water, Guillaume, quickly."

"Water?" William frowned. "Where?"

"Swimming, Pap, lovey?" Gaudet plucked the dog from the saddle and she dashed off, leaving him to grab the reins of his horse and give pursuit, sure she would find what they needed.

"Wait." William could be heard shouting as he did his best to follow. "Where in the name of all things holy are you going?"

"Pap loves to swim. If there is water, she will find it."

William's sigh was audible, yet he continued to follow along, muttering darkly as they went. Eventually they crested a hill beneath which there shimmered a small yet sheltered lake, the poodle bounding down to take a flying leap into the sun-dappled water.

"She is a marvel." Gaudet applauded, already pulling off his boots before he remembered the wounds on his back. All good humor suddenly deserted him at the realization that his scars would be laid bare and he said quickly, "I am so very sorry, sir, I quite forgot—"

"There is mud in my boots," William was muttering, preoccupied. "What are you sorry for? I have seen your back, Monsieur, and you need not be shy of it."

"But never in broad daylight." Gaudet blinked. He crossed his arms over his chest and admitted, "I am ashamed of my scars."

"Don't be." William's tone was suddenly serious. "Or he has won."

"You are kinder than you would ever admit." Gaudet peeled off the shirt tentatively, careful to keep his back to William. He was sure that there was more to this Englishman than he would ever share, a mystery that was too deep to traverse. "Thank you."

"I am not a blushing girl," William assured him gruffly. "And I am intrigued to see whether you swim as badly as you ride."

Gaudet forgot his apprehension, preferring instead to bristle once more at William's tone. Without a second thought, he stripped off his breeches and performed a showy dive into the lake, the sun warming his naked skin. Only as he entered the thankfully deep water did it occur to him that, for the sake of bravado, he might well have snapped his neck. William stood as if undecided for a long moment, yet the need to get clean seemed to overtake his reticence and he pulled his shirt off, hands hesitating again at his breeches.

"Get them off, Guillaume," Gaudet called as he broke the surface, tossing his head back to clear the water from his hair. At the sight of his companion's uncertainty he gave a shriek of laughter then chanted, "Off, off, off!"

"If it will stop that dreadful noise." William was already stepping out of his breeches, a moment later throwing himself into the water. It was a shame, Gaudet reflected, for he made a fine figure there in the sunlight.

"Strange," Gaudet teased, pausing for a moment before he laughed. "*I* didn't think it was cold."

"You had better be able to swim bloody fast," William warned Gaudet, making him laugh all the more.

"Why so, sir?"

"Because otherwise," William started to move with purpose, "you are going to find yourself dunked, *sir*."

"If you want to have some sort of watery horseplay with me, be my guest," Gaudet challenged. "Anything to get your hands on a slippery Frenchman, it would seem."

"More a case of wanting to silence one…"

"Then come and grab a handful of the Pride of Paris, Monsieur."

With a glare that suggested a less delightful intent than

grabbing, William swam toward Gaudet, who looked on appraisingly as he cut through the water. In fact, Gaudet mused as he watched, William cut a generally fine sight at *most* times, for an Englishman.

"This water," William spluttered as he approached, "is freezing."

"Is that your excuse for your diminutive state?" William's response was to splash Gaudet, who commiserated mischievously, "I cannot imagine what it must be like to be English — poor you."

"Better English than French."

"*Nothing* is better than French." When William responded with a disbelieving laugh, Gaudet added, "And being French and *stunning*, well, that is best of all. I'll wager you've never seen anyone quite like me."

"You'd be right." William trod water close by, his tone far from complimentary.

"The quality of my skin is second to none." Gaudet cast an appraising glance at his companion. "A fine bone china."

"If bone china were *red*."

"I am not..." The words petered out as Gaudet glanced down, eyes widening at the irrefutable proof that his fine white skin, so fashionable and cultivated, had caught the dreaded sun. "I look like a *farm hand*."

"Do I seem amused to you?" William's tone was deadpan. "Because I *am*."

"You are a beast." Gaudet splashed water at William in what he knew full well was a flirtatious manner, looking forward to seeing how this altogether too *serious* man would respond. "And I am a beauty, so we are meant to be a pair."

"I am not a beast." He was rewarded with a splash in return. "You may be red forever."

"Nonsense, Guillaume," Gaudet replied, enjoying the soothing water on his back, the carefree moments they were sharing.

"Forever," William continued, clearly warming to his theme as he swam after Gaudet, "and ever and ever."

"Red or not, I am still beautiful." A snort was the Englishman's reply to that, nearly catching up with Gaudet. "And I will always possess the finest arse in this or any other land." He glanced over his shoulder at William, adding for good measure, "Better than yours, Guillaume."

"Bloody well isn't," came the spirited reply.

In the middle of the lake, Gaudet turned, treading water as he examined his sun-reddened shoulders. Not that it mattered, he knew — if Alexandre Gaudet went to Drury Lane with red shoulders, then the following morning, *everyone* would want them.

"Are you admiring yourself?" William asked, disbelieving.

"Of course, the alternative is to admire *you* and I'm hardly going to do *that*."

"I'll have you know, sir," William was clearly affronted, "that I have been much admired in my time."

"By the blind?" Gaudet squawked with laughter, amused at his own joke. "No, no — by blind imbeciles."

"Not blind anybody." William gestured wildly in the water. "And if I put my mind to it, nobody in the room would so much as *glance* at *you*."

"Dreaming again."

"Think what you like." The Englishman turned and started to swim away, annoyingly serene.

There was silence then as William swam, apparently, and inexplicably as far as Gaudet was concerned, behaving as if the playwright didn't exist.

"You are ignoring me, sir?" Gaudet followed him. "How dare you ignore *me*, the man whose pout inspired the late queen to poetry."

"It inspired who to what?" William was clearly pretending not to hear.

"How *dare* you impugn Her Majesty's poetry, Bobbins, God rest her soul?" Gaudet huffed. "She was an *artiste* — we composed works together at the harp..."

"You and a harp."

"Me and a harp *what*?"

"I can just imagine it."

"Can you now?" Gaudet swam closer. "If only you might have known La Reine — such a gracious lady…"

There was a decidedly non-committal noise at that, William managing to shrug in the water. That was one step too far for Gaudet, the perceived slight to the queen he adored, *wept for*, one tease he was unwilling to take. He turned and set off for the bank, calling angrily, "Shrug at her orphaned children, sir, as they sit alone in their prison cells and see how far it takes you."

Gaudet heard movement in the water behind him but didn't acknowledge the other man until a hand closed on his shoulder, William suddenly near when he replied, "If you were truly that fond of her, then I am sorry for your loss."

"She was not as they would have you think." Gaudet turned then, the past too near once more. "Antonia was a friend to me, a fine mother to her little ones. *Democracy* is no excuse for barbarism."

William was silent for a moment and Gaudet saw a multitude of emotions play across his face. "The world," he settled for finally, "is an unfair place."

"Men are cruel." Gaudet shook his head, never more sure of anything. "If the world is unfair, then that is why."

"The end result," William told him, hand still on his shoulder, "is the same."

"It's a good shoulder, isn't it?"

"What?"

"My shoulder is a fine shoulder — the finest in France." William relinquished his grip in response to Gaudet's reply, muttering something Gaudet could not quite catch. "Second only to my *other* shoulder."

"You prefer one shoulder to the other?"

"Which of my shoulders do *you* prefer?"

"They both look the same to me," came the disinterested reply. "I've got two of my own."

"Yours are all right" — Gaudet shrugged — "for English

140

shoulders."

"*English* shoulders?"

There was, Gaudet noted, a definite pinkness to the Englishman's ears whenever he grew animated. With that realization, he howled with laughter, clapping and crying, "Your *ears*! They are pink!"

"Are not all ears?"

"They are pinker still now." He drew a little closer, just inches from William, and laid a hand on his shoulder, feeling the strength beneath his palm. "And now, red!"

"They are not."

Gaudet's other hand came to rest on William's opposite shoulder and he peered at the man who had saved him, studying his face. "You are troubled."

"I'm in a lake with a naked Frenchman." Something flickered across William's face before it was gone. "Of course I'm troubled."

"If you were a girl, you'd kiss me now," Gaudet told him coquettishly before, with a flourish of a dive, he swam away.

Clearly William had no response to that because a moment later he was climbing out, heading for his clothes.

"What on *earth*?" Dee's voice, stern and commanding, shattered the peace from where he sat in the saddle of an enormous black horse on the opposite bank. He turned to the young lady whose gray mount followed and told her, "Mademoiselle, avert your eyes. Monsieur —" With that, he pointed at William. "It appears we must *chat* once more."

With a tut the girl reined her horse round, the long plait she wore bouncing as she trotted away.

Gaudet, meanwhile, called cheerily, "Might there be clean clothes? Mine are terribly muddy…"

"We fell in a ditch," William protested, "We stopped to get clean."

"Clothes and provisions may be found at the farmhouse beyond the copse." The newly arrived figure pointed to the near horizon. "If your horseplay might be put off for a while we shall see you there shortly."

"Horseplay..." Gaudet heard the naked Englishman mutter, already pulling on his breeches as Dee left, his horse galloping away toward the trees. "We were getting *clean.*"

"I shall swim a while more. I shall not be dictated to," he decided, no intention of being barked at no matter how blue the eyes of the barker. "You may watch me, if you wish."

"Of course I don't wish." William scooped up his clothes, gesticulating quite absurdly as far as Gaudet was concerned. "We are wanted men, sir, and not in a good way—be so kind as to extract yourself from the water this minute."

"I will *not,*" Gaudet snapped, tired of the running, of sleeping in barns, of the constant, gnawing *misery.* "No."

"You would rather they catch up with us?" William stood at the water's edge. "Because that is what will happen if we tarry."

"Rubbish." The unfairness of it all hit Gaudet with the force of a slap. "How dare he bark at me, when it should have been *him* who was chained and flogged? How dare any of you!"

"This is not the time to have a tantrum." William gestured again. "Now are you getting out, or am I coming in to get you?"

"I will not be humiliated any further." Gaudet shook his head. "Go to your employer and let me alone for one *bloody* hour. Have I not earned some respite after all I have endured?"

"You can have your *respite.*" William was already moving to sit on the edge of the lake. "When we are in Le Havre, sir."

"Please." Gaudet felt suddenly exhausted. "Give me some time, please."

"You can have all the time you need once we reach safety." William was holding out a hand toward him. "There are others relying on you—if thought of them is not enough to sway you, then I am without further recourse."

"If they are relying on me"—the truth hit Gaudet too

hard, the reality of that terrible statement — "then God help the poor bastards."

As he swam to the bank and climbed from the water, he thought once more of Claudine and François, sure that he would fail them as he has always failed in anything that wasn't fashion and frippery, that it was for someone else to be their hero.

"We will see them safe," William told him more quietly. "You have my word."

"'We'?" Gaudet laughed bitterly, picking up the mud-spattered breeches and stepping into them. "Not we, sir, unless they need their styling or fashion advice or perhaps a farce to entertain? *You*, you and your employer, perhaps."

"They won't get very far without you."

"They have got all the way from Paris to Le Havre. I think they are doing well enough, don't you?" Gaudet murmured, feeling utterly hopeless. "I am...*lost*."

"Then come to the farmhouse." William held his hand out to him again. "Dee can tell me off and we will share that brandy."

"I worry that I will bring trouble." Gaudet curled his fingers around William's, needing the comfort, the kindness. "They are safer without me."

"You are all they have." The words were unexpected.

"An idiot dandy?"

"Perhaps this is your chance to prove that you are more than that." William's voice was low and Gaudet released his hand. He pulled on his shirt before reaching to scoop up Papillon and cuddle her close. "Or that what you *are* is enough."

"It isn't." With shoulders low, Gaudet glanced to the coat. Then he shook his head and, stooping to pick up his boots, walking away. After a moment, he heard William's footsteps following at a distance, trailing him toward the farmhouse where Dee waited. At the last, though, Gaudet faltered, the thought of going in there to face that stern demeanor, *more* questioning, more temper, one that he would not stand. He stood staring at the simple dwelling, shaking his head. "I cannot."

"You must." There was the barest hint of humor in William's voice as he came alongside Gaudet, the red coat slung carelessly over one arm. "You have the brandy, after all."

One of the windows of the house was opened from within and Dee appeared, no sign of anything stern on his face when he called good-naturedly, "My bread is proving. I will not see it ruined by a French playwright…into the house."

"One cannot get bread in France, they tell me," Gaudet murmured, feeling William's hand come to rest on his elbow, steering him forward, despite his reservations.

As they neared the door it was flung open and the girl with plaited hair emerged, beaming. He was surprised at her presence, the assured expression out of place in one who appeared no older than her teens.

"Papa has clean clothes waiting for you both and I must see the adorable little pup," she told Gaudet, so preoccupied with fussing over the poodle that Gaudet surrendered her to the girl. "He is not in *such* a fierce temper…"

"It stares," William called over his shoulder as he left the room. "Don't say I didn't warn you."

Chapter Eighteen

"Has it risen?" William enquired with as much levity as he could manage as he entered the kitchen where Dee was working his magic, readying himself for the Riot Act. "You wouldn't have wanted us in here with all that mud—your carpets would have been ruined. And a muddy Frenchman is a squawking Frenchman."

"As ever," Dee turned from the stove and regarded William with a deep frown, folding his arms, "this is not my house and it contains no carpets. I should not even *be* in France, putting my daughter in danger." Dee sighed, picking up an incongruous china teacup and taking a sip. "But a little discretion, perhaps?"

"For *swimming?*" William frowned. He peered at Dee, certain he was missing something of great importance.

"Better to save entanglements until you are safely back in England," Dee told him, those bright blue eyes too piercing. "Try to avoid naked embraces until then?"

"Naked what?" William blinked.

"Each man to his own," Dee said plainly. "But for God's sake, Knowles, keep a clear head."

"We were *swimming.*" William had the distinct suspicion that he was repeating himself. "To get clean."

"That diamond is going to pay for you and I to do *nothing* for the rest of our lives. It comes first." Dee took another sip of tea and observed, "Le Havre isn't so distant—don't get the playwright hanged before you get there."

"You think," William managed to keep his voice calmer than he felt, "that I am *buggering* a French playwright?"

"Well, if not yet, then looking at the two of you in that

lake, I doubt it can be far away."

"I need a drink."

Gaudet's voice sang out through the house, calling for his *Guillaume*, and Dee addressed William with a raised eyebrow and repeated, "Guillaume? You have told him your *actual* name?"

"That isn't my name," William protested, "my name is not French."

"Keep your breeches buttoned until you see the white cliffs of Dover," Dee told him, turning to open the oven with a smile of satisfaction before he retrieved a fine loaf of bread. "And I wish you luck, sir, because with a jewelry habit like his, you'll need it."

"What I need," William decided weakly, "is a drink."

"Guillaume!" came another shout. "Be a love and bring up my new coat."

"He's got you well-trained," was Dee's wry observation as he settled with his tea once more. "You're better behaved than Harriet."

With a roll of his eyes to the heavens, William turned for the door, certain that the day could not get any worse even as he scooped up the coat and called, "Give a man a moment."

"Monsieur Gaudet has spruced up very well," Harriet told William when she passed him on the stairs, still cuddling Pap. "He is in the room at the end of the hallway."

The playwright had indeed spruced up well and was once again immaculate, though the plain and simple shirt and breeches he wore were a world away from the fine suit he still carried in the portmanteau. Gaudet's hair was somehow perfect once more and he lay back on the mattress, hands pillowed beneath his head. He met William with a bright smile and declared, "*Chérie*, I may have had a moment outside, I do apologize—"

"I have your coat," William told the reclining Frenchman, "here."

"Did you get very badly told off? Isn't he *commanding*?"

Gaudet gave a rather wistful sigh. "I rather think he should have a dashing white charger."

The response that came then was something close to "Hmph," William setting the coat down none too gently on the bed before going to the window, the view of a field full of fat pigs doing little to improve his mood. "You won't say that when you hear what he thinks we've been up to."

"Do tell." Gaudet picked up a flask and threw it to William. "Brandy."

William needed no further telling, uncapping the flask to take a deep drink. He closed his eyes as the warming liquid burned its way down his throat and he wondered whether he could get drunk and stay drunk until Le Havre...until England, perhaps.

"I wonder if our new, tall friend might be tempted into a lake..." At his own words, Gaudet gave a hoot of laughter and William felt him leave the bed. Seconds later he heard the unmistakable sound of the playwright sliding his arms into the thick brocade coat.

"He thinks we're buggering each other."

"Did you tell him," William asked, even though he could almost *hear* the pout, "that it was only in your dreams?"

"I told him no one was buggering anyone." He took another swig, the very idea growing more absurd with every passing moment. "Good God..."

Gaudet was suddenly standing beside him, looking out of the window at the pigs. He took the flask from William and swigged from it. "You *were* virtually kissing me, Guillaume."

"I was not." William reached for the flask once more, fingers inadvertently brushing Gaudet's hand. "I have a job to do."

"Then do it." The playwright beamed. "And I shall do someone else."

Chapter Nineteen

"You never listen," Sylvie spat, slamming her fist into the palm of her hand. "Bastien won't be gone long, you can't arrest—"

"I *can* and will arrest them all when you tell me *where* this safe house is," Tessier interjected. Her eyes blazed as she fell silent. "And you will tell me or I will not let you leave this inn, Sylvie."

"If I tell you where I'm going…" She glanced around the bare room of their latest tavern. Her secret meeting with Tessier had not been hard to arrange in such an anonymous place. "You'll not be able to restrain yourself—you'll arrest the lot of them and never see your precious diamond. You know I'm right, and then what happens to me?" Sylvie shook her head, chewing her lower lip for a few seconds, then clasped her hands in her lap, pale against the dark fabric of a dress that had seen better days. "I've been on the streets too many times, I want more than that for us."

Tessier watched her silently and she knew that he was remembering a woman more than ten years ago who had been the light in his darkness. She had been the one spark of hope in a life that had been crowded with learning and politics, with dreams of a better future for all of them.

"What is it that you want, Sylvie?"

A tiny, barely perceptible shake of the head was her response.

He left his position at the window and walked the short distance to stand beside the bed. "Why did you leave me again?"

Sylvie lifted her head to look at him, resting it slightly to one side as though she didn't quite understand, then she said, "Because you don't want me, Monsieur Tessier – you forgot me as soon as you caught a whiff of revolution. All I'm asking is that you let us reach Le Havre – get your Star, get your playwright, your spy, the whole bloody lot of them."

"Then you disapprove of what I have done?"

"I might not have done it myself," Sylvie said. "But look at what you've become – I kept hearing your name and all the time I was thinking that I made a mistake in leaving, but what could I do? You weren't a student no more, you wouldn't want the likes of me now, would you?"

"But the other night –" Tessier began, suddenly alarmed at the direction her words had taken.

"Well," – she sighed, turning to offer him a smile – "I wanted to give you something and I don't have nothing, do I? All I have is my Bastien and what you see before you. I don't have a livre to my name, Vincent – you're somebody now, I'm still nobody."

"I would give everything I have if you would let me embrace you."

"My Bastien," she said as though he had not spoken, moving back to the glass and smiling down at her child in the courtyard. "He's so small down there playing with the horses and all… If you could choose between the diamond and the spy, where would you stake your claim?"

"The spy," he admitted without hesitation. "But where the Star of Versailles goes, Gaudet is sure to follow."

"Then we will meet at our next inn when *I* arrive and not before," she told him, picking up her bundle and pecking a kiss to his cheek. "Go there and wait for me."

* * * *

The Butcher of Orléans, Sylvie thought with a smirk as she and Bastien trudged on good-naturedly toward the farmhouse that was on Charron's list, *is soft as a babe.*

And there's no way he's getting that bloody diamond.

"Here we are, son," she said as they reached the worn, wooden door, twilight already descending and no sign of life within. "Our home for the night."

"You're *sure*," Bastien asked as she knocked heavily, "that Tessier won't find us, Ma? After what he did to Thierry, if I see him again—"

"Shhh," she hushed her son, knocking once more.

The door was opened by Dee, who regarded her for a long moment before he looked over her head through narrowed eyes, as though expecting to see something there. Finally, he said, "Mademoiselle Dupire and Bastien, I had heard you were free."

"Thank the Lord." Sylvie affected her most relieved expression. "Thank everything that we have found you—"

"Bastien." Dee smiled at the boy who had been his messenger in Paris. "Adam's round the back with the horses—go and say hello while your mother gets settled?" As the young man took off running, Dee offered the same smile to Sylvie and said, "Let's get the tea on?"

She nodded, watching Dee through lowered lashes as she followed him. "Tea and company, it's our lucky night— we're due some luck, aren't we?"

"If Vincent Tessier let you go," Dee commented airily, "You've had plenty of luck already."

"We're safe here with you, aren't we?"

"I would be *very* surprised"—he gestured to a seat at the kitchen table—"if you weren't."

Sylvie kept silent for a while as she waited, certain that this man, like any other, had a weakness, a way that she could bend him to her will, if only she could find it. And find it she would—she had a knack for that, after all.

"Charron is dead—I saw the dispatches."

There was a flicker of something that she recognized as remorse and she ducked her head. "Thierry…"

"And yet… Tessier let you go." Dee set a cup before her and took his own seat. "Why would he do that?"

"Who can begin to understand why a monster does things?" Sylvie dared to glance at him, surprised to find that he was staring *straight* at her, blue eyes piercing in the dusk. She recovered herself enough to say, "It's been a good long while since I had a cup of *anything*..."

"And, tonight, we have a fine meal planned," Dee promised. "I have managed to come by *lamb*, don't ask how, but it's a fine joint."

He was a useful man to know indeed. Sylvie smiled to herself, telling Dee demurely, "That will be welcome news to my boy. You are too kind, sir, too kind by far."

"Well, as the Bible doesn't quite say..." Dee retrieved a silver flask from his coat, adding a nip of liquor to the two cups. "Eat, drink and be merry." He held her gaze, taking a sip. "For tomorrow, we die."

Not if I can help it. She inclined her head at the words, however, accepting her own cup and holding it up to proclaim firmly, "I'll drink to *that*."

"And you at least have your boy, though I doubt you will see much of him now he and Adam have horses to groom."

"He's a good boy." There was no need to force a smile at that. "Better than I deserve..."

"The young ones are the best of us. They deserve more than a country going to Hell." He sighed, shaking his head before asking mischievously, "Would you believe that our hideaway has a piano?"

"Will you be giving us a little turn?" Sylvie tilted her head, peering through her lashes as she added, "I bet you play well."

"I play...*adequately*. I might be convinced to give a tune or two."

"Oh, you should," she pressed, taking another sip of tea. "We could all do with some cheer."

"Your playwright's safely upstairs." Dee left the table to cross to the oven and peer inside. "I'm sure he'd like a party."

"I'm sure you'd be right."

"Then perhaps we will have a little gathering." He smiled, glancing back at her. "I shall relish your good company, Mademoiselle. Paris seems a long time ago."

"Too long..." She chanced a slight flutter of eyelashes, mustering her best and bravest expression. "I'm well used to being alone, but that don't make it any easier."

"Well," Dee told her, "You are not alone this evening."

"I can't tell you how glad I am of that."

"I assume Charron passed his contacts to you? There's no other way you might have found us. "

"He told me everything."

"He must have trusted you completely," Dee observed as he began to assemble some fresh vegetables for dinner that evening, Sylvie's eyes never straying from him. "A true compliment from a fine man."

"He asked me to tell him that I loved him" — Sylvie fixed her gaze on the cup before her — "the last time we saw each other in that cell."

"Some men ask for a Bible." Dee turned to meet her gaze again, his voice soft. "Some for a last word from those they love. Tonight, we will toast his memory and your freedom."

It worked. She felt a surge of triumph, mingled, as ever, with the contempt she felt for all men to some degree or other. Allowing herself the slightest smile, she said in reply, "And your protection, sir — it's not often that I get such good company."

"Consider me at your disposal," Dee replied. "Do you need anything for the bruises on your face?"

"There's people" — she lowered her gaze — "who've been through much worse."

Dee crossed the room to rest his hand on her shoulder and say, "I understand, Sylvie — let me help you."

"You'll have me blubbing." She covered his hand with her own. "And I don't do that."

"Then let us pour the wine and speak of less serious matters."

Sylvie nodded, her hand lingering for a moment longer

than was strictly necessary before he turned away to pour the wine. She was surprised. Professor Dee had been so built up by Tessier that she had expected him to be so much harder to break.

"The work you do…" Sylvie began, lifting a hand to her lips as if catching herself. "Forgive me, it's none of my business."

"A simple traveler, Mademoiselle," he assured her, "of little excitement."

"Of course." She smiled inwardly. "Of course."

"And you, like me," Dee observed as he unloaded a sack of fresh vegetables onto the table, Sylvie's eyes widening at the very largesse of it, "have been somewhat pulled into events, I think? There are no innocent bystanders left in France, it seems."

"All I want is to be safe," she told him, getting to her feet. "Me and my boy. That's all I hope for now."

"Then tonight we'll forget it all…too much food, some music, perhaps a little more wine, too?"

"Ma!" Bastien rapped on the window and Sylvie turned, just reining in the angry retort that sprang to her lips. Instead, she waved at the boy, hoping he would take the hint and leave.

"Look!" He held up a coin, adding, "For sorting the tack for Adam!"

"Run along," Sylvie called brightly, thinking that at least he was doing something of use. "And have fun now!"

With another wave, the boy dashed away again, leaving Dee to comment, "He's a good lad, that one." As he spoke he offered a knife and gestured to the vegetables. "Get chopping."

Sylvie was no stranger to such work, and a moment later she was bringing the blade down, keeping half an eye on Dee. Long minutes passed in contented silence as they prepared the meal, Bastien occasionally returning to the window to show his mother a new treasure which she greeted with theatrical delight.

"We'll have a feast fit for a king," Sylvie observed presently.

"No kings," Dee told her with a mischievous smile, then he stooped a little, mouth very close to her ear when he whispered, "The Convention might hear."

She allowed herself to lean back just a touch until she knew her hair would be tickling his skin and whispered in turn, "And we wouldn't want that."

"Sylvie!" Gaudet's voice was an excitable shriek and a moment later the playwright bounded across the kitchen to take her in a warm embrace. "The most beautiful girl in Paris, I have missed you so!"

Just managing to keep her feet, she had no choice but to cling to the excitable Frenchman, telling him when she had righted herself, "Just waiting here for you, Monsieur."

"This woman is an angel, a saint," he told the man who claimed not to be Dee, but clearly *was*. "She fed me, washed my wounds, listened to my ravings. I had thought you lost."

Sylvie shook her head and murmured a denial, though it was true — she had bathed Gaudet's wounds and held his hand, watched him sleep in Charron's house, listened to the fevered mutterings as his body unconsciously fought its injuries. And a diamond was the reward she would take for her efforts.

"You'll be making me blush," she told him after a moment. "And that's all behind us now — look how well you are!"

"It is thanks to my good friend, Guillaume, and the professor, who carries a fine scotch and is," Gaudet dropped his voice, "a fine figure of a chap."

"He's been taking care of me *very* well since we arrived," Sylvie confided in a loud whisper. "Fine figure that he is."

Dee glanced at her with a smile as she spoke and Gaudet whispered, "You could do a *lot* worse, those eyes."

Sylvie allowed herself a demure glance, her expression suggesting that, although she remained silent, she most definitely agreed with him. "There's to be a bit of a party," she told him. "A celebration."

Gaudet clapped. "I shall recite a bawdy tale or two."

"Dinner will be ready soon," Dee told them. "Let the festivities begin!"

Chapter Twenty

A party. William shook his head as he fastened his coat, the worst of the mud splashes now removed. He would escape at the first opportunity. The thought of an evening with the assorted others in the house was not one that filled him with pleasure. He recalled again Gaudet in the lake, the expression on the other man's face before he pushed it hurriedly away, telling his reflection in a murmur, "And my ears are *not* pink."

With a final glance, he made his way from the room, muttering to himself as he reached the hall below, where Bastien was waiting to catch his hand and draw him toward the cozy sitting room, exclaiming, "Come and get some booze down you."

"I'm not—"

"All right, have some tea like the professor, just..." The boy's smile slipped momentarily. "Let's all have a laugh, yeah?"

A laugh. He thought he heard Gaudet's deafening bray at that, managing a smile for the boy. "It will be a fun evening, I'm sure."

"Uncle André's having a hell of a time already," Bastien agreed. "Come on."

The sound of merriment reached William before he entered the sitting room and he fought the sudden urge to run, even as he crossed the threshold. At the hearth stood a vision in vibrant blue silk, Gaudet swathed in the suit rescued during their flight from Paris, with the poodle held beneath his arm. Richly pigmented iridescent colors were blended into the fabric to create a jacket, waistcoat and breeches that appeared to shimmer. The white shirt he wore was a mass of frills and lace. Around his neck was a cravat tied into an enormous bow, fastened with a rock-sized sapphire pin. Matching buckles adorned mirror-polished leather boots and he was, William was sure, wearing *makeup*.

He blinked, and blinked again, but still the view remained the same, and he wondered just *how* this transformation had been achieved. "Bloody hell..."

"And here is my knight in armor," Gaudet exclaimed as his gaze settled on William, a slight narrowing of his eyes unmissable when they swept over the still mud-stained coat. "Or my knight in a muddy coat, but still a welcome sight."

"I dressed down," he told the Frenchman, "to avoid outshining you."

Dee laughed a touch *too* loudly in response to that and Gaudet declared, "I don't think we need fear that, Guillaume. "

"Well," he huffed. "Well!"

"Mademoiselle." Dee offered his arm to Sylvie. "Might I escort you to the table?"

"You're spoiling me."

 William watched with distaste as the woman laughed, head tilted to peer at her escort.

"Unless you would rather one of the other gentlemen," Dee said. "I am not *quite* a silk-clad playwright, nor a knight in armor, after all."

"I've no objections," Sylvie smiled coquettishly, eyes shining, "to a professor."

With Bastien running ahead, Gaudet turned to William and asked, "Will you escort me, *chérie*?"

"Will I—?" William found himself, not for the first time, staring at the playwright.

"Of course," Gaudet said with a dismissive wave of his hand. "Pap and I shall escort one another."

"There is no harm in walking together," William decided after a moment, realizing he might have seemed churlish, even as he wondered why he should care.

It was, however, something of a surprise when Gaudet slipped his free arm through William's own, beaming at him before he asked, "You'll note I was *subtle* with my makeup?"

'Subtle' was not the word William would have chosen, but he managed to keep that to himself, remarking instead, "How very restrained of you."

"If one is attending a function," Gaudet observed as they made their way through the house, "one makes an effort, Bobbins."

"I brushed the dirt off." William found himself defending his clothing, even as he reminded himself that he didn't care what this dandy thought of his wardrobe.

"I think it needs something." Gaudet stopped and withdrew his arm, bundling the poodle into William's grip. Then, with a frown of utmost concentration, he retied the cravat with a decidedly showier knot. It was then that William registered the heart patch the playwright wore, the slight fragrance of roses about him. After another close examination Gaudet glanced down at his own ring-bedecked hands and removed one large diamond. He threaded this carefully along the cravat and said, "There! A little impromptu perhaps, but *far* more fitting for the gentleman on *my* arm."

"Will I do now?" William sounded, he realized, almost meek. He hardly knew where the question had come from or why he gave a damn for the answer.

Gaudet peered *very* closely, lips pursed and said, "I think you will do admirably."

"Well, that's a relief." He managed *not* to roll his eyes, resisting the urge to fiddle with the cravat as they passed through into the dining room. Despite himself, William paused on the threshold, wondering if Dee was some sort of miracle worker after all.

Despite their reduced circumstances, the table was set for a feast, albeit one with mismatched crockery and cutlery, bright spring flowers colorful and fragrant in the candlelight. The scent of the roasting lamb, the first proper meal William could remember having in days, filled the room and bottles of wine and beer were an unexpected yet more than welcome sight. At the table, Harriet greeted them with a smile before she and Bastien fell to chattering and Dee told them all, "Tonight, we forget our troubles."

If there were ever a setting in which that could be possible, William almost thought it might be this one. He took a seat, wine the first thing on his mind as he reached for a glass.

"A little," Gaudet cautioned. "When the professor takes to the keys, *I* intend to give a song. I thought you might join me?"

"You want me," William realized with horror, "to *sing*?"

"Oh, dear." He pouted. "Perhaps you would prefer to remain in the audience?"

"You have not heard me sing." William shook his head. "If you had, you would know that the audience is the best place for me to be."

Soon the plates were piled high and Gaudet was in full flow, regaling the diners with all manner of shocking and amusing tales from his life in London. It sounded exhausting, his own social life having dwindled to nothing in recent years. Sylvie, however, had eyes only for the professor to whom she had so carefully attached herself, whilst Bastien and Harriet were engaged in their own conversation, each clearly taken with Pap. Despite the easy cheer of the atmosphere, William felt out of place, though he should not, he knew, let that bother him. After all, if everyone were merry and distracted it could only make it easier to slip away unnoticed once the meal had finished. There was no rush for an early escape when the food was this delicious but still William found himself flagging, glancing to the clock in the hope that the hour was later than he suspected.

"Papa will play the piano later," Harriet was saying excitedly. "It is like Christmas!"

William smiled at the girl who so resembled her father. He wondered again what she was doing in such a place, what *any* of them were really doing when the world was such a blessed mess around them.

"And this time next week we will be in England once more," Dee assured them. "Our Parisian companions included."

William's frown deepened at the grin that flashed across Sylvie's face. "I'll drink to that," was all he said, swigging deeply a moment later.

"*Guillaume*," Dee addressed William. "Help me with dessert? Harriet has earned a rest."

He turned to Dee sharply, the Frenchifcation of his name becoming, it appeared, a regular feature. It would mean escape for a while, though, and he nodded, getting to his feet with a sigh. "Of course."

"Come back soon." Gaudet beamed, catching his fingers momentarily before going back to his story.

The touch was unexpected and William snatched back his hand with an awkward murmur. Then he followed Dee from the room, breathing another sigh, this time of relief, once they reached the kitchen.

"The woman," Dee said quietly, even as he closed the door, his carefree demeanor gone. "I don't want her to have *any* suspicions — stop glaring at her, Knowles."

"You think," William realized, his own dislike of the woman now taking on fresh significance, "that she is not to be trusted?"

"I *know* she is not." Dee dropped his voice still further. "Intelligence has reached me that she and Tessier had an *assignation* in the past — *eleven years* in the past, if you catch the significance."

William considered that for a moment, doing some mental calculations of his own when he thought of the boy, of *young* Bastien Dupire. He had believed the boy fatherless, thinking now how wrong he was even as his eyes widened. "Oh."

"The boy has *no* idea, I am sure," Dee explained. "But Tessier does not just let prisoners *go*, especially prisoners who have harbored enemies of the state. He is nearby. I'm sure of it."

"Then why in God's name" — he searched Dee's face for some clue — "are we having a party?"

"Because Sylvie must keep her rendezvous with Tessier or he will move against us," Dee explained. "If we do *anything* to raise her suspicions, she will call him in. We must allow her to reveal herself, choose our moment carefully."

"Can nothing ever be simple?" William raised his eyes to the ceiling. "That poor lad, with *him* as a father — he must never be told."

"She's not as bright as she thinks." Dee clapped a hand to his shoulder. "Especially if she believes *I* am the sort of chap who falls for fluttering lashes."

"So we just wait?"

"Feel free to come up with another scheme. I would be more than happy to hear it."

With a sigh, William shook his head and said, "I knew I didn't like her."

"The playwright adores her, though I think his eyes are elsewhere. You might like to keep your wits about you tonight." Dee gave a hint of a smile. "Since you're sharing a bed with your admirer."

William stared at Dee for a moment, certain that the man was joking before he recalled that this was Dee and joking did not seem to be high on his agenda. Now he wished he had something to say, yet found he could only gape like the fool he seemed to have become.

"Shall we return and see what pudding awaits?" Dee's enquiry was far too innocent.

"Why not?" William felt as if events were carrying him along, powerless to stop it. "There are worse things than pudding."

With that, they returned to the dinner where Gaudet had, it seemed, not stopped to take a breath, still embarked on the latest tale of royal intrigue and scandal. William slipped back into his seat, reaching for his glass. Then Dee's words came back to him and he quickly set it down again.

With the food consumed and drink flowing freely, Dee whispered to Sylvie, "Shall we give that piano a try?"

"I thought you would never ask."

William bit back an exclamation of disgust as she fluttered her eyelashes at the professor once more.

"Escort me, *chérie*?" Gaudet offered his arm and William found himself acquiescing, even as he wondered exactly what he was doing. Eventually, he took the proffered limb, sure it was best if he just didn't think about it.

"Mademoiselle." Dee settled Sylvie in a chair with her son sitting cross-legged at her feet, Harriet settling beside him. He looked to William and Gaudet then said, "Make yourselves comfortable, gents, and we shall see what I can remember."

"Is your knee available?" Gaudet asked William with a coquettish blink.

"My knees ache terribly," he heard himself tell Gaudet. "I would end up pitching you onto the floor."

"Indeed, of course." The playwright smiled and nodded, settling himself in a chair with the poodle perched in his lap.

That left William standing awkwardly at his side, cursing himself and the Frenchman and everyone else in the room as he finally folded himself onto the floor, finding himself sitting at Gaudet's feet.

For the first and last time.

Dee began to play, revealing that he was anything *but* unsure at the instrument. Instead he was a more than competent player and the room was silent for a while, William stealing the occasional glance to where Sylvie watched in rapt adoration. He was so caught in his loathing of her that it was a moment before he registered the unmistakable sense of fingers in his hair, though when he did, he froze in place, heart suddenly quickening.

It would stop, he thought desperately, if he just ignored it. Gaudet would get bored of the joke, the attempt to rile him, and turn his attentions elsewhere. Instead, however, the touch grew more insistent with each passing second, smoothing gently over his scalp.

It would not do, William told himself, to make a scene. He would just move, ever so slightly, just a fraction...

Stop stroking me!

It was only as Dee finished the piece that Gaudet *clapped*. With two hands. Two hands clapping, yet something was still ruffling his hair, William realized, not entirely sure what fresh horror this could be. As carefully as he could he turned his head, receiving his answer in the form of a lick to the face from a very satisfied poodle.

"Oh, to be at the Pleasure Gardens once more." Gaudet sighed as Dee began to play again, quite unaware of the dog's cheek. "Dancing all night, singing bawdy songs... I cannot wait to be home."

"Will you get your dog out of my face?" William demanded of the playwright, wondering how the poodle's breath was sweeter than many he had encountered in Paris.

"*This*," Gaudet pointed out, "is not a *dog*. She is Mademoiselle Papillon Gaudet, confidante of the late queen, God rest her, and friend to the Dauphin himself."

"Whatever it is," William asked him, "can you get it out of my face, please?"

"*She* is not an 'it'."

"It... She... Does it matter?" William asked, baffled.

"Does it *matter*?" Gaudet's eyes widened and he shook his head, directing Dee, "Sir, play *Oyster Nan*, let us have a bawdy sing-song."

William gladly sat back in his place, carefully, to keep some distance between his head and the over-keen poodle. Whilst Dee began to play, Gaudet settled that same poodle on William's lap and went to stand beside the piano, one hand flat atop the lid, the other resting on his own hip. Silk suit shimmering in the candlelight, he launched into a rendition of the filthy song, handily translating it into his native language and adding a few vocal flourishes of his own, revealing a perhaps unexpectedly fine voice. Harriet let out a shocked laugh whilst Bastien gave a cheer, clapping along and whooping his approval at the more outrageous phrasings. William, not quite knowing where to look, found himself stroking the poodle as Gaudet sang with great enthusiasm and no small degree of talent.

"Another," Gaudet urged when the song ended, eliciting a cheer of agreement from the audience.

For the next several minutes, Dee played whilst Gaudet sang ever more saucy songs, clearly relishing his return to the spotlight. William found his eyes closing despite himself, the wine and the exertions of the day finally taking their toll as he dozed. Through the fog of sleep, he was vaguely aware of Bastien joining the song and, whilst the little boy took the lead on the filthy lyrics, Gaudet gave a shrieking hoot of laughter, that same laughter that might shatter the very glass in the pane. William's eyes flew open in response, his gaze fixing on the over-exuberant Frenchman with a mixture of awe and annoyance just in time to see Gaudet drop into a deep, courtly bow as the assembled spectators applauded his efforts.

"Have we had enough?" Dee's voice was rich with good cheer, just a hint of an Irish accent showing through.

Yes, William responded silently. *Most definitely yes.*

"I have bored the gentleman to sleep." Gaudet laughed, though his mirth was not quite convincing. "Perhaps we should say our goodnights."

"I was listening," William objected. "With my eyes closed."

"You were asleep," he said. "But I think the others were entertained."

"Resting my eyes," William insisted again. "I heard every word."

"Mademoiselle," Dee addressed Sylvie. "Are you ready for your bed?"

"Me?" Sylvie smiled, yet William saw only calculated scheming there. "I can go on all night."

"And yet, our young people cannot," Dee replied with a smile in return, telling his daughter, "Come now, miss, your bed awaits."

"I think," William decided, "I am likewise ready to turn in."

"*What*?" Gaudet fixed William with a glare. "The night is over so soon? It is still early. Why, it is just past midnight!"

"And that is why we should all be settled," Dee told him in a placid tone. "This house must rise early to travel on."

"You are welcome to stay up if you wish," William replied, getting to his feet, noting again how Gaudet had a knack for pouting and how much it seemed to suit him. "Some of us need sleep."

"Come on, Ma." Bastien was already pulling at his mother's hand. "Let me tell you about the horses me and Adam saw."

William watched as the woman reluctantly stood, her expression one of annoyance for a brief moment before she said, "Of course, tell away."

As the room emptied Gaudet retook his seat and told William, "I shall finish the bottle before I come up. I shall not wake you."

"If you finish *that*" — William watched the Frenchman, not sure about this new development — "you'll not make it up at all."

"But tonight has been so lovely." Gaudet pouted again. "I do not want it to end."

"Bring the bottle," he decided, certain it was the only way to get the Frenchman to bed. "You can party more yet."

"Come along, sweetie." Gaudet gathered up the poodle. "We are forced to bed by sensible Guillaume."

"I am *not* sensible."

"Pap says that you *are*, and she is never wrong." He swept past William, a vision in blue silk. "You may keep my diamond ring, as a token of my thanks."

"But I don't—" It was churlish to reject such a gift, William realized, even as he followed toward the stairs. "It really isn't necessary—"

"That ring was a gift from the Duchess of Polignac, may she rest in peace. I believe she would have adored you. She would want you to have it." Gaudet sauntered upstairs, trailing the enormous silk handkerchief along the banister as he went. "I have *many* gifts from Gabi, that is but one."

"That is most kind of you." William had no choice but to follow, captivated by the handkerchief's progress, wishing that he was in possession of the bottle and that Gaudet's suit did not shimmer so.

"She was a lovely woman."

"Keep walking." He found himself giving Gaudet a little guidance with his hand. "And keep drinking."

"Are you attending my derrière, sir?"

"It is attached to the rest of you, is it not?" William demanded. "I cannot help one without the other."

"If that diamond is not to your liking"—Gaudet turned to him, William seeing genuine concern on that powdered face—"you may choose another, of course. I have some wonderful pieces in London, and I do like to give gifts."

"Please." He found himself touching the playwright's arm. "Do not worry so."

"It is important to me to be liked," Gaudet admitted with an attempt at a careless shrug. "And diamonds usually do the trick."

"I do not need diamonds to like you." The words were out before he had time to think about their meaning, what they implied. For a second, they hung in the still air between them, their gazes meeting for that split second.

"Guillaume." Gaudet beamed and patted William's hand very gently. "You are a lovely man—shall we to bed?"

'Bed.' He recalled again Dee's words, the single bed, and found himself staring at Gaudet for a long moment before managing to nod. Gaudet led the way into the room, where a single candle burned in the window, barely illuminating the unbroken darkness. As William watched, Gaudet settled the poodle on the foot of the bed, cooing to her as softly as any mother might to her child, his attention entirely occupied by his 'girl'. Only when the dog was settled did Gaudet begin to remove the many jewels, humming as he went about the business of getting *out* of the monumentally ornate suit.

William found himself at something of a loss. To follow suit and undress was the obvious thing to do, but for some reason, he froze, uncertain, unsure. As the seconds ticked by Gaudet continued with the obviously well-trod routine, each silk garment carefully smoothed and folded, shoes set neatly together and jewels returned to their case. Finally naked, he crossed to the basin of water and washed the makeup from his face, still humming and clearly unaware for once of the still dark slashes across his sun-burnished back. Even now William couldn't quite bring himself to turn away, the sight strangely captivating, as he recalled once more his hands touching Gaudet's cool skin, the cloth he had used to soothe the vivid wounds.

"Well, bed, I think," Gaudet declared, once his face was clean of powder and rouge. He picked up one of the plainer shirts the professor had supplied then put it down again, deciding almost to himself, "Too warm, I think." With that, he crossed to the bed and slipped beneath the blankets, yawning softly.

William remained rooted to the spot, hands hovering at his own shirt, the thought of undressing and crossing the room to join Gaudet impossible to contemplate. If Gaudet noticed, however, he said nothing, instead snuggling into the blankets with an innocently sleepy murmur of, "What do you think of Sylvie?"

"Sylvie?" William shrugged, deciding that sleeping in shirt and breeches might be a good idea as he dropped his hands again.

"She's dreadful, of course." Gaudet's voice was more serious. "Philippe and Claudine trusted Charron above all others. What sort of woman sees such a man die and within the month is chasing another?"

"What do you know of her?" Dee's words came back to William once more, discomfort forgotten in place of curiosity when he approached the bed.

"I am not so silly as people might presume." He lifted his head, smiling. "This *stunningly* handsome body contains a keen mind... Sometimes."

William gave a small shrug, finding the desire to confide suddenly, almost overwhelmingly strong. He wanted to admit what had gone before, unburden himself of sin and wrong and *life*, yet he knew he could not.

"You look so tired — come and rest?"

William was, he realized, exhausted, the gentleness in Gaudet's tone throwing him into fresh confusion. He pulled back the edge of the covers carefully before getting into the bed.

"You are quite unlike anyone I have known before," the playwright observed as William settled. "Look at my mother's locket, an attractive thing to be sure, but the secrets, the stories...all hidden inside."

That cut too close to the truth, and he was silent for a while, eventually deciding, "I am merely boring, not full of *anything*."

"Nobody is boring, not one person." Gaudet reached out to pat his hand. "Tell me how you came to be here."

"Here in France?" He played for time. "Or here in this bed?"

"Both."

"I really do not know." He sat up again, muttering, "Where did you leave that bottle?"

With a languorous yawn and stretch of his arms, Gaudet responded by dropping one hand to fish beside the bed. After a few moments, he held up the missing bottle and handed it wordlessly to William, who took a grateful gulp, letting his eyes close for a second as he tried to gather himself.

"I miss my friends in England, those who have died here... My family." Gaudet's words, soft and heartfelt, were utterly unexpected. "But you and I are friends, I think, and I am glad for it."

'Friends.' He could, he knew without a doubt, brush the Frenchman's declaration off with a curt response, push him away and keep him out, and Gaudet would not make the attempt again. "I think," William heard himself murmur instead, taking another drink before passing the bottle to Gaudet, "you might be right."

"I'll drink to that." Gaudet's tone shone with happiness. "And if *you* ever need a hero, I will be there in full makeup and new silk stockings."

"With your poodle..."

"And my good friend, Guillaume."

"All in one bed together..."

"Even the locket." Gaudet lowered the sheet onto his chest to show the small trinket that hung around his neck. "Just in case Sylvie gets itchy fingers."

William was glad he was holding the bottle, thus removing the sudden temptation to reach out to touch the delicate necklace. "You think she would?"

"She already did when I was between this world and the next above the workshop — that boy of hers retrieved and returned it to me." Gaudet's hand closed momentarily over the exquisitely painted poppy. "Without it, we would not have found my sister."

"You will be reunited before very long," William told him with certainty. "Have no fear of that."

"I believe you will get us there — you put paid to Yves Morel, after all."

"Hm." William took a quick drink, that particular episode of his life one he would rather not remember. "It was hardly anything."

"To the *contrary* — the man was a devil, his reputation preceded him...and you put paid to him and stole his very name."

William almost laughed at that, the thought that he had acquired such a reputation when the act of dispatching the hated Morel had been nothing more than a rather fortuitously timed accident. "That is what they say."

"Tell me." Gaudet propped himself up on his elbow, green eyes glittering in the candlelight. "How did you do it?"

There were any number of lies he could have told, countless tales he could have fabricated to satisfy the Frenchman's curiosity. He might be a duelist, a swordsman, a cunning poisoner, anything he so chose. Instead, William took a breath, admitting in the next moment, "It was a mistake."

There was *something*, a flicker in Gaudet's face and the playwright whispered teasingly, "I know."

"Really." William shook his head. "It was an accident. A complete and utter accident."

"Any man who killed Morel would have shot Tessier's cook on the *spot*." Gaudet smiled. "So tell all."

"You must promise" — William wondered even as he spoke what on earth he was doing — "not to breathe a word of this to anyone."

"I swear it, and my word is as strong as my perfume."

"I *was* there." William took another long drink from the bottle. "I was gathering information and had been sent to meet Morel…"

Gaudet nodded, eyes still wide.

"We'd had an evening drinking, eating, you know how it is. I'd actually had a bit too much, in truth."

"And ended up in bed with a gorgeous playwright and his poodle."

William rolled his eyes. "Do you want to hear it or not?"

"I do."

"We were walking along, when I tripped — I still don't know over what." William took a deep breath, recalling the utter surreality of it all, the ignominious eye of the man who'd laid waste to the south. "I fell into Morel, hard, and he stumbled in turn — cracked his head and never got up again."

"So…" Gaudet's eyes narrowed as he processed this confession. "You killed one of the most feared men in France, the *icon* of the Revolution in the south, the man who slashed and burned through thousands…with clumsiness?"

William considered for a long moment. "Yes."

"Does Dee, who isn't Dee but we both know *is*, know?"

"Not exactly."

"Then we shall say nothing, either, *choux*."

"I didn't mean for people to think what they think," William explained earnestly, never having actually told anyone that he *had* killed Morel, after all. "It just… happened."

"And when you are done here in France, where will you go? More adventures?"

"I'll go"—he passed the bottle back to Gaudet with a sigh—"wherever I am sent."

"No more for me, or I will be giddy. Will you tarry in London long enough to see a play and take supper with me?"

"That depends." William closed his eyes briefly. "On a lot of things."

"Tell me them, and I shall solve them."

Could it really be that simple, he wondered as he met Gaudet's gaze, to just hand his problems over to a Frenchman? "I don't," he told him instead, "stay in any place for too long."

"*Why*? If you saw my house on Berkeley Square, you would not *want* to leave. It is a mix of Versailles and a seraglio."

Why indeed. William thought again of London, of the house that even the servants had long left, the dust-shrouded marble, the empty shell of a life that he sought with everything in him to forget. "Perhaps you might venture farther afield. I spend a deal of time in the country—"

"I have a home in Bath but…somewhere rural, you say?" Gaudet nodded, settling down onto the pillow once more and declared, "I accept your invitation, Bobbins. I would *love* to spend a retreat at your country home. I cannot wait. We will have such fun!"

Again, William found he couldn't bring himself to crush the Frenchman's enthusiasm, though he would not hesitate with any other. Gaudet was so very *happy* about the world, he realized, and it was becoming ever more difficult to shake it off.

"And a countrified Christmas is always magical." Gaudet clapped. "You and I, Claudine and François—*not* Queen Charlotte, though I know she adores Christmas with me. No matter, she can have me for Easter. How marvelous it shall be!"

"How marvelous," William managed. "Indeed."

"Such a warm night." Gaudet yawned. "One might almost forget the trouble we are in."

It was, he realized, warm indeed, the shirt and breeches he still wore uncomfortable in the summer that Gaudet so reveled in. He felt sweat bead his brow, sure the temperature must be all that was causing a surge of heat to course through his veins.

"Stuffy in here." William stifled a yawn, giving in as he loosened the neck of his shirt in a vain attempt to get cool.

"Take it off, Bobbins, you are sweating fit to drown—of course, that might be my presence."

'Take it off' indeed. The invitation suddenly seemed like the most decadent and dangerous in the world, though William hardly knew why, or was hardly willing to admit it. He resisted a moment longer then threw caution to the wind, pulling the shirt over his head and casting it onto the floor before making sure to cover himself once more with the bedlinen.

"Better?"

"Better," he confirmed. "Now, to sleep."

"To sleep," Gaudet agreed, adding for good measure, "Goodnight, Guillaume."

"Goodnight." William found himself already drifting.

"Goodnight."

Chapter Twenty-One

Two days after the impromptu party, the group traveled on in companionable silence and considerable comfort. No questions were asked as to *how* the inestimable Adam had secured a coach and four, but all were glad of it. The tranquil journey was broken by the occasional chatter of Bastien and Harriet, the little boy taking obvious comfort in the enthusiastic company of the older girl. Nights had passed without incident, days so peaceful one might have almost forgotten they were fleeing the forces of the revolutionary government. Now they sat outside their latest coaching inn, but Gaudet and Papillon were still inside.

Finally, as the sun emerged from behind a cloud to throw a brilliant ray of light onto the carriage, Gaudet emerged from the inn, Pap tucked under his arm and his handkerchief clutched to eyes that were wet with tears. A barmaid trotted with him, muttering obvious platitudes, gently patting his shoulder. Upon reaching the carriage he bid the woman a forlorn farewell and climbed into the vehicle, immediately sinking back into the squabs.

"Is there something in your eye?" William enquired, his tone businesslike.

"Little Louis-Charles." Gaudet shook his head, bringing the handkerchief to his eyes again.

He was surprised and gratified to find himself rewarded with an awkward pat to the shoulder from William, before, apparently realizing what he was doing, the Englishman cleared his throat and sat back in his seat. "Yes. Well."

"The king is dying," Gaudet managed to sob. "The poor little fellow, all alone in that terrible place."

He was aware of William and Dee exchanging glances, Dee finally commenting, "Sad news indeed."

"He and I used to have such games, the little mite."

"Would brandy help?" William asked.

"It is not yet nine. Brandy would not help at all," Gaudet decided, lost once more in the thoughts of times long passed, of friends long gone, of the world that had been smashed.

There was silence for a moment, then William passed a fine handkerchief his way. He took it in a delicate grip, preoccupied with the pressing thought of the imprisoned child, of the terror *he* had experienced as an adult in the hands of his jailers, let alone a boy of little more than nine years old.

"I have good friends five hours or so along the road and today is the start of their village festival," the professor told Gaudet with unmistakable kindness in his voice. "Harriet longs to see it and I believe you will find the celebrations a tonic, Monsieur."

"A festival," Sylvie piped up. "Just what we need."

"A chance to forget our woes." Dee turned to Bastien, who nodded. "Before we push on to Le Havre."

"Excellent." William's tone was far too cheerful. "Excellent!"

"And, perhaps," Dee chanced, even as Gaudet lifted his unhappy gaze to meet the professor's own, "you will toast the little king's name."

"Imagine being my age," Bastien murmured thoughtfully. "And a king — poor bloody bastard, who'd want that?"

Sylvie nudged him with her foot, saying, "No one asked you, did they?"

"Could've been worse." He fixed his mother with an insolent gaze. "They might've chopped his kingly block off."

"We'll be chopping *yours* off," came William's response, "if you say one more word on the matter."

"One day," Bastien shifted his mischievous gaze to

William, "they'll chop Vincent Tessier's block off and I'll kick it from Paris to bloody London, cheering all the way."

"Enough talk of chopping off blocks," Dee declared. "There shall be no blocks being chopped today."

"A child is a child whether he is king or rag seller," Gaudet said, watching the little boy, who shifted slightly, a glimmer of shame crossing his eyes. "And no child deserves the fate he has suffered, Master Dupire."

"So, let's all shut up," Sylvie added, nudging her son again, "and enjoy the view."

"I know what view you're *viewing*." Bastien shrugged, exchanging an amused smile with Harriet. "But I'd rather enjoy the scenery, thank you very much."

"Shut your mouth," Sylvie told him abruptly, before, cheeks red, she likewise turned her attention to the view outside the carriage.

As the minutes grew into hours, Gaudet remained silent, stroking the comforting coat of the poodle. He wondered why his back hurt more today than ever, why a man might be treated as the late king had been, what might become of the infant nephew he had not even met. He had no wish for festivals and dancing, wanting solitude and silence, somewhere to hide himself away until this sorry year had ended.

William remained silent beside Gaudet, perhaps just a touch closer than usual, and when he looked up he found the Englishman watching him, an unreadable expression on his face. For a moment, they regarded each other then, finally, Gaudet spoke.

"What they said of his mother," he whispered, still able to feel Marie Antoinette's hand soft in his as they had danced, hear her tinkling laughter. "She was innocent of it all."

"I have no thought regarding that," came the careful reply. "One way or another."

"You have no thought," his voice grew firmer, a flame of anger already rising unbidden in his gut, "on the matter of a mother accused of *congress* with her own son? You have *no thought* on it?"

"I merely meant that I give no credence to rumors," William replied stiffly. "As you told the brat, the loss of a life is a tragedy and I had not gone further than that."

At the slight against him, Bastien kicked William hard in the shin as Gaudet snapped, "Then you are a cool customer indeed." With that he folded his arms tightly and turned his eyes to the window, shaking his head once or twice to drive the point home. *Let them all be damned,* he decided, for no one could mend his humor today.

It was many hours later that the carriage rolled to a welcome halt in the courtyard of an unexpectedly large, rather ramshackle farmhouse. The yard was busy with workers and cattle and when their driver opened the carriage door he was not alone. Instead, Adam had one arm around the waist of a very admiring young lady who was already cooing over the fact that he owed her a dance from their last encounter at carnival.

"Monsieur Adam," Sylvie told him with a knowing smile, "you really *do* know *everybody*."

With a wave of his hand to the woman, her bosoms more prominent than any Gaudet had seen outside of a seraglio, Gaudet followed Dee into the farmhouse to meet their new hosts. They were greeted with warm embraces and booming salutations by a farmer and wife who certainly were not suffering from food shortages, each and every member of the party shown a welcome better suited to a long-lost friend, not a weary, carriage-sore stranger. Innumerable children darted this way and that and Bastien and Harriet were happy to join them, the whole family clearly well known to Dee and his daughter at least.

William hung back at the door, not quite joining the group even as he nodded greetings of his own. Gaudet, however, barely noticed where he was or who was with him, relieved when he was shown to a small, neat room. There he collapsed onto the bed, fresh sobs coming as soon as the door was closed, his body racked with misery as it had not been since his escape from the old nursery. The world was ending, and but for the poodle, he had never felt more alone, more desolate.

I am not used to such silence.

It was some time later that a knock came at the door, decidedly tentative, and Gaudet blinked into the present, catching the aroma of roasting meat on the air.

"I shall be down presently," he called with affected good humor, wiping the back of his hand across his eyes. "Never fear!"

"We're to share a room again," William called back apologetically. "Me and you and the poodle."

Trying to ignore the very slight surge of cheer that news gave him, Gaudet roused himself from the bed. Pap trotted beside Gaudet as he crossed to open the door and peered out, little caring what a sorry sight he made. "Do you wish to view the room, Guillaume?"

"I wish to hide in it."

"Then by all means do."

"If I had another handkerchief," William told him, slipping through the open door, "I would give it to you."

"Are you carnival-bound?"

"I doubt it." William sank down to sit on the thin mattress. Gaudet watched him, thinking that a shave might not go amiss. Or maybe it *would*, for the Englishman did have a certain rugged appeal with the shade of stubble that covered his jaw. "Because I have no wish to tag along after Sylvie making eyes at the professor, her brat *kicked* me, and the carriage man and I hardly have anything in common."

"The carriage man has the most delightfully cheeky look, don't you think? I have never *seen* such broad shoulders that were not carved in marble." Gaudet sighed, shaking his head. "Yet even *that* fails to cheer me tonight."

"You would rather I left you alone."

Gaudet hardly knew what he wanted, though he was sure now that solitude was the worst of it, that *being alone* allowed one far too much time and space to *think*. "What if

Claudine and her boy end up like *they* did? What if we are too late?"

"Of course we aren't." William's tone was firm. He passed one hand though his dark hair, ruffling it free of the road's dust. "They await you in Le Havre."

"What *stupid* sort of a sister would risk her life, her child, for a gemstone?" Gaudet asked angrily, pacing the room to peer from the window into the yard beneath, where Adam and Bastien were unharnessing the horses, the farm children dashing around them excitedly. "Antonia would *not* have wanted that."

Somewhere in the distance music struck up, a lone fiddle at first playing a jaunty tune that was soon joined by more, along with the sound of cheering, childish feet pounding along the hallway outside. It seemed almost ridiculous to hear the sounds of merriment in the midst of such misery — it was mocking, ludicrous, the cruel response of a world gone mad.

How could people be happy?

"You should go and have fun," Gaudet eventually whispered, though whether to himself or William was unclear. As Sylvie emerged into the yard, he watched the calculated manner she let her hand rest on her hip and tossed her gloss-black hair back over one shoulder, and he knew that this was the woman who had betrayed them all, had led his brother-in-law to the scaffold. "How I loathe that woman."

"And she has set her cap at our spymaster…"

"Don't be so sure." Gaudet had written more than enough such scheming minxes in his time, after all — women like Sylvie Dupire were never all that they appeared to be. "She would have him and the coachman in the same bed if she could, always skulking around the men."

"Don't waste a thought on her tonight." William shifted on the edge of the bed, testing it out with a small bounce before he concluded, "Well, it won't collapse under the weight of two, which is always a good sign."

"It will depend what we are doing in it."

"*Not,*" William blinked, "trying to get the professor and the coachman into trouble, that is for sure."

"Can you *imagine*?" Gaudet produced a fan, flicking it open with a movement of his wrist, as coquettish as any king's mistress. "One overheats just picturing it."

"That is not quite what I was thinking."

"You are very broad-minded." Gaudet smiled slyly, devilment just edging out misery. "For an Englishman."

"Is that a compliment?" William peered at him. "Or a criticism?"

"Oh, let us go to this carnival," Gaudet said. "Antonia adored such things. It will be our tribute to her boy. Should I wear my suit? Or perhaps a dress, in true masque spirit."

"Suit."

"You are right, of course—one cannot wear a dress without a wig." Gaudet frowned, tapping the fan against his chin, feeling far happier now his mind was on less serious matters. "And you do not think that my suit might *stand out* at a country fete?"

"Less than a dress would." William peered at him, their gazes meeting for one moment. "Wouldn't you say?"

"Then I shall change." Gaudet stretched his arms above his head, gaze still settled on William, on the strong jaw that seemed always so set, so *British.* "And so must you."

"Into what?" William's face crumpled into a frown and Gaudet tutted, wondering what barbarians were gathering on the other side of the English Channel. He did not reply but shook his head, moving to unpack the suit and jewelry, the makeup and scent. "These are clean enough, don't you think?"

"Then I shall dress"—Gaudet scooped up Papillon and dropped her neatly into William's lap—"for both of us."

"Good." William peered at the poodle. "Stop staring."

She did no such thing, eyes bright and beady as the long, long minutes passed and Gaudet went about the elaborate business of dressing. Shoes were buffed, jewels shone, stockings inspected for snags before he even *thought* about applying his powder and patch, let alone choosing which elaborate knot to use in his cravat. It hardly mattered whether he was visiting the pleasure gardens or the back yard of a tenement, one must *look* one's best if going out to celebrate, it was all part of the fun.

"Shall I have a nap while we wait?" William asked after a time. Gaudet ignored him, too busy ensuring his hair was just so, his rouge balanced. "The fun will be over before we even leave the house at this rate."

"Did you say something?" Gaudet glanced over his shoulder, pausing in his inspection of the powder he had patted to his cheeks.

"I said get on with it!"

"Wear your diamond," Gaudet instructed, tucking William's handkerchief into his coat pocket before, with a carefree swish, he pulled it out some way. That same careless gesture resulted in the handkerchief sitting *just* so, as though he had been dressed by the most expert valet society had to offer. He was not just a master playwright, after all, but a consummate creature of fashion as well. With a final glance to the mirror, Gaudet declared, "Come along, Guillaume, Pap and I are ready to leave and you are taking *forever*."

With a sigh, William righted himself, the diamond produced from a pocket before he told Gaudet, "You'll need to tie it."

"See how fine your kerchief is on a Frenchman?" He took the diamond and turned his attention to William's cravat, eyes narrowed in concentration.

"I am glad that it meets with your approval," came the dry response, William's gaze fixed resolutely over Gaudet's shoulder

"There." He patted William's chest lightly, hand lingering for a perfectly decent moment. "Perfect."

"Perfect," the Englishman murmured in response.

Chapter Twenty-Two

Thanks to Gaudet's unfathomably detailed preparations to leave their sanctuary, when he and William finally reached the ground floor the house was deserted, the rest of the party having long since made their way toward the delights of the carnival. The chaotic rooms stood empty, yet everywhere were signs of life and a family who lived it at full pace, the aroma of roasting meat still in the air, unclaimed until later.

"It looks like," William informed the decidedly decadent Frenchman, "we are going by ourselves."

"We shall enjoy the evening stroll," his companion said, opening the door onto the early evening dusk.

On the near horizon, a bright bonfire burned, the sound of music and cheer rising up from the village to fill William with trepidation.

He cast a glance at Gaudet, wondering when things had suddenly become slightly complicated. "A walk. Excellent."

"Away you go, Mistress Pap," Gaudet chirruped, setting the poodle down so she might trot ahead. "She can smell a hog roasting!"

"You seem in better cheer." William found himself with the absurd urge to take Gaudet's arm, the only way to fight it being to link his own hands behind his back. Something in the Frenchman's despair earlier had touched him, cut through his own quiet, long-festering dissatisfaction at life, and he wondered at Gaudet's attitude to this madness in which they were living. After all, he seemed so chipper now, so able to find cheer in even the most unhappy situation.

It was a hell of a skill.

"If one dwelt on it, one would be in Bedlam." Gaudet gave a soft sigh. "And none of those who have been lost would benefit from *that*."

"That," William agreed, "that is a fine way to look at it."

"And besides." Gaudet glanced to William with a cheeky smile. "Who else would bring such glamor to a village festival?"

"Don't draw attention to yourself," William warned, feeling belated misgivings as he studied the playwright. It seemed like a ridiculous request, he realized now, for a man so handsome, dressed in the finest silks and wearing just enough powder to appear as though he wasn't wearing any at all. How could Gaudet *not* draw attention to himself? He would catch the eye in a potato sack.

At that, William blinked, wondering at how the sun had affected him. He needed to catch up on his sleep, he decided, admire that bosomy woman and spend less time with playwrights, who definitely were *not* handsome, just a little showy.

"I intend to pose as a traveling player — any amount of flamboyance will be permissible." Gaudet's words were playful.

"You are not to be flamboyant."

"Look at me, *chérie*, how could I be otherwise?"

It was true, he realized — the Frenchman would not be able to pass anywhere unnoticed, even the simple handkerchief adding to the overwhelming feeling that one *must* be impressed. He was handsome, of course, but there was more than that, a magnetism, a presence that made him leap out of any crowd.

It must be hell.

The crowds in the village were a riot of colors and noise, dancing and cheer, the trials of life in a France in turmoil forgotten for tonight, at least. The coachman so admired by Gaudet lounged decorously at a table before the inn, half a dozen clearly besotted ladies hanging on his every word, whilst Dee, Sylvie and their plump hosts strolled through the crowd, greeting old acquaintances and making new. It was almost enough to make a man smile, William reflected, but not quite.

"What do you want to do?" William asked Gaudet, making sure that he and the Frenchman kept their distance from the rest.

"Dance, sing and not go to bed until dawn."

"And drink," William decided, craving suddenly the familiar, deadening oblivion of the bottle that had seen him through his darkest days. "Just a little."

"As you wish." Gaudet shrugged, dragging him farther into the fray.

It was a world away from the London parties that William no longer frequented, but a flicker of memory passed through his mind unbidden, of the young man he had driven to suicide. He remembered too clearly the cold rock of horror that had dropped into his belly when he had seen the words in print, the newspaper lamenting the sadness of a life snuffed out too soon. They had not named Viscount William Knowles, of course, but all of society knew whose hand might as well have been on the trigger of the gun that had dealt the fatal bullet. It was nothing but a silly gambling debt, a lost hand of cards between gamblers, yet William had crowed and hectored, had insisted that the youth pay his debt, pay off this man-about-town, the arrogant peer who showed no mercy to a young man in despair.

He'd had no money to pay...what choice but death or disgrace?

And William's debtor had chosen both. He had chosen to take his own life rather than admit to Viscount William Knowles that he could not pay the debt.

A damned waste of a young life.

"Whatever it is, forget for tonight." Gaudet's voice was soft and William was relieved to find a drink in one hand. His other was grasped quite firmly by the playwright as they passed fellow revelers on their way.

Somehow, without William quite realizing *how*, he found

himself in the center of a crowd of admiring women, all of them focused on the flamboyant traveling theatrical in the bright blue silk suit. Gaudet preened and pranced for them in obvious delight, telling endless tales of his dramatic pursuits, of the celebrities he counted amongst his *closest* friends.

It was good to see the playwright's mood improved, of course, but William could not escape the thought that *he* was redundant, neither Gaudet nor the women paying the slightest attention to him. The single drink he had promised himself was followed with a second and a third and he drank them down as though he was parched, gaze fixing on the handkerchief that bobbed in Gaudet's pocket.

"My good friend, Guillaume," Gaudet was saying to the women suddenly, seizing William's shoulder, "is my protégé. Together, we will have the *finest* theatrical company ever to grace the continent. He is a tumbler by trade."

"Yes," William declared. "I am very good at tumbling — especially after more drink."

His audience laughed, their requests for a demonstration silenced when Gaudet confided, "The gentleman cannot tumble just *anywhere*, he is an artiste."

"I am," he agreed, nudging Gaudet. "Though my talents are nothing compared with *this* man's."

"True, true — what I cannot *do* with a juggling club isn't worth doing."

"He speaks the truth." William found himself swept along in the story, Gaudet's silliness unexpectedly intoxicating. "There is no sight more glorious in all the land."

"The Pope himself was moved to tears by my mastery," Gaudet declared. "And awarded me the keys to the Vatican in thanks."

"Will he juggle for us?" one of the girls asked William, breathless with excitement. "If you will not tumble."

"He is not permitted to," William told her, voice lowered. "It is against the rules."

"The rules?" she asked, eyes wide with wonder.

"Oh, yes — and the rules themselves must be kept a secret, so I cannot possibly discuss them further."

"Even the rules," Gaudet confided, his hand tightening on William's shoulder, "have rules."

"And those rules" — William drank deeply — "have even more rules."

It all seems so simple with Gaudet, he thought as he closed his eyes briefly. Perhaps they could stay here forever in this moment of good-natured deception, and forget diamonds and sisters and ruined lives. Still, even as he knew he should intervene one song bled into another then, from somewhere, Gaudet was whirling one of the village girls round in a dance atop the table, the entire crowd gathered to cheer him on.

There's nothing like people enjoying themselves to make you realize how utterly alone you are, William thought as soon as the playwright's hand left his shoulder. One of his companions had been whisked off by someone else, the other leaning against him in a too familiar fashion, the way she kept helping herself to his drink something William did not agree with in the slightest. He took the bottle back firmly before downing a deep swig, telling himself that getting drunk was not a good idea.

"Guillaume." Gaudet helped his partner down and offered his hand to William. "Sing with me?"

He couldn't sing to save his life, he knew full well, but suddenly he didn't care, instead he accepted Gaudet's hand, allowing himself to be pulled up beside him. Under Gaudet's direction his talent mattered little, of course, because nobody was focusing on William with such an exotic creature beside him. The crowd carried the song with them, a riotous and raucous sound that lifted even William's sorry spirits, until he found he was leaning against Gaudet, certain that everything would be all right if they just kept singing and forgot everything else.

"Look." Gaudet nudged William as Dee took a fiddle

from one of the drinkers, the adoring Sylvie perched at his side.

"Bloody woman." He shook his head, turning away. Dee could handle himself, he was sure. "More singing. More drink!"

Both were supplied in ample measure, Dee's accompaniment on the strings was more than adequate and even Adam was convinced to leave his admirers to join a chorus, his female friends clapping decorously at his skilled efforts to carry a tune.

"Is this," William asked Gaudet, "what having fun is?"

"It is, indeed," Gaudet agreed, one arm around his shoulders and a party of girls took up the challenge on a table opposite, singing a song of their own with fine style. Gaudet laughed and reached down for a bottle before he said brightly, "Cheers!"

William repeated the sentiment, drinking deeply as he wondered how he had come to this—standing on a table in the middle of a carnival and getting drunk with a French playwright. He realized that he didn't actually *care*, because caring would take up valuable time in which he could be laughing, dancing, *living*.

There was more drink, more songs, more laughter, all of it making William feel as though, somehow, life *might* have the occasional chink of light. Gaudet's *joie de vivre* was in equal parts irritating and infectious. That braying laugh, the habitual clapping to signal his good humor seemed suited to a night like this, when *everyone* put their worries to one side beneath the bright full moon.

"I'm not going back to that house," William found himself telling Gaudet. "I'm staying here all night."

Gaudet beamed, starting on another song, and William joined in with, he suspected, entirely the wrong words, leaning against his friend as he did so.

Friend? Yes, why the hell not?

"You are happy, *chérie*?" Gaudet's gaze suddenly settled on him, green eyes twinkling with mischief and drink.

187

"I am ignoring everything except you," he told the Frenchman. "So yes, I suppose I am."

In reply, Gaudet threw his arms around William, hugging him in a way that felt almost companionable, if he could remember what that felt like after so many lonely years.

"There are too many people." William didn't push him away. "I think we are drunk."

"Gloriously, wonderfully so," Gaudet confirmed, voice teasing when he asked, "Too many for what?"

He found himself suddenly confused, caught in Gaudet's gaze and just a little too close. "To think…"

"Shall we adjourn to our farmhouse? We can still hear the music, after all."

"I said I wasn't going back there," William remembered. "Why is life so confusing?"

Gaudet sighed and released his embrace with a sigh of something approaching sadness, yet he covered it with another swig from the bottle, gaze settling everywhere but on William. He had said the wrong thing again, he knew, even as he struggled to explain exactly what he meant.

"My life, I don't want to go back to my life I—" William gave a sigh and took the bottle from Gaudet, throwing his arm around the other man's shoulders. "We'll go back, but only if you sing on the way and pretend that I don't sound as awful as I do."

"In everyone's past, there is *something*," Gaudet told him. "It is why we make our futures better."

"I think…" he peered at Gaudet for a long moment, "my knees have gone numb. Quickly, let us sing."

"Too late." Gaudet laughed, looping his arm though William's as the coachman and his pretty admirers took the stage. "Pap is tired, I shall take her to her bed."

"Take me with you." William steadied himself slightly before he stumbled. "But don't let it stare at me."

"Then let us away," he declared, the poodle trotting happily alongside as they began to walk, strolling through the revelers who swayed to the gentle ballad the party were crooning. "She is a she, not an 'it'. That coachman is a rare sort of devil, though, to chase ladies when *we* are in the vicinity."

"He's welcome to them," William decided. "All of them."

"He says he is waiting for the right girl," Gaudet confided. "And he always comes home alone."

"I am tired," William told him, his voice a whisper. "I am tired of being alone."

"I have had my fun, more my share of it." Gaudet laughed softly. "All I want now is the *one* who stays."

"The *one*?" William leaned more heavily against him. "Is there such a thing?"

"Yes."

There was no doubt in his tone whatsoever, William thought, wondering how he could be so bloody *sure*.

"And I know that, one day, I will find my *one*. It is precisely why I accept every invitation, never spend a night at home if I can be out and about because what if I don't, what if I decline a dance or a soiree and I miss them? What if, on the one night I *don't* go to Drury Lane, my *one* does? It is a risk I will not take."

"What if some missed their chance?" William asked. "What then?"

"Don't say such a thing." Gaudet's voice was gentle and he shook his head. "There must be a little romance left somewhere. It cannot all be chaos."

"Romance." It felt like a foreign word, one he didn't quite understand. "I used to be very good at that. You wouldn't believe it."

"I would like to hear all about your romances." Gaudet slowed to a companionable stroll, arm still through William's. "I adore my new handkerchief, Guillaume, thank you."

"I used to party." William gestured with his free hand as though the cream of society were lined up before them. "And dance and get up to all sorts in corners with ladies."

"Yet you and I…we never met?"

"That was all before you came to London." William shook his head.

"Really?"

He laughed then, the entire situation of his life so utterly absurd. "You have absolutely no idea who I am—of course you don't—no, not who I am, who I was."

"Why would I?"

"Does the name Knowles mean anything to you?" William wondered briefly what he was doing, where this was leading, but somehow he couldn't bring himself to care.

Gaudet pouted as he thought about that then said, "I don't *think* so...should it?"

"A viscount." He leaned closer to whisper. "There was an *incident* over a debt. A young man—it was most unfortunate."

"Ohhh..." The green eyes blinked again. "White's club— the chap took his own life. Some beastly peer pursuing him for money."

He felt again the sensation of sickness, the dread and horror that had accompanied that, the worst incident of his life. "Yes."

Gaudet nodded once, gaze still on William's, and he managed to hold it for a while longer, dreading what he might see cross those green eyes. There was no approbation or disgust, though, no outrage or malice. Instead, there was a smile of utmost tenderness and Gaudet tightened his arm on William's just a little.

"A bad business, to be sure." He shook his head, walking on at a strolling pace. "But any man who does what you have since done is not a man who should hide away. You made a mistake years ago, but you did not kill the boy, Knowles, and you must not punish yourself to your own grave."

I should have let the debt go — nobody should die over cards.

"I fear," he confided what he had never admitted before, "that I will never atone for it."

190

"What the young man did *nobody* could have expected—to die for the smallest gambling debt." Gaudet paused for a moment before resuming his stroll. "If not for you, I would now be minus my head and my sister would be without hope. I believe that counts for *something*."

"But is it enough?" William searched Gaudet's face, hoping desperately for an answer that would not leave him damned.

"Everything that was good in my world was gone—not jewels and silks, but my family, my little girl, my *freedom*... You lifted the darkness when all was lost."

He almost laughed but couldn't quite find the energy to, swinging round into Gaudet's arms as he declared, "Well, you're the only one to ever say so."

"I cannot believe that."

"Believe it." The Frenchman's face was again, he suddenly realized, rather close. "I am a *despicable* human being, everyone says so."

"We never had our dance," Gaudet whispered. "You and I."

"Then let's," he decided. "Now."

"Here?" The word was a gentle laugh as he glanced around the moonlit field. "Really?"

"Why not?" William gestured. "No one can see us, and we can hear the music."

"Lead on." Gaudet took William's hand. "I shall be your swooning partner."

William's own legs were hardly steady as he pulled Gaudet closer, musing that it had been a good long while since he had danced with anyone. That it should be Alexandre Gaudet was not half as ridiculous as he had expected, the other man's company filling him with an odd sense of cheer he had not felt in far, far too long.

"Don't you dare," the Frenchman whispered as they tentatively began the dance, "tread on my shoes."

"I have never," he replied, "trodden on toes in my *life*."

"You dance very well."

"I told you." William forced open eyes that he had not realized he had closed. "Plenty of practice."

"When we are home in London, we will go dancing."

"No one," William warned, "would dance with me."

"I said, *chérie* Guillaume, *we*," Gaudet pointed out in a decidedly decadent tone. "Why would we need any other?"

Why indeed? He closed his eyes again, noting as he did so that Gaudet was also a very fine dancer, that he moved as though air, not earth, was beneath his soles. In this field in the middle of nowhere, moonlight instead of a fine chandelier lighting their way, they danced to the distant music, worries forgotten for these stolen, drunken moments.

"I *do* dance very well," William realized. He found that he had slowed, he and Gaudet not really doing more than swaying together.

"Not as well as I. I'm a very nimble fellow."

"Nimble." Gaudet nodded silently in reply. "Are we very drunk?"

"Not me."

"I might be," he said, leaning closer until there wasn't really much closer to be.

"Probably." Gaudet slid his hand up, brushing through William's hair. "You're English, after all."

"And you're French," he pointed out needlessly, eyes closing slightly at the touch. "And we're dancing in a field."

"I have danced with plenty of Englishmen," his companion admitted. "But none as charming as you."

"You're my first Frenchman."

That sounded, he realized, more suggestive than he had meant. He discovered that it *was* possible to be even closer, stilling as his lips brushed the playwright's, finding them gentle and yielding. It was the first time in longer than he could remember that he had touched another person so intimately. Even by accident, the brush of Gaudet's lips on his was strange, enticing, and he found himself lingering there, every muscle in him frozen still.

"Well." Gaudet sighed. "Your first Frenchman indeed…"

"We should probably…" he whispered, realizing that he hadn't moved, gaze locked on Gaudet's.

"Probably."

Even as William thought about pulling away, he leaned closer instead, lips brushing Gaudet's again before he could think about it further. It was certainly a kiss this time, his eyes slipping shut when Gaudet's mouth moved tentatively under his. It could have been hours or mere moments that they stood like that until he finally had to stop to breathe, murmuring a soft apology as he did so.

"Not drunk *enough*?" Gaudet suggested lightly, letting his head shift a little to rest for just a moment on William's shoulder. "Let's get you safely back and into your bed."

"Our bed," he reminded him. "It's *our* bed."

"And it looks very cozy."

He nodded, holding the Frenchman's gaze before asking, "Then why are we still standing in a field?"

Gaudet smiled tenderly, taking William's arm again and murmuring, "Why indeed?"

It all seemed to make the most perfect sense when he led the way toward the farmhouse, silent as he pushed open the door, urging Gaudet to pass through before him. He watched the Frenchman do so, the poodle pausing to shoot him a beady glance before following her master.

With the door closed behind them, he caught Gaudet's arm again. "The stairs."

"Are you too drunk to manage them, *chérie*?" Gaudet teased, wrapping his arm around William's waist.

"If I said yes, would you help me up them?"

"I will do that anyway." The Frenchman stole another kiss to his cheek.

It really shouldn't have been so easy to accidentally find Gaudet's lips with his own again, he knew, but there it was, another kiss, less tentative than the first. This time, Gaudet deepened it, Gaudet's lips softly coaxing William's own apart. Somehow, his arms were around Gaudet's waist, everything else slipping from his awareness other than

193

Gaudet and the kiss that was growing in intensity by the moment, long and distinctly distracting. He was hit by the thought that Gaudet was as good at kissing as he was at dancing, the Frenchman's tongue moving gently as he slid his hands over William's back.

"Stairs," he remembered. "Don't forget the stairs."

"What of them?"

"We need to get up them."

"We do." Gaudet smiled against his lips, renewing the kiss.

"And into bed."

"Are you propositioning me, sir?"

Was he? He had no answer for that, and it was easier to kiss Gaudet again, all the time urging him toward the stairs.

"Go." Gaudet finally broke the kiss to set William on his way upstairs. "I will follow and admire the view."

It was a decided effort and involved some enthusiastic help from Gaudet before they were both safely on the landing, where William found himself somewhat confused over whether he should be kissing Gaudet or trying to get to their room as quickly as possible.

"Bedroom," the Frenchman urged as, downstairs, the sound of voices could be heard.

"Bedroom," he agreed, wondering when it had become so hard to open a door before it gave way and he pulled Gaudet into the room with him.

Papillon darted through the door. Gaudet closed it with a kick, his lips never leaving William's. He gave himself over to the kiss, sliding one hand into Gaudet's hair. Kiss followed kiss for long moments, the rest of the household forgotten. Finally, he broke for breath, forehead pressed to Gaudet's before he opened his eyes, certain now there was no way to make sense of this, and that he must cling to the Frenchman or else fall apart.

"You have kissed the finest Frenchman you will ever meet," Gaudet whispered playfully. "And I knew you could not be a *Bobbins*."

"Why?" William asked, curious despite himself.

"Bobbins is a farmhand—*you* are…well, lovely."

William blushed at that, covering the moment with another long kiss—again, it deepened, more intoxicating with every second. He tightened his arm around Gaudet's waist further, a gasp escaping unbidden at the press of the other man's hips against his own, his breath quickening.

"Will you…?" He drew back, gaze meeting William's. "Shall we go to bed?"

He couldn't find his voice for a response, aware of himself nodding as he held Gaudet's gaze.

"We don't have to…"

"Please…"

"Guillaume…"

The sound of his name made his breath catch in his throat and he kissed Gaudet deeply, urging him toward the bed. Gaudet went without another word, tumbling them both down, arms around William's waist as though they had every right to be there, as though men did this all the time. *And yet*, William thought as he kissed Gaudet over and over, *perhaps they did*. After all, he was almost lost in it himself, refusing to think, to do anything other than feel.

"Let me…" Gaudet's voice was breathless when he shrugged out of his ornate jacket, his arms around William again a moment later.

"Please…"

With another deep kiss, Gaudet settled back onto the pillows, drawing William over him. William had no idea what he was thinking of, the only important thing making sure his mouth was still on Gaudet's, his hips shifting instinctively against him. There was no question of the playwright's own desire in kind. Gaudet caressed William's behind as he slid the other hand beneath William's shirt, the touch warm on his back.

"Please," he gasped again.

"Too many clothes." Gaudet laughed breathlessly, unbuttoning his own ridiculously ornate waistcoat.

"God…"

"Get them off," William agreed, attempting distractedly to help him with just that.

It was, William realized, as he stroked over the waistcoat, the most buttons he had ever seen on a single item of clothing, but eventually, Gaudet managed to shrug the garment off, followed quickly by the flamboyantly tied cravat. He pressed his hand to Gaudet's shirt, mouth hungry against the Frenchman's, tasting brandy and scent and a heat that had to be desire.

Desire for him.

The simple gesture was greeted with a breathless moan of approval, Gaudet squeezing his behind *very* encouragingly. It was intoxicating as any liquor, the soft sounds of pleasure in Gaudet's throat wonderfully bewitching.

"Yes." He got his hands under the shirt, stroking Gaudet's chest where the locket still hung.

For a moment, no more, Gaudet withdrew his touch so he could cast his shirt aside, then he took William in his arms again, ducking his head to press kisses to his throat. He closed his eyes, hands running over Gaudet's back, the skin warm and inviting. Somewhere William realized that the soft moans and gasps must be from him, but he pushed the thought away, moving his hand with sudden boldness down farther to Gaudet's backside, pulling him closer.

"*Chérie!*" Gaudet laughed coquettishly.

"No one else calls me that."

"Then I will always call you it." A tender kiss. "Or Guillaume, of course."

"I'm not," a gasp as he rocked his hips, "French."

"I am French enough for both," Gaudet assured him, teeth grazing William's shoulder. "And you are so wonderfully English."

"And you are just wonderful," he said, reaching to pull at his own shirt.

With some urgency, Gaudet assisted in the endeavor, throwing the garment across the room before he moved his hands to William's chest, stroking and caressing.

He returned his own attentions to Gaudet's chest and back, tasting the saltiness of his skin, needing to feel his touch, his desire.

"I am sorry," Gaudet whispered with an uncharacteristic timidity, "about my back... Those scars..."

"What scars?" William breathed the words against Gaudet's lips, stroking firmly down his back and lower as he did so.

"Oh, *chérie*..." The next kiss was unmistakably tender, Gaudet's hips pressing to William's.

'*Chérie*'...

The moan was most certainly the viscount's own, he realized, slipping one leg between Gaudet's as he moved with him, swept along on a wave of feeling with all else forgotten.

"Take me," Gaudet whispered, nipping at William's ear.

His eyes snapped open at that, meeting Gaudet's as he tried, and failed, to find words.

"Oh, are you...?" Gaudet's voice was light, gaze meeting William's. "Forgive me, you prefer to be taken?"

He could hardly breathe, utterly incapable of anything for a long moment before the words, feeling woefully shameful, left his lips in a whisper. "I wouldn't know."

William waited then for the inevitable mockery, the witty retort. Instead, Gaudet kissed him again and replied, "Then, Guillaume, let us take all the time we need."

The kiss that followed was one of pure relief, soon forgotten in the tangle of Gaudet's tongue with his, the touch of his hands.

"*Chérie*." A gasp, one hand in his hair. "My *chérie*."

"I want..." He barely knew what he meant, eyes closing again as he continued to rock against Gaudet, breathing harder with each passing moment. Again, words deserted him, cheeks flaming and he gave a small tug to the top of Gaudet's breeches.

"Let me..."

Gaudet's words were soft and William nodded, feeling utterly absurd, but at the same time certain that Gaudet didn't mind, laughing as he whispered, "Please do."

"You are...*lovely*." Gaudet sighed, one hand moving over the front of William's breeches, pressing to him, tracing the outline of his hardness. He just managed to catch a whimper and slid his hand down to Gaudet a moment later, feeling the evidence of his own desire all too clearly beneath the silk breeches. William was vaguely aware of Gaudet's hand at the laces of his own clothes, of air touching his skin, then he was lost in another embrace, every kiss more heated than the last.

At Gaudet's first touch William bit his lip hard, his fingers tightening on the other man's back. It had been so long since he had been this close to anyone, the sensation one he had told himself he could do without. Now William felt an almost unbearable need and he gave an encouraging shift of his hips. His heart slammed as Gaudet curled his fingers around him, stroking softly, appreciatively, savoring his body. William closed his eyes and pulled at Gaudet's breeches, gasping when his hand encountered delicious, tantalizing bare flesh.

At the slight catch of Gaudet's breath, William renewed the kiss, deepening it, surrendering. He lost himself entirely in Gaudet's touch, their mouths meeting again and again for long, deep kisses. He couldn't think if his life depended on it, knowing only that he couldn't stop, didn't want to, and that he was murmuring utter nonsense, but too far gone to care.

There was nothing in the world but the two of them, no screaming children in the yard outside, no drunken singing from the merry coachman and his companions, not even the sound of the music to which they had danced beneath the moonlight. He heard his own heart, Gaudet's soft whispers and gasps close to his ear, felt the hand working at him, assured, tight and fast in its strokes.

William tried to slow, to prolong the delicious moments,

but he was powerless to hold back, nearing the end and gasping the fact against Gaudet's lips mere moments before release hit, body tensing as he cried out. Gaudet's own answering cry was just seconds behind him, his hips bucking hard into William's hand.

There was nothing but harsh breathing and a dizziness that had him clinging to Gaudet, face buried against his shoulder. The world should stop now, he thought, with everything perfect and just as it should be.

Before daylight.

"*Chérie...*" The word was a sated sigh, the arms around him tender.

"Thank you..."

"I have longed for you." The words could have been artful but were not, too much vulnerability in the tone of Gaudet's voice.

He couldn't answer that, he found, though he nodded wordlessly, stroking softly through Gaudet's hair. For a long time they simply lay there together, wrapped in one another's arms. He gave up trying to think and drifted a little, certain then of Gaudet's presence, the closeness they shared.

Eventually William was vaguely aware of movement as Gaudet gently shifted him onto the mattress, his embrace still as tender as it has been. Then the dandy snuggled close to him, sighing very contentedly as they allowed sleep and drink and happiness to claim them.

Chapter Twenty-Three

Then came the dawn.

Consciousness was not, William decided, something he welcomed at that moment. He fought it as best he could, cuddling close to the warmth at his side, shifting when something soft tickled his nose. He drifted again for a long while, the events of the previous night a pleasant blur as he dozed, everything soft and warm and very, very comfortable.

As with all good things, however, the long, contented moments had to come to an end. One nagging thought then another entered his consciousness, however hard he tried to push them away, and finally he opened his eyes, where he found himself staring at the sleeping face of Alexandre Gaudet.

The Frenchman's arm was flung around William's waist, hand still resting rather firmly on his bottom and somehow, despite sleeping in full makeup, Gaudet's powder and rouge managed to be utterly immaculate.

He wondered for a second if he might be able to extricate himself without waking his companion, to leave the bed and dress so that when Gaudet finally stirred they could both pretend that nothing had happened.

The thought was chased from his mind a moment later, though, when Gaudet snuggled closer, giving a contented sigh as he buried his face against William's shoulder. Gaudet's hand squeezed his bottom just a *little*, no doubt in response to some dream or other, and his breath caught in response, his body treacherously reacting even as he froze, heart hammering. Stirring slightly, Gaudet pressed a soft kiss to William's shoulder, causing his heartbeat to grow faster than ever.

Hell. He took a shaky breath, closing his eyes briefly. *Hell and damn everything.* With that thought, he pulled back as much as Gaudet's grasp allowed, telling him as firmly as he could, "We need to get up."

"Do we now?" The words were mischievous, and Gaudet slid his fingers lower, slipping them into William's breeches.

He almost gave in, wondering whether there could really be much harm in it, before he shook himself firmly and reached down to catch Gaudet's wrist as he remembered, "We have an early start."

Gaudet's eyes sprang open at the sharpness in William's tone and the strength of his grip, and he asked without any guile, "Something is wrong?"

"We need to go." William managed to keep his voice steady. "We've already slept in."

"No one has summoned us?"

"They will soon." William carefully but firmly returned Gaudet's hand to his side. "So we should be ready."

"Oh, I see."

There was no way that Gaudet really could see, for he was certain he didn't really understand himself, but he took the opportunity to sit up, scrubbing a hand through his hair. "And we'll need breakfast—"

"Will you kiss me?"

"We should be ready—" William met Gaudet's gaze before darting away again. "I don't think that's a good idea, do you?"

The very air seemed alive with *something* for several moments, Gaudet's eyes fixed firmly on William. Even though he refused to meet it, he could feel the furious gaze, and the Frenchman said, "Curiosity satisfied, was it?"

"That's not—"

"Go away." When Gaudet spoke, William felt a stab of regret at the words, at the hurt in his companion's eyes. Yet he forced himself to harden, managing a curt nod as he left the bed. "And tell your Professor Dee that I will not go to Le Havre or anywhere else with *you*."

"Don't be ridiculous."

"Tell him, please." Gaudet left the bed, fishing for his clothes. "You need not tell him why, just that I will not."

"Then what on earth do you intend to do?" William demanded. "You are being utterly *absurd*—"

"Get out of my room!" Gaudet shrieked with a stamp of his foot, Pap leaping to her feet and joining in with a shrill bark. "I will not be *used* to sate your drunken curiosity. Get out!"

Without quite realizing how, William found himself outside of the room, half-dressed, disheveled and cursing as he knocked on the door, shouting as loudly as he dared, "I need my shirt."

"Put some clothes on, man," Dee commented sardonically as ever as he strolled along the hallway. Clearly, he had not overindulged last night, or any night, the spymaster never more than utterly composed.

"He's thrown me out."

"Get dressed and come downstairs to the kitchen." Dee's voice was sterner and he knocked on the bedroom door. "Give the man his damn shirt or I shall put you through the bloody window, Gaudet."

At *that*, William gingerly tried the handle, relieved to find the door opening as he peered inside.

A moment later, the shirt hit him full in the face and Gaudet snapped, "Get out!"

William retreated with the shirt, pulling it on as he found himself, once again, outside the door. At least he had his clothes, he reasoned, and that had to count for something. He made himself as tidy as he could before he gave a final glance to the door and set off downstairs, hoping to eat and make sense of the things he was trying very hard not to think about.

As William reached the kitchen, he had no idea what he was going to say to Dee, who stood at the stove, watching water boil. The silence was a good thing and he hoped that it would remain, taking a seat without speaking or doing anything to alert the watchful spymaster to his presence. The rest of the house appeared to still be sleeping and Dee said nothing as he tended to his drink.

Minutes passed before he turned from the fire, cup in hand, and asked, "Well?"

"Are we just going to sit here and say that at each other all morning, or can I have some tea?"

"Do you forget, sir, who pays you?" Dee asked with studied politeness. "Is it above the call of duty to afford me a little civility?"

"My apologies." William got to his feet, managing to keep his voice calm — with effort. "I find myself no longer hungry."

"Oh, good Lord, my daughter is not yet fifteen and is less temperamental. What on earth has happened?"

He would not know how to begin to explain, William realized, even if he wanted to, as he could hardly explain it to himself. Instead he shook his head, anger deflating as he sank back down into his chair, asking meekly, "May I please have some tea?"

"Sure that coffee wouldn't clear your head more efficiently?" Dee's tone was softer and he added, "I knew he would be trouble — what has happened?"

"Coffee." He nodded, suddenly hoping that might solve everything. "Yes. Yes, coffee would do very well."

"So," he went back to the stove, "tell me?"

"I think," William managed carefully, "too much wine was drunk last night. That is all."

"Has there been an argument?"

"Yes." He decided that was the easiest explanation. "You know what these Frenchmen are like."

"Would you like to tell me anything?"

"Not particularly." The tabletop was suddenly fascinating, pitted and telling a hundred stories in its surface. "I would like to *forget* everything."

"Do you wish to leave the group?"

"Good God, no." William looked up sharply, the thought one he would not countenance now. "Why would you think that?"

"Because it is right you have the option." Dee set a cup down before William, the scent of coffee strong and a little sickening. "Otherwise, whatever has happened, mend it?"

He made it sound, William thought with irritation, so wonderfully *simple*. "That would be a good idea, yes."

"Good man." Dee patted William's shoulder, glancing to the door in time to see Bastien darting in. "And I shall leave you with young Master Dupire and go and prepare the carriage with Adam."

"When do we leave?"

"Later today—find me in an hour or so. We need to discuss another matter."

"Another matter?" He frowned, the words too innocent, too loaded, yet Dee's reply was a friendly nod, the conversation over.

As the spymaster left the kitchen, Bastien hopped up into one of the seats at the table and fixed William with his large eyes. The boy took an enormous red apple from the pocket of his tattered jacket and took a bite. "Adam married?"

"Probably a dozen times over." William took a long sip of coffee. "Keep out of trouble today, you hear?"

"You reckon?" Bastien sighed, scratching his head. "You married then?"

"Not a chance of it."

"I'm after for someone for Ma," the boy explained. "Professor's nice and all, but I don't see them as a pair—she likes someone a bit more...well, you know, cabinetmaker, boot mender, lamplighter. So, I thought Adam cos, apparently, he's got a stable yard and she'd do all right with him?"

"You're a good lad," William found himself telling the boy. "Enjoy your apple and spend less time worrying."

"We just need to find one that she'll stick with." Bastien

shrugged, taking another bite. "And will stick with her."

Or that keeps his head.

"If you come back to England with us," William said, "there'll be a place for you, I'm sure."

"She gets her hand on that diamond, you won't see her for dust," Bastien confided with a shrug. William was surprised at Sylvie's son's all-too-honest opinion of his mother. "But I'd settle for a yard like Adam's got."

"Plenty of those in England." He had to smile slightly. "One less thing for you to worry about."

"Do you want an apple?"

"No," William told the boy as kindly as he could. "But thank you for the offer."

"He'll come round," Bastien said as he slipped from his seat in response to a knock on the window from Adam, "when he stops shrieking."

"I should go and see." William sighed, getting to his feet.

"That pal of yours." Adam appeared in the doorway, leaning with one shoulder on the frame. "What's he shouting about?"

"He's French," William informed the coachman as he hurried to the door. "They are always shouting about something." With that, he hurried out of the room, taking the stairs two at a time as he hurried to their room. At the door, he paused to wince at the hellish noises from within then, gently, pushed it open to peer into the room.

Gaudet's ranting had taken on a more general form as he sat before the mirror applying fresh makeup, now in plainer clothes made rather more lively by the addition of the crimson coat he had retrieved from the molly house. At William's appearance, Pap began barking furiously and Gaudet's annoyance resurfaced, his voice enough to shatter glass when he shouted, "I have been ill-used, sir, most ill-used."

"Will you stop yelling?"

"I will *not*. Have you told him?"

"Told him what?"

"That I will not go on with you."

"Of course I didn't tell him that." William shook his head. "Because that is absurd."

"You have *used* me as surely as many a young lady has been used."

"There was no *using*." He felt a flicker of hurt despite himself at the accusation. "What happened — it was enjoyed. On both sides. But that doesn't mean —"

"After what I said to you, how I have wanted —" He turned back to the mirror, breathing deeply. "You looked at me this morning as though I were *dirt*."

"No."

"Yes, you did. Now Pap is distressed, nothing will calm her."

"I did not mean to cause any upset." William ducked his head. "For goodness sake —"

"I have no wish to speak to you," Gaudet replied haughtily. "I will travel on alone — please tell the professor I wish to see him."

"You can tell him yourself," he decided, temper rising. "I am not your servant, sir."

"No, because if you *were*, I would turn you bloody out." Gaudet rose to his feet imperiously, more than a hint of his Versailles background in his manner. "Summon the professor, *now*, and take mistress Pap for her toilette."

"I'll be damned if I'll do either."

The Frenchman was really more than beyond reason and William sat himself firmly on the bed, unwilling to be moved.

"I *beg* your pardon?"

"I said" — he glared at Gaudet — "that you can summon whoever you wish. I wash my hands of it."

"Come along, Mademoiselle." Gaudet scooped up his portmanteau in one hand and Papillon in the other. "Good day." With that, he stalked through the door and slammed it behind him.

"Well," William declared loudly. "Well, bloody well."

Finding himself alone, he did not quite know what to do next, his heart hammering as he resisted the urge to throw something across the room. Another door slammed elsewhere in the house a minute or so later, followed by blissful, empty silence.

He flopped onto the bed, covering his face with his hands as he wondered how on earth he was going to get out of *this* mess, much less sort through his own thoughts on the matter. Minutes passed before there was a knock at the door of the bedroom and Dee called, "Ready, gents?"

With a curse, William sat up, sighing heavily as he forced himself to open the door. "He's not here."

"He's what?" Dee peered around the room. "Then *where* is he?"

"He went, I thought, to find *you*." William gestured helplessly.

"No—he has simply *gone*." With that, Dee turned from the room, already calling, "Adam! Saddle a horse!"

Muttering under his breath, William found himself following, certain that there was no one who could get into more trouble than this Frenchman.

"You are off this job as of now," Dee told him with a glance back. "You'll still be paid, but you can sit it out."

"I've done nothing." This fresh outrage was more than he could stomach. "I'm not *off* anything."

"Horse," Adam called from the yard, children swarming from the house at the excitement, the promise of trouble. "Saddled and ready."

"He can't have got far," William protested. "He's on foot with a dog."

"He took the gray," Bastien helpfully supplied. "Fast one, that gray."

"Bloody hell." William was on his way to the horse prepared by Adam a moment later. "That bloody Frenchman—"

"Headed off to the village." The boy took a bite from *another* apple, larger than the first, and leaned on the doorframe in a clear imitation of Adam. "But it's a fast horse."

With an effort, William pulled himself up onto his own mount, certain Dee would have something to say but little caring as he made to leave the yard.

"Don't you get lost as well," the professor called after him, though there didn't appear to be any anger in the words. "And bring us back a playwright!"

Gaudet, however, had not got far and was sitting in a most stately manner atop the gray, declaiming on the benefits of a decent steed to three adoring young milkmaids who were listening intently to his words. From somewhere, he had acquired a pale blue scarf that was tied in a bow about his neck, whilst William could hardly help but notice his own handkerchief, once again spilling rakishly from the pocket of the other man's coat.

"Monsieur," William called, ignoring the women. Gaudet did not even glance round, though Papillon turned in his arms, dark eyes fixing on the newcomer, who now approached closer, determined not to be ignored. "You are to return with me immediately."

Gaudet dismissed the ladies with a few gentle words then reined his horse round to address William. "Pardon, sir?"

"The professor says," William forced his tone to soften, "that you are to return to the house, sir."

"I will come back because I will not risk my sister and her boy," he decided haughtily. "But I will not speak to you."

"Then ignore me all the way to Le Havre." William shook his head. "If that is what pleases you."

"You have used me," Gaudet said again, kicking the horse into a canter. "You are lucky that I am a chap who knows the meaning of discretion."

"I was not worried about that—"

"And I will tell you one thing," Gaudet declared. "You will never know what a *wonderful* lover you have turned your back on—there is no man like a Frenchman."

He had nothing to say to that, pushing away the sense of opportunity lost as he said gruffly, "Let's get back to Dee."

With a shrug, Gaudet urged his horse on, galloping away toward the house and leaving William with little choice but to follow, cursing as he did so the day he met this particular dandified playwright.

Chapter Twenty-Four

In the house that had become the hideaway of his tracking party, Tessier clutched the letter that bore Robespierre's signature in a white-knuckled hand. He had not thought his fury could grow any deeper, any more inflamed and yet he was wrong. This simple, curt note had achieved what any amount of sleeping in hedgerows, riding hours per day and existing on subsistence could not.

Recalled.

Recalled to account for your reckless actions in pursuit of a diamond that likely does not even exist.

He would not obey the command, of course, would not go back to Paris until the Star was in his grip, then he would ride through the city in triumph and that diamond, that royalist myth, to use Robespierre's words, would be proven as fact.

Tessier threw the letter into the fire, knitting his scarred hands before he returned to the window and stared out into the fields. He thought of Sylvie again, of how she had returned to his life, of what they might be to one another again if she could quell the ambition that so consumed her.

And she would — she would be *his* Sylvie again.

As if his thoughts had summoned her, a knock came at the door then, firm, assured, with a hint of impatience, heralding the arrival of the woman who held his thoughts.

"Enter!"

The door opened, and there she was, the day brightening as she entered the room, closing the door behind her. "What, no smile?"

"My correspondence brings no cheer," he told Sylvie

thinly, though her very presence was a balm to him. He crossed the room to greet her with the courtly bow that she so appreciated. "What news?"

"We are leaving today." She narrowed her eyes. "Once Gaudet stops his dramatics. What do your letters say?"

"I am recalled to Paris to *account* for myself before the committee." He reached out his hand to take hers before quickly withdrawing it, realizing too late he had forgotten his gloves. "I will do no such thing."

"You plan to hide?" There was a hint of steel in her voice. "To run away?"

"I plan to return to Paris with the Star of Versailles in my hand and the spilled blood of the playwright, the spymaster, the lady-in-waiting and her child fertilizing the soil of France," Tessier corrected.

"Now *that*" — a slow smile lifted Sylvie's full lips then — "is more like it."

"And that *filthy* bourgeois who dared to blacken Morel's name."

"What…" There was a definite flicker of something in her gaze as she reached out to touch his uncovered hand. "Will you do to *him*?"

At the brush of her soft palm on his own scarred skin he realized he could not summon the words of cruelty. Instead he felt himself tremble at her tenderness, the tenderness he had not known in too many years.

"You won't let anything get in your way." Sylvie's tone was gentle and she moved her hand to his arm, gaze fixed on his.

"And I… I am assured of your loyalty?"

"What" — Sylvie leaned closer by just a fraction — "do you think?"

"But you have your child. Your priorities cannot mirror mine."

"I would do anything." The hand was stroking his cheek, caressing with utmost care. "*Anything*."

"But your son." He remembered the boy he had once

been, the mother who had barely looked at him. "He must be your treasure above all."

"Don't you worry about him." Sylvie's lips brushed his. "If it comes to it, he can look after himself just fine."

The words hit Tessier hard as a slap, but he did not show it, never showed anything when it came to *her*. Instead, he nodded and asked, "And your destination is once again the next safe house on your cabinetmaker's list?"

"We'll be there by nightfall," she promised against his lips. "And I'll find you."

"We will leave shortly and be ahead of you." He nodded, this method of travel having worked so far. "And Le Havre is but days away."

"And then…" Sylvie smiled, the smile that always so beguiled him. "We shall have what we want."

"Oh, Madame." He bowed his head subserviently, battling with himself. "We will have that indeed."

"You can have *some* of what you want now," she promised. "Now."

Despite himself, he nodded, the memory of her hand soft atop the scars that maimed his own too beguiling.

"Sit down." Sylvie urged him back toward a chair as she spoke, sliding her hands downward to his breeches.

She would not betray her son, he told himself desperately as he settled into the chair. He had to convince himself of that, after all, because if she would, then what kind of a woman would she be?

What kind indeed?

The kind the nation had already driven from the throne, would drive from the land entirely.

No, Sylvie was not a woman like that, or where would Vincent Tessier be?

Chapter Twenty-Five

The news that they were not to travel on that night after all filled William with a definite sense of irritation, fueling further the feeling that life had gone off-kilter once again. In what would no doubt be termed a *sulk* he did not join the table for dinner, instead taking himself for an uninspiring walk around the farmyard, just *daring* the chickens to question him as he stalked among them. He must, he realized with trepidation, speak to Gaudet — whatever had happened had happened, but that was no reason why matters should continue with everyone in a bad temper. With that thought, he strode into the house, heading for the stairs where he believed the Frenchman might well still be concealing himself.

What greeted William from the landing was the shriek of the playwright's laughter, followed by the sound of children's voices sharing his mirth, and, for some reason, this antagonized him further. When he peered around the door of their shared room to see Gaudet completing a *very* elaborate version of Harriet's plait whilst a gaggle of farm children watched good-humoredly, his sense of annoyance grew still further.

All of the trouble was of Gaudet's making — *his* sulk had delayed their departure. His childishness had caused the argument earlier, and his ridiculous insistence that he had been used had been the start of the whole sorry affair. Yet here the dandy was, laughing and joking as though there was nothing wrong in the whole world.

"Having fun?" He sounded, he hoped, as put out as he felt.

"We *were*," was the pointed reply.

"Then I shall leave you to it."

"Then do."

A call from the farmer's wife summoned the legion of children and Harriet followed on, hugging Gaudet before she departed. Left alone with William, Gaudet settled at the mirror and regarded his face with a critical eye.

"I came to see if you were all right," William told him stiffly, hoping for some sort of a truce. "We can't be at odds all the bloody way to Le Havre."

"What do you want, sir? If it is a repeat of last night, you must find another *mark* to use."

"You enjoyed it— I—" William lowered his voice, feeling his face flame. "I enjoyed it, too. I did not mean to upset you. Can we not just carry on as before?"

"It is done and gone," the Frenchman told him as he powdered his face, though the warmth that had characterized their chats over the past days was missing from his tone. "And we will get along again, I am sure."

"Let me come with you," William suggested, in an effort to make a truce. "We can have a drink and put it all behind us."

"If you really must, but there will be no replay of last night." Gaudet announced, "Now away, I must change."

"What is wrong," William wondered aloud, "with how you look now?"

"I look," Gaudet said, frowning as though the question were absurd, "like a farmhand."

"Hardly!" William just caught himself before he could tell Gaudet that he looked very fine indeed, sure it would provoke just another crow of immodest derision.

With a shrug, Gaudet pronounced, "I shall see what I can do with this red coat and a few wildflowers—my blue suit is to be kept for occasions... You are dismissed, Bobbins, return in an hour."

Finding himself banished from the room, William took his leave. With nothing else better to do, he sat at the top of the stairs, doing his best *not* to focus on events of the night before. They would have a drink, he decided, and all would be well, and their liaison would be consigned to the mists of drunken encounters.

"And don't mope," came a shout from the bedroom. "I cannot abide misery."

He had nothing to say to that, settling for muttering something as he waited for Gaudet to deem himself ready. Yet long before the designated hour had passed, William nodded into a fitful sleep supported by the banister rail. Moments later, Gaudet nudged at his ribs with his shoe and instructed, "Awaken, Bobbins, if you are to join me."

The dream he had slipped into took a second to loosen its hold, and he could only blink blearily at Gaudet before telling him, "I'm awake—help me up."

"I will not," Gaudet declared as he swept past, gesturing with the pristine white handkerchief. "Come along, entertainments await."

William got to his feet with effort, wondering how on earth Gaudet managed to always look so fine, remembering again the touch of Gaudet's hands on him, the press of his lips, and the insistent, burning desire even as he followed his companion from the house.

The ever-present poodle seemed to be the one who knew where they were going and Gaudet strode after her, leaving William to follow in his wake. There were no milkmaids out now beneath the gathering dusk, yet the carnival seemed to still be going on, with a small bonfire picking out the village square, jaunty music sounding on the air once again.

"What do you want to do?" William called to the playwright. "Apart from drink, I mean."

"I wish to sing and enjoy the evening. I may also find someone to finish the task that was so abandoned this morning. You?"

"Me?"

"That is what I asked. What do *you* want to do?"

"Find some of those milkmaids for a start," William heard

himself utter the words even as he wondered what he was saying.

"Oh, back he scurries to the girls." Gaudet gave a toss of his head, clearly intended to show that he little cared. "Then I suspect the tavern is your destination. I understand one might buy some comely favors for little more than a few mugs of ale."

"As a Frenchman," he pointed out, "I would have thought you were duty bound to join me."

"I would not want to show you up."

"We'd give a girl a night to remember between us." William warmed to his theme, certain that was all that was needed. "Just think of it."

"Why a girl?" Gaudet challenged, glancing over his shoulder, those green eyes flashing. "I thought you'd got a taste for the chaps."

"A girl," he continued firmly. "Or have you forgotten what that's like?"

Gaudet almost physically bristled at that, a slight hint of tension showing in his movements when he turned to ask angrily, "Is it not enough that you humiliate me in the bedroom—must I now endure your idiotic comments in society, too?"

"We had fun," William exclaimed. "And we can have more fun—for goodness sake, man, let's get a drink down you and you may regain your sense of humor."

Gaudet's answer was to throw open the door of the tavern and storm into the crowded interior, transforming from a moody temper to the life and soul of the party in the space of roughly three seconds.

William rolled his eyes, letting out a long-suffering sigh as he followed. It was safe to say that all eyes were on Gaudet, so he busied himself with fetching drinks, surprised to find that it was relatively easy to turn on the charm that he had kept buried for so long with the barmaid. Feeling somewhat triumphant with his success he handed Gaudet a glass, telling him, "And there's plenty more where that came from."

"My tumbling friend," Gaudet took the drink without acknowledgement, preferring to address his admirers, "is seeking a lady to reawaken his slumbering manhood. It is his last chance. If it slumbers much longer, it will wither and die."

"Whereas he," William nudged Gaudet, "does not have one to wither in the first place."

"Not got one?" One of the bolder women pressed her hand to Gaudet's breeches, much to the hooting delight of her friends. She widened her eyes and announced, "He's got enough down there for two or three if you ask me."

At that, Gaudet *did* look to William, a note of amused *just try to better that* flashing in his eyes.

"My *colleague*," Gaudet pouted, "is bitter."

William simply blinked innocently before slipping his arm around the waist of the nearest girl, who was quite happy with the attention and giggled when he whispered something inconsequential in her ear. If Gaudet noticed he seemed to little care, perfectly happy with the adoring attention of his own gaggle of young ladies.

The next half an hour was devoted to drink and making sure the girl at his side was kept amused, with the occasional glance in Gaudet's direction. William noticed, with a twinge of regret, that he would not acknowledge that Gaudet hardly gave him a second glance in return. Instead, the playwright was dividing his time between his several admirers, which now included a couple of rather pretty young men, too.

Telling himself he didn't care, he redoubled his efforts, fresh drinks helping as he laughed loudly at something the girl, whose name he didn't recall, said and he barely even heard. Finally, as the night deepened Gaudet left his seat and, with a young man on one arm and a young lady on the other, made his way through the crowded bar and through a closed door.

"Will you look at that," William exclaimed. "Who does he

think he is?"

The girl shrugged, asking, "Jealous?"

"Jealous?" he demanded, the very thought absurd. "They aren't *that* pretty." He found, however, that he couldn't tear his gaze from the closed door, irritation growing by the second.

From within came a shriek of laughter, followed by an answering laugh from the young lady who had accompanied the playwright. A moment later the young man emerged, jacket and waistcoat already discarded, seized a bottle of claret, and darted back inside.

"They're very pretty." She laughed. "All three of them."

"Right." William huffed out a breath, already disentangling himself, and crossing the floor. What he intended to do he wasn't quite sure until he knocked loudly, waiting a moment before pushing the door open.

William was surprised to find himself in a small bedroom where, just as he suspected, Gaudet was certainly on the bed, though fully clothed and watching intently the scene of the young man and lady in front of him. The girl was sat on a stool before a mirror whilst the young gent, sleeves rolled to the elbow, tended her hair with utmost care under Gaudet's expert direction. In the closing stages of an elaborate chignon, none of the trio even breathed, let alone looked to the door.

"Hair?" William exclaimed. "You are doing *hair*?"

"Out!" Gaudet barked, waving a hand. "And close the door."

"Not on your life, sir."

"Close the damn door." Gaudet flew from his place on the bed and slammed the door, asking William, "Do you want *everyone* to see how the festival queen will be wearing her hair this carnival?" He turned his attention back to the couple, telling them, "That is *perfect*—you are a master."

Certain that he was in some sort of strange dream William found himself meekly taking a seat, glowering at the trainee hairdresser. "It's crooked."

Both Gaudet and his protégé rolled their eyes and the girl chirruped, "To balance the roses that I will wear on the day."

"Of *course*." William threw his hands up. "I shall keep my opinions to myself then."

"My colleague believes it unbalanced. Monsieur le Tumbler... Would you like a turn?"

"No." He gave Gaudet a look. "Are you nearly finished?"

"All done."

"Then for Heaven's sake, come and have some *fun*."

"I'll give you a good time." The girl who had sat with William appeared in the doorway. "If you're looking for something to remember the village by."

"Hear that?" William turned to Gaudet. "*That* is fun. You should come along."

"Perhaps I am just not of a mind to, but I can see that I will get no peace until I *perform*." Gaudet turned to the young hairdressing couple. "Good luck in the carnival. Now we will take our leave."

"Drink," William was saying to the girl. "We'll take some with us."

"Come on then, gents," she told them with a crook of her finger as she opened the door. "Upstairs we go."

"Don't look so glum," William told Gaudet and slipped his arms around the girl. "She's pretty enough, isn't she?"

"She is delightful." He shrugged, kicking at the straw-covered floor.

William reached back with his free hand, holding it out to Gaudet then, determined that he—they—were going to enjoy this and put things back on a better footing between them.

Instead, however, Gaudet placed his brandy flask into the outstretched hand and shrugged again. "I am following on, never fear."

With his own shrug, he opened the flask, drinking deeply as they made their way upward.

The girl led the way to a perfectly serviceable bedroom,

telling William, "You'd better have the money."

With an assurance that he had more than enough, he waited until Gaudet closed the door, then the woman looped her arms around William's neck and said, "A few coins first."

He rolled his eyes but rummaged for a moment before producing a more than adequate amount that he tossed down onto the bed. "Yours — with more to come."

"That'll do." She laughed, settling back on the bedcovers. "Come on then, gents, let's get to it."

William turned to glance at Gaudet, eyebrows raised in question.

"You first."

"I thought the point was it was together," William objected, something in Gaudet's expression troubling if he would let it be.

"Well, I don't fancy doing it 'together'," Gaudet replied, the way his gaze roamed the room betraying his obvious discomfort.

William let out a sigh, making for the bed. Moving to lie beside the waiting girl, he pulled her mouth to his, pushing aside the sudden comparison that came to mind when he remembered the night before.

"He don't fancy it," she lamented, urging his hand to her skirts. "Let him be."

"He doesn't know" — William glanced back at Gaudet once more, expression almost pleading — "what he's missing."

If he cared, it did not show, and as the prostitute made the occasional sound of pleasure to cover her obvious lack of interest, Gaudet was instead fussing with a curtain tieback, fashioning it into a flamboyant bow around the fabric.

William tried to concentrate on the girl, urging her hands to his breeches, but he found himself as uninterested in her as she was in him, even as he kissed her deeply.

"Better," Gaudet said softly, repeating the bow with the other tie. "One simply needs a little imagination."

"Then come over here and show us what a bit of imagination can do," the girl called. "Tell me what you fancy?"

"Him." Gaudet shrugged and stooped to pick up Papillon. "But it's not mutual."

William's heart lurched, the air suddenly filled with tension. His head snapped up, eyes wide and fixed on Gaudet.

Another shrug and the Frenchman left the room, leaving the girl to say, "It *is* mutual, isn't it, lovey? See it all the time."

"Of course it's not bloody—" He fell silent, a realization hitting him. Then William left the bed, throwing all the coins in his pocket to the girl as he hurried for the door, calling for Gaudet.

"Fasten your breeches!" She laughed and watched him go.

He did so as best he could, shouting for Gaudet again. The Frenchman had been faster, however, and was nowhere to be seen in the crowded, fire-lit bar where all of the village seemed to be congregating. Cursing, William forced his way through the mob, finally reaching the door and pushing out into the night.

There was no sign of his friend and William shook his head, wondering just how the man had managed to move so fast. What he would say when he found Gaudet he had no idea. The wash of thoughts, feelings and utterly contradictory nature of them all left him more in need of a drink than ever as he called Gaudet's name again, heading off through the village.

After a considerable time, and with dejection mounting, William was close to giving up when he finally caught sight of a familiar figure, anger surging once more and he stormed toward him, shouting, "Where the bloody hell have you been?"

"Go back to your whore, *Bobbins*," Gaudet spat as he turned to address William. "And prove to yourself that you're still a man."

"She's not my *anything*," William insisted. "And I'm now *penniless* with nothing to show for it after chasing you about for the last bloody hour."

"Then you are a fool as well as an idiot."

"I'm not the one who—" He gestured frantically. "Why did you say that?"

"Why do you think?"

"I don't know," William shouted. "I don't know, that's why I am asking. I was *trying*—"

"What? What were you trying to do?"

"Put things right." William did his best to ignore the other, less altruistic thoughts that insisted on flooding his mind. "So things could be—so we could have some fun."

"I had fun last night. I don't want to have 'fun' with a tavern whore who cares more for her tobacco. I prefer men, Guillaume, and I am very sorry that you seem so troubled by that."

"I *came* out here to find you—"

"Because if you lose me, Dee will skin you alive."

"I don't give a bloody *fig* what Dee thinks. He's on the verge of sending me back to England on my own, anyway, so he can bloody well—"

"Then good riddance to you. May you and your women be very happy and may you one day realize what 'fun' you missed." Gaudet turned, clearly intending to continue his angry promenade.

William had every intention of storming off, but instead he found himself grabbing Gaudet's arm, telling him furiously, "They are not *my* women, they are not my *anything*—I bloody left her to come and find *you*."

"Last night *meant* something to me." Gaudet's voice was quieter, eyes flashing with hurt. "And I feel *battered*."

"I've never," William heard his own voice, strange and unsteady, "ever—with a man. Before. I don't bloody understand any of this—"

"I thought you liked me," was the answering whisper. "I

really did."

"I didn't want her—"

"Nor did you want me, Guillaume, not for more than one night."

"What happens," William could barely breathe now, "if I say that you are wrong?"

"Kiss me again?" Gaudet's words were soft, breathless. "Please?"

It sounded absurdly easy, and as his lips found Gaudet's he wondered absently what all the trouble had been about, why he hadn't just done this with the dawn light, when it had been all he had wanted.

"I didn't want to share you tonight," Gaudet whispered into the kiss. William's heart leaped with desire and he rested his forehead against Gaudet's. "Was I terribly beastly?"

"No."

"Claudine says I am prickly."

"Forgive me," William implored. "I didn't mean to hurt you."

"Never say sorry." Gaudet's lips brushed William's again. "Never ask for forgiveness."

He was silent for a long moment as he kissed Gaudet almost desperately, everything feeling utterly off-kilter and confusing. The kiss went on for longer than ever, another following, then another as they sheltered in the shadows of the nighttime village. Needing the closeness of the man, the heady scent of his perfume, William slipped his arms around Gaudet and lost himself in their embrace, all thoughts, all worries, all 'sorrys' set aside for now.

"Guillaume…"

"Come back to the house with me."

Gaudet nodded breathlessly, setting Pap down before he whispered, "To our bed?"

"To *our* bed," William agreed, heart hammering so hard he was sure Gaudet must be able to hear it.

"Oh." The playwright laughed softly, no trace of the usual

shriek of mirth. "For a carriage."

"We'd better get walking."

It was after one last kiss that Gaudet pulled away to do just that, William's hand still held in his. He found himself silent as they walked along, his fingers laced with Gaudet's as if it were the most natural thing in the world. He couldn't think past each moment, the journey seeming to take forever until they finally, thankfully, reached the house.

As though she had been prompted to do so, Papillon trotted upstairs ahead of them and nosed her way into the room where Dee's daughter slept, leaving them at the foot of the staircase. The house lay in silence, all its inhabitants asleep or safely in their own rooms.

"Well…" William heard himself say, clutching Gaudet's hand and clinging to him as though his life depended on it.

"Well?"

"I really don't know what I'm doing," William whispered.

"What do you *want* to do?"

"I want," he admitted, "to go upstairs with you."

Another kiss, then Gaudet led him gently up the staircase, turning to steal the occasional kiss on the way. William kept close, realizing, as they reached the door, that he was trembling, praying Gaudet did not notice.

"We will just…?" Gaudet drew him into the room, telling him, "Whatever you want."

"Show me." He pushed the door closed. "Show me how it can be."

Gaudet answered that with more languorous kisses, his arms around William's waist and his hands sliding over his back. It was impossible not to sink into him, returning kisses and caresses as best he could, the heat between them growing with each passing moment. With softly encouraging whispers, Gaudet slid William's coat from his shoulders, exploring the kiss gently with his tongue.

He was happy to let Gaudet lead, relinquishing the careful control he usually kept over everything, barely caring when his coat fell to the floor before he ran his hands over the front of Gaudet's shirt.

"No waistcoat tonight," the Frenchman said good-naturedly as he shrugged off his own coat, "I had decided to try being *rustic*."

"I'm glad." He pulled Gaudet's mouth back to his. "Less buttons."

"Less buttons," he repeated, slapping William's bottom rather opportunely, sending a surge of heat through William's veins. With something close to a growl, he pulled Gaudet tight against him, the kiss that followed decidedly more desperate.

"*Chérie*," Gaudet declared, slapping him again. "My Guillaume."

"Bed…"

"Can we get," he tugged at William's shirt urgently, "all of this off first?"

"Mm…"

The next while was spent divesting each other of their clothing, William finding the process much hindered by the need to touch every fresh area of exposed skin, stroking, feeling, exploring this man who had bewitched him as no woman could.

"You are…beautiful," Gaudet told William, his gaze roaming over him. "Utterly."

A short laugh escaped at that, the word one that had never before been applied to himself. "No."

"Beautiful," he repeated, trailing one hand down William's chest before he pressed his lips to his throat, nuzzling softly.

In response, he closed his eyes and slipped his hand into Gaudet's hair as he murmured his name, arching to the touch, to the faintest scrape of teeth teasing his neck. He surrendered to it, heart pounding afresh when Gaudet trailed his hand lower over his chest, his stomach, moving to brush his thigh.

"Bed." Gaudet stepped back as he whispered the word, taking William's hands in his own and leading him to the bed.

He let himself be eased down to the simple covers. A moment later Gaudet's lips were on his again, his hands roaming over William's body.

What he wanted, how he felt, was almost overwhelming, Gaudet's name a gasp. He lost himself in a long, deep kiss. At the sound of Gaudet's soft breath of anticipation, his heart quickened still further, hips shifting restlessly when the Frenchman stroked his fingers over him.

"Do you want...?" William struggled for the words, flushing deeply at the suggestion that had almost left his lips. How did one say it to a *man*?

"Tonight is for you, *chérie*," Gaudet promised, hand moving against him. "Anything you might want."

"I want—" He gasped, closing his eyes at the touch, before forcing them open again. "I want you to have me."

"Guillaume," Gaudet whispered gently.

William held his gaze, sure once again that no name could sound so perfectly *decadent*.

"Just show me what to do."

"Oh, I think"—he kissed William again—"you will just *know*."

The thought was comforting, even as he kissed Gaudet hungrily, exploring wherever he could reach.

"Do you feel"—he dropped his head to kiss William's chest—"ready?"

Did he? He considered for a moment before nodding, watching Gaudet breathlessly in the dim room.

Still pressing soft kisses to William's throat, Gaudet moved between his legs, closing one hand over his hip. William felt as though he could barely breathe, gaze fixed on the man with him, the man who had occupied his thoughts for longer than he might care to admit.

"Please," he gasped, "I want—"

"I want *you*," came the answering admission, Gaudet's hip lifting him a little until he could press closer.

William closed his eyes at the words, wondering how

anybody *could* want him.

Gaudet slipped his hand down between William's thighs, softly stroking, caressing him. He was like a musician playing an instrument, practiced and intuitive. The touch was tender yet assured before, with exquisite care, Gaudet moved his fingers over his skin, heat building where they came to rest. For a moment, William tensed, but another kiss was all it took to relax him once more and with a soft breath, Gaudet pushed one of his fingers gently into him. He gave himself over to it, gasping as Gaudet whispered endearments, sliding a second finger into his body.

William moved his hips instinctively, lifting them in a silent encouragement to meet Gaudet's touch, to deepen it. His apprehension dissolved at the feeling of pleasure and he knew nothing but the night and them, this sensation that he had never even imagined. He gave a deep moan of pleasure that was stifled against Gaudet's lips. As he gave another moan, William clutched the Frenchman's back.

Still exploring with his fingers, Gaudet shifted to nibble at William's earlobe, brushing his tongue over the skin with each whispered sentiment. This seemed to go on for long, delicious minutes before Gaudet withdrew his fingers and slipped his arm around William's waist.

For a second, as Gaudet bought his other hand to his mouth, William didn't realize exactly what he was doing. It was then, as he licked his palm and rubbed the spittle over himself, that it dawned on him that the moment he had longed for had arrived. He felt that shiver of uncertainty again, glad for Gaudet's kisses when their lips met once more.

Still, his body tensed slightly in anticipation, a moan escaping as Gaudet entered and filled him. It was unlike anything he had felt and he tightened his grip on Gaudet's back, barely noticing the scars of Tessier's lash.

A soft whimper slipped from Gaudet's lips and he pressed a tender kiss to William's mouth before he started gently to move. Any discomfort quickly gave way to pleasure, and he was soon following Gaudet's lead instinctively, pressing his mouth eagerly against his lover's lips as he let his hands roam and explore.

For a moment, *more* than a moment, William felt the nag of discomfort. Not the sharpness of pain but a dull pressure deep within him. Gaudet's hips shifted and the sensation subsided, the ache giving way to something rather more pleasurable, something he couldn't quite describe. William hadn't known what to expect, yet it wouldn't have been this. This was a pleasure that was quite unlike anything he had felt in his life, far removed from those stolen liaisons with tavern girls and bored society wives.

Those women had been soft and yielding to touch, yet Gaudet combined that softness with an unexpected strength, firm muscles moving beneath hot, smooth skin. A faint sheen of perspiration covered them both. It seemed to glow on Gaudet in the candlelight, highlighting every contour, everywhere William found now that he longed to know.

William opened his eyes once more and met Gaudet's gaze, dancing flame reflected in the vivid green. He thought then of their own dance in the fields, the dance they had been doing since their first meeting, the delicious twists and turns that had led them here.

"*Cherie*," Gaudet whispered then he dipped his head once more, nuzzling his lips into William's neck. He arched into the touch, closing his eyes as he let his other senses take over, carried away on the ever-heightening feeling of pleasure. The only sounds were their soft whimpers and moans, the scent of Gaudet's skin as bewitching as any cologne. It wasn't the saddle soap and leather smell of a man on the road, nor the rosewater of a dandy at his toilette, but something entirely undefinable, silk and lace and *him*.

It seemed that there was no one else in the world but them, the sparse surroundings of the ramshackle house forgotten. William knew only the touch of the man with him, heard only their shared breathing, the occasional moans that he realized now were coming from him. He could have quite happily stayed like that forever, but his desire was mounting swiftly, release not far away as he gasped the fact against Gaudet's mouth, sliding his palms restlessly across his back.

"God." He bucked his hips, catching his lip with his teeth momentarily. "Yes!"

"*Guillaume*," Gaudet urged, thrusting harder. "*Chérie*."

He tried to say something but couldn't have gathered a thought and instead cried Gaudet's name before he lost all control, spending hard between them. It was just seconds then Gaudet followed, a crushing kiss claiming William's lips in the final moments.

William couldn't think, couldn't move, could barely breathe as he clung to Gaudet, happy to just let the world get on without him for a while.

Alexandre Gaudet was not a playwright.

He was a damned magician.

Chapter Twenty-Six

The man known to the small band of runaways as Professor Dee went by many names, each governed by the territory in which he found himself. His interest in the espionage business had, until now, been academic, a lucrative exercise in paperwork. After all, he was nothing more remarkable than a Dublin scholar with the occasional sideline in *acquiring* priceless treasures even if now and again he also contracted freelance agents to carry out the odd bit of work for the British crown. Not until this trip to France had he been *quite* so in the heart of the action, though. His first instinct, upon discovering that Gaudet and William were on the run, had been to gather up his daughter and the best friend who traveled with them and flee for safety, leaving the lot of them to it, but he would not, *could* not, as well he knew.

He was not a man who could turn his back on *anyone*, and he suspected that, one day soon, Bastien Dupire might need someone reliable when his mother showed her true colors and grabbed for the diamond.

Now Dee lay in the gathering dawn, half-awake and half still dreaming of a life without danger, no longer on the road but settled once more in his tranquil home, living a few quiet months after weeks of travel.

Soon, he promised himself as he rolled over and tugged the blanket up farther. *Soon we will be home.*

The sound from beyond the door alerted him to the presence of another in the second before the door itself started to open. He slipped his hand beneath the pillow for the touch of the pistol there as someone entered the room, the door closing a moment later.

The light tread of bare feet suggested that the intruder must be one of the few women in the house. He knew immediately who it would be and *why*. Gaudet's drama the previous day had delayed their departure yet when Sylvie had disappeared for her short sojourn that same morning, she could not have known they would be remaining here in the farmhouse. That Sylvie Dupire was passing information to Tessier's agents was beyond question—that she would now fear they would suspect her of betrayal might drive her to anything.

What that *anything* might be became clear a moment later as the covers shifted, the thin mattress beside him dipping with Sylvie's slight weight. There was a long pause then, the only sound the softness of her breathing beside him.

"I believe, Mademoiselle Dupire," Dee opened his eyes to look at his unexpected companion, words soft, "you have happened into the wrong room."

"On the contrary, Professor…" She lowered her eyes for a moment, he noted, before meeting his gaze again. "I'm exactly where I meant to be."

"You are seeking to…*secure* our alliance?"

"If you want to put it like that." She chewed at her lip, eyes wide with feigned innocence.

"Yesterday, just before breakfast"—Dee reached up to run his hand gently down her hair, gaze sweeping over her—"I searched the house but I couldn't find you—you were all I could think about." He met her eyes, asking, "Where did you run away to?"

Her gaze dropped briefly before she shrugged. "Sometimes you just need to get away."

"Do we really *need* the diamond, Sylvie?" One last chance to save herself, to prove his suspicions wrong. "We have our children, we could have a quiet life."

"With the diamond…" She leaned close enough that he could feel her breath. "We could have anything. *Everything*."

"Would we endanger our friends to get it?"

"Oh, they'd be all right."

"Tessier would look to them for his revenge." Dee held her gaze, needing her to say something that would convince him he was wrong about her traitorous nature. This pantomime of flirtation might have been ungentlemanly, but to send the party to their deaths was a risk he was not about to take. "And it would be brutal."

"We'd have the diamond." Nothing flickered in Sylvie's gaze. "As consolation."

"I think we will change our route to the coast," Dee commented idly, catching the flash of panic that crossed her delicate features. "Just in case we are followed."

"Why would we have been?" She shook her head. "Surely—"

"But why take the risk?" He stroked her hair again. "Charron knew *all* of the contacts. He might have given them away. He told *you* where to find us, after all."

"Which route will we take instead?"

"I wouldn't put you at risk by telling you."

"We're in this together." A flicker of something close to anger passed over her gaze then, her mouth tightening. "Remember?"

"Just you and me." He caressed her cheek with one hand whilst he slipped his other arm around her waist, a threat as much as an embrace. For a moment, they were so close it might have been the prelude to a kiss. "And Vincent Tessier?" There was no romance in Dee's knowing tone, nor his embrace when he tightened his arm around Sylvie.

"He'd never catch us." The hint of panic was brief but it was enough. "You know that as well as I do."

There was nothing worse than a traitor, he knew, and one driven by money was worst of all. Sylvie Dupire had no ideology by which she was guided, no radical fire, nothing but a love of avarice and influence. In a moment, he had drawn the pistol from beneath his pillow and told her, "Because of you, good people are dead—you are neither half so charming nor half so plausible as you think, *Madame*."

"We can talk about this." Fear was definitely the dominant emotion then, the color draining from her face. "It's not what you think."

"Your son loved that man. Charron was a father to him, Sylvie."

"There was nothing we could have done to save him." She shook her head. "He'd have wanted us safe."

"Did you *try*, Madam?" he asked frostily. "No, you did not—if you had, you would not be here today."

"I've got my boy to think of," she tried then. "You said it yourself, children come first—"

"And I believe *you* said that sacrifices must be made… your boy was among them."

"You misunderstood my meaning, Professor."

"Then clarify it, Mademoiselle, and let us understand one another better."

"What sort of a mother would I be?" Sylvie laughed, the sound hollow and desperate, before turning on the offensive. "You have played me most badly, sir."

"And you are an innocent in thrall to my cunning?" He could hardly help but smile then, wondering when the world had come to this. "In that case, let us travel to Le Havre by a different route. You will be free to come and go, but only with a chaperone. If I am wrong and no harm meets us at the coast, then I will offer you my abject apologies. If, however, I am *right*, then Tessier will believe you complicit in the deception and you will be the object of his vengeance." He watched her for a moment, reading a slight hint of fear in her eyes. "Of course, if I *am* wrong, then you have nothing to fear from the Butcher of Orléans."

"You'd make me a prisoner?"

He watched unmoved as she mustered outrage out of her panic, twisting in his grip.

"These are dangerous lands. I would not let any woman travel alone."

The laugh that followed was hardly reassuring, much less convincing him that Sylvie was in any way innocent. He tightened his grasp as from the corridor outside came the sound of cheery whistling. Recognizing Adam's manner, Dee called casually, "Adam, apprehend our traitor on your way down to breakfast?"

Sylvie flew from the bed at that, face flaming. "Traitor? There are many worse than me. What about the lies your man *Morel* tells?"

"Lies?" Dee slipped from the bed calmly as he heard Adam come to rest outside the closed door. He waited for her to elaborate, pulling a shirt on to accompany the breeches it was always germane to wear when sharing a house with a woman who had designs on spoils of one sort or another.

"If you knew the half of it."

"If it involves a drunken stumble and a deep ditch, believe me, I know." He shrugged on a waistcoat, well used to such empty claims once a villain found their back to a wall. "It won't buy your freedom, Madame, be assured of that."

"No." There was a pleased little smile then, "No, not that."

"God help you, Mademoiselle, if Tessier ever discovers your plan." Dee's words were not bitter, not gloating, only honest. "But as long as you travel with us, consider yourself protected — too many children have been left orphans."

"You had better watch your back." She met his gaze, brazen to the last. "*Professor.*"

"And if harm comes to me, *you* had better watch your neck." He shrugged, plenty of similar threats having come his way down the years. "Because that head won't be half so smart when it's resting in the basket."

Sylvie had, as he suspected, no response to that, the door slamming behind her before her voice, all sweetness, could be heard responding to Adam.

"Put her back in her room," Dee called. "And lock the damn door."

Chapter Twenty-Seven

Gaudet awoke from a very cheerful dream in a brighter mood than he had known in what seemed like years. The night had passed too quickly after their union, as Gaudet had drifted into a peaceful sleep in William's arms. Now, still tangled together in the sheets, he found his good mood abating too quickly as he gazed at the man beside him, wondering what his waking would bring.

He could not countenance another rejection, he knew, would not stand a second humiliation if it were to come. For long moments, he gazed at William, committing his peaceful features to memory, the face he had come to adore. When this all ended in heartbreak as soon as the other man awoke to the reality of the night just passed, Gaudet would not endure more sadness. He would simply gather up his bag, collect his little girl and find his sister alone, no matter the cost.

"Is it morning?" The words were barely a whisper, William's eyes still closed.

"A beautiful sunny morning," Gaudet told him gently.

He could almost feel the effort it took then as William's eyes opened and he pressed his lips to Gaudet's again before either had a chance to say a word. Gaudet met William's gaze, and returned the kiss deeply, a soft sigh in his throat. William slid his hands into Gaudet's hair, the kiss long and deep. *Perhaps,* he vaguely reasoned as he sank into William's arms, *this isn't going to go so badly after all.*

"Is this all right?"

"*Very,*" was Gaudet's response.

"You must tell me," came the earnest whisper, "if it isn't."

"Do not fret so," Gaudet advised, fingertips trailing down William's back. "It's wonderful."

He shivered at the touch, William's eyes slipping shut as he kissed Gaudet hungrily, his hands starting to wander. The time was lost to kisses and Gaudet fluttered his fingers into William's hair, tangling it softly. It did not take much before William was breathless and gasping in his arms, shifting closer in a subconscious, compelling fashion.

A memory of the night before swept through his mind, the tenderness of William's hands gentle on his scarred back, the sense of peace when they had drifted into sleep together. With a sigh, Gaudet ducked his head to nuzzle the Englishman's neck, utterly enchanted by the soft sounds of pleasure that escaped William's lips.

"You're so good at that." The words were unguarded, his neck arching to Gaudet's touch.

"And you...are inspiring."

"What," came the breathless reply, "do I inspire you to?"

"I could," he whispered, teeth just grazing William's neck, "show you."

"Please do."

Gaudet could hardly believe that this was happening, that William was still here, everything seeming to suggest that he was *very* happy with the current arrangement, too. With no thought in his mind other than William's pleasure he shifted farther down the bed, drawing the tip of his tongue gently over William's chest, reaching down to stroke him.

The whimper of pleasure that escaped William's lips was most certainly unbidden, his hips lifting as he pushed toward Gaudet's hand. "Yes."

He went lower still, whispering soft endearments before he withdrew his hand, moving his tongue against William very softly.

"Oh, *God*." William's hips jerked suddenly and he grasped the sheets.

At the reaction, Gaudet lost no time in taking him fully into his mouth, fingers curling around him again.

It was heady indeed to see the usually so restrained Englishman gasping and writhing under his ministrations, gripping Gaudet's hair as he moaned his approval.

He could hardly drag his gaze from William, could barely recall a sight so utterly *glorious* and it was with that thought in his mind that Gaudet slipped a hand beneath his companion and, without any attempt at a warning, pushed a finger into him.

"Christ!"

That was all the compliment Gaudet needed and he moved his hands and mouth in rhythm, teeth scraping gently now and again. He could, he thought, get *very* used to doing this for William Knowles.

It seemed that the Englishman was of the same opinion, gasps growing in intensity before he was suddenly pushing Gaudet away, a breathless moan warning what was to come. Gaudet, however, had other ideas. He was not, after all, the sort of chap not to finish what he had started and he tightened his lips, urging William on.

And finish he did a moment later, with a most loud cry of Gaudet's name, hips moving furiously before he spent hard and fast.

Only when he was sure that William was sated did Gaudet finally lift his head and withdraw his hands. He took his time returning to lie on the pillow beside the Englishman, placing tender kisses on his chest and stomach on his way back up the bed.

"Bloody hell." William's eyes were tightly closed, his breathing still heavy even as one hand smoothed shakily through Gaudet's hair.

"There is nothing so lovely," Gaudet whispered, nipping at William's ear, "as you like this."

"I think..." William said, "my mind has ceased to work entirely."

With a very soft sigh, Gaudet snuggled against William, finding, not at all to his surprise, that he could barely keep from touching the man at his side. He trailed his hand down

William's chest, resting his lips on his shoulder.

"I'm sorry," he admitted sleepily, "that I am an idiot."

"You are a ruffian, not an idiot."

"Is that better or worse?"

"It is *you*." Gaudet lifted his head to kiss William's cheek. "And that makes it wonderful."

"How do you do that?" William asked. "How do you always have the right words?"

"I am a playwright," was the answer. "Words and sauce are my stock in trades."

"Whilst I am hopeless at both."

"You could give the latter a try," Gaudet suggested, rather opportunely, the evidence of his own desire all too clear between them.

The Englishman's face colored considerably at that, William murmuring a moment later, "Do you want—?"

"I want whatever *you* want, *chérie*."

It turned out that what William wanted was much in keeping with his own thoughts on the matter, the next good while devoted to bringing Gaudet to a point where he was shuddering and gasping, given over completely to his pleasure. His hand was tight in William's hair, hips bucking hard as he surrendered to the man with him.

"Sorry." He was dimly aware of William whispering the word into a kiss, followed by a laugh. "I don't know what for—"

There was suddenly a thunderous knock at the door followed by Dee calling, "House meeting, gents, ten minutes—we travel within the hour."

Gaudet, however, barely heard it, far too occupied with deepening the kiss and when he did reply, "Indeed, sir," it was in a strangled tone.

"What did he say?"

"He said...*oh*..." Gaudet gave a whimper of pleasure, the words lost in a gasp of William's name as release swept through him.

He was aware of William's lips on his hair and he floated

for a long, blissful moment, thinking this was indeed a most perfect start to the day.

Chapter Twenty-Eight

At the discovery that Sylvie and Bastien were nowhere to be found, the window pane in her room expertly picked open, the house fell into an uproar. Search parties failed to find any trace and, with Dee declaring that time was of the essence, the party prepared to make its farewells. His warnings that Tessier's own forces may be nearby drove everyone along at some speed, yet Adam was distracted, something about Bastien's disappearance striking him as a little off-kilter.

Gone Sylvie may have been, but her son's belongings remained, including the walnut box so lovingly crafted by Thierry Charron, sat atop the tricolor flag that the disappeared woman fashioned into a sash when she fancied some flare. It was this discovery that caused Adam to search the yard and pastures, the pig field where the boy had taken to roaming, yet there was no sign of the child to be found. Adam was almost ready to admit defeat when he decided to look once last time around the yard, alerted to the child's presence in the corner of the stable block by the sound of soft sobs.

In the days they had known one another, Bastien Dupire had become a constant shadow to Adam. He was always somewhere nearby, watching, questioning, learning all he could absorb about caring for the horses for which he seemed to have such an affinity. Sure that he was not the sort of child who would welcome being caught with tears on his cheeks, Adam stood in the doorway to give him time to recover and called, "You in there, lad?"

There was a scuffling sound and a possible sniff before

Bastien appeared, sporting his usual swagger despite the redness of his eyes. "I was just checking the horses. They want to know what we're hanging around for."

"Got something for you," Adam told him casually, heart going out to the boy whose mother had left him without a second thought as the child dragged his sleeve across his nose.

"What is it?" Bastien's words were studiedly careless.

"One thing about being a coachman, I always seem to have these hiding in the pocket of every coat I own." He held out a single key. "So this one's for you."

"What's it for?"

"My house in Dublin." Adam shrugged. "So you've always got a place to call home."

"Why would you do that?" The boy peered at him, curiosity and suspicion warring in his eyes.

"Because that's what mates do — they help other mates."

A flash of something that looked like pleasure passed across Bastien's face, chasing away the misery for just a second. He took the heavy key in his hand, examining it for a moment before slipping it into a pocket. "Better hang on to it then."

"Just don't bring too many girls back," Adam told him. "The beds squeak."

"Not too many," Bastien agreed with the slightest hint of a grin. "One or two."

"I know you Frenchmen."

"Put you English to shame." The boy sniffed. "As it should be."

"*English*?" Adam drew in a deep breath, looking with comical shock at the boy. "Did you call me *English*, laddie?"

"Might've done!" Bastien turned, the swagger he had already learned from Adam evident as he started to whistle the coachman's favorite tune.

"Aye, well, maybe I'll start calling you a...a bloody Prussian."

"You'd better bloody not."

"I'm Irish, you cheeky bugger."

"You and that professor both." He rolled his eyes. "I know, I know."

"You going in the carriage or up at the business end?" Adam reached out to scrub Bastien's hair. "We get the guns and the brandy at the front."

"All those hours in a carriage?" The boy shuddered. "I've had enough polite conversation to last a lifetime."

"And before we hit the road, you got anything you need to get off your chest?"

Something passed across the youngster's face and for a moment Adam didn't think he would answer.

"I hope—" Bastien admitted, his voice small and soft, that of the child he tried to hide. "I hope she's all right."

"We'll keep an eye out for her." Adam scrubbed the boy's hair again. "And for each other."

"Sounds good." Bastien ducked away, familiar grin firmly back in place. "Now get to work."

"Me?" Adam shook his head. "I'm the foreman, lad. *You're* harnessing the horses, so get to it."

With a roll of his eyes, the boy did so, whistling and decidedly more cheerful than he had been.

Chapter Twenty-Nine

For all that had gone wrong, Sylvie could at least take satisfaction in the fact that she had chosen her mount for the escape well. The animal had carried her admirably on her journey, fueled, it seemed, almost by her own grim determination to save herself, to find Tessier at all costs. As she rode, she allowed herself to think of nothing else, self-preservation the only spur necessary as they went on, covering mile after mile. It was hard going, but perseverance paid off when the familiar ebony carriage came into view in the distance. She kicked the horse on, drawing closer.

Followed by six men on horseback, the carriage drew to a shuddering halt at the sight of her, the outriders pulling back their mounts in well-trained formation. Seconds passed before the door of the vehicle opened and Tessier emerged, a shadow in rook-black, silver buttons glinting sparks in the sun. He regarded her with a face that betrayed nothing, knitting his gloved hands behind his back.

"You made good time," Sylvie called, bringing her mount to a halt as she neared him. "I knew you'd find me."

"Your safe house is gone…it is burning still."

Sylvie kept her expression calm, asking, "Why?"

"Because this game is over—we are bringing all of you into custody *today*," Tessier snarled. "The playwright will hand his sister over when I am done with him—he will *beg* to hand her over."

"All of *us*?" Tessier's words filled her with a jolt of fear, hidden in the sharpness of her tone. *He wouldn't, not to me.*

"Not all—those who have no value will be executed where they stand."

"I came to find you—"

"You have betrayed me at every turn...humiliated me with your *professor*, sent me along the road for nothing but sport." He shook his head, face hard as marble. "What lies do you bring me now?"

"Harsh words, indeed"—Sylvie met his gaze squarely—"when I've been so sorely mistreated already. That meddling *professor*—who is no more mine than the playwright, I'll have you know—changed plans at the last minute, and I've been a prisoner from then until the moment I managed to escape. I've chased along this road for hours in search of you, and this is how you greet me?"

"And you have left your son?"

"They'll look after him." She nodded to remind herself of that fact. "He's safer there for the time being."

"Get into the carriage." He turned to one of his men to bark, "Take the horse alongside."

With a surge of satisfaction and relief, she slid down from the saddle, allowing Tessier a smile as she climbed inside the carriage to take a seat.

"And are we to collect your boy *now*, or would you like to leave him a little longer?"

"He'll be fine," Sylvie decided. "We'll get him when the time is right."

"The time for action has come. I am recalled to Paris." Tessier slammed the carriage door and it began to roll along. "We shall see how much *stamina* the playwright has this time."

"It was his fault we didn't leave when we were supposed to," she remembered, certain he was at least partly to blame for what had happened.

"Why?"

"Him and your *Morel* had a right argument. He was yelling for hours."

"Why would they argue?"

"Oh." She gave a sly grin. "They'll be all made up now, I imagine."

"Do not play your games with me, Sylvie, speak plainly."

"They're fucking each other." Sylvie watched for his response and saw none. "Is that plain enough for you?"

Despite herself, she still saw *nothing* in the stone-cold expression, the only movement the knitting of Tessier's hands before him. She wondered again at the innocent young man he had once been, the shy student who had burned like a firebrand on the political stage, yet had barely been able to string a sentence together when faced with a pretty girl.

"Enough of them." She let her voice soften. "We shan't quarrel, shall we?"

"Never."

"Never," she repeated, smiling softly with satisfaction before turning her gaze to the window.

Chapter Thirty

"Might I have a word?" William rehearsed the question a couple of times under his breath on his way to the kitchen, entering the room a moment later where he spoke it for real, determined that he and the professor would have more than one before the interview was over.

"There's no time," Dee told him, busy loading an assortment of pistols that were ranged on the table. "We need to be away."

"'We'?" He shook his head impatiently. "I fear I am uncertain where I stand after my *dismissal*."

"You are with us to the coast, of course." The professor frowned. "I would not abandon any one of you, you know that."

"I don't need a bloody nursemaid." William's ire rose once more, despite Gaudet's best attempts to calm it earlier. "Let me do my job."

"One thing I told you, *one*." The words were stern, the tone as infuriatingly level as ever. "You keep things professional—I do not think that you are cut out for this work."

It felt like a punch to the stomach, even as he told himself he shouldn't, *didn't* care. "And so again, you prove yourself to be wrong."

"I have been informed by a contact in the south of the facts in the death of Yves Morel."

Now William was silent, this new revelation unexpected.

"You have put yourself in danger, Knowles, and I would not want that. I thought you had killed Morel. I learned he died thanks to a drunken accident—you are not ready for a job of this importance."

"I don't need your concern." William scrubbed a hand over his face, mortification adding to his anger. "I can take care of myself."

"There will be other work for you, but, I think, something a little less intense."

"Do you want to know," he asked, "what you can *do* with your *work*, sir?"

"There is no need for—"

At that moment, the door to the yard opened and Harriet hurried in, followed by the ever-present poodle. "Papa—"

"Will you leave us be?" William snapped, the unwelcome intrusion the last straw. "What kind of a *mission* brings damned children along for the ride?"

Without a word, Harriet turned on her heel and walked quickly back into the yard as Dee told him, "You will not speak to my daughter in that tone, *sir*. I may put up with your rudeness, but I will not expect her to do likewise."

"I don't want *any* of you putting up with anything." He just managed to keep from stamping the floor. "I have had enough of all of it."

"Believe me, that is mutual. My party and I were bound for home, yet I find myself forced into France to mop up a mess that should never have been made." Dee's calm facade cracked just slightly. "She should not be anywhere *near* this country."

"Nor should she be walking in on other people's conversations, sir."

"This conversation is over, Knowles." Dee's words were silenced by the sound of Papillon's frantic barking from the yard, followed by a cry that could only be from Harriet. Despite his last words, William was at the door moments after Dee, the sound of distress all too unmistakable.

There was no time to think anything, an ebony carriage hurtling along the track away from the farmhouse that William, with a stone of pure horror in his gut, recognized all too well from those nights spent under the same roof as Vincent Tessier. Whatever Dee thought or knew went unsaid, the spymaster already hauling himself onto the untacked back of one of their own carriage horses and urging it into a gallop after his abducted daughter.

With a curse, William had no choice but to clamber onto one of the remaining horses, giving chase a few seconds later. Dee had made good time and was thundering after the carriage, William close enough to see but far enough away to be unable to do anything other than watch helplessly as one of Tessier's men turned in his saddle, the sudden flash of a pistol brightening the muzzle as a single shot sounded.

The professor's horse reared back with a whinny, for a moment standing tall in the air before it toppled over, trapping Dee beneath it for a few, terrible seconds. As the animal scrambled onto its feet and cantered back to the safety of the farmhouse the professor was left on the ground, William hoping that the unmoving man was nothing worse than unconscious.

Bringing his own horse up short, William scrambled down, hurrying to crouch beside the fallen figure. The poodle that had followed them both unnoticed licked at Dee's face, William noticing with relief the rise and fall of the professor's chest before telling Papillon, "Go and get help, quickly."

Much to his amazement, she gave a blink of her glittering eyes then turned and scampered back to the house, barking wildly once more. With that, William turned his attention back to Dee, tapping the man gently where Papillon had licked a moment earlier, before forcing himself to look at the wound. It was not as bad as he had feared, the bullet having missed Dee even though the weight of the horse had smashed his knee into the stony ground.

Dee's eyes flickered open, the memory of the horror that had confronted him all too evident there when he said, "Harriet—"already struggling to sit up.

"The poodle has gone for help." William wondered at the words even as he uttered them. "Stay still."

"Stay still?" He looked at William as though he was mad and attempted to rise to his feet, an exclamation of pain bitten back as he did so. "My daughter — oh, God, Harriet."

"You're hurt," He was, he felt, doing a wonderful job of stating the obvious and instead went to support Dee in his futile attempts to stand.

"Get me a *horse*." Dee's tone was low, face white as though all the blood had blanched from him. "Please…"

Dee was, William was certain, in no state to do anything, blood already pooling on the left knee of his breeches. A glance down the road rewarded William with the sight of Papillon and those she had summoned fast approaching. Making a snap decision, he got to his feet and pulled himself up onto his waiting horse, knowing only that there was a girl in need.

"Knowles, *please*," Dee told him urgently, glancing down at where his own leg was red with fast-spreading blood. Only then did he clamp a hand to the wound in his knee and gasped, "Help her."

Determined to do just that, William had time to shout an assurance before spurring the horse to action and chasing after the distant carriage. He rode the horse into the ground in pursuit, sure he could, *must* do something to help the young lady. At first, it seemed as though the five outriders hadn't seen him but then, as they crested a narrow bridge, they turned as one and galloped straight toward him, each man already reaching for his gun except for one, who held in his hand what appeared to be a roll of paper. With no other choice, William slowed, wishing he had his pistol to hand as he waited for them to reach him, to *kill* him.

Yet, the shot didn't come.

As the riders drew closer, he realized that their leader was Jacquet, the jailer whose son had died at William's own hand. The man slowed his horse, the smallpox scars that marked his face worn deeper with grime from the road, and he regarded William with a dark frown, holding out the paper wordlessly.

"What's this?" he asked, even as he took the note, unfolding it and examining the fastidious writing therein. A quick glance gave him the answer all too soon—a simple exchange of father for daughter was the deal Tessier proposed, the implications of *that* all too clear to William as he skimmed his gaze over the words for a second time.

"If his lordship is *amenable* to the exchange," Jacquet told him, "the address to come to is in Harfleur." He gestured to the name of a street on the back of the letter. "No games neither. The people there are *very* loyal, if you get me, and anything amiss...*his* girl will get what *you* gave my lad, understand?"

He understood too well, managing a grim nod before pushing it into his pocket and wheeling his horse around.

"Tell him she'll be a pretty sight on the scaffold, citizen," Jacquet bellowed after William as he galloped away. "The girls always do!"

The ride back to where he had left Dee felt like the longest William had ever known, heart seemingly in his throat as he turned the note over in his mind, a plan already forming. It was with a surge of relief that he saw Gaudet standing there in his red coat. The playwright rushed to meet him, his hand outstretched toward the reins.

"How is he?" William called as he approached, pulling the horse to a halt and noting, even in the panic, how at the sight of Gaudet things were not quite so bad.

"Stubborn as a mule. Terrified as any father would be." Gaudet caught the bridle, gazing up at William. "What news?"

"Tessier." He swallowed hard. "Demands a swap. Dee for his daughter."

"But they only have one another..." Gaudet shook his head. "*I* shall go—he believed me to be Dee once, perhaps he might still."

"No," William said firmly, sternly almost, the thought of sending Gaudet back to Vincent Tessier one he would not even contemplate. "No—I will go, and you must stop Dee from getting involved."

"No!" The utter horror on Gaudet's face, the reflection of it in his voice, struck William unexpectedly hard and the Frenchman shook his head, saying urgently, "Never, Guillaume, not you."

"It's the only way." He took a deep breath. "Not a word to Dee."

"*Chérie, please*! I cannot go on alone, Claudine and François need someone like you, not a silly playwright."

"I'll be back before you know it," William assured Gaudet, not quite sure how he would keep the promise. "I don't intend to stay very long—being Tessier's houseguest once was more than enough."

"I will not let you go."

"I'll fare better than the girl," he pointed out, remembering Dee's words when he added, "And Dee will get you to Le Havre—I've done nothing but get things wrong since this mission started. I can at least do this to try and do *something* right." He reached out to Gaudet's hand for a moment, their fingers touching before he urged, "Now, we must hurry. And remember, not a word."

"Please, *chérie*," the words were a whisper, William sure Gaudet had already accepted that he must go. "I will not say a word."

"I will come back," he promised, knowing he must, somehow, now keep his word. "I swear it."

"You had better." Gaudet gave a brave smile. "Because I—"

"Oi!" Bastien's distant voice silenced whatever Gaudet was about to say. "Can either of you two drive a carriage?"

"As well as I can do anything else," William shouted back before turning to Gaudet. "Which isn't saying much. Up for giving it a go?"

Gaudet nodded mutely, apparently just a little lost, but now Bastien was running toward them, the moment they had shared over all too soon.

"Didn't you catch them?"

He had to tell the boy that he had not, adding quickly, "But we will get the better of them. Where is that carriage?"

"You need to come and tell the professor what's going on first."

The boy was right, of course. William gathered himself for the confrontation, to tell the professor that his daughter was lost. He could not panic, he knew, could not rush — that was, after all, how mistakes were made.

"See that the boy stays out of trouble," he told Gaudet, meeting his gaze before heading into the house to find the professor.

The sound of raised voices was uncharacteristically audible as he entered the building, both Dee's and Adam's usually impeccable French *distinctly* Irish now, despite the language both were speaking. With an expression of utmost gravity on her face, the farmer's wife bustled into the sitting room carrying a pail of water and bloody rags and told William, "Through there, calm them down."

William had about as much chance of that, he knew, as keeping a snowball from melting in Hell, but he smiled grimly at the woman before entering the room.

"You can't even bloody walk." Adam was reasoning furiously whilst Dee sat on the sofa, breeches slit from ankle to knee as he busied himself with dressing his wound, from which blood still flowed.

At William's appearance, Dee glanced up. For a moment, his gaze shifted to the empty doorway where he obviously hoped to see his daughter.

What little color remained drained from his face and he asked, "Tell me all?"

Feeling this fresh failure deeply, William handed the note to Dee, standing back to allow him to read.

"You did all you could, Knowles." Dee took the letter. "There was nothing one man could do against so many."

He fell silent then, eyes moving over the page as Adam, face set in a mask of anger and worry, crossed to the window to look out into the yard. Finally, Dee turned to his friend and asked, "You will care for Harriet, if I cannot?"

William remained silent, more certain than ever that his plan must succeed as he waited for Adam to answer. Instead of words, Adam turned and crossed to Dee, peering over his shoulder to read the note. He too was silent for a moment, scrubbing one hand through his hair before he asked William, "Did you read this?"

"It was not addressed to me," he pointed out.

"He doesn't know you." Adam turned to Dee and William realized that he'd had *exactly* the same idea as him and Gaudet. "Let me go."

"What good," William asked, "will that do?"

"I've no one relying on me, no daughter, no lass. I'll tell him I'm his man."

William waited, silently, cautiously, intrigued to hear what Dee would say to that, whether he would capitulate.

"Nobody's going but me," Dee finally replied in a measured, calm tone. "Nobody dies on my behalf."

"Nobody is dying at all," William objected. "Unless it is Tessier."

"We need to get underway," Dee replied, white-faced as he finished fastening a bandage around his leg. "Thank you, Knowles, for bringing word to us."

William nodded an acknowledgement, the kind words fueling the feeling of failure and also of determination that he would be the one to put things right.

The sun was warm when he strode out into the yard searching for Gaudet, needing his company. He whipped his head from left to right, calling the playwright's name and finding himself even glad to see Papillon at that moment. Her presence meant that her master could not be far away. He set off across the yard, trying to push the memory of Dee's face out of his mind as he searched for his lover.

Lover.

Thank God for it.

Gaudet met him coming across the yard, face ashen when he asked, "What did Dee say?"

"He says he's going to swap himself for the girl."

"Then he will have to join the end of the line."

"Will you help me" — William held Gaudet's gaze — "to do it without him noticing?"

"Please, *chérie*," Gaudet whispered, touching William's hand very lightly, "we have just found one another. Please do not get chopped up or boiled or turned into jam or anything silly like that."

"I would make," William told him as solemnly as he could, "very unpleasant jam."

"I thought you very tasty." Gaudet gave a saucy smile. "And you must come back because you haven't seen my amazing bed yet."

"That is reason enough in itself." William touched Gaudet's hand in turn before he murmured, "Do not worry, please."

"You might as well ask the sun not to shine" Gaudet attempted a smile, though it was a weak effort at best. "Anyone would worry, but I know you will come back safe."

"You won't get rid of me that easily," was the bold promise. "Now, let's go and rescue a maiden."

"You have already done that in Paris. I am rather fetching in a gown."

"Perhaps you can show me," William called as he turned to inspect the carriage, "when all this is over."

Minutes later they were on the road again, the farmer and his family sending the group off with supplies, bullets and good wishes. The plan, Dee had told them, was to find safe lodgings in Harfleur, then he and Adam would go to the meeting point, where the professor would surrender himself and Adam would return with Harriet. No one was to take a risk, he warned, no one to try to be a hero.

Leave the stupidity to me and Adam.

William concentrated on making sure the horses remained on the road, more glad than he could say of Gaudet's comforting presence at his side. With Adam, Dee and

Bastien traveling inside the coach with Papillon, Gaudet made the occasional admiring noise about William's prowess as a driver, but his heart was clearly not in the good humor, worry mapped across his handsome face.

"When we reach the town," William told Gaudet, "drive them round, buy me some time."

"I will do what I can."

He nodded grimly, watching as the ghostly shapes of buildings approached in the distance. "Slow the carriage as we enter, I'll slip away then."

"Of course."

"And remember," he whispered, "smile."

"Smile," Gaudet repeated, attempting to do so. "I will try, Guillaume."

William managed a small one of his own as the carriage approached the entrance to the town. Gaudet took the reins and drew them back to slow the vehicle as promised and, with a final touch to Gaudet's hand, he slipped down, praying he wouldn't be seen by Dee or Adam as he did so. For once his luck held and the carriage rumbled on, leaving William alone in the bustle of the street, Gaudet watching over his shoulder until they could no longer see one another.

Then he was alone.

William felt suddenly and utterly bereft. Closing his eyes briefly, he gathered himself, knowing he had little time to put his plan into action. For a few moments, he stood calming his nerves, reminding himself that he was a professional, that, if he could steal Gaudet out from under Tessier's nose, then he could definitely do this. With that thought in mind, he set off, asking a passerby for directions to the street before he went on his way.

As William walked he perfected his story—the shot had killed Dee, leaving William to take his place, and the girl was to be set free immediately. He repeated it over and over to himself, the thought of Gaudet and that bed of his keeping him going when he approached the address.

The building was a tall, well-appointed house in an expensive street, the only indication that anything untoward was happening the man at the door, who shouldered his rifle with all the self-importance of a military general. He eyed William suspiciously as he neared and asked, "What's your business, citizen?"

"My *business*," he told the man, "is with Citizen Tessier."

"What name?"

"Morel."

The guard knocked three times on the door and it was opened from within by another. For a few moments, they conferred quietly, then William was ushered into the musty hallway, which was surprisingly ill-kept, given the fine exterior of the building. He peered around, heart pounding despite himself. If something were to go wrong, if it did not play out as he had planned…the thought was too horrible to contemplate.

"Are you carrying any weapons?" the guard asked, polite yet frosty in his tone. "I must ask you to surrender them if so."

"I am carrying nothing." William held up his hands. "As you can see."

"Secure him," Jacquet's voice sounded along the hallway and the scarred man emerged from the gloom, gripping a length of thick rope. "He's slippery, this one. Kills folk soon as look at them."

"It takes more than a look," William assured him. "There'll be no need for tying anyone."

"We fasten your wrists," Jacquet said again, "or I start shouting that there's someone out here causing a nuisance and the girl wouldn't want that, would she?"

She wouldn't, he knew, even as he held his hands out. Freeing Harriet was what mattered, the only thing at that moment to concentrate on.

William recognized the gleam of triumph in Jacquet's eyes as he tied the rope roughly, far tighter than was necessary, until it bit into the skin of his wrists. The guard stalked ahead, pulling at the end of the rope as though he were walking a dog on a lead.

Another knock at another door and Tessier called, "Enter!"

William kept his head up, ready to meet the other man's gaze as he entered the room.

"Ah, *Morel*." the room was an unremarkable middle-class study that had clearly seen better days. Harriet sat on a chair in a corner, apparently unharmed but fastened with a pair of heavy iron manacles about her wrists. She lifted her tear-streaked face to William, gaze imploring. "You may see the young lady is quite unharmed — quite *uncommunicative*, but unharmed."

"I am here" — he forced himself to watch Tessier instead of Harriet — "to take her place."

"No." Tessier shook his head, cracking his knuckles with the gloves he wore. "*You* are not the one they call Dee."

He kept his expression as neutral as he could at that, praying Harriet would forgive him when he told Tessier, "Dee is dead."

"Dead?" Tessier ignored Harriet's cry of horror, a sound of utter desolation escaping her lips before her head dropped, chin resting atop her breastbone. He held up his hand to her for silence and narrowed his eyes, though William saw a flash of *something* pass across his cold gaze. "How?"

"One of your men shot him." He refused to blink.

For a long moment there was silence, punctuated by the sound of Harriet's sobs, then Tessier nodded and turned to her to say, "Do not cry, Mademoiselle — if one's parents are not of the finest stock, one is often better to find oneself relieved of them."

"So you see," William pressed on, "I'm afraid you must make do with me."

"So I shall." Tessier nodded and turned away, clearly contemplating matters. When he swung round it was at a furious speed, his fist landing solidly in William's stomach as he spat, "And *you*, sir, will have to do."

The shock of it made William's knees buckle, just

managing to catch himself with a hand to the edge of the desk, the world suddenly spinning.

"Jacquet," Tessier bellowed, "The horsewhip."

"Let the girl go," he gasped.

"Are you making demands of me, *Morel*?" Tessier dragged William back by his shoulders, flinging him down to the floor, breath blasting from his lungs with a gasp.

"Let her go." William refused to stop, even as the wind was knocked out of him. "That was the deal."

"And where will a girl with no father go?" Tessier landed a solid kick to his stomach, snatching the horsewhip from the newly arrived Jacquet. "Better that she stay here, don't you think? Stay where she is safe until trial?"

He couldn't speak, managing barely more than a moan, the force of the betrayal, the lies hitting hard. Sylvie had given them up. Tessier had lied in his offer.

They were lost.

"I know," Tessier crouched beside him, voice a low whisper, "what *you* are…you and your playwright."

"You don't," he whispered, "know anything."

Tessier slowly peeled off the black leather gloves, the melted, knitted flesh revealed bit by bit as the sometimes-pale, sometimes-pink skin glistened before William's eyes. "They tell stories of how I came by these scars," Tessier told him. "I feel the fire even now, deep in the bone."

William remained stubbornly silent, the only sound his gasps as he tried to steady himself and catch his breath.

"What I did to Gaudet"—Tessier rose to his feet, a silver buckled shoe flashing in front of William's eyes in the second before it connected—"will seem like a dream compared with what I will do to you."

William was dimly aware of a noise that must have come from himself, the pain tearing through him and his eyelids falling despite his best efforts not to surrender.

"Stop it!" Harriet suddenly shouted, pulling wildly at the manacles that held her, but if Tessier heard, he little cared, his foot landing again and again in William's stomach.

Let her go, he tried to say again, but the pain was overwhelming, Tessier's hatred knowing no limits as he vented his anger.

"He is a British spy." Tessier stalked across the room to where Harriet was sobbing, near hysterical. "Come from London to France to usurp the people, to spread dissent and terror and I will smoke out the nest." Tessier leaned in very closely to the girl, inches from her face when he promised, "And you, girl, tears will not bring him back now."

"Let her go," he managed to whisper, the world black around the edges. "Please—"

"I will let her go on the day you die," Tessier said, turning back to address him. "She is my guarantee. Only a fool would attempt a rescue while I have her in my custody."

"I'm sorry," he tried to say, certain now that he had failed yet again. "I'm so sorry."

William was dimly aware of the ropes on his wrists being replaced by manacles, then, with a shout for Jacquet to lock the door, Tessier was gone, leaving William and Harriet alone.

"He's…" He paused, tried again. "Your father—"

"Papa said you were brave for saving Monsieur Gaudet." She sniffed back her sobs, voice a whisper. "Papa was very proud of you, sir, but not able to speak such sentiments."

"I'm not brave." William lifted his head to meet her gaze. "And he's not—he's not dead."

"Don't…" Harriet rose from the chair, her manacled hands before her as she walked to the desk and picked up a blotting cloth. "You're bleeding."

"He's not dead," he repeated, needing her to understand. "Leg wound, that's all."

She dropped to her knees, awkwardly holding the cloth to his forehead as she whispered, "You don't have to say that."

"I thought he'd let you go—"

"That is because you are a man of honor. He is a monster."

Honor or not, they were now in a very bad position indeed

and he gasped, "I'm sorry."

"Being here." She renewed her pressure on the cut on his forehead. "That is worth more than you can guess."

"I swear I will see you safe." William met her gaze with effort. "What he said about Monsieur Gaudet…"

"It doesn't matter." She smiled gently. "Not to me."

"I have messed up everything I have ever done," he told her, touched by the innocence of her words, "but I won't let you down."

The door opened with some force to admit Jacquet, who stared at the pair of them for a long moment. Finally, he said, "This one don't like girls, darling—he likes Frenchmen."

"I don't like *you*," William pointed out, certain that politeness wouldn't get him anywhere with this one. "Leave her alone."

"Boss wants to see you. Girl, you're to sit with the lady, keep her company."

William considered refusing, but the thought of putting Harriet in any more danger stilled his tongue and he nodded gingerly, getting to his feet.

"You're to help the lady with her hair," Jacquet informed the girl as he reached out to grab William's bound hands and pull him across the room. "So behave."

"I'll be back," William promised Harriet, pleading with her with his eyes not to do anything that might endanger her further. "Don't worry."

"I will behave," she assured him. "As well as any girl raised by a father like mine."

With that reassurance, William allowed himself to be led away, steeling his nerves for whatever was about to come after he had been half-walked, half-dragged along the oppressive hallways to the kitchen. Here William's hands were wrenched up until the manacles were secured to a meat hook that hung from the ceiling, arms stretched so high that eventually the tips of his toes rested on the floor. Things were, William knew, about to get very, very bad. His muscles screamed, the wounds already inflicted smarting as his stomach ached, yet he found himself focusing on the fear that much worse was to follow.

"Strung up," Tessier commented in a pleasant voice as he followed into the room. "Like a British pig."

William kept his mouth shut and his gaze fixed on the wall, refusing to give Tessier anything.

"A deviant." He snapped the horse whip against his boot. "British pig."

Fuck you, William kept the words to himself, fear growing.

"What do you know the death of Yves Morel?"

William concentrated on breathing as Tessier spoke, taking reassurance from each breath, in and out, in and out. He could do this, he could see it out.

"Tell me your name?"

"Why?"

"So we can correctly record it for trial."

"You will never" — he felt a surge of anger at the arrogance, at what this man had done to Gaudet—"learn anything from me."

Tessier's hand shot out with the speed of a striking snake, the horsewhip slashing across William's chest twice in quick succession. He wasn't quite quick enough to bite back the gasp of pain, body jerking at the impact. There followed another slash with the whip as outside, a cry went up from the people in response to the shout from a newspaper barker that, "Citizen Robespierre is dead!"

"You," William managed to groan, "you'll be next."

"Jacquet! Jacquet!" Tessier bellowed, the whip striking again. "Fetch me the news of Paris."

"They'll do to you what you've done to so many," William gasped, certain the pain was worth it if his words proved true. "Justice. That is justice."

"If they *do*," Tessier closed his scarred fingers around William's chin, spitting the words into his face, "then mollies and traitors will follow me to my fate, and you will be first in the line."

"You don't frighten me." He met the icy fury of Tessier's

gaze. "Neither do your threats."

Tessier, usually so considered, so *proud* in his violence, let loose with a volley of strikes of the whip, his fist punctuating the blows. Faced with the onslaught, William could only screw his eyes shut, triumph and agony and the desperate hope that this might soon all be over mixing together as he struggled for breath.

This is where I will die.

The thought occurred to him as the door opened and the guard slipped into the kitchen, a sheet held in his hand. At Jacquet's return, Tessier snatched the paper from him, ceasing his assault to read the report of his friend's death. His gaze raked frantically over the page and he whispered, "My God."

"They want you back in Paris." Jacquet tapped his yellow fingernail to the page, eliciting a sound of pure disdain from his employer, whose colorless eyes then slid back to William.

"You've lost," William gasped out. "You will pay for everything you've done."

"Everything I have done" — Tessier grew calmer — "has been in the cause of righteousness, for the good of my nation. I will ride into Paris with the Star of Versailles in my hand and your body dragged behind my horse."

William actually laughed at that, opening his eyes to meet Tessier's gaze again. Once he started, he found he could not stop, the baffled fury on Tessier's face fueling his sudden mirth.

"You..." He tried and failed to gather himself as another wave of laughter engulfed him. "You — oh!"

"The girl is — " Sylvie burst into the kitchen, hair at right angles. "What on earth?"

At the sight of the Frenchwoman's hair, William laughed harder, tears streaming down his cheeks as he told her, "Oh, Madame, if only you knew."

"Out," Tessier bellowed at her.

"Run along," William spluttered. "Run along like a good

girl there!"

Sylvie seemed about to argue when she clearly thought better of it, turning and hurrying from the room, the door slamming pointedly behind her.

"You find this funny?" Tessier asked quietly.

"Yes," he told him truthfully. "Oh, God, yes, I do."

"Explain?"

"You've lost," he told the nonplussed Butcher of Orléans with a fresh wave of laughter. "You've lost and you don't even realize it."

It seemed to William, through the haze of pain and mirth, that Tessier's rage was so great as to paralyze him, the Frenchman simply staring through hate-filled eyes. He neither moved nor spoke for a long time, as though he had no idea how to cope with laughter, so used to screams was he.

"I would say that I am sorry," William finally managed, "but I'm not."

"After twelve hours on the meathook" — Tessier slashed the whip across William's stomach — "you will be."

"And you," William gasped sharply, "will still be lost."

"No, sir — I will rise higher than Robespierre and his puppets ever dreamed."

He laughed afresh at that, though he was fast running out of energy now, the agony starting to make itself felt in a way he could not ignore.

"And tomorrow, when the hours have weakened you to a babe, we will talk again." With that, he cast down the horsewhip and stalked from the room, Jacquet following after.

Left alone, William closed his eyes, amusement fading to worry and pain as, once more, he wondered what the night to come would bring.

Agony and the end, he knew, *but I will have known how to feel and that, that has to be worth something.*

I will not die having never lived.

As the hours passed, the world plunged into darkness,

even those barking the news outside the house growing silent eventually. Left suspended by his bound wrists, William lost track of the time, of the footsteps that passed the closed door now and again and even of the occasional sound of voices from floors above.

He heard a clock strike each hour, concentrating on the chimes in his fugue and counting ten, yet still there was no sign of life until the door opened and Harriet entered, her head bowed low. Her narrow wrists were no longer bound, though she was not alone, Jacquet following with a gun trained on her back. The girl glanced to William with eyes filled with concern, crossing to the dresser as Jacquet lit candles, his gaze barely leaving her.

"Visitors." William tried a smile for her sake. "Just what I was hoping for."

"I cannot dress hair," Harriet told him carefully, "so I am set to work being a maid to the *lady*."

"Don't talk to the likes of him, girl," Jacquet snapped. "He's the sort of man as kills youngsters like you – my own boy."

"I would offer to switch places with you." He ignored Jacquet, addressing Harriet again. "But I fear I have the marginally worse position here."

"Might we loosen his arms a little?" Harriet asked Jacquet appealingly. "Or at least place something beneath his feet so he is not so…pained."

"No, lass." Jacquet shook his head and she nodded, lower lip quivering until he said, "Citizen Tessier'd have my guts."

"Citizen Tessier has been recalled," William told them both. "His days are numbered. You should take care of your own guts."

"Monsieur Jacquet, will you go back to Paris?" Harriet looked to Jacquet and William detected a softening of the guard in her presence, perhaps reminded of his own lost child. "He will expect you to stay at his side – his belief in his cause is very strong."

William stayed silent, thinking not for the first time that the young woman was wise beyond her years.

"My own father is dead, Monsieur Jacquet, he was all I had in this world." Harriet's head dipped as she, apparently, battled with her emotions. William found himself admiring her ability, thinking her well-trained. "I am so sorry for your boy but please, can we not do something to make this man more comfortable?"

"Mademoiselle—"

"The hook seems none too secure in the ceiling," Harriet implored, wiping at her eyes, and William let his head fall again, doing his best to appear harmless. "Might it not just...*fall*? He is manacled, sir, he can do you no harm and nor would he, with me held here."

"This much and no more." Jacquet pushed a bundle of sacking under William's feet, just enough to relieve the pressure on his muscles. "Now gather the food and let's leave him to it."

The relief was instant and William shot a smile of gratitude to Harriet, wishing that the girl could stay with him, even though he knew it to be impossible.

"One more favor?" he asked Harriet as they turned for the door.

"What's that?" Jacquet's tone was suspicious, eyes narrowing.

He smiled at the guard before whispering to Harriet, "Before you give anything to Sylvie? Make sure you spit in it."

"Of course," she told him earnestly, turning to Jacquet again and asking, "If you were to fasten my hands again when the lady and gentleman are eating supper, might I come and sit in the kitchen later?"

"Not a chance." Jacquet shook his head.

She frowned, a deep sigh escaping her lips as she nodded.

The guard watched her then amended, "Maybe—we'll see."

The exchange gave William comfort on one level—Harriet,

however unhappy, was, at least, not being mistreated.

A moment later, he was in darkness again, the house silent once more. He closed his eyes wearily, pain sinking in now he was alone. William drifted, thoughts of Gaudet mingling with the less pleasant memories of the last few hours, the Frenchman's name a gasp on his lips when he jerked awake, only to drift again moments later.

William heard the door opening, though whether in a dream or reality he wasn't sure. Light footsteps were followed by heavier boots and he heard Jacquet say, "No going near him, no passing anything."

William opened his eyes to look at Harriet. Jacquet settled into a seat at the table with a bottle of beer. The girl seemed tired, he thought, worry and fortitude vying in her expression.

"I still cannot do hair." She eventually smiled, lifting herself to perch on the work surface so William did not have to move to see her.

"Then we have that in common," he managed. "Where's a playwright when you need him?"

"Hmph," Jacquet said to that, unfolding a newspaper and settling to read.

Harriet met William's gaze with a rather meaningful one of her own, then looked down at her manacled hands for a moment.

"Those hairpins, they get *everywhere*, horrible, sharp little things." Harriet sniffed. William watched her as she went on. "Everything is so *small* and fiddly. Hair grips, silly little tiny scissors—I am afraid Mademoiselle Dupire is not so impressed with my efforts as she might be."

"Nothing small about that diamond she's after" — the guard didn't look up as he spoke — "and when they've found that, it's back to Paris for you."

"And what about you?" William asked Jacquet.

"Me?" He glanced up at William. "I'm just a man doing his job for his country."

"That is probably what the man you all called *Dee* would

have said," Harriet reasoned innocently. "Yet, I doubt the defense would go very far were he to be put on trial here in France—a defense is only as good as the person who hears it."

"They'll have your head on a pike next to Tessier's," William told Jacquet firmly. "Don't say you weren't warned."

"I had never thought Robespierre would fall...one realizes how far things have gone already." Harriet shook her head. "After Danton, Desmoulins—Citizen Tessier's student circle is growing smaller by the day."

"Doesn't look good." William met her gaze. "Does it?"

"Not to me." She shrugged and Jacquet shook his head, going back to his paper.

Harriet contented herself with chatting with William about nothing in particular for some minutes and he wondered whether she had a plan or if she really was *that* relaxed despite the heavy manacles that held her hands.

Eventually, Jacquet finished the bottle of beer and yawned.

Seeing this, Harriet asked, "Can I get you another bottle?"

"*I* wouldn't say no," William replied before gathering himself enough to watch Jacquet.

"You don't have to wait on me," the guard told her, though his sincerity was undermined by the fact that he didn't lift his eyes from the paper he was reading, squinting through the candlelight.

Harriet hopped down from her perch and retrieved one of the bottles, humming to herself as she crossed the kitchen to where Jacquet was bent over the page. She glanced to William, a second in profile in which she was the very image of her father, then she lifted the bottle and slammed it with a sickening thud into Jacquet's unsuspecting skull.

My God.

William stared for a long moment, feeling a swell of respect for this deceptively strong girl. As Jacquet slumped over the table, Harriet set the bottle down. She brought her wrists to her mouth, teasing a long hair grip from inside her sleeve. Holding it between her teeth, she worked with a swiftness that he could scarcely countenance to pick the lock of the manacles. He found himself thinking with new respect of this girl's father, wondering at exactly *what* their adventures across Europe might have encompassed.

Free of her chains, she fastened Jacquet's hands behind his back and, tucking a sharp kitchen knife into that same sleeve, crossed to where William was chained to the hook.

"Papa always said one never knows," she mused, applying the grip to the keyhole of his manacles, "when one might need to pick a lock."

"I would have to say," William told her, as he found himself freed, arms so stiff he could barely lift them, "your papa is right again."

"There are at least five guards somewhere else in the house, as well as Tessier and that bloody woman." Harriet's eyes widened and she said, "You must not tell Papa that I said 'bloody'."

"I will not," he promised, hoping that he had enough strength left to make his rescue worthwhile. "Now let's get back to your father."

Chapter Thirty-One

In the hours that had passed, Gaudet had witnessed Dee's fury at William's self-sacrifice burn bright for some hours until, settled in a nondescript lodging house with Adam setting out the common sense facts of the matter, the professor finally began to calm. After all, Adam pointed out, the fall of Robespierre had suddenly weighted the scales firmly in their favor.

As the men laid out their plans, Gaudet stole from the house and hurried through the nighttime streets in search of the spy he now knew he adored, the pain of William's absence and the fear for the man and girl almost too much to bear. Reaching the building, he stared up at it with a frown, realizing now that he was no more able to breach its walls than if it were the Bastille itself.

But look what happened there.

With that in mind, he hurried down the lane at the end of the row of houses and picked out the back of the house, where a guard waited. For a moment, he watched then set off into the shadows, trying in vain to see if there was any way he might gain access by another route, but all appeared impossible.

All the time, Gaudet studied the buildings, circling them and peering up into the darkness. He felt the sense of dread increasing, each lost moment another in which William was in Tessier's scarred hands. Suddenly, he wondered whether his father had been right in decrying him as a wastrel, sure now that he had not really mastered the correct skills to perform an operation such as this.

Hardly a task for a playwright.

Then today I shall be something more.

"So what's the plan?" He jolted at the sound of the child's voice and glanced back to see Bastien rounding the corner. "I've come to save my girl. Want me to get you in?"

"In there?" Gaudet could hardly believe that Bastien would ask such a thing. "Go back to the others, Bastien, this is no place for you."

"I got something for you," he whispered, his eyes wide. He drew a pistol from his pocket and handed it reverentially to Gaudet. "You might need it."

Gaudet's stomach lurched, yet he took the weapon from the boy, weighing it in his hand until he said, "I have nowhere to put it—you keep it."

"I've already got one." The child grinned, holding up another firearm as Gaudet slipped the pistol into his coat.

There was slightly too much enthusiasm in Bastien's face when he retrieved his own pistol. Gaudet gave him a brave smile. Then, taking a deep breath, he walked along the alley until he could see the house in which the pair were being held.

"Wish me luck," Gaudet said to nobody in particular, reaching up to take hold of the window ledge and lever himself nimbly up.

Using the ivy as a handhold, and with some effort, he scaled the facade of the house, hardly daring to look down or even think about exactly what he was doing. No candles burned behind the glass and, as he reached the upper floor, Gaudet glanced at Bastien and instructed, "Shoot!"

Bastien didn't need telling twice and, as he pulled the trigger, Gaudet punched through the window, shattering the glass with a sharp gasp of pain. After a moment to ensure there was nobody in the room, he climbed through the broken window to find himself in a richly furnished bedchamber, still filled with the possessions of the unfortunates who'd once called this place home. He hardly dared to breathe, but trod on tiptoe across the floorboards toward the door, pausing to listen for any sign of life. When

Gaudet heard nothing, he moved through the three upper rooms as silently as he was able, until a deep mattress tempted him and Gaudet sank down to catch his nerves, dropping his head into his hands.

As soon as his thoughts turned to William and Harriet, Gaudet was on his feet again, listening at the door before slipping from the room. He might have thought the house deserted were it not for the sudden sound of a voice from downstairs.

Gaudet pressed his back to the wall, creeping along as he tried to work out whether he could recognize the voice, hardly daring to hope. A moment later he was sure it was William. His heart leaped at the sound of his lover's hushed tones, followed by a feminine voice that sounded just a touch exasperated.

Reminding himself *not* to shriek with the thrill of finding them alive, Gaudet hurried downstairs to the darkened hallway where the pair could be found. At the sight of William's injuries, he gave a mute gasp of horror, barely worrying what Harriet might think as he threw his arms around the Englishman.

"I shall return within the hour," Tessier's voice split the silence from upstairs. "Admit no one."

"*Chérie,*" Gaudet began, still holding him close.

"Shhh!" Harriet pressed a finger to her lips and drew them back along the hallway.

The seconds, as Tessier descended the stairs with two of his men, seemed like hours. Gaudet was sure he would hear their pounding hearts over the marching boots. The figures paused at the foot of the stairs before Tessier opened the front door and, with the guards flanking him, left the house.

"I could kill him," William murmured. "I could kill him with my own bare hands."

"*Not* today," Gaudet told him, taking Harriet and William's hands in each of his own. "Now let us get the lady home to her papa and you, *chérie,* home to bed."

"How much does Dee want to kill me?" William gasped

as they made their way toward the door. "Just so I know."

"He will probably want to take you to bed when you walk in with his daughter on your arm," Gaudent decided warmly. "I think, perhaps, the front door is guarded. And the back."

"Then how do we get out?"

"One guard." Gaudet released their hands suddenly and drew his pistol. "Versus one French playwright. We leave through the front door, *chérie*."

"Don't you dare get yourself killed," William instructed. "Do you hear me?"

"Me?" Gaudet asked playfully at the front door, sure that nobody could tell how terrified he was.

A moment later, he dragged the door open, though he could feel William's tension behind him, heard him mutter something comforting to the girl, something she would probably be a fool to believe.

Before the guard had even registered what was happening, Gaudet had the gun pointed at him, yet the playwright knew even then that he could not possibly *shoot* another human being. The soldier likely had no such reservations and Gaudet landed his own pistol hard on the man's head. In fiction, they always fainted, but this man did no such thing, instead swearing rather loudly until, on the third such hit, he finally crumpled to his knees.

Suddenly there came a shriek from Harriet and Sylvie barked, "Nice try, *Monsieur*!"

She had a tight hold of the girl's plait in one hand, the other clutching a sharp dagger with a lethal point.

Harriet froze at the sight of it, urging the men, "*Go.*"

"Go," William repeated to Gaudet, before, in the next moment, he lunged toward the armed woman, the force as he fell into her enough to knock her to the floor.

Harriet went with her, twisting in Sylvie's grip to land a startlingly firm punch on her jaw. She scrambled to her feet and grabbed William's hand, dragging him to the door, where Gaudet hit the now-stirring guard once more for good measure. The three of them hurtled out into the street, Gaudet catching their hands again to pull them along with him as he called, "Don't collapse yet, Guillaume."

"Collapse," came the indignant response. "Englishmen do not *collapse*, sir."

"Nor do they shout about being 'Englishmen' in places loyal to the new regime," Gaudet told them, not entirely sure where they were going even as they ran.

"Gaudet." William seemed to have read his thoughts. "Where are we going?"

Gaudet froze as Tessier's black carriage glided out of a side street and stopped right in front of them. He would not, he decided, get caught now, even if he had to rip Tessier's head off with his own, very delicate hands.

"Back," William hissed. "Quickly!"

The black-shrouded driver of the coach turned in the moonlight to peer at them for a long moment, then he lowered the scarf that covered the lower half of his face. Gaudet's mouth fell open at the sight of Dee's best friend sitting, somehow, at the head of Vincent Tessier's carriage, and Adam laughed. "You three look a sight for sore eyes — climb in."

It was less a matter of climbing and more one of being dragged, in William's case, but the trio were finally ensconced, the door shut and the carriage rolled on its way.

Gaudet fussed around both William and Harriet, encouraging both to settle back into the squabs, the carriage surprisingly luxurious for a citizen who claimed to favor austerity. He hardly knew *what* he could do to help, all too aware of the blood that stained William's tattered shirt, the bruises on his face and deep cut on his forehead. He eventually reached into his pocket and found the blue scarf the milkmaids had given him, pressing it tenderly to the wound on William's skull as he took Harriet's fingers in his other hand. "Monsieur Guillaume was your hero today, Mademoiselle!"

"No," came the weak denial from the man in question.

273

"Not at all."

"He was," Harriet cut in. "He was very brave."

"Gaudet saved you—saved us."

"And I almost lost my plait."

William mumbled something which sounded like, "Bloody woman," before slumping in his seat.

Gaudet slipped his arm around William, drawing him close as he whispered, "You're safe, *chérie*."

"I thought I was going to die," came the slurred reply. "I laughed at him. Couldn't stop laughing."

"Because he is a *ridiculous* creature," Gaudet declared, every limb shaking. "And, Mademoiselle, your father is on the mend already. He has missed you dreadfully."

"I'm sorry I told you he was dead, I had to." William was rambling now.

"He is not the sort of man to die," Harriet whispered, snuggling against Gaudet, too. "He is far too reliable for that."

"You must tell him I am sorry."

"Hush, both." Gaudet reached into his coat to pass the brandy flask first to Harriet, who took a deep sip, then to William, holding it to his lips. As he drank, his eyes slipped shut, a shiver running through him.

With one arm around each of those he had thought lost, Gaudet finally let himself begin to relax, sure that *nobody* would intercept the carriage of Vincent Tessier. Eventually, they rolled to a stop in a quiet lane and Adam pulled the door open. He peered in and said, "We can't be seen arriving by carriage...up to the end of the alley, first right, fourth door on the left and Dee'll be waiting for you. I'll dump this then see you in a bit."

"Not long to go," Gaudet promised William, taking his weight as they began to walk.

Harriet produced the lethal-looking knife from her sleeve once more as she went.

He felt a sudden, overwhelming rush of emotion, taking a deep breath. "My sister is so close, just an hour or so away.

You will meet what is left of my family and we will *all* be safely home in England soon."

There was a hint of a laugh at that, and a murmur of 'home' before William tightened his hold on Gaudet's arm. Harriet left them behind, already hurrying ahead to find her father.

They were barely into the house, however, when Bastien and Dee, leaning on a walking stick, emerged from a closed door. He seemed as though he had not slept in weeks, yet at the sight of his returned daughter, the look of fatigue visibly lifted. Harriet threw herself into his arms, Bastien letting out a cheer. Gaudet, however, took care with the delicate man on his own arm, telling him, "Into bed and let our Dee have a look at you."

"I'm fine." The very words proved too much and, no doubt much to the Englishman's chagrin, William slumped against him.

"I shall settle my swooning damsel," Gaudet told the others even as his heart blanched with concern, hefting William over his shoulder like a sack of potatoes. As Dee promised to be with them shortly, he carried William through the house, wondering suddenly what he would do if this was worse than he thought, if he lost this most precious man so soon.

The room he found contained a bed, simple but clean, and as he settled William upon it he murmured, eyelids flickering.

"You will be all right." Gaudet pressed a fierce kiss to William's hair. "I swear it."

William's lips lifted in a small smile of delirious response, followed by a pained gasp of Gaudet's name.

"Boots off, no boots on the bed," Gaudet chided good-humoredly, slipping William's boots off. "Can you slip your jacket and shirt off, *chérie*, and we shall clean you up."

"Do I look a mess?" William tried his best, getting the jacket off with effort.

"You look like the ruffian you are." Gaudet helped him

with utmost care. "And still lovely."

"I couldn't stop thinking...about you..."

"Well, naturally." He kissed William's hair again, gently helping him with his shirt. At the slashes and bruises left by the horsewhip, Gaudet's stomach lurched and he whispered, "Oh, *chérie*."

"It's not as bad as it looks..." When William spoke, Gaudet knew that he should go and summon the professor. For now, he could not bring himself to leave his lover alone, stroking one hand through William's hair whilst the Englishman murmured, "I'm glad that you are here."

"I have been so worried..." As Gaudet spoke, William lifted one hand to his cheek. At the touch his eyes flickered shut for a moment and he whispered, "I thought I would lose you."

"You won't get rid of me." There was almost a smile in the words. "Not that easily."

"When we are home, you are not leaving my sight, sir. Besides, I have the most *enormous* – " Gaudet dropped his voice to a whisper, eyes wide when he finished the sentence, "bed."

A flicker of something other than exhaustion and pain crossed William's face at the unspoken promise and the hand that trembled on Gaudet's cheek slipped up into Gaudet's hair. He pressed a gentle kiss to his lover's lips, the worry and fear and love he felt all mingling as the hours just passed finally washed over him.

"*Chérie*..." Gaudet whispered, hardly noticing the door open nor the figure of Dee stepping into the room, a heavy medical case under one arm.

William broke the kiss, voice barely a whisper when he murmured, "It hurts..."

"Well," Dee commented, as though nothing was unusual at all in this new departure, "it *will*."

If he minded in the slightest, William gave no sign, still clutching at Gaudet even when he sank back into the pillows with a weary sigh.

"You must be gentle with him, sir," Gaudet told Dee, gaze still on William. "And lovely though he is, he's mine."

"It's all right," William murmured, eyes closed, "he's too Irish."

"Are you Irish?" Gaudet was genuinely stunned. "Your French is flawless. What about the roguish one with the twinkle? Is *he* Irish? Do you wield a *shillelagh*? *Chérie*," he gasped with the very thought, "are *you* Irish, Guillaume?"

"No." The Englishman's eyes snapped open at that suggestion. "No, I most certainly am *not*."

"This poor chap is English," Dee lamented, resting his stick against the wall. "Well, *Guillaume*, Gaudet, I should be furious. Instead, I wish I could pin a bloody medal on the pair of you."

"She is a wonder with a hair pin," William remembered.

"And a beer bottle, from what she tells me." Dee sat on the edge of the bed, bringing the candle closer as he examined the wounds left by the whip.

"You have taught her well."

"She is a fine young lady," Dee agreed with obvious pride. "I think you will live. I shall clean the wounds, dress them and then I recommend some bed rest. *Rest* being the operative word," Dee told Gaudet. "As in, *actual* rest, Gaudet, no bouncing off the walls for your friend just yet."

"And afterwards?" William's voice was sharp and Gaudet took his hand. "Am I still to be relegated to less *challenging* work?"

"Afterwards," Gaudet cut in before Dee could, glancing to the door as Pap bounded in and hopped onto the bed, "you shall not be doing *any* work, for we shall be enjoying life for a while."

"That sounds…" William didn't get any further, words trailing off in a yawn as his eyes slipped shut again.

Gaudet watched Dee work in well-behaved silence, glad for Papillon's presence when she snuggled into his lap, tail wagging softly. Finally, the professor declared that William would mend soon enough and, setting a bottle of claret on the nightstand, took his leave. After settling Pap on the covers, Gaudet slipped off his own boots and coat and lay beside William, drawing the blanket over them as he kissed his lover's hair.

"Sleep," he whispered, holding William in a careful embrace. "I will be here."

Chapter Thirty-Two

With a good few nights' rest and the benefit of Dee's healing salves, William felt sore but distinctly more alive than he had in days when the carriage arrived in Le Havre. Sitting as close as he could get without being in William's lap, Gaudet was a bundle of nervous energy, his excitement writ large as the carriage rolled on, the sight of ships at the dock marking the closing days of their journey.

"I have not seen Claudine in many years," Gaudet whispered, peering from the window at the dingy buildings with a frown. "And have never *ever* seen the little man. I have written, sent stories, drawings, but this is a world away from Versailles."

"What is she like?" William asked, curious to know more of the woman who so occupied Gaudet's thoughts.

"She is *beautiful*, the most beautiful woman who ever was at court—wonderful hair." He shook his head. "And quiet and intelligent and I wish she would laugh more."

"You will make her laugh." William was certain of that. "And the child, too."

"Well, Monsieur Roucelle awaits," Dee announced. He and his daughter exchanged a few words then he gestured to the small house before which they had stopped. It was tiny, unremarkable and best of all, easy to miss. "Go and find your sister, Monsieur."

With the carriage door opened, William hung back, certain that Gaudet would want to enjoy his reunion in private, yet it seemed that he had no such plans. With Pap safe beneath his arm, he knocked at the weathered wooden door and urged, "Come, *chérie*."

William climbed down to join Gaudet, standing close beside him, hands knitted behind his back. They did not have long to ponder, as the door opened to reveal a man who, William's first impression noted, had a head as round as his belly, as stout as he was short in stature.

"Roucelle?" Gaudet asked and William noted that the man peered around him, seeming to recognize Dee. "I believe you have a guest who is awaiting her brother?"

"I have a lady who has just about given up on the lot of you." Roucelle stepped back to let them enter. "There's been not a smile nor a snicker in this house for longer than I can recall."

Gaudet slipped into the house, William following as they made their way along a narrow hallway and into a tiny sitting room. There, a woman as large as Roucelle was knitting in a threadbare armchair, though she barely glanced up at the new arrivals. What struck William as utterly, almost comically, incongruous was the presence of another woman, who sat straight-backed in a rocking chair with a little boy perched in her lap, a book held in his small hands. Dressed all in black with a silver crucifix shining at her throat, she did not lift her gaze to them, her dark hair scraped into an unruly bun that seemed at odds with the soft beauty of her pale face.

The child, no more than three, was dressed as simply as his mother in shirt and breeches, bare feet kicking happily as he pointed to something in the book. She peered closer, smiling before she kissed his hair very gently. Only then did her gaze shift to look over the new arrivals, her hand flying to her mouth before she gasped, "André!"

William stepped back at the word, certain in that moment that Gaudet's sister would not welcome any intrusion into this moment of reunion.

"It's Uncle André," she told the little boy, who peered at them with sparkling eyes.

William was so used to referring to the playwright as Gaudet that the name sounded strange, as if it belonged to someone other than the man who stepped forward to greet them. He closed his eyes briefly, wondering what it might be like to be so cared for, to be so welcomed.

And now, of course, now I have Gaudet, I know what it is to be cared for.

To be loved, perhaps?

The little boy flew across the floor and leaped into the playwright's arms as Gaudet declared, "And *this* is my wonderful friend, Guillaume, to whom I owe my very life. He is an honorary member of our family."

"Oh," William interjected. "No, I've not, I just—"

Claudine rose from her seat and greeted him with a polite nod, her eyes glittering. "I had thought—oh, sir, where have you all *been*?"

"Your brother got here as quickly as he could, Madame." William bristled just slightly at the tone. "At much peril to his person."

"My brother is an oaf," Claudine replied without any conviction and a moment later she flung her arms around Gaudet, leaving William somewhat taken aback when François scrambled from his uncle's embrace and held up his arms to William.

When he didn't immediately respond, the little boy asked in a manner so imperious that he must have learned it from his poised mother, "Cuddle?"

He approached the child with the utmost care, gingerly bending as best he could to be in reach of the small arms that demanded attention.

"Guillaume," the child tried the name out. "Uncle?"

"Oh, no," William told the infant quickly.

"Quite so," Gaudet cut in. "This is Uncle Guillaume, my best friend of all my many friends, and this is your cousin Papillon." He raised one of Pap's paws and waved it. "My little girl."

At least he had not said our *little girl*, William thought as he smiled for the boy, trying to avoid the gaze of Gaudet's formidable sister.

"Well." Gaudet reached across to take William's hand and whisper, "she is *ours*, really."

William's eyes widened even as he patted Gaudet's hand reassuringly, wondering what on earth this suddenly adopted family would make of him now.

What would everybody *think?*

Claudine's gaze did not falter. She took in the sight, then she released her hold on Gaudet, clapped once and said to William, "What is—?" The words were stilled however, her gaze moving to the opening door to widen at the sight of Dee and Harriet's appearance, eyes flickering back to William when she asked, "You have come for the Star of Versailles?"

"We have indeed, Madame," William informed her. "And to bring you to safety."

"We have come," Dee corrected carefully, William wondering exactly *what* the meaningful look he and the woman exchanged might mean, "For the *diamond*. The Prince of Wales awaits his trinket."

"And you will see us safe to England?" Claudine asked as François began patting at William's cheek, saying *something* about rouge.

"We will," William assured her, watching the woman. "You have my word on that."

"Although I do wonder…" Dee frowned, chewing his lip before he asked the householders, "Sir, Madame, might I have ten minutes with the party?"

"Come on." Roucelle heaved himself to his feet, gesturing for his wife to do the same.

With a glance back at the assembled group, they left the room, William telling the child he held, "No, no rouge. I do not do rouge."

Leaving Harriet to steer Bastien from the room after the couple, Claudine gathered her son back into her arms, where he immediately began telling her of the rougeless new uncle. Smiling rather brightly at the child's chatter for just a moment, Dee ushered them all to sit, his face taking on the very grave look that William never liked to see.

Trouble is coming.

As they sat he found himself overwhelmed by the sudden, and only just suppressed, urge to take Gaudet's hand, instead folding his hands in his lap to relieve the temptation when he asked, "What terrible matter are we to discuss now?"

"I think that the time has come for honesty," Dee told them.

God — not this, not such public revelations. It doesn't matter who I bed, surely, who I care for — will Dee really tell the world of our liaison?

Why?

William recalled Dee's presence while Gaudet had comforted him, the indiscretion seemingly so trivial at the time now momentous in the cold light of day. Whatever Dee was about to announce to the assembled group he would not apologize for, he decided. If he never worked again, faced public shame, faced a life in hiding, then he would gladly do it for Alexandre Gaudet. The same went for whatever he stood to lose from not profiting from the diamond they had come to collect. Being with this French dandy, rouge and all, meant more than any money.

"The Prince of Wales is…well, to be polite, a boor." Dee knitted his fingers in his lap, looking for all the world as though he was in the finest club on the Strand and not a dingy sitting room barely large enough to contain his height. "I propose that the diamond is officially *lost*. The *Star*, however, must be protected at all costs."

"So…" It took William a long moment to process this unexpected and relief-inducing development, the realization that his sex life was not the topic under debate. "We have to keep the diamond safe but pretend to the Prince it is missing?"

"I have a buyer for the diamond, a gent of the east, and propose a split of the spoils between us in Madame Plamondon's favor, of course." Dee met Claudine's gaze with a polite nod of acknowledgement. "There is something more, however."

"The diamond is grand enough, but it is not the Star of Versailles," Dee went on, Claudine giving an imperceptible nod of her head in consent. "When the royal family fled to Varennes they left a precious treasure with Madame Plamondon and her husband, entrusting it to her keeping along with the diamond that is so sought after…"

"This child, my beloved boy, was given to me as a newborn by her late Majesty, and it broke her heart to say goodbye to him, to have the world know nothing of his birth," Claudine took up the tale. "When this *regime* collapses, he will be rightly called by his proper title as our sovereign King Louis XVIII, chosen by God."

It took a moment, a rather long one, for William to process that, to realize that the small child who had so imperiously patted his cheek and waffled about rouge was in fact the rightful dauphin of France. "Bloody hell!"

"He was born premature," Dee went on, as Claudine drew the child into a loving embrace. "The flight to Varennes could not be postponed any longer and the intention was to follow the family when the little one was stronger. It was not to be."

"And what happens now?" William asked, thoughts flying. "He grows up an English boy and no one is any the wiser?"

"Your king has promised us protection," Claudine explained, the boy reaching to clamber into Gaudet's arms, where he was happily received by the playwright, who, William noticed, had shed one or two fresh tears. "François will be raised there in safety until the time comes when he might be restored, for they say Louis-Charles is wasting away in his prison. Until that day, his uncle" — her lips twitched distastefully — "*Louis Stanislas*, God help us, will serve as Regent. Perhaps it might even convince his wife to brush her hair in celebration."

She is very much a Gaudet, after all, despite the black and bun.

"His existence must be revealed to no one outside this room. There are plenty of people who have reason to want this little boy to *vanish*, and not only those who cry revolution," Dee told them. "As far as we are *all* concerned, the Star of Versailles, as the prince calls his diamond, never made it as far as Le Havre—it was lost when Tessier stormed the Plamondon home. Agreed?"

William knew that it was not something to agree to lightly, the whole matter one that he found disturbing for a number of reasons he couldn't quite place.

"I have no need of money." Gaudet waved a hand, seemingly far *less* troubled as he told Dee, "I shall find some foundlings in need of it instead."

"I do not want the money," William decided, getting to his feet. "And you give me no choice but to keep your secret." With that he bowed politely to Claudine before making his way to the door and through it, thoughts racing.

"What's going on?" Bastien leaped to his feet from where he sat outside the room, crunching another apple. "What's the news?"

"No news." William shook his head, certain that what he needed was air. "No news at all."

The door opened again and Gaudet made his tentative way into the hallway to ask, "Are you terribly angry, *chérie*?"

"Angry?" William frowned, certain that was the one emotion he was not feeling. "No, not angry."

"Bastien," Harriet whispered, beckoning the boy along the hallway and out of sight as Gaudet peered at William, reaching for his hand.

"That child"—he accepted the touch gratefully—"knowing who he is—that's a big responsibility."

"Not," Gaudet told him softly, "when it is shared."

"I am not used to that," William heard himself say. "Sharing."

He thought again of the gambling debt he had enforced, the young man who had taken his own life rather than choose shame and ruin, then he shook his head, sure he would never be a man who shared anything.

"But when one is in love, one shares everything," Gaudet whispered tenderly. "And I love you, so what I have is yours, too."

The words made William freeze, his grip on Gaudet's hand tightening as he wondered how he had reached this, the urge to tell Gaudet that he was mistaken almost overwhelming. "You can't—"

"You do not have to love me in return." Gaudet shrugged with affected casualness. "But I love you, nonetheless."

"How can you be so sure?"

"Because I feel frightened and blessed and as though I am *not* on the run for my life, but somewhere near Heaven." He raised his free hand to William's cheek. "And you are my every thought."

"I don't deserve this." William reached to cover Gaudet's hand with his own. "I've never met anyone like you."

"Well, naturally," Gaudet told him and William had to laugh, his gaze locking with Gaudet's as the laughter faded, leaving them inches apart. "I thought I had lost you in Harfleur."

"I'm here," he murmured in reply, still not quite able to believe it. "And I'm not going anywhere, though I don't think that your sister likes me."

"She doesn't like anybody." Gaudet stole a lingering kiss. "Do you like me a little? Or a little bit more than a little?"

"A lot more"—he found his hand in Gaudet's hair—"than a little."

"When you have seen my bed and my room *full* of clothes, you will want no other," Gaudet teased. "And wait until I show you my collection of shoes, and I haven't even *mentioned* my boots. Then there are my rings, though I have already given you a diamond."

"I haven't given you anything," he realized.

"Your handkerchief…"

"That is true." He kissed Gaudet again.

"I am so glad to have found you," Gaudet told William and he nodded, somewhat forgetting where they were as he kissed Gaudet deeply. "And just *wait* until I get you alone."

"Is that a promise?"

"I thought I might start by kissing every *gorgeous* inch of you," he said conversationally, brushing his hand through William's hair. "Then we'll see where we go from there."

William found himself unable to reply. Instead he concentrated on kissing Gaudet hungrily, several ideas for future liaisons already in his mind.

"Could we tell them," Gaudet asked as they broke for air, "that the patient needs to be in bed?"

"I think," William responded gravely, "that I *am* feeling somewhat lightheaded."

With Gaudet's most charming manner deployed in the direction of Madame Roucelle, they were soon upstairs to a room so tiny it was barely the size of Gaudet's fabled shoe cupboard. It was filled with a bed that had probably, like much of the furniture in the house, been *liberated* from a grander abode and, as the door closed, Gaudet said, "They should forget the house and move into the bed, it's bigger."

William was sure he had murmured an agreement, holding Gaudet close again for a long, deep kiss.

"I love you, *chérie*, so much..."

"And I love you," William whispered in turn, feeling his ears flush. "I want you."

"I am yours," Gaudet promised, meeting his gaze. "And only yours."

Ignoring the pain of his healing wounds, William urged Gaudet onto the bed, mouth hungry on his. As Gaudet slid his hands over William's back he let himself forget where they were, safe in the knowledge that they had each other.

"What do you want?" Gaudet asked gently.

"Make love to me."

The words brought William up short, gaze holding Gaudet's before he murmured, "It would be an honor."

Gaudet gave a soft sound of contentment, slipping his

palms beneath William's shirt, then the world seemed to stop delightfully once more, long moments lost to kisses as they undressed each other.

"I am no longer pale," Gaudet realized breathlessly. "What *will* people think?"

"That you are utterly glorious," William decided, ducking to let his lips caress across Gaudet's chest.

"I shall have to cover myself in powder." Gaudet lost the thought in a sigh, combing his hand through William's hair.

"I'll help," he promised, heart quickening in response to Gaudet's whispered words of love and he realized, with something close to contentment, that he would have to get used to compliments now. He would probably, William reasoned, have to get used to Gaudet's very enthusiastic ministrations, too, not to mention the Frenchman's talent for removing his clothes with him barely even noticing he had done so until Gaudet was touching his bare skin.

"It's funny." William sighed. "You've quite taken my mind off the pain."

"And you have taken my mind off fashion — so it *must* be love."

Chapter Thirty-Three

"Let's see it then," Roucelle said, sitting in what looked like a dangerously insubstantial chair for his bulk as thunder raged overhead.

With a glance toward François, who slept on the rug before the fire, Claudine stepped toward the table and loosened the ties on a small velvet bag. She tipped it up gently and, as one, every eye in the room seemed to focus on the single, flawless diamond that tumbled onto the table, Bastien muttering a most unchildlike oath at the sight.

Roucelle darted out his plump fingers and seized the gem. He cupped it in his hand as he pressed a jeweler's glass to his eye. Squinting, he turned the diamond this way and that, occasionally muttering something unintelligible or tapping it here and there with a yellowing fingernail.

"Fit for a queen, indeed. I never thought I'd see it." Roucelle shook his head, letting the glass tumble from his eye to the tablecloth. "Professor, you were *not* wrong."

"Well" — Dee held out his hand and Roucelle placed the diamond there — "I get it right on occasion."

"The diamond," Claudine explained, "is as priceless as they say, but it meant nothing to the queen, nothing at all."

"While the gentlemen were resting, I made contact with Captain Pascaud," Dee commented innocently. "The first dawn after the storms break, we sail for England."

Bastien's gaze moved over to the chair where François slumbered, wondering what life must be like to be a child like that, one with *such* a family to call one's own. Bastien tightened the tricolor flag that he wore as a sash and whispered to Adam, "I'll be back in a bit, boss."

"You don't go far," Adam replied, scrubbing the boy's hair affectionately.

Bastien pushed the door open and darted out into the rain, his pace slowing to a walk when he made his way through the streets, head bowed. He barely noticed the woman who emerged from the tavern opposite to walk alongside him. He was lost in his thoughts until he heard Sylvie's voice say, "Hello, son."

With wide eyes, he turned, tears clouding his vision. She lowered the scarf that covered her face, and he whispered, "Ma?"

"Bastien." She stooped to embrace him before she drew him into a side street. "You didn't think your old ma would leave you to it?"

He shook his head, overwhelmed at the sight of her, by the fate he had imagined befalling his mother at the hands of Tessier, and yet here she was, unharmed and vibrant as ever.

"He doesn't know I'm out," Sylvie whispered, searching his face. She seemed to read his very mind. "He'd kill me if he did."

At that, Bastien shook his head, clinging to her skirt as he whispered, "We can go now, Ma — go and tell the others and —" It seemed so obvious to him that he could hardly understand why they were still standing there. He took her hand, tugging it helplessly. "They'll help you, Adam and the professor."

Sylvie shook her head, gaze darting around. "You think they'd let me go free when we got to England? No, boy, you've got to help me."

"What?"

She kneeled before him and whispered, "I need that diamond." Sylvie was obviously ready for his shocked response and she silenced his blustered complaints, saying, "No, no, listen. They don't need it, do they? All they want is to get to England, so why not?"

"No." He shook his head. "I won't take —"

"If I haven't got that diamond by the time they leave, I'm dead." Sylvie's eyes were fixed on him, unblinking, and he thought then that she would *never* betray him, this mother who had been through so much. "Bring it to me and we can go back to Paris. He don't care about nothing but the Star. You've got to get it for me."

"I'm going to tell them, get Dee's help," Bastien declared, sure that someone would know how to solve this awful problem, that they could somehow save his mother. "He's nobody to fear anymore, is he?"

At that, Sylvie drew back, her face slackening. "You don't know him," she said fretfully. "Fetch it for me, please."

Bastien nodded earnestly and threw his arms around her neck, holding her closer than he had in years.

"I love you," he whispered in a small voice, hearing her return the sentiment. "And I'll get it."

"Good lad." Sylvie smiled. "Now go on, I don't know how long he'll be out. You can find me in the rooms behind Bertrand's butcher. Bring it my way tonight and then we'll take the bloody thing and be gone *together*."

Bastien simply gazed at his mother, heart wrenched as he found himself rooted to the spot. She wouldn't leave him, he told himself, yet not so long ago, hadn't she done just that? He remembered the pain of waiting in the pig field for the mother who never came, eyes full of bitter tears, his heart torn in two.

Not again, she wouldn't.

And what would Adam think?

But if my ma's life depends on it…

"I'll do it."

"Good lad." Another kiss and she whispered, "Now go."

Bastien returned to Roucelle's house at a far slower pace than he had departed from it, watching the ground sadly where the thick mud slurped and pulled at his boots. The sun was setting by the time he pulled open the door, his shoulders sloping when he dropped into a seat at the table and stared at Roucelle's sleeping face.

"Bastien," Gaudet called in welcome as he hurried downstairs, greeting the boy with a smile. "Where have you been?"

"Thinking about Ma," he muttered, wanting to tell the man who had shown him such kindness exactly what had happened, what she had asked of him.

I owe you all so much, he knew, *but she's my mum.*

What the bloody hell would you *do?*

"If I come to England, what's going to happen to me?" Bastien already knew the answer to the question, of course, but he wanted somebody to make the decision for him, to say the right thing.

"Monsieur Adam has given you the key to his home. You are practically brothers," Gaudet told him kindly, no doubt about that, and when he spoke again, it was with humor. "And if you fancied something more exciting, there is my own house. Whatever you wished, you would have a family to call your own."

Bastien nodded, feeling his lower lip tremble for a horrible moment before Gaudet saved his embarrassment and asked, "Supper?"

For some reason that was the thing that pushed Bastien over the edge, tears suddenly coursing from his eyes. He could hardly speak, deep shudders running through his thin body and he sobbed, "My ma—"

"What is it?" Gaudet put his hand on his shoulder and Bastien bolted forward, resting his face against the playwright's shoulder just in time for Dee and William to emerge from the kitchen. "Bastien, tell me all."

It all came out then. Bastien finally told them what had happened, how his mother had reappeared and appealed to him to steal the diamond. As he talked, Gaudet, Dee and William said nothing but simply listened, occasionally nodding, but no more than that. He gabbled until he had nothing left to say, collapsing back into his chair.

"Well," Gaudet mused, folding his arms over his chest and glancing over at Dee. "We can't have this."

"Give her something else." William shrugged. "Tessier's never seen it and she won't know either. I'm sure *you*," he gave Gaudet an indulgent look, "have something suitably flamboyant to hand."

"But what about Ma?" Bastien looked from one to the other, searching for any hint of optimism. "If he catches on, he'll kill her."

"We'll kidnap her," was Dee's response, as though it was the obvious option. "Leave her with no choice but to join her boy in England."

"Don't worry, Bastien," William decided and Gaudet agreed with a nod. "Your mother will come to no harm as long as she stays with us. There is safety in numbers, after all."

Chapter Thirty-Four

Trusting little lamb.
Just like his dad.

Sylvie had no doubt, as she waited, that the boy would come — where else could he go, after all? One thing she was utterly certain of in life, along with the selfishness of men and the fact that anyone would do anything if the price was right, was Bastien's loyalty. *He had better hurry*, Sylvie thought. *Vincent never stays out for long.*

Her mind roamed and she thought again of the diamond, what it would mean when she finally had it in her grasp. She could almost feel it, imagining the weight and sparkle of the all too elusive jewel that would, at last, be hers.

There came a soft knock at the door, the rhythm familiar from the boy's scouting missions in Paris, and Sylvie hurried to admit her son. He looked haunted, as though he had not slept.

He'll be all right, she told herself. *Time to make his own way.*

"I got it," Bastien exclaimed as he crossed the threshold, panting for breath.

"Show me," she demanded. "Show it to me now."

The boy proudly held out the velvet pouch. She snatched it from him, heart hammering, hands shaking. Sylvie tugged at the ties of the bag, the diamond heavy on her palm a moment later. She found herself almost speechless, certain that her life was about to change beyond her most extravagant dreams.

"Now get your gear and let's *go*." Bastien reached to take her hand. "Come on, Ma."

"About that." She held up a finger to pause him, the final

part of her plan yet to be put into action.

In response, he frowned, asking in a suspicious tone, "Yeah?"

"You're not coming," Sylvie told Bastien, caressing the diamond with the pad of her thumb before slipping it back into the pouch.

Bastien's face fell, eyes widening as he reached for her again with a small hand and whispered, "You what?"

"That lot, they've taken you in — you'll get on much better in life if you stay with them now. They won't see you want for nothing, especially if you're alone."

"But…" His hand followed her own even as she shifted it away from his reach. "You're my ma…"

"And you're better off without me." Sylvie pocketed the diamond, wondering why he couldn't see the sense in it. "You'll thank me for this one day, just you see."

"You're my *mother*," Bastien shouted, voice cracking. "You can't just say 'live with them' and run off with a bloody diamond."

"Well I *have* said it." Sylvie's voice rose and she saw the look of dumbfounded horror on his face. "Now you bloody well do as you're told this one time, you hear?"

"They said you was bloody rotten — I bet you sold Thierry out, too." He reached for the jewel, Sylvie lifting it high over her head, far out of his reach. "You bloody old cow."

"Don't you dare." Sylvie's anger flared and she darted out her hand, slapping him across the cheek, the sound loud and sharp.

"Cow!" Bastien bellowed again, tears flowing down his face.

She raised her hand once more, sure that he should have been taught this lesson a long, long time ago.

Chapter Thirty-Five

Tessier stared at the raging surface of the ocean, hardly feeling the rain that fell upon his shoulders. It dripped from his hat onto the ground at his feet, the letter he held gradually growing wetter in his hand. The dark ink that now ran in wordless streams had carried his death sentence just minutes earlier and he barely breathed, a lump forming in his throat that seemed likely to choke him.

There was the suggestion of movement in that hard line of a mouth as Tessier chewed at the inside of his lower lip until he tasted blood and, even then, he bit down harder, tearing at the flesh.

You are urged to return to Paris…

We are all to be called to account…

Citizen Robespierre is dead.

He screwed the paper into a ball and closed his eyes tightly, his arm at full stretch as the letter rolled from his palm into the waves. Then his eyelids flickered again and he threw his head back to stare into the clouds. Above Le Havre, the sky itself was cracking, lightning flashing in the heavens as Tessier finally recognized the joke, heard the laughter of the very gods. His scarred hands seemed to burn in their gloves. He stretched the fingers out as far as he could, feeling the joints crack, yet even when a gasp of pain escaped his lips he continued to exert himself, to test the limits of his own body.

…called to account…

They would abandon him, Tessier knew, the men who had been so loyal already scattering at the news of Robespierre's hurried execution. Only now did he regret leaving Jacquet in Harfleur to fend for himself, turning his men away as he sought this final lone triumph. Too late he recognized that he stood alone, halfway between the sea and the scaffold.

A crash of thunder split the raging sky and Tessier drew in a deep breath. His heart slammed in his ribcage as again and again he thought of the man who had been fastened to the kitchen hook, had been there in the next room. He'd hardly seemed like a spy and less still like a spymaster. No, he was nothing more than one of those inconsequential loudmouths who'd crowded the streets of Paris before the revolutionary flag had flown, polluting the air with the inane chatter, the braying voices, drinking dry their wine bottles and dishonoring the women.

He was one of the rich men who'd stepped over that child Tessier had once been, one more obstacle on their way to sell themselves to the Lord.

And even if I am to go to the guillotine, I will burn them before they take my head.

Let them call for him, send letters and soldiers and the very hounds of Hell, but nothing would take him back there before he had seen them all suffer, had torn the lying tongue from Dee's very mouth.

"Monsieur," a woman said, a gnarled finger plucking at his hand. "Monsieur."

Tessier turned to the beggar who crowded him and he hardly hesitated, a silver blade flashing for a moment as it bit into her stomach. Before she had even crumpled to the ground, he was striding away, returning the knife to his coat as he went.

"My horse," he instructed the boy with whom he had entrusted the animal. "Now."

The child bolted forward and handed him the reins, eyes widening at the small crowd of people who drew in around the stricken woman. Tessier dropped a coin on the ground at his feet and drew himself up into the saddle. Then he turned the black horse to them, the Butcher of Orléans returning as he barked, "Clear the street."

For a moment, his command was obeyed, and he pulled back on the reins. The horse reared as he shouted again, "Clear the damned street!"

The final warning came barely seconds before he urged his mount forward toward the gaggle of filth that blocked his path. Flashing hooves cleared the blood that had pooled around the prone beggar and he galloped through the crowd.

I have nowhere else to go, though — he turned the horse back toward his own home — *so here I will remain.*

Tessier's transformation from the Butcher of Orléans to a man who could pass unnoticed on the streets of Le Havre was not difficult. He kept up his vigil hour after hour, searching for the party, the diamond with which the queen had tormented him. Still he haunted the taverns, the slums and the docks in search of the playwright and his debauched party, yet still there was no sign. He knew that they would hardly leave without the remainder of their group and neither sibling would abandon the other, but he had that slight suggestion of doubt, a hundred explanations for their absence swirling in his head.

And no one would sail in this storm.

In the lane behind the house where he and Sylvie were lodged, Tessier dismounted and bowed his head against the storm that battered him. His feet sank into the sludge, the once feared politician showing no interest in the people who walked abroad on such a night, so swallowed was he by his thoughts. Silently he opened the door of the building and slipped inside, just in time to hear the sound of a child's voice raised in fury.

"Get out," Sylvie's voice could be heard then. "Get out of here. Go back to bloody Roucelle like Thierry told you."

Pace increasing, Tessier threw open the door, eyes growing wide at the scene. The presence of the boy meant one thing. He murmured, "You have brought them here?"

"He's leaving." Sylvie bristled with rage before turning on her son again. "If you're not out of here by the time I count to five—"

"We cannot have our whereabouts known." Tessier slammed the door shut. He dragged Bastien toward him by one arm and searched his jacket for the still-bloody blade. Only then did the Butcher drop his gaze to the pouch in Sylvie's hand. He whispered, "*You* have betrayed me."

"You've got it wrong." There was fear added to her anger. "I don't know how he found me—"

"Where is Dee?"

Bastien twisted helplessly in Tessier's grip as he pressed the knife to the boy's throat.

"He doesn't know." Sylvie's hand clenched onto the pouch she held. "Let him go, he knows nothing, never has."

"Then I will kill him." Tessier shrugged, the blade already beginning to move.

"You'd kill your own flesh and blood?" The words, so utterly unexpected, shot from Sylvie's lips like a bullet.

"My...?" The word was a whisper and Tessier dropped his pale gaze to look at the boy. The he lifted it again to stare at Sylvie. "He is *mine*?"

"Of course he's bloody yours," Sylvie, ashen-faced but defiant to the last, spat out. "Who else's would he be?"

Tessier froze for a second before he threw Bastien across the kitchen, the child's head striking the edge of the table with a sickening blow and sending him sliding, unmoving, to the floor. He advanced on Sylvie, glowering. "I have no son, woman."

"He's yours," she repeated, taking a step back, then another. "I swear it."

"You should have—" Tessier shook his head and fell to his knees beside the small, prone figure, seeing now the child he had once been, the child who had no one but a whore mother. It was like looking through a mirror back in time, seeing Vincent Tessier before the world had made him a man. "Why did you never tell me?"

"Because he'd hold us back." She raised the pouch. "And now we've got the diamond, we can do what we said. He'll stay with Dee. He won't get in our way…"

"You raised my child as a bastard," Tessier muttered, putting his hand on Bastien's shoulder for a moment. "Dragging him from house to house behind you as you *whored* yourself?"

"I *raised* him," a note of affront entered her voice, "as best I could."

"With a cobbler, a landlord," he whispered, rising to his feet. "A cabinetmaker? You left me a student, *Madame*, but you find me a leader of men."

"And I'll leave you again," she threatened, white-faced and shaking, "and take your precious diamond with me."

A duplicitous, lying whore…

Filth on the street.

Tessier snatched out and grabbed for her, catching long hair in his fingers. Sylvie gave a shriek, feet skittering on the tiles. He dragged her toward him, hissing her name furiously. He had intended to stab her but it didn't seem enough, the punishment too quick. Instead he closed his fingers around her throat, squeezing the very life from her.

"My son, a bastard?" He shook his head, tightening his scarred hands. "I would rather he were dead."

Sylvie struggled in his hold, one hand clawing at his in desperation, eyes wide as the realization of what was happening finally sunk in. She tried to speak but no sound came out. He kept tightening his hands until those eyes bulged and grew dim, the woman in his arms suddenly and finally limp.

With a long sigh, Tessier saw the life go out of her, Sylvie's struggling body sagging beneath his. When he released her throat, she dropped to the floor with a heavy thud. Tessier remained beside her for a few moments, his gaze fixed on that ashen, still beautiful face, then he reached out and closed her eyes for the final time before turning, shocked to see that the boy was gone.

And yet the front door has not opened.

As he snatched up the diamond, Tessier heard the creak

of the boards beneath the kitchen table where the little boy had scrambled to safety. He turned to face it, smiling softly.

"Come out, child," he called gently. "Why prolong things? Come out and join your mother. Come out or I will burn you as I burned Orléans."

When there was no movement, he strode through the door and pulled it shut, turning the key. The fire in the sitting room grate would provide all he needed to burn this house to the ground, the woman and her child with it.

"Open the bloody door!" The child's voice was a terrified howl despite his obvious efforts to disguise the fear. "I'll bloody kill you, you bastard."

The word jarred more than it should. He took a deep breath, closing his eyes for a moment and seeing again Sylvie's slackening face, the very life leaving her.

I have no son.

And this house must burn.

Chapter Thirty-Six

"That woman," William muttered to Gaudet, "had better appreciate this."

"She won't." Gaudet yawned, inspecting his fingernails, though William knew that being in such close proximity to Tessier could hardly be easy for him either. He peered along the dark street and shuddered in the rain despite his cloak, asking, "Where *is* he?"

"Perhaps he's run off with the diamond," William suggested, though he didn't believe his own words for a moment. *Yet he should be back by now.* An uneasy feeling settled in the pit of his stomach.

Something has gone wrong.

The door opened and the figure of what looked like a man who had reached the end of his tether emerged. Huddled into a heavy cloak, he moved as though the weight of the world rested on his stooped shoulders. The two men paid him no heed, such a sight hardly unusual in this part of the town. It was as Gaudet was beginning to elucidate for William's benefit on exactly *what* he intended to do when they were alone that night that he peered more closely at the building and said, "Oh my…smoke!"

And smoke there was, far too much of it for a mere cooking fire. William widened his eyes and in the next moment grabbed Gaudet's hand before they both ran toward the house.

"That man…" Gaudet turned to stare after the vanished figure before the sound of Bastien's voice could be heard, raised in alarm.

The door opened with relative ease, William thanking

any powers that were listening as he burst into the house, calling for the boy. He did not have trouble locating him. Bastien was kicking and hammering, desperate to be freed from a room beyond a hallway that was overwhelmed with thick smoke, flames licking throughout the sitting room and out into the street.

Without a thought to anything other than rescuing the hollering child, William held a hand to his mouth and nose. Breathing as lightly as he could as he reached the door, a rattle of the handle found it well and truly locked.

"Get me out!" Bastien howled. "Fucking hell!"

"Your shoulder," Gaudet fluttered, attempting to do just that with little success as Bastien continued to shout terrified oaths. "Knock it down, *chérie*."

The Frenchman was, William decided, every bit as quick-thinking as he was good-looking. He added his own efforts to Gaudet's, their combined weight and force causing the door to burst open a few moments later.

"Help me get my ma," Bastien told them in a panicked voice, running from the door to the unmoving woman. "He killed her, help me get her."

Without a word, William advanced on the child, swinging him over his shoulder and turning more slowly with the burden back to the door to tell Gaudet, "We need to get out. Now."

Eyes fixed on the flames that surged into the hallway and cut off their exit, Gaudet froze momentarily. Then, with yet more of that admirable quick thinking, he took off the cloak he wore and used it to bat out the fire that had caught on the rug, providing at least a modicum of safety for their passage as he shouted to William, "Quickly!"

He didn't need telling twice and, yelling for Gaudet to follow, he ducked his head, holding the boy as he made blindly for the door. The kitchen doorway was thick with black smoke and the cloak caught alight beneath Gaudet's very feet. He dashed after William, the beams crashing down behind them.

The night air was almost painful as William dragged deep, shaking breaths into his lungs, feeling them fill with clean oxygen. He held a struggling Bastien in his arms, relief welling through his heart at the sight of Gaudet, just a little sooty, leaving the burning house behind them.

"He killed my ma," the child bellowed, fighting in William's grasp without much success. "He killed her!"

"And getting yourself burned along with her isn't going to change that," William told him more roughly than he meant, his next words softer. "You're safe. You're going to be all right."

"I am so sorry." Gaudet handed Bastien his brandy flask, his voice soothing, compassionate. "Truly, Bastien."

"Let's get him back to the house." William found his voice just about steady. "We need to tell Dee."

The child grew limp in William's arms, the fight drained from him until he was absolutely still. He clutched William's coat with white knuckles. Bastien sagged into the embrace, body shaking with soft, uncontained sobs. William met Gaudet's gaze over that smoke-scented head with its mop of unruly hair, wondering then why life did this to the innocent.

Why bring such horrors to the people who least deserve it?

"Let's get you both to safety," Gaudet said, offering William a loving look, "and out of the rain."

Chapter Thirty-Seven

It was, Bastien told himself, nothing but a bad dream. He would wake up soon and find things as they should be. There'd be no diamond. He'd be cold and hungry and Sylvie would be telling him off for helping himself to a gentleman's watch or some other knickknack. All he had to do, he knew, was open his eyes.

"Wake up," he muttered to himself as he sat, arms around his legs, on the stable straw. "Wake *up*."

The smell of smoke still lingered about him and he took a deep, wrenching breath. He refused to let the tears escape again, to think of the man Sylvie had named as his father. He would think of none of that, only of waking from this nightmare into the gray, empty gutter of Paris.

Bastien pressed his face to his knees, closing his eyes tightly. He wondered whether, if he stayed where he was, everything would just vanish. Even better, perhaps he might vanish himself, putting an end to all his problems once and for all.

At the sound of the door latch lifting, he remained unmoving, willing himself to disappear and be free of all this. He barely heard the sound of boot soles crossing the earthen floor, hardly felt the straw shift as someone sat beside him, then Adam asked, "What're you doing all the way out here when you've a bed inside?"

"Not tired," Bastien managed, keeping his head down.

"There's a poodle looking for you."

He shrugged in reply, certain the dog, along with anyone else, didn't care what he was doing or where he was.

"I'm really sorry about your ma," Adam told him. "It's

rotten."

"She didn't deserve that," he whispered, "whatever she'd done."

"Nobody deserves that," Adam agreed in a gentle tone. "I know it's no help to you now, that it feels as though the bottom's dropped out of your world, but if you ever need a friend, you've got one right here."

"A friend?" Bastien wiped at his nose, barely daring to look up at Adam. "I'm not used to friends."

"Well..." Adam patted Bastien's shoulder. "You've got this *loveable rogue*, a sensible fellow and two chaotic gents about town. Not to mention the young Miss Dee, who's taken a shine to her new best pal."

"What'll happen to me now?" Bastien asked after a long moment. "Where do I go?"

"I could a use a livery lad at my yard if you fancy a change of air?"

"In England?"

"England? Not a bloody chance, lad...Ireland."

Bastien let the thought settle for a moment, weighing it against remaining here, alone, living from one stolen mouthful to the next, exchanging the familiarity of the street for what sounded like a settled existence. "What if I make a mess of it? You'd send me back here on my own?"

"You'd get an extra shift on shit shoveling duty, maybe." Adam shrugged. "No worse than that, though."

"That all?" Bastien peered at Adam, searching for any hint of dishonesty.

"If it's really bad, maybe two shifts?"

"I think," he decided, "there might be worse places to be than an Irish stable yard."

"And it's *my* Irish stable yard...it's never dull."

"Lots of ladies?"

"Everywhere you turn."

"Pretty ones?" Bastien sat up straighter.

"Try *stunning*," Adam confided in the boy. "But they're *all* the finest you'll see."

"Maybe I'll give it a go then." He felt a tiny flicker of something that might, perhaps, be hope.

"One thing you need to agree to."

"What's that?" Bastien narrowed his eyes, betraying his suspicion—there was always *one thing*.

"If ever you think I'm not paying you enough...you make sure to tell me?"

Bastien felt his eyes grow wide, disbelief clear in his voice when he demanded, "What, I'll be getting *paid*?"

"You'll be working, so you'll be getting paid."

"Well, then"—he almost managed a smile—"when do we go?"

"As soon as these storms clear. We'll have to go via England." Adam pulled a face. "But we'll be in Ireland soon enough and *you* can get on with admiring the lassies—just don't let Miss Dee catch you."

"I won't," he vowed, "and I'll leave you the prettiest, of course."

"Well, I'm the foreman, so you should."

"I might," Bastien decided with a smile, slowly uncurling from his unhappy bed of straw, "be ready for that bed now."

"Come on then." Adam offered his hand. "And have a nip of brandy to see you to sleep?"

A pause, then he reached out, closing his fingers gratefully around Adam's before he got to his feet. "If I told you something," Bastien found himself venturing as they made for the door, "would you tell anyone? If I told you not to?"

"It'd be tough to know until you said it," Adam mused. "But if you trust me, you can give it a try."

Bastien battled with himself, not quite able to bring himself to name Tessier as he told Adam, "That *man*, the one that killed my mum—she said he was my dad."

"If that's true, then he's got a finer lad for a son than he could *ever* deserve," Adam said after a moment's thought. "The best lad I know."

He had nothing to say to that, feeling once again that

everything *might* somehow be all right, his hold on Adam's hand tightening as they walked out into the fresh air.

Chapter Thirty-Eight

Gaudet awoke before the dawn the following morning, listening for any sign of the storm that had raged as they'd slept fitfully. He heard nothing, breathing a sigh of relief that, perhaps, they might be safe in England within the day. As he opened his eyes, his gaze found William immediately, settling lovingly on the man who rested in his arms, who had saved him in more ways than he could ever say. Now, in the gray light, he told himself that whatever happened, William would be saved, no matter what new hazards faced them in these closing stages of this long, arduous journey.

I would give my life for you, he promised silently, stroking William's hair. *I love you.*

"In a moment," came the sleepy response, William stirring to cuddle closer, "I promise."

He kissed William's hair in reply, smiling at the characteristically unexpected observation. Those closed eyelids flickered a second later, William blinking awake to just gaze sleepily at Gaudet.

"The storm has passed, *chérie*. We will sail for home today."

"Home." The Englishman actually smiled. "It will be good to find out what that is."

"You are welcome to my own nest," Gaudet whispered. "It will be yours, too, if you wish it. I have *marvelous* people who look after *me*."

"Then I look forward to joining the household," William whispered, snuggling into Gaudet's arms "If you will have me."

Gaudet's answer was a lingering kiss, his heart fit to

burst with happiness, and when he spoke again, it was in a whisper. "I feel that for all of us, things will be righted when we are home."

"And the boy," William added after a long pause, "he'll be all right, too."

"To lose one's mother to violence…" Gaudet ducked his head, pushing away the wave of sadness before he concluded, "We must make sure that *both* of our young charges are kept safe and happy from this day forward."

"Your sister still doesn't like me." There was a definite smile, though. "Is it treason to refuse to wear rouge when commanded by the king?"

"My sister has lost her husband, her friends," Gaudet commented between soft kisses. "And she liked few enough people as it is. She will soon warm to your many wonderful aspects."

"My aspects are indeed somewhat warm as we speak," came the grave response.

"We have a little time before that rather dashing professor whisks us away to safety. Shall we use it wisely?"

"What exactly," the decidedly breathless murmur told Gaudet that William was more than open to suggestions, "did you have in mind?"

The discussion soon turned rather more practical and as the sun rose over a beautiful day in Le Havre, as their party prepared to flee for its very life, Gaudet was *less* aware of his surroundings. Instead he was devoted to having as much fun with as little noise as possible, given the close confines in which the lodgings had placed them. What the morning would bring mattered not for now. All that mattered was these moments together.

"Well," William finally gasped, eyes closing briefly as he gathered himself, "that was highly instructive."

"And *you*" — Gaudet let out a long, delighted sigh — "*Chérie*, you are my dream come true."

"You have to say that," William observed, "now that we're —"

"I say it because you are *mine* and I love you."

"I am," came the admission, "I *am* yours."

"Gents!" Gaudet took William in his arms as there was a heavy knock at the door and Dee called, "We sail for home today — out of bed and into boots."

"*Home…*" Gaudet could barely believe that the time had come, that he would soon be happily back in the salons and theaters, with William on his arm. "I have missed my house so. When we get home, I shall wear a dozen outfits a day and I shall have my tailor enhance my lovely red coat with some silver adornments."

"When we get home," William corrected, "you won't wear any outfits at all."

"Just perfume and a smile?" He slapped William's bottom gently. "And the occasional dab of rouge."

"I can't see a problem with that," was the contented reply. "I suppose you have to get dressed now?"

"I *could* go like this, but I don't think it counts as keeping a low profile." With that, Gaudet sprang from the bed, pulling William along with him. In fact, William's spirited efforts to help him dress proved something of a hindrance, fresh kisses and embraces taking precedence over urgency. Eventually they were dressed and ready to leave, William pausing at the door to look around the small room with a sigh.

Gaudet slipped his arm around his companion's waist and murmured, "It has been quite a trip."

He left unsaid the part about this man, who he had once thought the torturer of the south, changing his life. No mention of how he had taken a creature of vanity who'd lived for the next moment in the footlights, the next note of appreciation from the queen or some other notable, and turned him into a man who could love, could *be* loved.

"You have changed me" — a kiss to William's cheek — "for the better, my love."

"You have made me," came the reply, "want to live again."

"André!" Claudine knocked firmly on the door. "Come on, man."

"He'll be there in a moment, woman," William called back, eyes widening. "Now she *really* won't like me."

"Woman?" The door flew open, Claudine wild-eyed as she juggled an assortment of luggage. "You may address me as Madame Plamondon, sir. André, come along."

"Yes, *Madame*." Gaudet laughed, exclaiming to William, "*Well!*"

"Well!" William repeated before shaking his head and following Gaudet from the room.

Downstairs, the party was gathered in the kitchen, the odd atmosphere of anticipation and anxiety palpable. Bastien was the only one to seem anything like cheery, sticking close to Adam as he loaded pistols on the kitchen table, giving the lad a quiet instruction on how to do so. Dee stood by the filthy window, peering out keenly, and at the arrival of the final party members, he turned to greet them with the ghost of a smile.

"This is the end of the adventure, thank the Lord," he told them. "You are to go ahead. I shall follow behind. This limp, you know."

"What about Tessier?" William asked the question with obvious care, noting the shock on Harriet's face at her father's words. "We should all go together."

"We know from what the young man told us" — Dee offered Bastien a supportive smile — "that he is alone."

"You know me and I'm not one to argue." Adam addressed his best friend. "But let's stick together this time, so we *all* get on that boat?"

"Together," Gaudet agreed. "I am sorry, Professor, but I would not want us to separate. You have saved us all. We would not leave you behind for the sake of a limp."

"I'm on a stick." Dee sighed. "I will slow you all down if there is trouble."

"We go together." William's tone was one that brooked no argument. "Stick and all."

"I will follow along." Dee patted his daughter's hand. "Tessier's quarrel is with me."

"We will not take no for an answer. We go together," Harriet told him softly and, after a moment, he nodded and kissed her cheek very quickly.

"Come on then"—Dee turned for the door—"Captain Pascaud awaits."

"If anything happens," William murmured to Gaudet, "you must make sure your sister and that boy get to the ship."

"No, *chérie*." Gaudet shook his head urgently as they made their way to the door. "I place them in *your* care—you are the hero, I am simply a playwright."

The party made their way out into the new dawn, Dee leading them from the house of Roucelle and down toward the dock. The streets were already busy, the sound of the waking quay filling the air. Gaudet found himself studying every face, examining every passing figure for *him*.

"I'm armed," William murmured from his side. "Just keep going."

Gaudet nodded, pressing on through the streets.

Chapter Thirty-Nine

Despite the seeming ease with which they made their way, William found he could not quite shake a feeling of anxiety. They outnumbered Tessier easily, of course, and the chances were he had more on his mind after his recall to Paris without worrying about this small group. Yet, at the same time, there was something in the air, like a storm coming in. He peered around, alert, staying close to Gaudet as he felt for the reassurance of the gun he had under his coat.

The little dauphin in Claudine's arms seemed to sense his anxiety and grew increasingly fractious during the walk, griping and reaching out to his uncle and Papillon, grumbling that he wanted to be with the dog and her *papa*. Eventually, Claudine turned to her brother and asked, "Would you mind taking him, André? He will not settle otherwise?"

"Of course," Gaudet beamed, patting William's arm as he stepped forward to take the child from her.

Once again, William glanced at the people around them, noticing all too casually the cloaked figure who seemed somehow different to the other beggars who were similarly clad. Something in the bearing of the figure was too *upright* and beneath the tattered cloak, the shoe that peeped out was familiar, the leather toe one he had seen before.

It was with a jolt of horror that William realized *where* he had seen it, remembered that same shoe flashing past his face as it had kicked again and again. It had been adorned with a silver buckle then but it was the same shoe, the one that had adorned the foot of Vincent Tessier.

His step faltered, mind whirling as he tried to work out what to do. The moment to shoot on instinct had passed, and now he was left with the sudden realization that he had no choice but to follow.

Tessier had obviously deduced the party's destination and, swirling the cloak around himself, disappeared into one of the many labyrinthine alleyways that would lead him to the docks. Dee led the group through those same winding lanes. With a last, longing look to ensure that Gaudet was fully occupied with trying to settle the increasingly unhappy child, William took a deep breath, whispered once more his love for the Frenchman and hurried after the disappearing Tessier.

I will be with you on that boat, William told them silently, *and we will soon be home.*

Hand on his weapon, he could not remember a time when his senses had been so heightened, every movement, every sound a possible clue as to Tessier's whereabouts. He would find him, he was certain, and he would make sure the man never troubled them again, whatever that took.

It became obvious as he rounded a corner *why* Tessier had chosen this particular route to the dock. It ended in a high wall that had long since become the dumping ground for all manner of harbor rubbish that was simply thrown over it, piling into a mountain of filth that sloped up to the lip of the wall. It was here that Tessier scaled the mound of rotting waste with no problem whatsoever. As he settled at the edge of the brickwork, he cast his cape aside to reveal a concealed rifle, perfect for picking off a more distant quarry.

There was not, William was certain, much time. He approached as quietly and quickly as he could, heart hammering as he followed the path Tessier had taken. His pistol was drawn and ready for the inevitable moment when the Frenchman would sense his presence and turn, finger tightening on the trigger even as he felt cold steel on his throat and heard Jacquet hiss, "Looks like I found a lost *spy.*"

William froze, wondering if Dee and his party would hear if he shouted a warning, the impossibility of that hitting him even as he said, "You stay with him, Monsieur, and you lose."

Now, in the closing moments of his life, William comforted himself with the knowledge that if nothing else, he might have caused *just* enough of a distraction for the party to reach and board the vessel. Indeed, Tessier had turned from his single-minded intention of aiming the rifle and appeared torn, eventually slipping down from his perch to stand before William.

"Thirty seconds to gut a spy." His smile was cold. "I believe I can spare *that*."

"Thirty seconds?" William asked. "You're nowhere near as good as you think."

Tessier met that challenge with another smile and reached into his coat for a knife, plunging it toward William's stomach with alarming speed. He was not, however, *quite* fast enough to sidestep the poodle that flew around the corner in a whirlwind of white fur, weaving through the collected limbs with enough speed to completely wrong-foot Jacquet. Even as the guard moved to avoid her, she sank her teeth hard into his ankle and he pitched sideways, twisting William clear of Tessier's blade. William hit the floor hard right in front of his own discarded gun. He scrabbled quickly to retrieve it.

"I told you," Gaudet told William as he, too, rounded the corner, pistol drawn, "*don't* wander off!"

Jacquet was on his feet again in a second, head whipping from left to right to look from the men to Tessier, clearly weighing up ideology versus freedom and, when it seemed ideology was wanting, he took off running from the alley. He hadn't gone far before there was the sound of a pistol shot and Adam's voice calling their names.

For Tessier, however, ideology was all and he flung himself at William, the knife slashing wildly before him. It was sheer luck that he managed to lift the gun, pulling the trigger on the advancing Tessier.

He couldn't miss at such a range. Tessier let out a howl of fury as the bullet hit home, the Butcher of Orléans sprawling back across the alleyway. Summoned by the sound of the gun, Adam's voice grew nearer, then Bastien darted into the alleyway and yelled, "Come on, they'll go without us!"

"The wall," William managed to shout. "Over the wall!"

Snatching up the poodle, Bastien called to the unseen Adam, "We'll see you at the boat." He dashed nimbly up the pile of rubbish and, with a spirited cry of excitement, vaulted over the wall, leaving Gaudet to let out a cry of, "Papillon!"

"Come on." William grabbed the Frenchman's arm, the next moment dragging him upward to follow the little boy.

"Do I look like a man who jumps walls?" Gaudet had time to shriek before he did just that, landing with a cry of surprise on his feet, safe in view of the boat.

Harriet, Pap settled in her arms, and Adam and Dee were standing on the gangplank of the vessel that was now held in place by just one mooring rope, the professor remonstrating furiously with the captain who, in a raised voice, was telling him, "I can't have bloody delays."

"Here are the gentleman and lad now," Dee replied serenely, stepping aside to let Bastien dart aboard. "There really is no need for shouting, sir. Have you never seen an escaping playwright before?"

William's own leap was less dignified, a loud curse escaping as he let Gaudet pull him along, yelling, "If that boat goes, I'll shoot everyone on it."

"Come on." Dee beckoned with just a hint of urgency.

Gaudet seemed set on tearing William's arm from its socket as he hurtled along, racing up the raising gangplank and onto the deck of the ship.

"Go, go, go!" William heard himself yelling even as his feet hit the deck. "Go!"

"Monsieur," Claudine said from where she stood, the child in her arms regarding him with a regal look, "there is nowhere *to* go from here."

"Quite right," Gaudet agreed, voice full of nervous energy. "We are safe!"

"Safe?" William demanded, the pain in his ankle suddenly hitting full force. "Bloody hell!"

"Not in front of the boy," Claudine chided, though she softened somewhat when she added, "You saved us today, sir. Let us hope my brother has chosen well."

"In the name of Vincent Tessier," a weak voice called over the creaking of the now unmoored ship, "drop anchor."

On the dock, Tessier stumbled on buckling legs toward the edge, a slick slug trail of blood following along with those whose interest was piqued by the name. "You will return to the dock." Words failed him, blood gurgling somewhere deep beneath his voice. He crumpled to his knees on the edge of the land. "Turn back."

A cry went up of something between fear and disbelief, someone calling with disgust, "The bloody butcher?"

William had, he realized, dropped his gun in the chase. Without a thought, he put himself between the child and the widening patch of water between them and the dock, gesturing for Gaudet to get back as he did so.

"It's all right," Gaudet told William gently, whispering, "I love you *so* much."

The cries of discovery had given rise to shouts now, Tessier faced with a barrage of obscenities from the mob who seemed determined not to return him to Paris, but to lynch him where he lay. As the crowd advanced, spitting fury and fire, he gave one final movement, his black-clad figure plunging into the pitch waters of the dock, where it sank like a stone.

William heard himself returning the sentiment, reflecting that it was considerably easier than he had worried it might be, adding as an afterthought, "I don't think I'm going to be able to walk for a week."

"That's all right." Gaudet turned to him, their gazes meeting as he said, "I have a *very* nice bed, after all."

More books from
Pride Publishing

Book one in the Gin & Jazz series

It's the silent film era of Hollywood, and young, innocent Jack fights for love amid the heady allure of fame, gin and easy money.

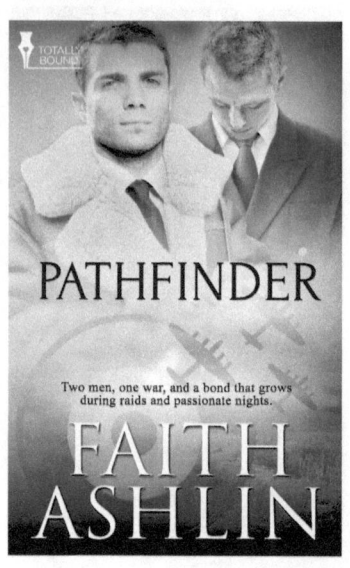

Bobby is fighting fervently amid the planes and bombs of World War Two when events take a passionate turn with the arrival of a new pilot. Can Lewis offer him more than he thought possible?

Nathan Stephenson died seventy years ago and he'd like the world — or at least one person — to think he stayed that way.

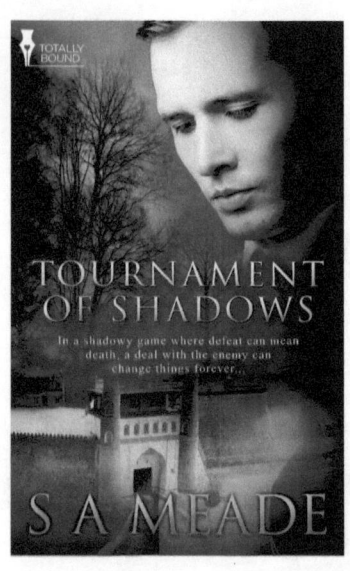

*In a shadowy game where defeat can mean death, a deal
with the enemy can change things forever.*

About the Author

Catherine Curzon

Catherine Curzon is a royal historian who writes on all matters of 18th century. Her work has been featured on many platforms and Catherine has also spoken at various venues including the Royal Pavilion, Brighton, and Dr Johnson's House.

Catherine holds a Master's degree in Film and when not dodging the furies of the guillotine, writes fiction set deep in the underbelly of Georgian London.

She lives in Yorkshire atop a ludicrously steep hill.

Willow Winsham

Willow Winsham brings readers regular tales of witches and witchcraft at her blog. Combining a passion for research and history with a love of storytelling, she dedicates her time to investigating some of the most intriguing stories from the history of the British Isles. When she isn't digging out tantalising historical titbits or tracing elusive family members, she is busy writing historical fiction and home educating her two children.

Our authors love to hear from readers. You can find contact information, website details and an author profile page at https://www.pride-publishing.com/